THE EMPIREID

THE EMPIREID

ILVARIO

editor@vagabondbooks.net

Published by VAGABOND

VAGABOND
Collection

Intellectual Property
Ilvario
The Empireid
1st ed. / p.cm.

ISBN13: 978-1936293-40-7

Library of Congress: 002134087

Made in the USA.

To Patrick and Susanne, for sparking the fire,
and to Eta, for feeding the flame.

Time, our everlasting ally and foe...

BOOK I

THE SLEEP OF THE GODS

For love and the destiny of man I sing,
of those compelled by Fate, to fulfill the goddess's journey
and lift an Atlas weight. In the house of Priam, forward bring
those beleaguered sons of Troy, who fled across the Aegean Sea,
harried by the unfathomable hatred of Queen Juno,
and the accursed sorrow of Greek led tragedy;
set adrift on Neptune seas, a floating human cargo
suffering beyond all measure to Lavinian shores,
surmounting brutal wars and many foes
to found a home once more,
have at hand one final test,
greater than all that have come before,
before claiming their well earned rest.
O Muse, and to Apollo, sun god, who sees beyond all,
whose beloved lineage this telling does attest
to follow, through peril and great toil, I pray for the merit to recall
how the empire finally ended, and the gods themselves did fall.

Was it by some grand design maybe?
Or that frivolous Chance did lend a hand?
For in here lies the story, set forth by dark and mighty Hades,
of how the lovely Venus, made her final stand.
It began long ago, before the counting of time and swelling tide,
an old grudge, born from the careful, cunning plan,
forged between the brothers three, committing patricide.
For the stars they do remember, and the lesser third could not forget,
let alone forgive, the untold longing and crafty slight that cast aside
he, the unfortunate, to his eternal banishment
into the realm of everlasting night, to go
where all souls go, to burn with regret.
Patience, the Virtue, enjoyed by none who know
greater than the immortal gods themselves,
was a constant and stall-worth friend to Pluto,
the Lord of the Underworld, from the heavens expelled,
who forever in darkness dwelled.

Ever stronger did his powers swell, more so
than for all of those above; Time, his lasting love and only treasure.
Through endless ages of wanton death and carnage his ranks did grow,
buoying his power, beyond all scope and measure,
whilst Jupiter and Neptune, God of Thunder and Master of the Seas,
were constrained to the prayers and sacrifices of the living, it was sure
in the end would all belong to he, for Plutonic Hades drank richly
from the grave, foe and ally alike, both the master and slave, poor
and rich the same, peasants and heroes of new and old, finally
all fell unto his power, till now hark, at last befell the hour
of his rising triumph, a revenge so sweet,
beget from an eternity in the waiting, as a flower,
at last his time did come. As cold is to the winter, and in the summer heat,
a new season was approaching, that none could disavow.
A thousand years and more had passed, since the crossing of the seas,
to the founding and rise of Rome, since poet put ink to task, to tell of how
came to pass the joining of Troy and Latium, for Aeneas alone the crown.

To east and west, the houses of Gaul, of Spain and Thessaly,
even far away from Italy, the ruling voice of Latin could be heard
to echo, in Jerusalem and on Cleopatian sands, all to surrender eventually,
for none could stand to challenge the might of Roman thunder.
Even Carthage, the enemy of ancient wound,
twice defeated, under salted sands, too would fall asunder.
For once across the Rubicon, and Pompey within the fold and bound,
the entire world lay at her feet, for Caesar's grasp alone.
Yet, in a world united, beneath the eagle's banner, from underground,
there rose an opportunity, even all-powerful Jove could not hone.
Ever watchful did the brother, biding time and breath, steady to his course
find himself a catalyst in the most unlikely of all men grown.
The carpenter for him would build a second Trojan Horse,
the old wound once again would open,
as blood would run its course,
releasing teeming hordes upon
sacred Mt. Olympus, home of the gods anon.

Despair followed the newly slain,
while Confusion filled their minds,
across the boatman's threshold they strayed,
two coins given at a time,
payment for their passage
to the other side.
On this day of ancient age,
the line was long with newly dead,
for many souls had fallen to Roman rage,

the rivers running red.
Yet, among their ranks was one
that stood out among the rest being led,
who was neither thief nor rapscallion,
evident it was, as so often happens here,
the visible proof of innocence done,
was the punishment being most severe,
a telling sign beheld most clear.

Upright he stood before the mast,
while crippled and broken his comrades lain beat,
each and every man to the very last.
Through his palms and on his feet,
the corpse did bare the mark,
upon his chest tears did bleed,
and a wounded crown did arc.
Off the surface of River Styx,
with skies an inky dark,
a thick fog rolled in, like some ghostly trick
just as the boat had reached the other side.
Blinded by the heavy, misty mix,
before the craft, Doubt began to rise.
A bony finger stretched out long, pointing at last
towards the one who stood astride.
"You are summoned," the desolate voice called out from grayed overcast.
"Come stand here by my side," removing him from the craft.

Beneath his wing, the fog consumed the two,
as they vanished from all sight,
to a destination no one knew,
leaving the crippled cargo behind to blight
upon the banks of the river's shore
and to their eternal plight,
of them we'll hear no more.
As the fog it lifted, alone he stood before a darkened throne,
the father of the underworld looking, as in biblical lore,
down upon the newcomer to his home.
"Welcome, my child," a grim benevolence
exuded from bearded Pluto's tone.
A gentler cut he tailored hence
what was proceeded by earthly reputation.
Of all the gods misunderstood, here sat poor Pluto, whence,
by circumstance, the least of all forgiven throughout creation,
and for that the most deserving of mention.

"What is it you want from me?"
the man spoke, his a voice most discerning,
trusting less in what his eyes could see,
for the sound of his heart's fair warning.
"Ah," the god laughed and bellowed.
"Not so much the lamb, I am learning.
There's more in you the fighting fellow,
and to that all the better. Worry not your bones
however, you are quite safe here below.
I have called you here not to break against the stones,
but for the completion of a task,
one in which you are suited for alone.
You are the carpenter, are you not?" he asked.
"That I am," came the carpenter's reply.
"And," Pluto pressed a second question fast,
"for others' sins is the reason why you died?"
"Yes, it is true that I am free from guilt. Why?"

"Splendid," the god applauded.
"Then you are the one for whom I've been searching."
"So you know then, already have I been tested,
and yet still you are not answering,
what is it that you want from me?"
Pluto stretched a broad smile, reaching
out his hand. "The answer should be obvious to thee,
to build for me a new kingdom, of course. That is the sole requirement."
"I shall do no such thing," the carpenter was curt in his testimony.
"I admire your courage," the god enjoying his entertainment,
"though it will do you no good to resist. The task is your own father's will.
What's to be is already set into motion. You may not deny the commitment,
any more than may I control the oceans. The act is your own to fulfill,
and will be done by your own doing, for your kingdom,
hear me, lies in heaven above, still
it is only through I that you may obtain what is to come.
In this way, you and I are one.

"We're partners in this dance,
think of it as a business arrangement.
I set you free, easing the path of your entrance
and you do what comes naturally, following your father's commandment.
A win-win situation if ever there was one. Now, let us get you cleaned up.
A bath I believe is called for to seal the sacrament,
before we can have you sent back up.
Hades this may be, but let it not be said that we are uncivilized.
What kind of host would I be, allowing you to still reek of vinegar from the cup,

whence you rise? Oh and one last thing I shall require from the circumcised,"
Pluto paused the demon nymphs, escorting the carpenter from the hall.
"A memento of you is what I desire realized,
before you part in three days hence, so that I may recall
the flavor of your recompense, and the pleasure of this time.
Worry not, my friend, the payment is quite small,
a gentle slice of your noble flesh, and a chalice of blood for wine,
the rest, of its own accord, will come all in due time."

And so the Fates
and course of history were thereby set in motion.
Rome enjoyed its glory days,
the envy of every nation.
So too the years they passed,
like waves upon the ocean.
The wars they raged, each one the last, until at last,
the god of the under-cast, buoyed at every bastion,
obscured by shadowy reason, playing the faithful, his guise surpassed,
all the while preparing his infernal potion,
until ready to unleash the lamb, upon the unwitting race of men.
It began slowly, as one would imagine,
a virus of the spirit, devote and solemn,
eating away at all that was held dear,
casting Doubt upon the wind, till when
nary a prayer the gods could hear,
only too late did the danger become clear.

From man to man the message grew,
to all those who would hear it,
passed on by the chosen few,
of a great Lord in the sky, of a spirit,
more powerful than all the Olympians on high,
of one who could relieve mortals from their final judgment,
who would release them of their sin, and free them by and by
to escape from Hades' punishment. A shrewd and careful plan was this,
a sacrilege to the established order, in which they carried the lie,
yet so simple too in all its genius,
was the awakening of a new spiritual order.
Pluto, cunning, feigned the most to lose, demanding a heavy penance,
for directly threatened by such news, and in due order
the loss of his rightful inheritance. Plead
to brother Jove, to reestablish order
he did, and all the gods agreed,
righteous was the need.

Unforgivable was the loss of faith,
to prop up an imposter in their place,
a penalty must be paid, they saith,
by all those who would dare to replace,
the old and proper ways. So late that night,
while all did sleep, father Jove, with Olympus grace,
in the form of a mist, did descend right
upon the emperor's chamber,
appearing in a dream that would incite
and in his ear did so whisper
instructions, to punish those who refused to honor,
as duty did require, the deities of old, while he slumbered.
For those who kneel at the cross would be left to ponder
the risk of lifting their own. The cloud did rise
and on the morrow, with the waking sun, the emperor,
granting the gods their desired prize,
established a new decree, as a warning for every eye.

All those caught in the act
of serving this Christian god,
by grace of the simple fact,
would at best be flogged,
and if found to persist, crucified,
if not simply fed to the lions. While the gods
they cheered and drank to their victory on high, defied
they were, as more was in store than what they had expected,
for hidden deep within the Jovian command, by the guide
of Pluto's hand, was a new form of devilish trickery, erected
so subtly that even the thunder god himself was blind to the plan.
Yes, there would be some temporary relief, yet unsuspected
it would not last, for it was a faith renewed on the sorrow and grief of man,
and when the final die be cast, the old gods would perish to another belief.
Now Pluto was patient, we've said this before, he was willing to wait a thousand
years and some more, for the final subterfuge he had in store, in brief,
was just brilliant in its simplicity, it fell from the tree like an autumn leaf.

Having planted the seed, he let it grow,
knowing full well the frailty of man, sin was bound to happen.
He stoked their fears and gave them hope,
using their mortality as leverage against them.
The thought of escaping death to claim eternal salvation,
in exchange for worshipping this Son of Man, then,
in the end, was too great of a temptation.
And so it began, one by one, becoming penitent
the race of man began to divert their attention.

None more so than the line of Rome, descendant
of noble house of Troy and Aeneas seed,
did fight to preserve the glory of Olympus and
the gods of ancient home, brought over sea
and hardship to Latinium. Yet Pluto, Lord of the Underworld,
was cunning in his ways, poisoning with greed
the minds of emperor and commoner alike, unfurled
with blood soaked wine and manna flesh for bread, they sold.

The stomachs of the poor
he fed with religion,
plying with promises for
an afterlife and forgiveness,
so they would suffer every strife in earthly life,
prayer and sacrifice becoming their opiate addiction,
while those on high, for lust of power sake, rife
with excess and personal adoration, their thirst would never slake.
The more the empire grew the more it must be fed, as a knife
cutting through their heartstrings, all the rest they would forsake,
until even Earth's own frontiers could no longer satisfy
those at apex crest, hearts so filled with lead, knew only how to take,
with appetite that knew no rest, crowned upon their heads lie
a godly mantle, and so began their own undoing.
So filled with self-importance, every whim a command, to glorify
their own existence, surrounded by courtiers schooled in wooing,
with bronze and gold and marble idols of themselves for viewing.

Protected by purple coated praetorian,
the mighty line of Caesar, forgot on whose shoulders
stood their greatness. As rotted carrion,
with minds polluted by earthly delight, becoming bolder,
offerings they let subside, the poor all but neglected,
turned their prayers to a newer divinity, forsaking the older.
Now befell the times of growing hardship, infected,
disillusion turned to abandon, the gods began to weaken.
No longer were bullocks slain in Minerva's honor, tributes deflected,
and so they lost their wisdom; no calf and wine were taken
to place upon Apollo's alter, and so their sight diminished;
no longer were statues erected in homage of Lord Neptune,
so the seas of plenty ebbed, safe voyages were finished;
and Jove, master of thunder, lightning and the heavens
received not a word of prayer, all honor was relinquished,
and so over Rome the skies began to darken,
their glory, no longer for the world a beacon.

Yet, the blood of man flowed ever more increasingly,
greater than the length of Tiber, for the trinity of the carpenter.
With every execution his influence strengthened exponentially.
Born from persecution, his followers ever more petitioners,
determined to spread the word from ear to ear,
boldly making their declarations, became arbiters
of salvation for all those who could hear.
As his power grew, so too did that of Pluto, his arch-rival.
Jove, weakened and in a state of near
panic, called the gods to council,
for a plan must be devised. If faith were to be revived,
it would require a concerted effort, from their combined will.
Juno, retaining unending grudge, unquenched, deprived
of retribution for ancient offense, was the first to bring forth her solution,
one that she most longed for, for the line that she despised,
nothing less than complete and total destruction
to punish the Trojan lineage. "Let them burn," she made her declaration.

"Release your wrath, O husband Jove,
father of the sky, with lightning strike
them where they lie, in the very heart of Rome,
as they fiddle in their folly, smite them with your thunder spikes,
for their growing praise of this usurper king.
If you ask of me the course to take, this is what I like,
with fear of the true gods, let every last one of their hearts wring.
Make example of this treacherous race, release on them your anger."
Venus, gentle Goddess of Love, flying on mercy's wing,
for mother of Aeneas and Rome, most stall worth defender
of Ilium tribe, was quick to argue the opposite line.
"Revenge shall not renew our strength," she was swift to counter,
"but only turn more hearts away. It is the promise of love that binds,
for why so many have turned their prayers and succor
to this god of the cross, welcoming the price of penance, leaving us behind.
For love alone shall return the offerings of man to Mt. Olympus, that is sure.
How much more suffering must the Dardanian seed still endure?

"It is on the blood of man
that this carpenter thrives,
on death's wings only can
his angels fly. If we are to survive,
we must take away his chalice."
Love's plea brought a murmur of agreement, yet with their lives,
and all they held dear, hanging in the balance,
there still remained disagreement amongst the gods,
split between Juno fury and Venus reason. Mars, most callous

God of War, no stranger to slaying the lives of men, with a nod
fell to the side of the queen's command, where Apollo, Neptune and Vulcan,
stayed faithful as the seasons, in their support of Ilium's seedpod.
Jupiter, torn as always on this Trojan question,
knew it was time to end his neutrality, and though
leaning towards Venus fair, one final voice began
to rise above the din in hopes of swaying kingly opinion. Thus Pluto,
in somber voice then spoke, without even a hint of bravado,

"This situation, the fate of Empire Rome, affects us all.
There was a time, to these mortals' favor,
when honest argument could fall,
when they remained with noble honor
in their homage to the gods who bore
and protected them. But now, look at how they waver.
These mortals care not for the gods anymore.
Listen to how these Nazarenes preach about their own immortality,
about joining the one true god in the next life. Even more,
they would void us from all thought, memory
and existence. They threaten to steal my very kingdom
and free those rightfully destined to my keeping. Additionally,
they would go as far as to forgive their earthly acts and become
as gods themselves in place of us and dethrone even you, my great
brother, Jupiter. How should we tolerate such debauchery? Come, come!
If we don't act now, I ask you, when shall we? Do we just leave demise to Fate?
Be warned, the hour of Olympus now grows late."

Pluto was cunning in his speech,
playing to their deepest fears, whispering notions like a snake.
"Hear! Hear!" Juno applauded the Lord of the Underworld, eyeing each
of the gods in turn. "How true your brother speaks. Take
note, wise is his council." The other gods around fell silent,
while Venus bit her tongue, even she unable to make
fault of Pluto's declaration. Moved by the evident
threat to them all, Jupiter finally conceded. "So be it then," he rose.
"Lightning shall strike Rome tonight, as punishment
for their sacrilege. Let these faithless Christians all know
and finally repent for angering the gods." The decision made,
searing fire then fell from the sky, from his hand a thunderbolt he did throw,
which set the great city ablaze. The flesh of man fed the flames,
while the earthly emperor played. From the ashes a cry rose up, however
it was one that none but crafty Pluto had foreseen, the pain
and angst of Rome, in wake of such horrific destruction, in that hour
fell not upon the godly skies in penitent reflection, but towards the emperor.

Man blamed one of their own,
pointing their fingers at the careless cruelty of their earthly ruler
for his own illicit schemes, while Olympus was shone
no prayerful remorse for all its righteous ardor.
The gods succeeded only in further weakening
their own influence, making their position that much harder.
The heavens now stood upon the precipice, balancing
on crossroad's edge, despite all their righteous intentions,
a clear line had been drawn, for faith once sworn to this Judean king
could not be turned nor forsaken. It went beyond mention
how loyal and steadfast was their pledge. Between the heavens
there stood a wedge, a new god had been awoken. The only option
now at hand, a bitter pill to swallow, co-habitation, a shared haven,
amongst the gods, each camp to reinforce its followers.
For now, as much as they tried, the gods themselves even
were unable to quell the spiritual rebellion from their high towers.
A new immortal born was receiving all callers.

Pluto, while outwardly draped in sorrow,
in secret he rejoiced. The plan devised went off
like clockwork, his revenge loomed on the morrow.
No longer subservient, the lowliest third, one to be scoffed,
soon a full half and more be his, just to wait a little longer,
to stoke their anxieties and fear, and he would sit aloft.
Time was now his ally, in the shadows he would linger.
On Earth, the domain of man, the empire continued to expand,
but internally it reeked of division, no longer the stronger
as all the greatness they had built, unable to command,
now stood upon the brink of oblivion. The strife
between two camps had taken a bloody toll; the demand
beyond all reckoning in the loss of life.
A civil war was threatening to split Rome in two, once and for all.
And so it happened, after many years on the edge of a knife,
with six co-mingled emperors and a second capitol,
founded in the city of Constantinople.

All the elements were set in place
for the great downfall. An edict was cast to change the course of history.
Constantine the Great, steered by faith and all the Fates,
to save his monarchy, secured a baptismal pact, to serve a single deity.
Rome, by dictate, forever changed, opened the doors
to a papal theocracy. Nothing short of blasphemy,
the ancients they'd serve no more.
While the gods on high, from time immemorial,
watched helpless in their misery, for what was now in store.

Pluto, unable to conceal his joy, prepared the final memorial.
Gloating in his shadowy craft, at last, with ear against the wall,
ascended to Mount Olympus, to have a final
laugh. The torches around the great council hall,
once bright, as a radiant, glowing dove,
now dimly lit and fading an eerie pall
upon them all, while Jove
himself lie limp, as did the other gods above.

Once so full of power,
now helpless as a log,
exuding his final hour,
eyes overcast with a cloudy, lifeless fog.
"Hark, O brother Jove, you arrogant wretch,
greatest of all the gods, how lowly you sit now, curled up like a dog,
prostrate, unable to lift a finger, know that it is I, the architect
of your undoing, the cause of your misfortune,
and like this forever shall you linger, the longest bitter stretch,
for you see before you the one fooled by your own cunning tune,
cast forever below by Jupiter's blind ambition,
now risen to claim my rightful throne and all its boons,
while you, I curse to suffer an eternal retribution.
Sleep now brother, sleep, you and all your kin,
fulfill your death march, your comatose mission,
while alone I live to revel in
a world designed to sin."

The heart of Jove burnt with rage on being betrayed,
yet like the lamb, carefully led to slaughter,
he lie helpless beneath his brother's blade.
Upon his lips there rose a whisper,
the most that could be mustered for his part,
"Curse you, forked tongue devil and shyster,
you vile seducer of the mind and heart.
Woe be upon you the day I do return
to claim revenge upon your head, and that just for a start,
for none in all your kingdom shall ever suffer and burn
greater than the punishment that is in store
for you, dear brother, on that you have my word. One day you shall learn."
"Boldly spoken for one lying at the foot of the door,
in the throes of death," Pluto laughed. "Now sleep all
you gods of the past, the future no longer needs you poor
relics, while I, for the new heavenly order am integral,
an antagonist most indispensable.

"The only praise you shall hear
raised is that of your former glory,
and that merely an echo of the past. So adieu brother,
we shall never meet again, here lies the end of your story."
With that Pluto took his leave, descending, into the expanding chaos
he'd created below. Stirring, most needed and lovely
Venus, a mere flicker of her former flame, yet not lost,
a breath she still maintained, more so than the rest above,
for the last to perish in the hearts of man, in his soul embossed,
shall always be that of love.
Weary, she had strength left for one final command to bestow.
"O darling son, dear Cupid, who flies as like a dove,
hear me, for I have need of your reply. Pull back upon your bow
string and let one last arrow fly. Be for me an envoy
to the last of Aeneas line. Seek out my grandson, Horacio,
delivering this message with a kiss, it is urgent to deploy.
Behold, there remains one final duty for the House of Troy."

BOOK II

THE FALL OF ROME

Let no joyful voice be heard,
sing no merry song,
for Rome of ancient glory be dead,
the gods have come and gone.
A new purpose now fills the hearts of man,
a dreadful bitter one,
a crusade against the ancient plan,
they lie prostrate before the son.
Baptized in blood, through sword and
shield and every manner of pain, a rage has come,
unlike any other seen. From papal palace they wield
their reign, ushering in the darkest age, an unholy kingdom.
For this they fight, to this is what they kneel,
in the name of their deity an unholy war they wage.
It's in these times of cursed plight, when all that's good does reel,
in which our story shall unfold, released from memory's cage,
for in the darkest hour of night, there's the turning of the page.

With one's back up against the wall, behold
that like a star up in the sky, shining clear and bright,
courage shall return to the hearts of man, to once again unfold
and in their time of greatest need, show to them the light,
when one amongst the rest shall
stand against the grain and fight,
heeding to the pressing call.
Civil wars divided once all powerful Rome,
every corner rising, gathering at the wall,
to rebel against their formerly united home.
In the north the barricades fell, abandoning Britain for Arles,
the Franks invaded Belgium, taking it for their own,
while barbarians swept across the fields of Gaul.
In the east, the Visigoths, they rose, a terrible and mighty clan,
pillaging and raiding outlying posts, before them much did fall,
opening the doors for Attila to take away Milan.
And so, like this, is how it all began.

The world was changing every day,
lines redrawn on the map. Rome herself fair
game, was not immune once the pirates came
sacking the eternal city, stripping the temples bare
in the raid, before they went away. Through all of this,
the papacy, better than all the rest, did fare,
for the followers of the Son of Man were ferocious
in the name of their savior, they launched upon a quest.
Riled by old Pluto, who sent his Fury, Allecto, evil goddess,
sorrow bringer, up onto the earth, to stir the hornet's nest,
now she would prove her worth. Needling with rumor and plot,
empire Rome, under new holy banner unfurled, rose to the test,
in honor of the cross, with more souls than could be counted lost,
a twenty thousand score army bearing down upon Jerusalem.
Gorgon of black coiled serpent hair, tongue, full of complot,
a fiery funeral torch, bound to enrage once again
with deepest, darkest thoughts, the people of Latinium.

Wrung with fear and hatred,
in each and every heart,
the seeds of warfare planted,
to yield a bloody crop, her craft, the darkest art.
Disguised as an old hermit, bearing in name
that of Peter, after the first pontiff, she made her start,
transforming snaky coif matted into locks of twisting gray;
scaly flesh turned to a toughened bronze, with sun and burden;
face lined with grizzle; back, bent and weary,
in such a manner did Allecto present her mischief, when
upon the papal feet in Rome, did she plant her poisonous kiss,
with stories of such persuasion and eloquence, with such a zealous zen,
fervent, glowing with indignation, bearing a weighty crucifix,
she relayed the suffering of noble pilgrims and native factions
in the far off land of Palestine, until all who gathered were transfixed.
For the anguish of their tormented brethren, hearts melting with compassion,
all together did their voices rise and clamor for retribution.

"God wills it. God wills it,"
thousands exclaimed in unison.
In such ways wars are made, with anger roasting on a spit,
a nation, blinded, in a fit, stealthy Allecto's work be done.
Having successfully applied her trade, she slithered back unto her lair,
to watch the trouble she had made; a twisted type of fun.
Back in Rome, from every corner, men prepared for warfare.
Under the influence of Allecto's poisoned caldron,
"To arms" the cries rang out. The blacksmith's wheel there

did turn, swords were sharpened, and new ones
forged on anvil; javelins glistened in the sun; equipment
for siege and battering walls were constructed; bludgeons,
maces and shields were made strong with iron ore; helmets
and breastplates fastened; axes were hone,
and prepared were all sorts of battlements.
War horses were bridled, immense they were grown,
while fierce were their riders, in armor, brightly shone.

From the provinces, France and Lorraine
numbered sixty thousand in a clamorous flock,
while the lands of Danube and Rhine
added fifteen thousand on foot to the stock.
Twenty thousand more came in from Germany,
following Godescal, a fanatical monk in a frock,
and bringing up the rear, full of debauchery and rapine, a great many,
two hundred thousand savages, a drunken, depraved devotion their lot.
Some three thousand horsemen road up in front, all at the ready
to partake in the plunder, their mouths they fed on this looted rot.
All that intersected the path of those champions of the cross,
whether it be commoner, farmer or village, have or have not,
either by negotiation or pillage, found themselves at a loss,
and so go the spoils to the strong, while the rest only get the hunger,
and a nation of wealth before very long becomes one of lowly peasants tossed.
The empire however would survive just a little longer,
stretching out its demise, as the east kept growing stronger.

While the great Khan
captured everything far to the east,
every battle his army easily won,
closer to home the Turks began to seethe.
The final blow took place when hope
met its end, as the barricades fell and a fleet
of invaders rushed in. The mighty city of Constantinople
shifted from the west to the east, as the marauders victorious,
captured sixty thousand children, women and men, in one swallow.
Tidings of misfortune on rapid wings they do fly, the glorious
empire of Rome was lost, in a thousand pieces it lie crushed.
Yet, from tragedy a new hope may begin, humble, inglorious
at first, like a spark in the forest, a fire may rush,
rekindling the gods' favor, a new destiny for man,
there came along a hero, when one was needed so much.
O Muse, stay faithful, I pray. Tell us now of the divine plan,
of how this adventure, designed by the gods, really began.

It was in the year that Constantinople fell,
with an empire broken to great Turkish rage,
when the earth was turning towards Hades and hell,
after crusades had plundered, and known world, at this stage,
lie in flame, that the hero of our story, a child of Time,
the gallant Horacio, finally came of age.
Citizen of Rome by birth, descendant of faithful pagan line,
against all opposition, hidden from inquisition's eye
true of heart, last of noble Priam kin and kind,
and goddess Venus's womb, had secretly survived
to restore hope to the race of man and heal the ancient wound,
bringing forth a balance that would at last their hope revive.
On the night of his thirteenth year, at the strike of highest moon,
with stars shining down, through sky silent, clear and dark,
as he lie there sleeping, quiet as the tomb,
did Cupid's arrow, tracing the slow arc
of eons to his room, from godly Olympus above, find its mark.

Granting him a dream, a gift and a test,
from the Goddess of Beauty and Love, did the arrow lay.
"For me," she whispered and blessed
his ears, "and for all the gods you praise,
a quest must be fulfilled, so put aside your fears,
and set upon the path, else all will fade away."
Promises of glory, songs for a thousand and more years
be his. Moreover, the eternal gratitude of Jove
and all his lineage shall be restored, and for all of Ilium's tears.
Even Juno, Queen of the Heavens, shall forsake her trove
of rage upon the Trojan line, the goddess Venus pledged there and then.
"Great shall be your reward, for greater still be the danger wove.
To save the soul of human kind and renew a faith forgotten
would require a strength beyond all measure and season,
one not seen in a mortal's age, nor in the years of ten;
courage in the face of peril beyond all reason,
greater than that of all the heroes, you shall be their beacon.

"For it was you, who to roam
it has been chosen, to honor an ancient oath,
a new Achilles, born of mighty Rome
and Trojan stock, here upon the earth,
to break the locks of Pluto's home, to smash his wicked loom,
releasing from death's most guarded keep, unearth
the father, you must, from his abysmal tomb
and in so doing we gods will be liberated
from our eternal sleep filled doom."

Venus showed to him a secret passage in the dream, protected
by the most monstrous of beasts and foes,
a portal that would lead him undetected
to the bowels of Hades' inferno.
Here it is that he would find Lord Saturn, who had become
father of all the gods, creator and ruler of time itself, who long ago
gave birth to the tribes and race of Latinium,
now a prisoner himself, ad infinitum.

Slain by brothers three,
placed into Infinity Glass for all of time,
and into the hands of the god Pluto's keeping, he,
now in the underworld, cut off in his prime,
resides with the rest of the dead, and must be released.
"From goddess nape, into a turquoise sea, a necklace of fine
gems once did fall." The image she made vivid for Horacio to at ease
perceive. "Seven in total they count, sprung as enchanted isles of Italia,
off Lavinian coast, by Tuscan sea, the centerpiece,
most precious jewel of the string, by the Greek name Aethalia,
Pluto's Shrine is what you seek. Follow the trail of blood for safe landing
the omens are there to betray. Dread not the geologia,
although weaker hearts will curse its meaning,
from this path you mustn't stray. Many obstacles will surround you;
much there will be to overcome. The path will be most demanding,
yet through all your turmoil remember these words be true,
the greatest of all power is that of Love and that is what I give to you.

"More gifts you shall receive from above,
though we gods will be powerless to directly assist.
Trust in your heart, for above all, my love,
this is where your greatest ally is.
Search out the navel of the earth,
the gate, Enfola, the umbilical cord is this.
When in the darkest, moonless hour, look up from this hearth,
unto the vastness of the heavens in the sky,
and your path shall be unearthed.
Remember, with favor, you are regarded by the gods on high."
There, with a kiss left upon his cheek, the dream it faded.
Before departing, a gift goddess Venus laid by his side,
a reminder of his people's destiny, there with him in his bed,
the only tool with which the darkest prison he might destroy.
Then disappearing, with these final words she said,
"To smash the glass that captures time, employ
the long lost Sword of Troy."

BOOK III

HORACIO'S QUEST

Horacio woke from his dream, his head torn,
still spinning, groggy from the vividness
of his apparition, his chest still sore, worn
from where Cupid's arrow had stung, the rest,
all around silent in the early morning air,
except for the sound of swallows in their nests,
chirping outside his window, waking there
to the new day's light, he might,
as often happens, simply shake the sleep from his hair
and let be forgotten this vision of the night,
if not for the proof lying there by his side,
a sword glimmering and bright.
In the blade, sharpened to a fault, his reflection did shine
back upon him. Lifting it by the hilt,
unable to believe his eyes,
heavy in the hand, standing square and still,
the Sword of Troy before him, ready to do his will.

More than a sign, or some simple request,
his life's destiny, his people's history,
forged within that blade, in his hands there did rest.
He thought back upon all the stories,
of all the struggles and hardships
endured by his very kin, to return glory
to the house of Priam, and the gods he still worshipped,
over countless waves and the relentlessness
of Queen Juno's wrath, through wars and endless bloodshed, stripped,
to finally emerge victorious, at the very point of this sword no less;
to be now entrusted to his hand's grip,
for him to carry the destiny of his people's progress,
was both an honor and a duty that he could not simply skip.
Then and there he knew it was no mere shadow
playing tricks with his mind, to whip
him into foolishness, but a sacred quest he must follow,
the gods had willed it so.

Without a sound, full with the impetuousness
of youth, having no formulation of a plan,
other than the acorn planted in his consciousness,
he prepared a small satchel of trivial necessities and
a loaf of bread, wrapping his prized sword
in a thick oil cloth, wound with a chord to band,
placing it secure, until a proper scabbard
could be found, he strapped these contents to his back.
Soft on foot he passed a final glance, without a word,
upon parental chamber, where mother and father napped.
Sharing by appellation, both the father and he,
the name Horacio, the Keeper of Time. On track,
without a glance back, left his home to seek his glory
and fulfill the gods' request.
Come what may be, his destiny
now lies entwined unto this single quest.
Until complete his heart would know no rest.

Recalling stories of old,
of how ancestor Aeneas located their promised home,
knowing full well his journey be twice as bold,
without a guide to tell his feet the way to roam,
a memory entered his head of a powerful oracle
hidden in the cliffs far south of Rome,
on the outskirts of Naples, one beloved by Apollo,
where lived, he hoped still, the one who might
show him his path, the wise and wondrous Sibyl.
Many days and several nights
this journey would take, with much pain,
he knew, before gaining sight
of the Cave of the Cumaean
Sibyl, yet his steps were light as dewy rain,
and in his heart grew a gentle refrain
reminding him of how his ancestors came,
to see him through the bane:

"O, sons of Troy, do not despair.
Though skies be dark,
the seas be fair.
O'er the waves, there lies our mark.
The gods guide our way,
so lift your hearts.
O, sons of Troy, we'll have our day.
New home be promised
so beat back them waves.

O'er there, just through the mist,
you can see the light,
it can't be missed.
O, sons of Troy, our time be nigh,
so row, row, with all your might.
There be no time to sit and lie,
so row, row, with all your might.
O, sons of Troy, row, row, with all your might."

The world, for the first time to his eyes,
did open, every step a new adventure,
as life can only reveal itself to those guised
in their waking youth. Miles he ventured,
for days on end, sustaining himself on what nourishment
nature and the trees did bare. Indentured
to Fate, and his growing commitment,
knowing for the first time his share
of hunger, what it really meant,
at times eating only air, yet without a care,
the sun at his back
and wind in his hair,
there was no turning back.
Forward, he continued on his journey
into the unknown, with no lack
of fortitude, he embraced the destiny
set forth by mother Venus and the tide of history.

After seven days of lonely footed voyage,
Horacio came upon the vast rocky cliffs,
separating Neptune's infinite domain from the edge
of Earth's frontiers. In the air, a whiff
of sea salt rose up to greet him,
a reminder of his kinfolk's long shift
across the oceans, from exile to the Lavinian
coast and their heroic struggle
against Juno's longstanding anger, to finally win
a new home for their people
and the founding of the greatest
empire known to man. Here, just north of Naples,
at the precipice of the abyss,
it was that grandfather, Aeneas,
passed the crucial test,
passing through the fires of Avernus,
to Hades' gate, for his own quest to bless.

Horacio paused, and taking to his knee,
lifted prayers and praise to Apollo,
protector of the Ilian family.
Burning sage in his honor, so that he too may follow
in ancestor's footsteps and find in his time of need
the path to the rocky hollow,
which bore the oracle, Sibyl, who might lead
him unto the next step of his appointed task.
Through devotion's deed,
wearing the supplicant's mask,
a boon was granted and the skies did open,
parting clouds to reveal at last
a single stream of light, where upon
it rested on a shallow trapezoidal crevice.
Apollo's favor shone on him, like a beacon,
guiding his way along the precipice,
safely across the jagged, jutting cliffs.

On the path, a shrine he saw there,
formerly dedicated to Jupiter,
sitting abandoned and in disrepair
converted now to a basilica
for the new Christian deity.
Sweeping clean the alter,
he placed there, as a show of his piety,
a cluster of wildflowers.
A poor offering, yet, for one travelling in poverty,
also a gift rich in spirit and honor.
In times of great hunger and drought,
a gentle word can seem as ambrosia,
more so than can be brought about
by the slaying of a hundred bullocks,
from all the kings flaunting their clout.
So, with that simple gesture, for just a moment, the clocks
they stopped and joy floated down onto those assembled rocks.

Then Horacio came upon the entrance of the cave,
haunted by the absence of presence.
Yet, as if a spirit rising from the grave,
somewhere, just beyond the entrance,
he sensed that he was not quite at all alone.
Feeling the rising winds of Avernus,
blowing across the eaves, hoping that would hone
the spirits to his favor, he placed one careful step
beyond the portal, whence from within could be heard a moan.

"O Sibyl, prophetess great," Horacio kept
his breath at bay, "reveal yourself I pray.
Speak of the future once more. Long have you slept
and the need is great. Wake now, cast me not away.
For Troy, for man, and most of all, for the gods we serve,
I ask you show to me the way.
O oracle, hold not your voice in reserve.
Bless with me your guidance, for which I hope only to deserve."

The wind blew warm from the hundred directions,
from the hundred passages that cross-sectioned the cave,
filling Horacio with a sense of foreboding for a fraction
of a moment, which just as quickly did wane.
A spirit then surrounded him with fiery breath
that urged him to remain.
"O Trojan child of Venus breast,"
a chilling, ghostly voice called to our hero,
from where no living eye could attest.
"You arrive at the crossroads,
seeking my aide, which I will barter to give.
Pledge to me your word, with unbreakable oath,
O Keeper of Time, that if
the path required I do show,
in return you shall present me my gift.
Answer me now, son of Aeneas and Rome.
Shall I grant your request, or send you back home?"

To his knees, Horacio did drop,
pledging his word without delay.
"If it be in my power, nothing could stop
the fulfillment of this equitable trade.
Tell me the price required to be given,
O Sibyl, and on my life, I do obey."
The wind then blew hot and seared his abdomen
as a constant reminder of his sacred vow.
With that they struck their bargain
and the Sibyl, formless spirit began to howl.
"When your quest reach its end,
and you be near the father of time, as we are now,
the moment before you break the glass, and
Saturn be in the position to offer you a gift,
demand that bequest be that my torment he must end,
to turn back time and my curse to lift.
Too many years have I roamed this Earth, and desire no longer to live."

Struck in the heart, Horacio did fall,
moved deep inside by the Sibyl's sorrow and grief.
Not once had it occurred to consider at all,
the torture of endlessly diminishing, till the only relief
be that to simply lay down and die.
Empathy filled him beyond all measured belief,
whence hearing the prophetess's agonizing cry.
It was no longer a question of striking some deal,
but caring for another being was the reason why.
With a sigh, Sibyl saw his aver was real.
Only a true child of Venus
could produce such a compassionate zeal,
so filling herself with the air of Avernus,
a tempest swirled and vision fed,
hotter than all the fires of Vesuvius,
and in a cavernous voice full of portent and dread
all hundred doors flew open and on the winds the answer be said:

"O Trojan, Horacio, child of Love, hero of Time,
long is the road that lies before you.
Greater wars, bloodier than ever seen, and years equal only to mine,
must be overcome before rest finds you.
Many are the paths that lead beyond Hades' gate
yet only one, winding and narrow, through
which you may find the prize you seek, destined by Fate.
Chosen you are, the one to ancestor Aeneas I did speak,
equal to mighty Achilles you shall become before too late,
yet in the spring of your youth, still humble and weak,
stand you today and full a man must you become
prior to undertaking this venture. Therefore, seek
the road to Napoli, by which way will come
in three moons hence, under blackened sky, by ocean's gate, the tide
of your destiny. Remember, by Aethalia only may you come,
through that portal alone shall you find your guide. Bear in mind,
when others prepare to die, hold your ground and look the Gorgon in the eye."

With that the winds they lowered and died,
and old Sibyl returned to the vile in which she rested.
Her spirit gone, Horacio, as much as he tried
could not revive it, so instead of further testing,
he left a prayer and then himself retired from that place.
A direction he'd been given and all sorts of clues festered
in his mind. He had a million questions that raced
through his head, yet leaving with many more answers,
some to make use of in the moment, to trace

his path of the present, and still several others
that he hoped later to recall
when the need for recollection would tether.
For now, his road led to Naples
and in three nights hence,
gods willing, a first taste of the apple,
and his future would open, from whence
he may fulfill sacred mission and earn from the gods his recompense.

BOOK IV

RAID OF THE BARBARY CORSAIRS

Arriving in Naples, a first to his eyes,
Horacio stared out in wonder at this Renaissance seat.
In every direction, a spring of vitality energized
the teeming populace, as they haggled to compete
for the latest wears, arriving on merchant vessels,
from Pisa and Genoa and far away Crete.
The markets they bustled, while, under the shadow of the castle,
the port busily unloaded more goods.
No stranger to turmoil, the Kingdom of Naples,
was the center of shifts in regional power and it be understood
that in time all that comes will too one day be gone.
For the moment, from there where he stood,
Horacio could see flying, the colors of the Order of the Dragon.
From the House of Trastamara, surrounded by gothic architecture,
sat Alfonso the First, ruler of Naples and King of Aragon.
These were the times of upheaval, discovery and adventure,
a perfect place, Horacio thought, to commence his new venture.

Aiding Chance and the Fates, Horacio decided
to canvass the merchant ships at port,
in hopes that by actively pursuing the gods' design,
he might find work and passage of some sort
to his destination, and therefore speed up his prospects
to find the Isle of Aethalia. Yet, for all his effort
naught was to be found, except to collect
a handful of scorn and abuse.
None it would seem had any need to select
a youth with no seafaring knowledge to use.
With his spirits and the sun riding low,
discerning neither the right nor wrong way to choose,
he consoled himself, trusting that the prophecy before long would show,
and with it the direction in which his fortunes lie.
Feeling the weight of his days travelling the road,
he found a quiet spot near the port to rest for the night,
and letting his eyes close, he drifted to sleep there with a sigh.

The moon rose black that night
and nary a star could be seen in the heavens above.
An eerie silence filled the sky,
pitch in its darkness, as if wrapped in a glove.
The stillness woke Horacio with a shudder,
heart beating so fast, as if one in love.
In the next instant, an eruption of thunder,
shouts and cannon fire came from every direction,
the port was surrounded by marauders.
In they rushed, a tidal wave of destruction,
pillaging every vessel, looting all within reach.
Before he could even consider his options,
Horacio was taken captive, there on the beach.
Bells they tolled out, too late in their warning,
the bulkheads had already been breached.
By the time the soldiers arrived to fight back their storming,
escape had been made out to sea, far from the port and its moorings.

The Barbary Corsairs were known for their boldness,
a plague to settlements throughout the vast sea.
Now caught in their net, shivering from coldness,
Horacio and the rest of the captives were down on their knees.
The galley moved fast over the waves,
the oarsmen rowed hard, else was their backs that would bleed.
The pirates, hard lined, fierce looking naves
gazed upon the new comers with menacing posture,
ready to strike the first daring to misbehave.
One among the rest stood tall in his stature,
with a long midnight beard and skin, a bronze toughened hide.
He examined the booty that had all just been captured,
content, he was gloating, now riding high.
Snarling out orders, the men snapped to their duty,
the captain was he, none could deny.
It was then that his eye turned towards the captives, no longer free,
their fate in his hands, destined to be sold for another handsome fee.

In total the prisoners numbered a dozen,
seven men, four maids and Horacio, barely more than a child.
He examined them closely, his manner quite brazen,
in his eyes, a jaded kaleidoscope, there resembled something ferociously wild.
In his good time, after a long pull on his pipe of tobacco,
he turned once again and gave a sinister smile.
"I'm Reis-el-Kahn, and ye curs be mine, give up all hope fer the morrow,"
he cursed, accent thick with a heavy Turkish brogue.
"Do as yer told, and et'll save ye much sorrow,

but attempt te defy me, any of ye pathetic rouges,
and et'll be the hot end of the bosun's whip
that'll taste the flesh off yer bones."
The Barbary captain paused to stroke the steal of his sword's hip,
letting the terror he imbued distill to its full breadth.
"Let there be no doubt en yer minds," his words rolled along with the ship.
"I've not a lick of pity fer ye Christian dogs," there was spit on his breath,
"I'd just as soon look at ye, as throw ye te the depths."

It was not by intent, but a spontaneous reaction,
that Horacio did speak up, "I'm not a Christian,"
he simply said, but that was enough to draw unwanted attention.
"What'd ye say, boy?" Reis-el-Khan's head to him did spin.
"I'm not a Christian," Horacio repeated, wishing he had stayed silent.
An eyebrow lifted, as the captain contemplated the youth in front of him.
"Is that so?" he shifted to the other eye for a moment,
considering if punishment was merited for the outburst.
"So what be ye then, a Muslim per chance?" curiosity lent
a hand to fate. Perhaps, he thought, this one may have some worth?
"No sir," Horacio looked up mustering what courage he had,
"I serve Jove and the gods of old," he said, remaining true in his word.
Reis-el-Kahn turned with a great bellowing laugh,
"Ye hear that?" he addressed his crew of buccaneers.
"We've got a pagan on board, what a fortuitous catch.
Perhaps Neptune will bless our voyage te the slave markets of Algiers?"
The crew joined in with a round of chortles and jeers.

"Captain," one of the brigands stepped forward,
the pirate who'd captured the boy. "We found this in with his belongings,"
he said hoping to gain in favor, presenting the cloth covered sword.
"What be this?" Reis spoke with surprise, on unbinding
the parcel, lifting the foil up to the night.
"How come ye by such a magnificent blade?" he asked of the finding,
to which Horacio replied, "That is a gift and mine by birth right,
presented to me by my grandmother, the goddess Venus herself."
"That so?" there was scorn in the captain's voice. "Kin te those on high?
That should fetch me a pretty sum," he laughed to himself.
"You should be careful not to mock the gods," Horacio rebuked him.
"And ye should be careful not te be givin' orders on me ship, young whelp,"
Reis spun around, pointing the sword towards the boy's chin.
"I've got a right mind te carve out yer tongue fer yer insolence."
"Well," Horacio didn't know what came upon him, for no way was there to win,
"be warned, anyone but a Trojan to wield that will be cursed." With a tense,
"Ha," the captain scoffed, yet as a seafarer he paused at the tale. "Nonsense."

Reis-el-Kahn admired his captive's grit and comportment.
Perhaps he wouldn't damage him, yet there were more ways
than one for him to exact his punishment.
"Well, that line be dead," he spoke of Dardanian days.
"So none but ye, I suppose, would have much use fer this sword?
Ef that be the case, et might serve me best te send et back te whence et came."
Thrusting the blade back to the brigand who found it, "Throw et overboard,"
he gave his command. "No wait," Horacio cried.
"Hold yer tongue! That be twice ye've been warned, there won't be a third."
On that the captain gave his word, and nodded that his command be applied.
To that the sailor, regretting the loss, cast the weapon to the waves.
Neptune, in his own watery sleep, was at that moment unable to rise,
yet the nymphs of the ocean, in his stead, did what they could to aide,
from whence underneath they gave a gentle rock to the starboard
side, just as the sword had been cast to its watery grave,
lifting the ship just enough so that the hilt, striking the ascending oar,
spiraled back up, to lodge in the throat of he who had cast it, now no more.

Blood strew across the ship's deck,
as a panic ensued from all who witnessed the curse, like a burst,
instantly fulfilled, the proof gorged in the dead pirate's neck.
Reis-el-Khan blew a furious anger, he swore and cursed
in a rage, his eyes, they burnt with glowing fire.
"What devilry be this?" he shouted. Horacio prepared for the worst.
"Te the brig with the lot of 'em," the captain barked. Then, adding to the mire,
pointing a finger, "Not ye," he looked menacingly towards Horacio,
who suddenly felt the situation growing much more dire.
"Take this one below," a new command then rose.
"This one be not fer sale, shackle 'em te an oar.
Ef he give ye any lip, flog 'em back te his precious Jove.
That should give 'em a good taste of what lie en store."
The crew bustled furiously, roughly taking charge of the prisoners,
leading them away with a commotion and threatening roar,
while Captain Reis-el-Kahn contemplated his young pensioner,
removing the bloodied sword from the victim it had recently punctured.

Alone in his stateroom, by the light of a burning candle,
Captain Kahn, stared at the sword, reflecting a bright orange hue.
A gift, or a curse, he was trying to determine, gripping it by the handle.
The double blade cuts both ways, he saw, yet which direction be true?
If only one may use this, then the weapon also has a will of its own.
Already he'd seen its power and so had the crew.
Should he slaughter the boy and be rid of a dangerous foe,
or gain his trust, and thereby groom a future powerful ally?
These are the answers a good captain must know,

and he, descendant of the grand master Kublai,
was a great captain. His very name, Reis-el-Kahn,
meant Ruler of Kings, his ship, the swiftest galley
in the fleet, the Crescent Moon, under his command, had won
a hundred battles outright, yet this child perplexed him.
He would have to be hard on the boy, before it be settled and done,
ten times harder than on any of the warriors trained before him,
then alone would Khan know his true nature, whether he should die or live.

Down in the bowels of the galley,
Horacio was strapped, chained to a long wooden bench.
Five astride they sat, rowing oar eternally,
defecating right where they sat, was the life of these lowly wretches.
For six hundred miles his arms would burn,
pushing the sea, hardly ever earning a rest, he wrench.
Faster they barked, whips snapping at each in his turn,
until all hope of safe return was gone.
Such were the seafaring lessons to learn.
Then one day, during their voyage so long,
a sun baked strip of land came into sight.
Around the ship, as it landed, scores of people they thronged,
with multiple shades, from darkest dark to lightest light,
they chanted, with rhapsodic voices, using words he'd never heard before.
This was Algiers, where slaves would be auctioned at the going price.
Horacio prayed to the gods that here they might open the door,
but soon he would learn, that for him, another outcome they had store.

Above on deck, Horacio could hear, the other captives
being herded, through cries and pleas, they squeal,
off to be sold on the markets, praying for the Lord to forgive
their trespasses. For himself, he tried to fathom the reason for this ordeal.
Just then, a rattling of keys foretold of some new impending wreck.
"The captain wants to see you," the overseer balked with zeal,
loosening his shackles, grabbing him roughly by the scruff of his neck.
He was hauled to his feet, body aching and stiff with pain,
pushed ahead to comply, keeping his emotions in check,
lest he be whipped for an insolent refrain.
Alone in the stateroom, he stood silent before the captain,
who eyed how in these weeks he'd physically changed, from the strain
of pushing water. "Ye be a quandary te me boy," Reis-el-Kahn began.
"Yer not a Christian, so not me enemy, still yer not me friend.
So neither slavery nor freedom be a fit fate fer ye, understand?
Now, unless ye prefer yer work en the galley, where I promise yer life will end,
I've got another proposition te make te ye, ef yer ear ye care te lend?"

Considering his options, Horacio was listening intently.
"Seven years of service, that be the price," the captain laid out his offer.
"Ye swear te me, fer that period of time, yer fidelity,
and en exchange, well, first ye get te live... that already be a gift fer ye...
and moreover, ye'll be trained en the seafaring ways,
pirate that tis. Make no mistake about yer lot here,
ye'll be sailin' with a hardened crew, all of yer days.
Make a reckonin' man out of ye et will.
Fightin' and lootin', them be our ways,
and ye'll need te do the same. Bust yer arse and show yer steel,
or they'll be the devil come down on ye, that be the arrangement.
Speak up boy, are ye with the ship, or should I haul ye over the keel?"
It didn't take long for Horacio to think over his commitment.
"Aye captain, I will pledge my loyalty under those terms,"
he said, confirming the corsair's agreement.
"Very well then," taking his hand, Reis looked him in the eye, square and stern.
"As fer this cursed blade, et'll be fer me te decide when ye've earned ets return."

BOOK V

IN THE SERVICE OF REIS-EL-KHAN

Seven years be a long time to wait,
but longer still pushing an oar,
with no hope of escaping his fate.
If this truly be the path the gods had in store,
if somehow it be all part of the plan,
then he had no choice but to follow, for
it was controlled by destiny's hand.
The first year was the hardest,
he worked back breaking hours, more than
ever before. His service was not just a test,
constantly under a watchful eye,
being driven greater than all of the rest,
fearing that one mistake might cost him his life,
there was no option other than to give it his all.
Yet, in his heart, through all of the strife,
he never once forgot his pledge to the goddess's call,
regardless of what may come, in that duty, never would he fall.

The Crescent Moon
was a ship like no other, more than a galley,
a galleass, it was known, the Turks they called it a *mahon*.
Ahead of its time, the fastest ship on the sea,
it was said to be of Reis-el-Khan's own design,
with multiple desks and masts numbering three.
It had thirty-two oars, sixteen to a side
and fifty guns, twenty-three port and starboard each,
with two fore and aft, the only on the water to cover its behind,
no other had such a deadly, terrible reach.
It made port in Algiers, Rabat and Tripoli,
and all along the Barbary Coast, in each,
selling what they stole for a handsome fee,
with ten percent of the share going to the sultan
as homage, the standard duty for all ships of the fleet.
Hunting for treasure, Christian slaves and all that they can,
it was run by a crew of bloodthirsty pirates to the very last man.

Life on board was hard, fast and cheap,
seldom were there restful moments,
for maintaining the ship, their home and their keep,
was of the greatest importance.
For his part, Horacio was placed under
the direct supervision of the boatswain, of Moroccan decent,
Suleiman his name, a towering moor, with a voice of thunder.
As such, his duties were vast, from swabbing the deck
and repairing the sails, to hauling cargo and weighing the anchor.
Every aspect of caring for the ship fell on his neck,
and for that, in short order, both his body and value grew.
Of all his responsibilities, his preferred place on deck
was standing at the helm, steering the Crescent Moon,
setting her course, by the light of the stars,
learning the secrets of navigation that very few knew,
thus being able to cross the sea to points both near and far,
leaving only one item from which he was barred.

Being indentured in service and not truly free,
the captain forbade him to ever leave the ship,
whether it be at port or with a raiding party.
The temptation he felt would be too great to skip,
especially when near the coast of his homeland,
to find a way to give the others the slip,
so on board he must remain, unable to touch dry land.
That would all change though one night off the coast of Cartagena.
It was somewhere near the end of his third year of service and
the moon was dark as it'd been on the night he was captured in the arena.
Now the corsairs ran heavy, with a full contingent of bodies
in order to overwhelm the lightly crewed merchant vessels in the marina.
Plundering in this fashion, they would secure their booty.
However, on this particular night in question,
with a score and a half silently rowing out on their dinghies,
a trap was being sprung which caught them not paying attention.
From a hidden cove, Spanish soldiers were heading in their direction.

The attack came as an utter surprise,
with the raiding party caught half way to their target,
the Crescent Moon herself was now compromised.
With only a third of her crew on deck, guarding the parapet,
a boarding party of Spaniards jumped over the railing,
while the merchant vessels, militarized, began to set
their own cannons' sights on the smaller boats, now flailing.
The master gunner and his men were busy returning fire,
while above, on top deck, a furious battle was ensuing.

Hamid, the first mate, was the first to expire
taking a sword thrust direct to the heart,
while Reis-el-Kahn fought gallantly with his rapier,
slaying two soldiers immediately, just for a start.
The rest of the pirates were busy trading blows,
while those in their boats, made of rowing an art.
"Faster you dogs!" Suleiman yelled out his prose,
as cannon fire rang all around their heads, to heighten their woes.

At the peak of the battle, with the situation quite dire,
from the most unlikely source, came a turn of events.
Horacio, taking to arms, fought like infuriated spitfire,
a lion loosened from his cage, in a rage, an army hell bent.
With a blade he'd acquired from a soldier who fell,
he killed three at a time, to Hades they were all sent,
striking two in the head, and one through the lapel.
A fourth, a sergeant, most gruesome, he gorged in the neck,
just as the captain he was making ready to quell.
The returning crew, they scrambled to deck,
with shrapnel flying through the air, and not a moment to lose,
two Spanish war ships, were gaining on them, moving in to check.
"Hard a starboard," Kahn shouted commands like a hot fuse.
"Trim that sail. Gimme flank speed on them sweeps. Today!"
The boatswain doubled his orders, ready on the cues.
"Man those aft guns," the captain called out, above the fray.
"Be ready on my command, or there'll be the devil te pay."

The Crescent Moon tacked hard,
as a frantic chase then got underway.
Cannon fire blasted the rear quarter, in its wake leaving shards,
while the order was given to return fire the Spaniards' way.
Ringing the air with thunder, two shots were let off from the stern,
one crashing into the lead ship's bow, while the other went astray.
Catching the Spanish by surprise, it was now Kahn's turn,
"Give 'em another round," he yelled from his place at the helm,
as the gunners reloaded and once more let the fuses burn.
Two more blasts could be heard, as the Spanish, from their realm,
fell behind, and fortune be their ally for one more day,
though at a cost the entire crew felt in their hearts to whelm.
Sailing hard, with sweat and strain, they just managed to get away.
Coming to a safe distance, they began to assess what they'd lost.
Fifteen of their crew dead, with a rowboat sunk on the waves,
both the port and stern raked with holes, in total a heavy cost,
with nothing to show, but on the sea to be tossed.

"Bosun," Reis called, the ship in disarray.
"Get me a damage report," he ordered,
"and assemble a party te bail out the bilge right away."
"Aye, aye captain," Suleiman for his part concurred.
His top priority was to ensure they stayed afloat,
it was over two hundred miles before being safely harbored,
and they had to hope there were no more patrol boats,
for they might not survive a second encounter.
"And clear up this deck," he made another note,
while the carpenter, who doubled as a doctor,
tended to the wounded, and separated the dead.
Kahn finished off a still breathing solider,
with a thrust of his sword, his eyes seeing red.
Then, as he pitched the Spaniard overboard into the sea,
"Get their valuables, and send 'em all te the locker," he said.
It was a hard night for them all, as the ship listed towards the lee,
"Get them buckets working on the double," he shouted. "Nay, make that three."

Horacio was put in charge of a party of six, each with a pail,
as they headed straight to the bilge, down below deck,
and scooping up buckets of water, began they to bail.
The port side was leaking, so in order to prevent a wreck,
he busily filled the holes with oakum and hot pitch.
They worked through the night, the speed was breakneck.
Yet by the time they had finished mending each glitch,
the ship was now out of danger, again sitting upright.
Returning to top deck, drenched and covered in filth, every stitch,
they saw the sun on the horizon, having made it through the night.
Dawn now upon them and work complete, the ship was again sailing clear,
as Captain Kahn, tall in red turban, called Horacio to stand on his right.
With a look in the eye, he slapped Horacio on the back, drawing him near.
"Ye saved me life en battle, when instead ye could have let me die,
no greater pact 'tween men can be made," he spoke for all the crew to hear.
"So en return fer yer valor, that which no man may deny,
let me offer back te ye what et tis ye most prize."

With that the Sword of Troy he present,
handing it over to Horacio, as a sign of his own trust,
in honor of their longstanding agreement.
"En my culture, pagan, the saving of a life is a debt which must
be repaid. As captain, from a line of warriors, both powerful and great,
et is beneath me te neglect this responsibility, thus,
I've decided, en light of the demise of Hamid, our first mate,
you shall be elevated te take up his post."
Surprise and grumblings could be heard from the crew, "Wait,"

the captain demanded. "Who better te be me second coats,
than the one who guards me back?
B'sides, a fine fighter ye be, as evident en how ye joust,
but by me side ye want te be, ef I be te train ye en what ye lack."
The decision was final, the crew saw that to be true.
No friends it earned Horacio, yet none had a bone in the back
to contest their captain's command, for with their own eyes they knew
Horacio had faithfully paid with honor his due.

It was no favor the captain gave,
making Horacio his second in command.
As such, his work was now doubly grave,
having to both fulfill his current functions and
oversee the crew, of whom he'd just recently been subservient.
It was either swim or die, his path to becoming a man.
Yet, along with the added commitment,
his new post also came with special benefits.
No longer was he acquiescent,
a scabbard's dog, a lowly misfit,
but being trained as a leader,
with his own authority of writ,
learning the subtleties of wielding power,
of how to inspire without being despised,
to win the hearts of the crew, to flower
in their eyes was most greatly prized
and the mountain that must be sized.

It was a grueling week at sea
directly after the battle.
They had to travel at speed.
Supplies were low and nerves rattled
and still repairs needed to be made,
work crews to be assembled
and between Horacio, Suleiman
and Ali Abbas, the ship's carpenter,
the three were responsible. Yet, at the end of the day,
Horacio alone sat by the captain's side to receive new orders.
This is when they would parley, until the hours wee,
when all his strength he would have to muster,
for as grueling as the physical duty may be
the intellectual held no less importance.
Here it was not just charts and strategy,
but religion, philosophy and political stances;
to shape the world, one must first shape his own intelligence.

After ten days, they finally arrived in Algiers.
Memories of his first moments in that port,
chained to a bench and oar, filled with fears,
came rushing back, as will such thoughts report.
Horacio prayed to his patron, Apollo, for the strength
to continue. For now, esteemed in the pirate court,
how simple it would be for him at length
to abandon his pledge and all other care,
and just give himself over to a life spent
on the high seas as a buccaneer corsair,
mastered by none but his own heart's whim,
to be a scourge to all that is good and fair,
as the life chosen by all those around him.
It would be dishonest for Horacio to say
that he too did not share a taste for blood within,
that he would not prefer to choose this way.
This was the struggle he wished to stay.

Algiers, also known as *al-Jazā'er,*
a magnificent port city of glistening white,
lying at the crossroads of two empires,
was quickly reaching its height
of influence and power in the region.
It was sought by Spaniards and Ottomans alike,
as a rich trading ground, with no formal adhesion.
Under the amir it maintained a large measure of independence.
At the gates there was no occupying legion,
and though the Spaniards did hold a presence,
passage was allowed to all those wishing to enter and leave.
It was here, past the islet of Peñón, whence
the Crescent Moon did come to weave
a path to safe harbor for essential repairs,
and for the crew a much welcome shore leave.
"Heave to," Horacio called out, bringing the ship square
with the dock, slowing it into position with care.

Watches were assigned and work crews organized.
Ali Abbas, their carpenter, an Ottoman Turk,
would oversee the repairs, while Horacio itemized
the needed supplies; all those not on call to work
were free to go ashore at their own discretion.
For his part, Reis-el-Khan kept an eye on his handiwork.
Silently, he pulled at his beard, deciding on a direction.
"That's settled then," he declared, if for no one than himself.
"Enough of that," he called Horacio to attention.

"Come with me," his thoughts seemed to be engulfed.
"Aye captain," Horacio responded, falling into line.
"And ye too," to Suleiman he commanded, "bring yerself."
What the captain was up to they'd discover in due time.
For now, the three made fast for the gangplank.
"After ye," Reis motioned for Horacio to go by.
"Captain?" he looked at him, wondering if he was playing a prank,
three years had it been since dry land his feet had drank.

"Aye advance," the captain gave the order.
"Ye be a bona fide member of the crew,
there be no restriction on ye now and ashore
is where ye be needed fer what we have te do."
Horacio took one tentative step and then another,
until a full stride placed him upon the long wharf, onto
the gulf separating sea from land. Striking earth with a shudder,
he stood still, motionless for the first time in years.
"Will ye look at that," Reis laughed with bluster,
"the boy's land-sick. Aye, welcome to Algiers."
The three walked side by side, under the early morning sun,
pacing their steps through the throng that there gathers,
bartering goods and human flesh and what may be spun
in the trading markets, outside the fortified city walls.
"This be just a taste," Khan's voice beckoned, having begun
their journey through the city's gate, standing tall, it sprawls
upward in defense of the white city and her majestic halls.

"Welcome te the Kasbah!"
Kahn exclaimed, jubilantly.
A thick and twisting labyrinth ran far
up the hillside, built at an angle, vertically,
separating the Low city, that of the people,
from that of the deys, the High city,
home of the rulers, a virtual citadel.
The Kasbah was the beating heart of Algiers,
with markets and squares, brothels and temples,
where people from every walk of life and all spheres
came together. "Have ye ever seen the likes?" Kahn inquired.
"Never," Horacio replied, in awe of the fodder that appears
before his eyes. "Of course, ye haven't young squire,"
Reis rejoined. "There's nothin' te match this anywhere."
He was excited now, his pace it quickened, his eyes on fire,
as they ascended the hill, carving a path to some secret lair,
"Where are you leading us?" Horacio asked, and Khan, "Te see the amir."

BOOK VI

THE BATTLE OF ALGIERS

Up the winding hillside they climbed,
Reis navigating the twisting alleyways
all by memory. The bell of adhan then chimed,
as they came through a passageway
to a large public square.
Suddenly their momentum gave way
to a mass of supplication, where
hundreds of bodies turned towards the east,
all falling into line. "Mid-morning prayer,"
Suleiman whispered in Horacio's ear, as Reis and he
joined in the ceremony of touching their foreheads to the ground,
reciting the ritual of prayers, four times each.
Horacio had of course already seen this around
the ship and was familiar with the daily homage,
this however was quite different from anything he'd previously found,
an entire city stopping in mid-stride, people of all ranks and ages,
together lowering their heads to the sun, here in the heights of Algiers.

It began by standing touching hands to the ears
with the words, *Allāhu 'akbar,* "God is Great,"
on their lips for themselves alone to hear.
Hands on chest they continued the rakat,
quoting scriptures from the Quran.
Bowing, then three times did they iterate,
"Glory to my Lord, the Most Magnificent" and
standing again, "Allah listens and responds to
the one who praises him." Then, *Rabbanā wa-laka al-hamd,*
"O our Lord! And all praise is for You."
Now lying prostrate with head and palms upon the ground,
"Glory to my Lord, the Most High Most Praiseworthy," three times they do,
from whence they sit before again lying down for another round.
When complete they sit once more, recite a prayer, then stand and repeat.
For the final raka'ah, while sitting on the ground,
to the right, then the left, a blessing do they offer from their seat,
"May Allah grant you peace and security, and upon you may His Mercy be."

Horacio watched the practice in amazement
and could not help but feel compelled
to join in, not for some stirring commitment
to the Muslim god, but for how they resembled,
in their honoring, his own dedication to the gods he praised.
Dropping to his knees, he followed those assembled,
offering worship to Jove, Venus and Apollo, he raised
words of thanks for seeing him thus far safe upon his journey,
renewing his pledge to fulfill the quest, on this he prayed.
When complete, they then took to their feet and turned towards an alley
to continue their climb, passing brightly robed, bearded merchants
and the odd camel chewing its cud, their footsteps they rallied.
Reis was eager to make the assent, he had an obvious penchant
to complete some mission, his haste betrayed the fact.
Arriving at the pinnacle, to their eyes opened the magnificent,
a towered palace with fortified clefts and a spire cap.
Before an archway opening, huge tents, proffering wares, lined the tract.

Tales of Scheherazade would not seem as vibrant
to Horacio's eyes, for all the splendor before him.
A cacophony filled the air with voices and accents,
while in the background there lifted chants and hymns.
Everywhere an explosion of color, from orange terracotta,
to turquoise and jade, to the deepest of crimsons
filling his senses, as bright as the white of day. The palace, a basilica,
with domes and detailed mosaics, every facet
a work by craftsmen, skilled in their trade, like the Kasbah,
in itself unique to this world, impossible to recreate, 'cept
for in the expanding eye of the imagination,
where all things become achievable in concept,
yet in the tangible, for what can be touched and true, duplication
fell outside the realm of the feasible.
Here alone in the Algerian nation
stood an image completely unimpeachable,
for the sole fact that it be singular to this Earth, non-reproducible.

The three passed through the arched gateway without interruption,
Reis-el-Khan, to the eye himself would pass for royalty,
dressed in scarlet turban and the finest linens. By interpretation,
none would dare question his writ of authority.
Inside, they came upon a gardened courtyard,
where a guard and secretary protected the inner passageway.
Here, Khan was most direct. In the eye, he looked the secretary hard,
"Tell the dey, Reis-el-Khan is here and must speak te 'im now."
The secretary, a middling man of plump stature floundered,

coughed and stepped back, accustomed only to those who kowtow,
was unprepared for such a direct command.
"Just a minute," he spoke with a nervous tone,
and disappeared into the inner chamber, according to Reis's plan,
then a moment later, reemerged with doors open wide,
"Right this way," the secretary gestured with a wave of his hand.
"The dey is please to have you once again by his side."
And with that he led the party of three inside.

The audience chamber was even more impressive
than the outer trappings, with marble floor
and vaulted ceiling, the space was expansive,
able to hold a thousand and more.
The inner dome was an intricate golden mandala,
while pink and sandstone colored columns bore
the memory of eons past, dating back as far
as Mohammed. Elaborate scrawls in Arabic
decorated the walls, with words to remind pashas
of their own frailty and subservience. A tonic
for the soul, the whole scene presented itself
with perfect symmetry. At the far end of this epic
sat the royal dey, Abu Abbas Ahmad, himself.
Of the Zayyanid dynastic line, a Berber tribe,
that maintained with difficulty its power and wealth,
internal struggles having marred the entire line,
he ruled with caution, nearing the end of his prime.

Long bearded he sat, with flowing amber tunic
and an aged authority. He was surrounded
by courtiers, petitioners, slave girls and eunuchs.
Seeing the approaching company of Reis, he grounded
himself with a broad smile of salutation.
"Welcome, dear cousin, captain of the seas," he expounded.
"*As-salāmu 'alaykum*," he offered the greeting of tradition.
"*Wa 'alaykumu as-salām*," and peace be upon you,
Reis-el-Khan returned as custom demanded, a precondition
of their faith. "Hopes me visit finds ye well, O great amir?" he continued
the necessary preamble. "Very well, thank you for asking,"
the dey responded. "And how are the seas treating you?"
"Couldn't be better, praise Allah," Khan bowed his head, reaching
the end of his patience. "I come though on urgent business
and must speak with ye en private," unmasking
his true intentions. The dey's hard lined face tightened, as witness
to his internal discomfort of being in Khan's presence.

Although unquestioned in his right to rule,
the amir always suffered a slight tinge of anxiety,
when Reis came to visit. Not as though they were locked in duel,
but more the sense of being confronted by one who was truly free,
when he himself was a prisoner to his own responsibility, and therefore,
while fully in control, he still felt compelled to comply with the decree.
Exhaling a breath, as though if to consider for a moment more,
"Very well," he nodded his assent. "As you wish," he clapped his hands.
"Leave us," the dey commanded, to which all those who sat before
him, except for the guards and lowly servants, he disbands,
ushering into the adjoining anti-chamber to await further instructions.
"Come now, my old friend, why all the theatrics?" the amir demands,
once they were alone, wanting to hear straightaway the induction.
Khan bowed once more with exaggerated flourish,
"Fergive me intrusion, but I come te warn ye of yer pending destruction.
Hear me words, fer all ye hold dear and cherish,
else et be yer kingdom shall perish."

Reis-el-Khan was most direct with his charity,
never one to mince his words, he got right to the subject.
"Them damned Spaniards be preparing te attack the city
and take et fer their own," his words had an immediate effect.
The amir's cinnamon complexion began to pale.
A long history there'd been in the borderlands, where empires intersect,
and the imagination did not need to stray too far to believe such a tale.
His attention was captured. "Tell me what you know," the dey implored.
"Just ten nights past," Khan began, "I got a glimpse behind their veil
and narrowly escaped with me skin. There, behind the doors
of Aragon, off Cartagena coast, a fleet of ships be massin'
with only one purpose, te take them straights, I've seen this all before."
The amir listened carefully, letting not a word go in the passing,
"Indeed this is grave news, but how do you know Algiers is their target?"
"Ah," Reis caught his eye, "fer something that cannot go missin'.
They be already en yer port, standing at the ready, I regret,
fer the right moment te turn yer streets scarlet."

Abu Abbas Ahmad, Amir of Algiers,
no stranger to intrigue and diplomacy,
thinks carefully upon the words he hears.
Reis-el-Khan, he knows is a master of strategy,
but the question in his mind is, what be the actual target?
"It is true, the Spaniards have a few ships here," he admits freely.
"Yet Algiers remains an open port now for years, do not forget,
and the trade that flows through these doors depends," he panned,
"upon us maintaining our position of neutrality, so I regret,

without clear evidence, caution must prevail, you understand?"
"Aye, yer words be just," Reis knows he must joust to prevail.
"So consider the position en which yer city now stands.
A fleet be massin', their steps be bold," he then told the tale
of how his ship came under attack. "Et be no coincidence
that the largest port, and en strikin' distance, would be buildin' te scale.
They be armin' heavily, and not te repel a raidin' party. There be no innocence
en what them infidels be doin', mere days away from yer capital's entrance."

The amir took a heavy breath,
Khan was no fool in military matters,
his lineage spoke of that at length,
he would have to weigh seriously the factors.
"What is it that you would propose, my friend?"
"Te drive 'em from yer shores, te scatters
'em across the seas, te harry their forces te no end.
This ye know cannot be done alone, therefore
allies must we have, a pact with the Ottomans," Khan bend.
"This is what you'd have me do?" the dey sounded sore.
"To exchange one foreign rule for another; to risk
open war? Nay, that I cannot afford."
"Aye, not en yer name, fer sure," his speech was brisk,
"but remember we be Berbers from the same clan,
Ottomans of the same blood and religion, the real risk
es te let these Christians get a foothold on our land.
Te repel 'em," Khan looked shrewd, "fer that I has a plan."

Hearing him out, the amir did agree,
it was a bold act, more daring than anything yet tested.
To challenge an entire empire and theocracy
with a rag-tag corsair fleet suggested
that war could be waged without a flag
or sovereign, who could be directly contested,
while still reaping the benefits, and as always, snag
a percent of the pillage. With little direct risk, a sound investment.
"What is it you need?" the dey inquired, contemplating the price tag.
"Stocks, provisions and twenty strong seamen, who'll make the commitment."
Khan was not greedy in his request, his reward was glory
above all the rest, he took only what was required to make a dent,
and with that most importantly, a pledge to support as a signatory,
an appeal to the Ottoman Empire, for their participation
in such a venture. The real capital, the ships and crews, obligatorily
he knew, must come from the sultan, yet confident in his station,
with Algiers securely at his back, he could unite the various factions.

"Take what you need from my stores,"
the amir agreed to Khan's requisition.
"As for men, you may have your score.
Review the ranks and make your selection.
Be a guest here in my home, while your repairs
are being made. You and your men have a welcome reception.
Carry out your war. All this I grant you, but take care,"
the amir was clear on this point, "in no way shall I support
open battles in my harbor. I cannot afford to let tensions flare
between Algiers and the Spaniards. Keep the fight clear of my port.
In all other ways I'll support you as I can, but we must maintain,
at least for now, the illusion of neutrality. I'm sure you can comport
yourself to this one restriction." Khan bowed, knowing better than to strain
the point, he'd take what he could in the present moment
and let the rising tide conduct the oncoming train.
"What was that all about?" Horacio asked, once clear of the compartment.
"Politics, me boy," was Khan's sole rejoining statement.

With official writ in hand,
the training grounds were their next stop.
Passing an eye, it would be understated to say that Khan
was less than impressed by the prospects that dropped
from the royal tree. "No wonder he has no nerve fer a fight,"
Khan was direct in his assessment of the crop.
"I need men who can handle a rope and brawl all night,
who won't lose their dinner en a gale
and this bunch don't even know their left from their right."
Horacio's eye though was caught by something a bit less frail,
a reminder of ancient glory, from the line of ancestors,
of those from Trojan stories and heroic tales.
"That one," Horacio pointed towards a group of archers.
"What be en yer head?" Khan was quick to rebuke the request.
"Bowmen be no use onboard ship." Still Horacio replied, contrary to protestors,
"Perhaps not for sailing, that much is true, but if battle is your quest,
that one's yet to miss his mark. Imagine what he could do in the crow's nest?"

"Aye," Kahn lifted a brow, seeing the point.
"That could pose a serious threat indeed,"
the captain applauded his second's viewpoint.
"Yer've got a good eye fer flesh, but let us see,"
he desired a higher test, "ef he can hit a movin' target?"
"Ye there," he called approaching, "young steed
with the quiver. Yer've got some talent, but ferget
them stationary objects. See that swift doin' them loops,"
he pointed two hundred paces away to a fast flying bird curving an orbit.

"Can yer knock that down, or are yer just good at shootin' hoops?"
The young archer, by name of Avranos, took up a challenging stance,
not one to let his pride or reputation suffer ridicule, an arrow he scoops.
"Oh, so you want to see some shooting," he smiled, taking his balance
and without hesitation pulled back the string of his bow, aimed at the sky,
and, as though if watching a guru in some spiritual trance,
stopping his breath, he released the line, letting the arrow fly,
as the bird it fell dead to the ground with an arrow in its eye.

"Yer hired," Khan grinned. "Welcome te the crew."
"Excuse me?" Avranos was taken aback by the situation.
"Ye seek adventure, glory, te make a name fer yerself, ye do?"
Khan cut straight through the confusion.
"Yes," the bowman answered in truth, "but I..."
"Excellent, then by order of the amir," Khan answered the question,
"ye belong te me. Gather yer things, the time be nigh.
Report te the Crescent Moon within the hour."
"Well, that's one down, only nineteen more te find,"
Reis was happy the search hadn't been all sour.
Horacio had once again proven his worth, to see merit
in the unconventional, his own value was beginning to flower,
each day growing as a leader, showing himself as a true asset.
By day's end, they had found half of the needed stock.
Four brawny men, Evhad, Davud, Butrus and Kismet;
three good swordsmen, Etci, Kasim and a Pashtun named Baloch;
finally to round off, a pair of fighting twins, Isa and Nebi, each solid as rock.

Later that night, while at banquet
in the amir's palace, they continued their banter.
"We got some good fighters today, that be an asset,
but what we really need is a few real panthers,
some scallywags and savages," Khan ate his meat right off the bone.
"There's only one place to find that lot, to be sure," in answer
Suleiman responded to the captain's groan.
"Aye, yer right on that," Reis replied.
"Where's that?" Horacio asked, aside in his tone.
"Down on the ships in the harbor," Suleiman confided.
"That's where all the seafarin' men are," Reis agreed.
"On the morrow," to the boatswain he guide,
"go canvass the port te find what we need.
Press inte service ef ye must, te complete the quota,
while the two of us raid the pantry," he nodded to Horacio, his steed.
"We sail on the mornin' tide after next. Have the ship ready fer muster."
"Aye," Suleiman agreed. Then Horacio he eyed, "Et's time te earn yer diploma."

That night, with all in the palace at rest,
a footfall sounded softly outside of Horacio's chamber.
He stirred from dream, half asleep, heart pounding in his chest,
yet alert, still feigning sleep, he reached quietly for his dagger,
at the sound of door creaking and approaching footstep.
Perhaps, he guessed to be victim of some plot, so as to surprise the intruder,
he spun quickly in his sheets, taking hold of the uninvited guest, who crept
in closer. With blade an inch from the throat, a muffled gasp the only sound.
A girl it was, no older than himself, with hair a swirling raven nest that swept
past shoulder and eyes a grey ocean tempest, mesmerizing and profound.
She trembled in his grasp. "What's the meaning of all this?"
Horacio asked the maiden in his hand, knife he laid to the ground.
"I am offered to you, from the amir, as his gift.
If I do not please you..." Horacio stopped her there, heart beating fast
"A gift from the gods no less," he corrected, thumb caressed her kiss,
as he felt the tan of her cheek blushing in his hand, yet had to ask,
"Is this also your desire?" Returning his gaze, "Oh yes," she said at last.

He took her there as only can those in the passion of youth,
with a gentleness and strength and unbridled yearning.
For him it was a first, so he could not say in truth
if it was indeed love that kindled within him, burning,
yet in other circumstances he could see himself risking all for her.
As it was, two slaves, caught in a moment of freedom, learning
what it meant to be happy in the arms of the other
would have to be enough to last a lifetime.
As dawn edged upon the horizon, so too must they suffer
the final minutes of what precious time
to them had been granted, both a blessing and a curse.
"Tell me your name, before you depart," the bells began to chime.
"Medea," she whispered, with a farewell kiss.
"I shall not forget you," never had he spoken more true.
"Nor I you," she returned his gentle promise,
before departing, slipping from his embrace, as must she do,
and he, to prepare for another long journey, bid her a fond ado.

The day was already busily underway
by the time Horacio and Khan met at the storehouse.
Servants and porters were lined up, helpfully in the way,
while the sounds of merchants and tradesmen announce
in the distance that business was ready to be conducted.
Algiers lived and died with the sun, as how it did rouse
the white city going back centuries. The servants, as instructed,
were preparing the carts and mules to transport the needed cargo
to the port, all to be loaded upon their vessel as contracted.

Horacio, though concealing well his thoughts, let forgo
his usual attentiveness, preoccupied with the memory
of his nocturnal affair. "Aye, snap to, time te go,"
Khan gave him a nudge, recognizing his slowing functionary
motions. "Didn't get enough sleep last night?" the captain jibed
with insinuation. As with all those who ruled, and he especially,
Khan, even when he saw nothing, he knew everything, besides
it was he who'd sent the girl. "No, of course, I'm fine," Horacio lied.

"Aye, that be good," Reis encouraged,
"fer I want ye on the midnight watch t'night."
"Aye captain," he already felt how the oncoming challenged.
It wasn't punishment, Horacio knew, merely the right
course of action. On the final night in port,
with enemy ships sharing the harbor and in sight,
there was no room to chance a retort,
all eyes on duty would have to be vigilant.
With the sun now riding low, back on board,
with cargo stored in the hold and a full contingent,
Reis-el-Khan called the crew to quarters.
"Listen up," he announced to the body of pirates belligerent.
"Many of ye be on yer first voyage, some trained only as soldiers.
Goin' forward ye must ferget all about yer past life.
From this moment, ye be only corsairs. Them be yer orders.
Learn quick and remember this ship be yer wife.
Take good care of her and she'll guard yer life."

With that the order to fall out was given,
all hands busied themselves, making final
arrangements, the only thing missing
was the command to make sail,
and for that the captain had made his decision,
to wait until first light, till then they'd stay idle.
Horacio and Suleiman made their inspection,
with Ali Abbas, who'd overseen the needed repair.
Then, with night taking over and black covering the horizon,
something they hadn't expected arrived to their lair,
a shipment of barrels and an extra rowboat.
"Aye, get that loaded up on the double," the captain came to declare,
emerging from his cabin. "Captain, we've already replaced the lost boat,"
Horacio questioned. "Aye, there be yer good eye workin' again,
well done. Just strap et all te the aft fer now," Khan passed the note.
With boat and barrels hitched astern, the crew settled back in
making the most of their rest, before the voyage begins.

In the still of the night,
Horacio, hours into his watch,
with Avranos, the bowman, by his side,
doubling as lookout, for eyes being topnotch,
he could at a great distance detect any disturbance,
making him doubly valuable in a tight notch.
Originally from the Aegean, his people were Thracians,
noble allies to Troy in the great ancient war.
His father, Acamas, a scout in Suleyman's resurgence,
during the Ottoman Interregnum, fought bravely in Bursa
and later distinguished himself at the battle of Kosmidion,
aiding in the defection of Vuk Lazarević, a vassal of Musa,
helping to win the day for his side. Ties going back eons,
the two quickly bonded as allies and friends.
At the midway point in the watch, the two Aegeans
surrounded by silence, as the second hour came to its end,
were suddenly jolted into action, as Khan appeared to them.

"Rouse the crew," Reis commanded.
"Get ready te make sail," his voice near to whisper.
"Sir, against the tide?" Horacio contended.
"Aye that be right, against the tide, mister.
An' keep yer voices low, I don't wanna hear so much as a peep."
"Aye captain, right away," Horacio confirmed the order.
"An' ye, come with me," he eyed Avranos, "Time te earn yer keep."
With that the entire crew was set into motion.
All hands at their stations, "Hold off on them sweeps,"
Khan, from the helm, was quick to mention,
as the order to cast off was then given.
Against the tide, with sails alone, they slowly changed their position,
yet silently too they crept through the harbor, only the heavens
as witness, while all others slept, unaware of their game.
Seeking position, Khan maneuvered until they were even
with a pair of Spanish ships tied to the dock. Stealthily he came,
not too close, but on passing kept in line, eye taking careful aim.

Gaining some distance, timing his action,
Khan gave a nod to Suleiman standing ready at the aft.
"Now, loosen them ropes," to which the boatswain
let go of the line, cutting the dinghy below loose from their craft.
The small boat, heavy with barrels, drifted with the incoming tide
back the way they had just come, where at last
it approached the space between the two ships parked astride.
"Ready on them sweeps," Khan called when the proper time came.
"Light 'er up," he ordered Avranos, who with pitch set his arrow on fire.

A shot flew across the sky, as a star descending in flame,
lighting upon a heap of loose gunpowder in the dinghy,
a great explosion from which then rang,
crippling both vessels, cutting holes both large and fiery.
"Row ye dogs!" Khan then commanded, eyeing open sea.
The Crescent Moon lurched forward with speed. "Well done, matey!"
"I thought the amir forbade fights in his harbor?" Horacio asked quietly.
"That implies they can hit back," Khan gaffed. "This be aggressive diplomacy."

BOOK VII

AT WAR

Having reached the Ottoman seat
in Constantinople, now renamed Istanbul,
conferring with the power elite,
and Mehmed II, the sultan, directly, adding fuel
to his story for the urgency of action,
Captain Reis-el-Khan, became the center of the whirlpool.
Mehmed II, known as the Conqueror, already desired an expansion
of his empire further to the west
and this timely arrival set off a chain reaction.
Khan was commended, his vision blessed,
backed by additional resources, the Barbary Corsairs
now had official sanction to pillage and wrest
as much as they could capture from the Christian spheres
of influence. Khan himself protected by letters of marque,
was named admiral and granted authority over the affairs
of all other pirate vessels, to direct and embark
into battle, as representative of the monarch.

Though primarily ceremonial,
knowing the anarchist nature of pirates,
the honor itself was testimonial
to Khan's own influence and merit.
Having gained his suit and advanced position,
Khan desired no further delay to forfeit
the accomplishments he'd made. Action
was now, above all else, required.
Word would quickly spread to every nation
that the Mediterranean was mired
not just with corsairs, but with a fleet
and a mission to crush the western empires.
For certain, retaliation the kings would seek,
that a price would be put on their heads,
for the daring to challenge their royal seats,
that if caught bloody would be their deathbeds,
yet fight they would, the enemy to taste their lead.

Embarking with new found bravado,
Khan, and the crew of the Crescent Moon,
charged into battle, with a daring do
that even excelled their own former exploits, gaining boons
tenfold, as they raided port after port, striking the enemy,
directly targeting fighting ships of the line. Soon
enough they became the most feared ship on the sea.
None suffering more than the Spaniards
and the Kingdom of Aragon, who paid a heavy fee
for the past injury, one which Khan always remembered,
as a point of honor, having been caught once unawares,
it was not a mistake he would again repeat, a hard
lesson learned. The bluster of the corsairs
though was not without consequence.
In retaliation, Spain targeted Algiers,
increasing in the harbor their naval presence,
to deny a safe port to the accursed pirate pestilence.

Khan however was unfettered,
"Et just shows they're scared," he'd boast,
which was not absent of some merit. Undeterred,
he pressed the course, mapping out targets all along the coast.
"The trick," he schooled his young apprentice,
"is te be unpredictable. Ye can take out an entire host
with a single ship, ef ye know their patterns. These Spaniards be novices.
They follow the very same routes every time
and that gives us the advantage."
Khan to the contrary, stayed ahead by redrawing the lines,
suddenly changing direction, skipping obvious targets,
"Be everywhere and nowhere at once," he chimed,
which led to the circumstances of their present harvest,
coming up fast on the tail of a Spanish galley.
"Let rip the long guns, Give 'em a blast they won't soon ferget,"
Khan grinned, speed and cunning being his ally.
"Prepare fer battle," he advised Horacio. "Yer sword be needed today."

The fore cannons echoed,
tearing holes in the stern of the Spanish war vessel.
as the distance between the two ships narrowed.
In hand, the strongest held the grapples,
while the boarding party stood at the ready.
Swerving course the Spanish attempted to wrestle
for better position, yet the Crescent Moon was too steady,
matching each turn and maneuver.
Gaining, Khan eyed his prize already.

"Take out 'er mast!" he gave a strategic order,
preferring to cripple the ship than sending it to the depths.
A shot rang out with devilish fodder,
two cannonballs linked by a chain, slicing the breadth
of air that separated them, cutting the enemy's center mast to splinters.
The Spanish man-of-war, was dead in the water. Christendom wept,
the day they made Khan their enemy, for none could hinder
his purpose, driven by a vision that was singular.

The battle was won before it even began.
The boarding party, fierce as any ever seen,
had taken the main deck and the ship's captain.
Any resisters, who threatened to intervene,
were cut down by Avranos, high up in the crow's nest,
with arrows that until too late went unseen.
Another ship they'd been able to arrest,
another crew taken for ransom,
yet this was just the beginning of the unrest,
Khan had a plan for bigger things to come.
After two years of concerted effort,
creating havoc on the seas, every skirmish won,
it was time for the next phase to erupt.
With reputation and Ottoman backing secure,
with more ships coming on line to support,
with more pirates being drawn to reward's allure,
finally all the pieces were in place for what he had in store.

It was in his sixth year of service,
Horacio, now a skilled seaman
in his own right, no longer the apprentice,
but a natural leader, and with sword in hand
one to be feared, that the war on the seas escalated.
Having attained a fleet of a hundred galley ships to command,
Khan could now directly threaten those who grated
upon his ambitions and sense of freedom.
While the sultan pressed his forces from the east, Khan concentrated
on wreaking havoc in the west, disrupting trade from the major kingdoms,
scattering their energies across the Mediterranean.
Just as shipping had reached its height of tension,
together they shifted their focus to another plane,
in a move unexpected, like a sudden Halleluiah,
their eyes turned back towards the Aegean.
For Horacio a gift, for Troy would now return to Sparta,
to attack the enemy of old; their mission to capture the Kingdom of Morea.

The Peloponnese peninsular
was a major strategic asset,
connecting three seas in a position globular.
By taking control of where Morea sat
gave the empire a foothold to the entire west
and would eliminate the last remaining targets,
being claimants to the Byzantine crest.
Ruled by a pair of despot brothers,
the factions and clans of Morea were a hornets' nest
of discontent; oppressed and smothered,
they were ripe for insurgent rebellion.
Of all the territories, Sultan Mehmed eyed this like no other
and Khan was more than ready to join him,
as were many of the Greek and Albanian tribes,
having been plied with promises they could revel in,
of independent governance, of religious freedom and other bribes.
And so they prepared the field for the battle that, like night, must arrive.

From the east, the Turks they gathered
bringing in a contingent of eighty-thousand men:
from Anatolia alone, twelve-thousand into battle they stirred;
with Thessaloniki and Kosovo each adding ten;
from Macedonia another five-thousand soldiers on foot
and from Thessaly, the great Omer Bey, loyal to the sultan,
who would not be outdone, rallied fifteen-thousand to put
on the line; contingents from Syria and Antioch
accounted for another eight-thousand men, dark as soot,
while at the head, Mehmed II rode with twenty-thousand of his best flock.
At the opposite end, the brothers Palaiologos, Demetrios and Thomas,
after years of incompetent rule, were nearing the end of their dock.
Their strongest ally, Venice, protecting its own interests, cast
ninety ships into the water, with Spain adding another forty.
For men though, other than their garrisons, numbering at last
only half of the Ottomans', their position was purely a defensive story.
Khan, tasked with clearing the seas and landing troops was in his glory.

They launched from the northeast
on a clear morning in the early part of May,
sweeping through the isles of Greece
capturing a few in strategic locations along the way.
The main vanguard depositing a torrent
of troops, led by Mehmed II himself, with Omer Bey,
his chief lieutenant, onto the beaches of the Gulf of Corinth.
To take Morea, holding this important position would be a must,
for at the top of a monolithic rock sat the Acrocorinth,

with its high wall gates, overlooking the city and isthmus.
From here they could control the entire northern crest,
and have a commanding view over two gulfs, thus
this would be the first and most crucial test.
At its very peek, on top of the hill, sat Venus's temple.
Though Horacio would not be partaking in this contest,
he felt the ominous potent of this moment, so from his vessel,
dropped to a knee, and with the Sword of Troy raised, prayers he leveled.

"O mother Venus," he reverently declared,
"I pray you watch over and bless this expedition,
for righteous be our cause. Once these hurdles cleared,
my bones speak of a turning point for the sacred mission
you have bestowed upon me. Though the path be hidden
to my eyes, I feel the call to return to Sparta, as if a vision
has awoken that the launching point be on the shores where Helen
and brother Paris, had first declared their ill-fated love,
setting into motion the beleaguered destiny of we Trojans,
and our noble rising from the ashes and the windswept glove
of oceans, through sacrifice and sorrow, to found the greatest empire
known to the history of man, sanctioned by ye gods above.
It is not for I, but for your glory, for your love, I implore you not to tire
in your favor, but to guide my hand, my sword, our crew to victory
on this day, to rekindle hope and Olympus fire.
Let this be not the final hour of our story,
but merely the start of a triumphant journey."

Stirring, as at times will occur
when such humble prayers be lifted,
lovely Venus woke briefly from her slumber,
for all that be truly needed to renew the gods' gifts is
the simple act for mortals to remember
that they themselves are not alone gifted
but subject to another, higher power,
one beyond their scope of reason.
So, with a gentle smile, love blossomed as a flower
and returned to Horacio a sign of hope, a beacon
in the form of an eagle, carrying a snake from the high cliff
in its talons, a clear indication that the enemy would be beaten,
the eagle being the symbol of Rome. Flying swift
over the Crescent Moon, the great eagle loosened a feather
from its mighty wing, which lighted down upon the skiff
coming to rest by Horacio's side, better than any treasure,
this gift announced a great victory beyond measure.

Horacio giving praise for the sign
and to Venus mother, sheathed his sword,
and placed the goddess's gift safe within the lines
of his frock, preparing for the oncoming battle in store.
Providing cover from the sea, he watched the opening movements,
as Mehmed and Bey, side by side, drove the lines forward.
Riding a white steed, in a shining body of armor, Mehmed
led the army uphill with fierce bravado towards
the defenses. Reaching the plain, from castle above, a torrent
of arrows, slaying many a soldier with piecing chards,
rained down upon their advancing position.
In return, Khan's ships launched a storm upwards
of cannon fire, striking the Acrocorinth's high bastions,
sending the Byzantine archers retreating from their wall.
With approach secure, siege equipment was quickly fastened
and up the towers Mehmed's men began their climbing crawl,
till battering down the doors, the fortress was soon to fall.

Easily acquiring a foothold in the north,
the fleet continued their sweep along the coast.
To this point, before reaching the turn to the south,
having encountered no resistance. Yet the Christian host
there was waiting, defending their own claims to terra firma
and it was here, on the sea, that the true battle would with fire roast.
Here, in the straights between Damala and Hydra,
forming a picket, did the Venetians and the Spanish ships of Aragon
station themselves in an attempt to surprise Khan's flotilla.
Hidden behind the jutting cape, past the Isle of Poros, their guns
stood in ready ambush. Rounding the peninsula, there came the exchange.
With shots sounding the opening salvo, sixty ships made a veering run
to establish a skirmish line, beyond the Venetians' firing range.
There they waited in challenge, for to prevail all they required
was to deny Khan's troops a safe landing. Their game to arrange
was to either delay the enemy, or to draw them into their fire.
"Aye they be sitting ducks," Khan grinned, playing on a level higher.

With the sun lowering on its western arc,
Khan, in an outrageous move, gave the order to advance,
heading straight for where the enemy was parked.
"Ready on the guns!" Horacio doubled the captain's cadence.
With all eyes focused on the approaching fight,
neither Venetian nor Spaniard had bothered to check on the stance
of their stern. From the southwest, with sun still shining bright,
a sudden terror arrived, in the form of forty galleys approaching
from the Myrtoan Sea, closing from behind, they wedged the enemy tight.

"We got 'em boxed en now, mates! Full speed!" Khan shouted, closing
the distance, signal flags relaying orders to the ships of the fleet.
Now in range the ambush reversed, "Fire!" the order chosen. Encroaching,
with a succession of cannonade glare, forward guns flared across the sea,
in an exchange of shrapnel. Pinned on all sides, the Western Alliance
was forced to scatter its ships and make for open sea, as they flee,
yet many remained hemmed in, the Isle of Hydra preventing their chance
of escape, to which the Ottoman navy intensified their stance.

"Prepare te board!" Admiral Khan bellowed,
the order passing from ship to ship, as the corsairs
made ready to do what they did best, raiding enemy vessels.
Horacio cheered, encouraging the men, with a powerful glare,
as he took position, sword in hand, at the front of the line.
"Hear me now!" he began with an authoritative flare,
"Many battles have we seen together and each time
you have all proven your metal, your courage and worth.
We go where we want and take what we want," a howl began to chime,
spreading amongst the men. "Today though is the birth
of a new era. The deeds we make today will ring through history.
It is we who strike fear in the hearts of those on Earth.
It is we who rule the waves. You are not men, but lions of the sea!
There before you lies your destiny! Reach out and take it!
Let your actions echo throughout all eternity!"
A roar then rose from the deck that would split
the skies in two, as a hurricane blown through a trumpet.

Khan aimed directly for the flag ship of Aragon,
with red and amber waving from the top mast.
Eyeing his prize, "Take off ets head!" he bawled before long.
Like the Crescent Moon, Aragon's man-of-war was fast
and heavily armed. To counter their extra guns,
Khan used his own practiced maneuver to avoid their blast.
Approaching fast, he retracted the starboard oars and the ones
to the port he ordered to drag. With a sharp turn on the rudder,
without dropping anchor, they clubhauled, to the left they spun
and fired cannons from the aft, letting the enemy's fore taste their fodder.
With the shock of surprise the Spaniards fired all,
yet without proper angle, the majority only struck water.
Now, with a forward pull from the port, Khan swung tall,
coming about even to give a blast to their aft.
The Spanish, struggling, half crippled, now felt their grapples.
"All aboard!" Khan bellowed, giving the cue at last.
With thunder they came, the die being cast.

Horacio, the first over the rail,
threw himself into battle, cleaving off the head
of the first victim to cross his trail.
No better fared the second, who a moment later was dead
with a mighty thrust to the gut, spilling entrails raced
across the deck. The colossal Suleiman following, led
a column of pirates over the side, carried a heavy mace
in hand, swinging wide to crush the skull of an ill-fated sailor.
The battle raged with more than a hundred ships engaged in chase.
Isa and Nebi, the twins, hailing from famed Cairo of ancient lore,
distinguished themselves fighting back to back, with double head and neck,
they fought as one beast with four arms and legs, and a tail of bloody gore
following behind them, as they carved their way along the deck,
slashing away with one curved knife for each of their four hands.
Second by sword only to Horacio came the Pashtun, Baloch,
who grew from the sands of the far east desert, tribal clans.
Jousting from right to left to right again, red the early evening ran.

Avranos, from his perch, proved over again
his great value, picking off Spaniards with his bow,
though too late on one occasion when one of the crew of Aragon
impaled Davud through the liver with the point of his blade, a mortal blow.
Avenged he was before his life bled out, as Butrus, the strong,
lifted the villain by the neck and broke him in two with his bare hands, so
together, as brothers, they parted this Earth for Hades before too long.
The sun, a fiery crimson, rode deep along the horizon
before the battle subsided, ending with a valiant push through the throng
by Horacio, cutting his way through lesser men, as though they were fauns,
with Avranos, in this matter, faithfully guarding his back,
until reaching the captain and master of the ship, whereupon
circling one another they finally fell into single combat.
"Surrender now," Horacio offered, "and I will spare your life tonight.
As captain, you're worth more to us alive than dead," delaying the attack.
"Never!" the captain's honor would not allow such an ignoble flight.
He lunged hard, to which Horacio spun, dismembering the hand on the right.

The captain's sword fell helplessly upon the deck,
with the right fist still clasping fast the grip.
The captain dropped to his knees, Horacio's sword at his neck.
He clutched the bloody stump, an agonizing curse upon his lip.
"Go on, finish me," he spat, his eyes fearlessly indignant.
Horacio, not yet the cold, hardened soldier, admiring the courageous quip,
instead of slicing the throat, which he easily could have in an instant,
slid the tip of his sword along the side of the captain's head, removing
his threefold and fitting it upon his own head, retorted, "Nice hat.

Take him away," he commanded Suleiman and Butrus, who were guarding
his back. With the captain captured, all remaining resistance faltered.
In a final capping gesture, Horacio scaled the center mast, cutting
off the ship's colors, waving it in the air to cheering bluster.
The day's battle won, with thirty ships taken and over two thousand
prisoners in chains, they had much to celebrate in the nightly hours.
For their losses, twenty ships sustained serious damage and three sunken,
yet with the enemy retreating, the morrow would see their troops on land's end.

With the Christian fleet routed
and the Ottomans in control of the Argolic Gulf,
they were able to deposit their soldiers unhindered.
Landing near Argos, just to the south
they easily took Nauplia without a struggle.
The entire coastline of Tsakonia they could now engulf
with cutlass and cannonade, their victories double
as they streamed upon the western coast.
It was only upon the very most tip, where met by trouble,
their momentum was halted. In the land of Monemvasia, a host
of defenders, in the high fortress town, defied their conquest.
At a hundred meters above sea level, the city could boast
to be impregnable, being out of range for the canons to test
their walls. The only approach possible was to assail by foot,
and this a long and arduous path, difficult at best.
Khan though remained undeterred in his quest to root
out every last holdout, so with red in his eyes, he laced up his boots.

Seeking to crown his undeniable glory,
Khan himself would lead the charge into battle,
so certain was he of his forthcoming victory.
In council, the evening prior to combat, he assembled
his best men and captains of the fleet to plan the attack.
"The Rock has never been taken," argued Captain Selim, of Tunisian mantle.
"We face the Gibraltar of the East. It may serve us better to turn back
and isolate them as the rest of the peninsula falls."
"Rubbish," countered the hefty Turkish captain, Hizir Bey. "All that we lack
is the courage to take what is sitting in front of our eyes. Their walls
will not protect them from the one powerful hand, *Inshallah*." God-willing.
The exchange prompted a heated ruckus of back and forth catcalls.
"Enough!" Khan silenced the stateroom, the quite now chilling.
"What say you, Oruch-el-Din?" Khan called upon the sultan's tactician,
who sailed with the fleet, representing the royal billing.
"Strategically, it commands the doorway east. This is an important partition,
yet there still remain many challenges to taking this fortified position."

Oruch-el-Din laid out the primary obstacles
the army would face in taking the city. Drawing out a map,
"There is only a single path which leads uphill,
it is winding and narrow, offering many possible traps.
Once reaching the plateau, our men will be easy targets for arrows.
Then, if we surpass these tests, we must still prove to be apt
in defying their walls. After all that, at the apex, where the rock grows,
there is yet the fortress to contend with. There is no dishonor
in going around. Considering the difficulty, to the empire still a hero
you stand, even if you decide to circumvent this most defiant corner."
Khan reflected long on this advice for the attack to halt.
In the corner, Suleiman seemed to disagree with the warner.
"Speak up, bosun. Don't hold yer tongue, ye've earned yer salt."
Khan encouraged his man to talk. "Well admiral, it just seems a shame
being the stronger, with the men all behind you for making the assault,
to come all this way, just to turn around to go back to where we came."
Khan, to himself, admitted that he felt the same.

"What if," Horacio then spoke up, from memory's eye seeing,
with knowledge of standing on the defensive end
of impenetrable city walls engrained into his being,
an alternative course for which they might fend,
"we went about this from a different direction,
something unexpected? Instead of trying to contend
with the city directly, we sent a small party to scale this section
of rock here," he pointed to a shallow sloping crevice
on the far end of the island. "With the main body as a distraction,
out of range of the bows, in the shadows facing the gate, no one may notice
us climbing to the fortress. With ten men we'd be able to take it
and then descend directly into the city and open the gate by force."
A deafening silence ensued, followed by a bellowing laugh that broke it.
"Aye!" Khan roared. "Ye be crazy as the day is long.
Alright," he then said after all had settled, "we have a plan. Do et.
Assemble yer men, make 'em fast and strong.
Ye leave tonight, them gates need te be open before the dawn."

BOOK VIII

THE SIEGE OF MONEMVASIA

The garrison of Molaio, the town seat
of Monemvasia, was standing on high alert,
with watches doubled at the gate and tower peeks,
all eyes set on the ships of the Ottoman Turks,
preparing to repel the pending invasion.
"Are we sure of this?" the Despot Thomas seemed irked
from his throne behind the high walled fortification.
"Yes, your majesty," confirmed his deputy, "our source was very clear."
"Very well then, make it so," he confirmed his sanction.
"And for the terms of engagement?" the deputy drew near,
in a muffled tone. "Yes, yes it is acceptable." Thomas exhaled,
playing the cards he was dealt, feeling himself the poor gambler here.
With word that his brother, Demetrios, was taken prisoner, having failed
to properly defend his lands, Monemvasia was one of the last holdouts
and barring a miracle, surrounded, he too may find himself jailed,
or worse. That he would not let happen. Giving benefit to his doubt,
a pact he would seal to hold on to what remained of his clout.

Meanwhile, the corsairs prepared their assault.
Darkness was upon them, with the only light
a waning moon under a starlit tapestry, to a fault
it was a friendly omen that befell upon their sight.
Horacio, selecting his best men for the mission,
filled a small rowboat, and under the cover of night
they silently rowed out to the far corner of land, where a division
in the rock's side jutted an angled slope upward.
Beaching their craft, the ten began their accent towards the heavens.
"Keep pace," Horacio instructed his squadron, "we must go both forward
and back down by daybreak." With him was mighty Suleiman,
along with the strong, Butrus, Kismet and Evhad.
Isa and Nebi, never to be parted, scaled along like caimans.
Fast with a blade, Etci and Kasim, also both joined the crew,
however Baloch, their finest, Horacio ordered to stay near Khan.
Last and not least, Avranos, with quick bow and sharp eyes like a crow,
climbed at the head. Being scout for the group was the honor he drew.

The slope was an arduous task
for even the best mountaineer.
With every foothold they'd unmask
a new obstacle was there to clear,
yet a steady determination guided their progress.
With luck and the gods' favor, by the wee hours, near
the top they would be. They could settle for nothing less,
failure was not even a consideration to bestow,
for everything depended upon this one success.
About a third of the way up, they reached the first plateau
overlooking the sea. From there they could see shades of the fleet,
beautiful, sparkling upon the tide, bobbing to and fro,
as if Neptune's gentle nymphs were frolicking beneath their feet,
though nothing was gentle upon those ships that night.
As our climbing party enjoyed a well earned pause, the drum beat
of war was pulsing in the hearts of ten thousand men ready to fight,
sharpening their swords, grabbing their oars, the beach was now in sight.

By twelve bells, the army had disembarked
on the eastern flank and assembled for the long march uphill
along the main road, while on the western side, under the cover of dark,
Horacio and his party continued their treacherous climb by shear will.
Upon reaching the second flat niche, catching their breath, in an upward etch,
the rock turned straight towards the sky. For lesser men dread would fill
their hearts, having to surmount such a dangerous, nay impossible, stretch.
For this hurdle ropes were unfurled, as they broke off into pairs,
one light and nimble to lead the assent; one strong, the anchor, to catch
the other in the chance that calamity befell upon those virgin stairs.
A length of rope, connecting each duo, as an umbilical cord,
made one life of two. Isa and Nebi, protested the need to tear
them apart, each trusting no other better in being their ward,
yet seeing the reason, where of the group they were the best climbers,
they finally succumbed, following orders and moving forward.
To quell their concerns, each was matched with the strongest arms of timber,
Suleiman took Isa, while Nebi and Butrus became partners.

Kismet and Etci tied their tether,
while Evhad and Kasim also matched up.
In the lead, Horacio and Avranos would climb together,
the two Aegeans cutting the path. Turning, Horacio whispered a heads-up,
"Remember, be as silent as you can, the slightest noise may draw attention
and we don't know how close the sentries may be." Then, looking up,
they began the assent. This was the most precarious section,
straight up the cliff rose, with a drop of perhaps two hundred meters.
The only path forward was what handholds they could pension

from the rock face. They moved slowly, with caution, centimeters
as feet, while the ticking of time constantly worked against them.
About halfway towards their goal, they reached a menacing feature,
a purely smooth segment, with not even a finger-hold, much less a stem.
From their position they would need to traverse horizontal
across a rocky cleft for ledge, along a fifty meter bend,
to a crevice that ran back up the side, slicing vertical.
Their arms burned from exertion. One look down would end it all to vertigo.

Finally making it to the crack
they recommenced their movement upward,
not a second had they to even think of looking back.
Then, just as all seemed to be striking the right chords,
from a hole no larger than a man's fist, a serpent
slithered across Nebi's hand. Startled, he lost his grip forward,
slipped and tumbled towards Hades' door. "Nebi!" Isa jolted in that moment.
With pure instinct he reached out, taking hold of his brother's wrist
as Nebi dropped past, being himself pulled off the edge on an angle bent.
Butrus, seeing from below the looming tragedy, gripped hard his fist
onto a thick root that grew out of the stony fissure.
Suleiman, not so fortunate, with a double weight falling past, in a twist,
was also pulled off balance, and likewise cast to his death for sure.
If not for the incredible might in Butrus's right arm,
all four would have rode the River Styx that night. Yet secure,
by nothing less than a miracle of strength, the three dangled like a yarn,
twisting in the wind, Butrus, holding fast, keeping them from harm.

With a gasp, Butrus pulled on the rope
with his free hand, swinging them with care
back in towards the rocky knoll and one last hope
of clutching onto the craggily surface that presented itself there.
Suleiman, with both hands free, hanging at the bottom of the line,
the only link of safety being the tight clasp of the brotherly pair,
was the first to find a rock, a jutting boulder, which he clung to like a vine.
Isa and Nebi, scrambled, each with their free hand, to secure a point of earth.
Out of danger, having obtained their footing, just barely in the nick of time
"Let's not do that again," Isa chided his brother, struggling for breath.
"You have my word," Nebi concurred, then giving praise to Allah,
"*Al-hamdu lillāh,*" he said. "You might want to also praise Butrus's strength,"
Horacio mentioned, seeing his men were now out of harm's way, so far.
"Ah but," Nebi countered, "who made our good friend here so strong?
And yes," he quickly added, "thank you too, by all the stars."
"It was just fortunate I had this root to hold onto, or we'd have all been gone,"
Butrus thanked the earth. "Enough," Horacio hushed. "We climb, it isn't long."

The top of the mountain was now very close
and they scaled with care to avoid further incident.
Reaching the base of the fortification wall, which rose
three lengths a tall man upward, it appeared not even a dent
compared to the last three hours. Silently, they took stock
of the defenses. Here, the wall pointed to a sharp angle, which bent
along the narrow western border. Hidden behind a group of rocks,
Horacio eyed a single sentry, who in the late hours appeared not so attentive.
With a finger to his lips, he signaled Avranos with his bow to knock
him out of commission. Here, the bowman was inventive,
shooting a dart straight through the guard's throat,
silencing him as he fell to the ground, unable to raise a superlative.
With coast clear, they raced to where the body wrote its last note,
and in the still of the night, prepared their grappling hooks.
Suleiman cast the first line which clipped the stone like a garrote.
Horacio, the first to go, climbed the knotted rope, feet finding rocky nooks,
peered his head above the rampart, his eyes in the scene they took.

"All clear," he gave the signal,
hoisting himself over the edge in silence,
as the others prepared to ascend the stone shingles.
From the parapet, the wall V'd on a narrow balance
along the cliff's edge. The length stretched for a full kilometer,
with the widest section at the far end, like the sack of a phallus.
Along the angle, facing each other, at a distance of two hundred meters,
sat opposite guard posts, each looking out to contrary points on the sea.
Both would have to be taken out for their passage to go undeterred.
Lightest on foot, Isa and Nebi would again be thrown into the breaching spree,
having to cross the converse end, dispose of the soldiers, then double back.
For his part, Horacio, along with Suleiman as his second, would scurry
to the north facing station, to do away with the lookouts on their path.
The rest were to wait and hold their position for the sign to advance.
Approaching light-footed, Horacio and Suleiman made their attack,
the first slicing a throat, the second breaking the neck, as the sentries danced
to their deaths. For their part, Isa and Nebi readied their fighting stance.

Without a struggle both of the guards died,
as Isa and Nebi secured matching bronze helmets,
before pitching the two bodies over the side.
Then, in the process, their eyes were met with new frets,
struck by something unforeseen. In a private commotion,
they hurriedly retraced their footsteps,
meeting the pack and together all raced for the position
where Horacio and Suleiman, attended their arrival.
"The Spaniards," Nebi gasped for air. "Out on the ocean,"

Isa finished his sentence. "They're gathering, preparing to rival
our forces. They've got thirty ships there at least."
"A trap," Horacio cursed, "we have to warn the others." Survival
was now for what they played. However, this far in, there ceased
to be an alternative other than to keep moving forward.
With several hundred meters yet to clear towards the east,
it was now a race against time. "Draw swords,"
Horacio ordered, moving on the double they poured.

Working their way quickly along the edge
of the northern perimeter, one final obstacle
stood between them and the passage
into the city, a guard house and domicile
with four lookouts on duty. "Etci, Kasim," you're with me,
Horacio choosing his best swordsmen to handle
the task before them. "Cover us," he called Avranos to the ready.
"With pleasure," Avranos took aim, fingering his bowstring.
"We have to do this quick and quiet," Horacio counseled. "On three."
Storming the guardroom, they struck as lightning,
Horacio, plunging his sword into the heart of the one on the left,
while Etci and Kasim, splitting the two on the right, and with a freighting
shot Avranos, felled the soldier on the far side. Just then, from a cleft,
a fifth appeared at the opposite doorway, about to strike the alarm.
By instinct Horacio launched his blade, impaling the guard through the chest,
then leapt on him, hand over his gaping mouth, and with sword arm
twisted the steel, until at last he expired, buying the farm.

A trail of blood followed their path
to a stone staircase which etched down from the fort,
through the Rock, zigzagging fore and aft,
to the city below, this was the trail they needed to cut,
and the darkest hour was already upon them.
Down below, covered in the black of night, the court
of corsair warriors waited for the cue to come.
"How can you be sure your men will succeed?"
Captain Selim questioned. "Ah, cuz ye don't know 'em
like I do," Khan spat. "Et's already a done deed.
Just make sure yer men are ready fer fightin',
when the time comes, and that goes double fer ye."
"Oh, don't you worry, we're ready," Selim was biting
at the bit. Moments later, "Admiral, there's the signal,"
it was Baloch who spotted the torch above the gate's tower waving.
"Aye, that et be," Khan slapped Baloch on the back. "Be nimble
men, fast like the wind." He gave the order to advance to the open portal.

"Ye of little faith," he jibed Selim.
"Not true, Admiral," Selim countered keeping pace.
"I was sure this moment would come," being the last from him,
as they broke into a run. To the gate it was a race.
"Look there!" Avranos pointed to the signal torch,
their party only half way down the cliff's face.
"We're betrayed," came Kasim's voice, beneath a rocky arch.
"Faster men!" Horacio pushed nearly running down the stairs,
and Butrus, "I can see the gates opening," in a sprinting march.
At full speed they were still beyond their prayers,
for once descended they would still need to cross the city's width.
Emerging from the Rock, as the exploding flares
of dragon's breath, they ran at top speed cutting down all in their path.
At the same moment the front lines had reached the open gate.
However it was not the sleeping village according to their math,
but a full garrison that greeted them en masse debate,
having fallen into a trap, discovered too late.

Two rows in an arch of solid pikes,
halted their advance to a dead stop,
as Khan's men, the first through to strike
were surrounded. From the rampart tops
a battalion of archers rose like the sun,
taking aim at the growing field of hostile crops,
with an avalanche of arrows, the rain had begun.
Behind Khan's troops, cutting off escape
was the crew of Selim, turncoat and dung,
with arms at the ready, blocking the gate.
"What foul treachery be this!" Khan caught by surprise.
"Where's the disloyal blaggard? I'll eat 'im alive," discovering too late.
"Right behind you," Selim announced himself, with a knife in the side,
stabbing him hard in the vitals. Baloch, the closest ally by was unable
to assist, with four swords pointed directly at him, was immobilized.
Khan, dropping to the ground looked up at his assailant, Cain to his Abel.
"Selim, ye scurvy bastard! The lowest realm of hell will be yer stable."

"Save it for yourself, Ottoman dog,"
came the reply. "You'll be there soon enough.
And the name is Mendez, know that it is I who flogged
you, to the glory of Catalan and Christendom," he spoke all gruff.
"Die knowing that thirty of my finest ships are approaching as we speak,
to finish off your unsuspecting fleet and all your men here will be snuffed
out by fire at the stake before too long." The future indeed was looking bleak,
as the sound of agonizing cries rose from the opposite side of the well.
The pirates, pierced and scuttled, were dying where they fell and in retreat.

Just as all hope had faded, from the flank a loud commotion befell.
Horacio and his men, attacking from behind the lines with furious anger,
threw the whole square into disarray, as if the arrival of hell.
Suleiman and Butrus, hitting the ramparts, tore through the archers,
while Avranos cast his own flying darts into their ranks.
On the ground Horacio, and the rest, redefined the meaning of danger.
Slicing left and right, a dozen fell before they even knew who to thank
for meeting their maker, their own blood it was they drank.

Baloch was the first to take the cue,
raising his sword, he parried with all four at once,
stabbing first once and then another, till all in his way he slew.
A mêlée then broke out, to the death the crew began to pounce,
Yet Baloch, with his eye on the prize, went straight for the traitor Mendez,
with a sweeping blow, slashed his face through a bloody trounce,
taking out one of his eyes. The Spaniard fell back, losing his imitation fez,
retreating through the ranks, with a bloodcurdling gasp,
hand clasped to his cheek, he barely escaped, leaking a scarlet forest.
On the opposite side of the crunch, the best of the lot was taken to task,
Kismet taking a lance to the thigh, hollered out in pain,
falling back, in trouble, was then filled with the devil, and holding fast
ripped the shaft from his shank, and turned the pike upon his vain
assailant, gorging him through the thorax, he lifted him high
and pummeled him back down to Earth like a thunderous rain.
"Take that to your grave, you worthless trash," Kismet said with a fie.
Though weakened, the wound would heal, his spirit refused to die.

Outnumbered they were, but skill
and strength were their allies. In rally,
Isa and Nebi could not count how many killed,
as they slashed away with their knives brutally.
Etci and Kasim, with their swords in hand
each competed for the highest tally,
while Evhad bashed his way through a band
of defenders, taking out three at a time,
with fierce blows not of this land.
Yet it was Horacio who stood at the top of the line.
With singular vision, he cut his way through the corps,
heading straight into the ranks of soldiers, sublime
were his movements, striking at one before
even finishing with the other, leaving nothing but a trail
of dead bodies in his wake, and a crimson river of gore.
Memories of Achilles manifested in that moment, as he sail
unhindered to where his captain lie, already growing pale.

Kneeling, he cradled Khan's head
in his powerful arms. "We'll get you fixed up,"
he said. "Don't you worry." Yet he could not hide his look of dread.
"Ah, I'm dead already, food fer them crows," blood he coughed up.
"Et's Allah's will. Don't mind me, save the ship, she's yers now."
"Nonsense," Horacio protested, "this is no time to give up."
Khan clasped a hand to Horacio's, "Betrayed we were," he lifted a brow.
"Yes, I know," Horacio confirmed. "That damned traitor, Selim,"
Khan spat a blood filled curse, "faithless Spanish cow.
Save the ship," he gave his last command. "They're comin' te box us en."
And then, as the sun began to rise, "Do ye see that?" he asked. "The light..."
Khan let out his final breath, "Allah be praised." Horacio's head began to spin.
From the distance, he could hear the reinforcements arriving for the fight.
As much as he could have slaughtered a thousand in that moment,
he knew better and had his orders. "Fall back to the ship!" he felt the bite
and sting of shame in the command, but he had no time to lament,
lifting Khan, he rushed back to fulfill his final commitment.

BOOK IX

ESCAPE

All the storms were now converging,
a cyclone of sweat and blood and flesh,
in every direction swirling, surging,
rallying each to his own mesh.
Three camps were in disarray,
nothing had gone according to sketch.
Scuttled, the garrison of Molaio,
in lieu of reinforcing Mendez as ordered,
retreated from the walls to seal the entrance way,
concerned more with being cornered,
with ally and foe dressed in the same manner,
closing the gate most importantly factored.
For his own part, Mendez, in a clamor,
with a gaping wound, and left eye cut from socket,
was delirious with pain, could barely stammer,
and fell unconscious when a hot iron was brought to seal the pocket.
His men would be leaderless, for twice an hour held on the docket.

For the corsairs,
that would be what needed to save the day.
As it was the pirates had been hit square,
routed and in full retreat, having broken through the fray,
those not lost on the field scrambled down the hillside,
racing back to their ships without delay.
Defending the rear, the last to escape alive,
was the fighting contingent from the Crescent Moon.
Horacio, with Khan's lifeless body straddled astride
his port shoulder, found himself suddenly strewn
into the unenviable position of command,
with a fleet of ships sitting unaware that soon
they would be plunged into battle, a plan
for survival must be devised on the double.
Meanwhile, while all the preceding fanned,
the flames of war burning, the Despot Thomas made use of the scuffle
to escape the city by use of an underground tunnel.

It was a narrow passage,
lit only by the torches they carried.
Sweaty, the stone blocks reflected orange,
the pace of heavy breath hurried
until they came unto an opening
with a set of stairs, down the slope they quarried.
Coming to a tiny dock, with a rowboat tied to its mooring,
they loaded the few odd chests of gold,
and cast off without further warning.
Rowing oar, through the dark and cold,
they followed the slivering waterway crevice
along a jagged spilt where the mountain did fold,
until the sea revealed its presence
through a crack in the far side of the Rock.
There appearing too in that pre-morning blemish
was a tapestry of seafaring war hawks,
as the Spanish fleet sat, awaiting only the clock.

"Why the delay?"
Thomas queried, on boarding
the lead ship. "The battle is already underway."
He was met by a crisp lieutenant supporting
a heavy accent and a list of rules.
"Ah, welcome your eminence. According
to orders, we are to await first light before entering the duel."
Thomas was flustered, "Well, I'm bringing new orders!
Take me to your captain at once," he commanded the fool.
"The battle will be over by first light." They marched to the captain's quarters,
where he lit a fire. "Get these ships moving now!" he burst into the cabin,
as only royalty can. The captain, a military man, was hunched in the corner,
studying a map. In a flurry, he snapped too, as all soldiers do, out of habit
when being yelled at. Upon hearing the monarch's command, his training
prompted the proper response. "Si señor," he said, like a rabbit.
With battle order relayed, the fleet weighed anchor, sails and arms positioning.
"Not us," Thomas held the captain at bay. "To Naples," he said to no arguing.

"Si señor," came the captain's enthusiastic reply,
as they led the armada from the rear.
Back on land, odds would defy
a timely return to vessel, clear
of a miracle, the pirates would be unable
to reach their ships and the sphere
of battle, prior to the coming attack. Survival
drove them forward along the edge of the cliff.
The sky, already with a pink hued variable,

would soon be turning red, while their fleet of ships
though at the ready, unaware they sat, facing the beach.
From the gable, where the path turned towards their landing slips,
Horacio could see the Crescent Moon, with its rear in the breach.
"Look there!" Avranos with the hawk-like eyes pointed long.
Mendez's ship, Os Dentes Serpente, lingered there just in reach.
Slithering, it was positioning itself behind the throng,
to the stern of the Crescent Moon it would be before too long.

"They must be unaware of the traitor
within their ranks." Baloch, lifted his voice.
"They need to be warned," Suleiman was in accord.
In moments of life and death there is seldom choice,
there is only what is possible, and in the end only action
decides, sometimes there is nothing one can do but be devoice,
and sometimes, sometimes one is struck with inspiration.
To Horacio now befell the decision of their next move. Win or lose,
the duty of that moment was alone to his imagination,
and then, gazing above the horizon, over the ships and their crews,
into that last black patch strip of night he was struck by a spark of light.
Having studied the stars and constellations, he knew this point he muse
be true, that this red flare in the distance be none other than Mercury's light,
the messenger most needed now, in times of hardship and despair.
"Here," Horacio passed Khan's body to Suleiman to hold tight.
He tore a strip of cloth from the admiral's chemise, "I have an idea."
From within the seams of his own frock, he removed the gifted eagle's feather.

Sharpening the tip
upon the edge of his sword,
he then dipped the nib
into where Khan had been scored,
a sacrilege most forgiven on such occasion
was the converting of blood into warning chords,
he marked the parchment with purposeful determination.
"Avranos," Horacio called at last.
"It's an awfully long way," the bowman sized up the calculation,
while securing the message to the arrow's shaft.
Horacio shared his confidence, "If anyone can do it..."
"Just tell me where you want it?" Avranos asked, and Horacio, "Aft mast."
"Next to the helmsman?" "Yes... no wait, there, Oruch-el-Din, he's your target."
"Yes, I see him," Avranos confirmed, adjusting his angle for the Mistral Wind.
Horacio lifted a silent prayer to Mercury, messenger of the gods, to let
their bowman's aim be true, for much would be determined
in that breathless moment of hovering.

With a thunderous snap,
the arrow rocketed through the air
as the line released rang with a crack.
The projectile sailing on a high arched affair
cut a whiz right through the aerodynamic currents;
banking thirty degrees, it caught a ride on a cold stream of air,
increasing in speed as it began its descent,
piercing a puff of cloud, it curved straight for the Crescent Moon,
in line directly with Oruch's head, until at the last second, by crosswind bent,
up ninety more degrees, to lodge itself square upon the mast with a boom.
Horacio and his whole crew exhaled and began to breathe again,
while on deck Oruch-el-Din flinched and ducked, shocked by the boon,
spun to see the dart, that had used his head for a weather vane.
From their perch on high, the crew could see the rising commotion.
Finding the note, Oruch eyed it twice. "Behind you," read the stain.
Twisting around, he saw Os Dentes Serpente quickly approaching.
Understanding the situation, the chief tactician called the crew to stations.

Warning bells rang out,
signaling the fleet to action.
From behind the Rock, as they turned to come about,
the first of the Spanish vessels appeared upon the horizon.
Without hesitation, to their boats the crew ran,
while Os Dentes Serpente, themselves captain-less, made a retraction.
having lost the advantage, and seeing spoiled their plan,
still flying Tunisian colors, turned their stern, hoping to yet be undiscovered.
The maneuvers required and general chaos which ensued in that span
guaranteed a wide berth of confusion conferred
upon those waves in that silver morning bath,
yet those precious moments of forewarning deterred
a much more gruesome aftermath.
By the time the Spaniards had made their position,
the Ottomans were able to counter with their own offensive path.
Through salt spray, Horacio and crew raced the ocean,
to war they rowed, head long into the fire's ignition.

In two staggered columns
the Spanish ships of Aragon
presented themselves the problem,
sweeping in picket to form a firewall along
the northeast corridor, the Ottoman corsair fleet
was penned in between coastline and cannon.
Though superior in number, double on the sheet,
the tactical advantage was against them,
as they needed to advance their retreat.

Oruch, seeing the situation dire before them,
signaled the fleet to adjust their course,
by cutting a forty-five degree, south-easterly bend,
they could avoid the brunt of the enemy's force,
while steering their ships towards open water,
the only downside being to this recourse
that the Crescent Moon herself at the tail quarter
would be the most likely target to be sent underwater.

Heaving hard through cresting tides,
the crew rowed as if their lives depended on it,
having to return on the double, else they may be left aside
without a vessel, for the battle for them would not idly sit.
They came upon the ship's starboard flank,
making with haste to climb the parapet.
"Just in time," Oruch called, as the first rank
made it safely aboard. "We don't have a moment to lose.
Where's Khan?" and then from his own eyes he shrank,
as Suleiman lifted the body aboard. "Dead," he said sharing the news.
"It's Allah's will," he turned a hardened jaw towards the approaching armada.
"Now what?" Oruch questioned the sea. "We fight!" Horacio drew
himself up onto the deck. "Bosun, bring the ship to order,"
he commanded. "Aye, captain," Suleiman made clear his reply.
"Prepare to change course," he added a new twist to the drama.
"But..." Oruch was about to ask, when Horacio came up to his side.
"You see that," he pointed to the slant of enemy guns, "that's our demise."

"Now," he drew a line
to their ten o'clock angle.
"You see that," to Os Dentes Serpente he made a sign,
"how it maintains our same course, yet wrangles
closer adrift towards the Spanish fleet?
It's no accident she's moving to close the triangle,
that's the ship of the traitor who killed Khan, now in retreat
and, by the way they're sailing, they don't know we're on to them.
Signal Hizir Bey, to fall in line, we're going to render them obsolete,
but first they're going to lead us a little further in." Then,
"Agreed," Oruch baldly nodded, with respect in his eye.
Seeing Horacio's plan, he flagged the message therein,
bringing two more ships in for their forces to magnify,
while ordering Os Dentes Serpente to lead the attack,
thus employing deception to confuse their quarry,
they lined up their spearhead to the enemy's back
and drove them in towards the Spaniard's line of attack.

Knowing that Os Dentes Serpente,
the Serpent's Teeth, was a ship of the rival,
Horacio's plan hinged on the bet that they
would not fire on their own vessel.
So driving them with fear, he would use their ship as a wedge,
to break through the Spanish columns and to open sea their arrival.
"Ready on the forward cannons," he called, preparing the sledge.
"Let me know the second they drop their colors."
"Aye, aye," crewmen confirmed the order, sensing they had the edge.
They positioned extra cannons at the fore for added firepower,
while the three ships came together into a pyramid formation,
creating a lethal vanguard with which to challenge the others.
"Let's see the range on those chasers," Horacio called from his station
at the helm. "Give 'em a shot over the bow."
Aiming long the cannon erupted with vexation,
as flying shrapnel struck water just short of the Spanish fleet's prow.
"Hold tight," Horacio readied the crew, "it's going to get hot any moment now."

"There she goes,"
Avranos called from the crow's nest,
as Mendez's ship dropped her colors and Spanish ones rose.
"Right on time," Horacio sounded with confidence. "Signal the rest
to target the ships of the line, but this one's ours."
"Aye," Oruch confirmed, flagging along the bequest.
"Open fire," he gave the command to light the fores,
as their guns rang with thunder, casting cannonballs aloof,
into the violent throes and watery trenches of Mediterranean wars.
The first shot sailed past the starboard flank, with only water to reproof,
while the second scored the upper deck shattering glass and timber.
Now, with all ships in range of fire, they would see the proof
of using such tactics, as driving head long into an overwhelming number.
As it was, so far, the Spanish center held up to expectations,
withholding fire, so as to not shoot one of their own, they felt the hammer
of the Ottoman guns, with flanking ships targeting their bastions,
they'd be raked without being able to present their own counter projections.

"We must return fire, captain."
Aragon's first mate pled, as they came under bombardment.
Here rose Captain Cardenas's dilemma, as it would happen,
for Os Dentes Serpente was not simply a ship of Spanish endowment,
but, unknown to the Ottomans, the command vessel for the entire flotilla.
For Cardenas, it was still possible to survive this current hostile movement,
yet, if he were responsible for the sinking of Mendez's own ship, Attila
would not have his head on the end of a pike any faster.
"Come to port thirty degrees," he called to the helm, there was still a

chance to re-maneuver for a position that was better,
effectively opening a hole in the Spanish line,
in order to free his gunners from the fetter.
"Target the ship closest to port and return fire," he let chime,
with their long guns flaring, as they roared into action.
"In coming!" Avranos called from his nest up on high,
as the iron fodder missed their flanking ship by a fraction.
"All ahead full!" Horacio pushed the crew forward, gaining traction.

The distance between the two forces
was now rapidly closing, as the pursued
raced for the opening made by the change of course.
Into the breach they fled, while Horacio on their heels, perused
his options. "Give 'em another round!" he bellowed.
"And make ready those forty-fives," gauging the latitude
between the vessels, Horacio calculated the coming blows,
to time the attack most efficiently.
The resonance of cannon fire, a deafening vibration, flowed
across the waves, carrying death in its metallic effigy,
striking hard against the enemy's stern.
Cries rose up to a bursting splintered cacophony,
as crimson striped shards through the air burned,
impaling one sailor through the lower deck.
Bracing for more, Os Dentes Serpente cut a ninety degree turn
behind the Spanish line, just barely avoiding a wreck.
Now, for Horacio, was the moment of check.

With the enemy clear of the battle line,
and open water now standing between opposing navies,
their most perilous moment did arrive upon the vine,
as the spearheaded triumvirate entered the broken levee.
The Crescent Moon, leading the charge,
flanked aft astride by two of Hizir Bey's bevies,
the three between two would wedge,
faced long by a single war vessel.
The numbers even, yet the margin large,
Horacio's bet came off so far the most part successful,
sustaining relatively little damage, this close to danger,
to the edge, while inflicting much already to the first into battle.
Horacio had one final salvo ready to better the odds of the wager,
"Hold steady," he cautioned the anxious, slowing his breath,
awaiting the precise moment. "Let me see his eyes," spoke the arranger
before giving the command, weighing the width and breadth.
"Fire, all fore cannons!" he cried, as the coming of death.

With guns facing the angle of forty-five degrees,
the Crescent Moon, at the head of the vanguard,
with the luck of the gods and no short supply of steady knees,
managed to cripple two enemy helms with one volleying cannonade,
while the chasers fired long to greet their dueling partner.
Retorts abounded in flying shrapnel and splintered facades,
no one escaped unscathed, yet clearing the first line of departure,
the Crescent Moon fared better than the rest.
Having disabled the ships to each side, defeating their armor,
no need was there to slow their advance and in combat test
the broken further, a hole it was they needed to punch
and with three against one, it was too much to best,
so the remaining obstacle in their path fled, escaping the crunch.
An opening now made, through it the fleet would rush,
as more Ottoman ships, filling the gap, expanded the outward lunge.
The Spaniards, in disarray, their ambush no longer flush,
fought a retreating battle of their own in that early morning blush.

"Give me eyes!"
Horacio cried, still hot for battle,
searching fruitlessly for where his prey flies.
"Where'd they go?" the saber did rattle,
as Os Dentes Serpente slid back behind the Rock,
taking cover in their retreat, abandoning the mantle.
"I can't spot them," Avranos confirmed, taking stock
of the clustering enemy forces. In the rush to regroup their ranks
and regain clear passage, the mouse had escaped the hawk.
"Curse that viper's luck," Horacio held back his thanks,
frustrated at having come so close to gaining his vengeance.
Still themselves not out of danger, urgent it was to cover their flanks,
with the Spaniards recovering, rallying to a defensive stance
and their ships divided in two directions, they needed to unite the fleet.
"Coming about, southeast," he finally called. Deciding not to risk chance,
their ships would rendezvous at Cape Maleas in a tactical retreat.
"Well done, captain," Oruch acknowledged, having been saved from defeat.

Hizir Bey agreed later in council,
"That was some inspired seamanship.
Khan was right to put faith in your counsel."
"And we all mourn the loss of his leadership,"
Oruch added, pausing for his own somber reflection.
Now at the end of battle, he had to decide the next stewardship
of the fleet. In the sultan's absence it was for him to make the selection.
"What's our next move?" Hizir questioned the assembly
and Oruch, after a moment of thought, "That's up to your discretion,"

promoting Hizir there on the spot to complete the present duty.
"It was the correct choice," Horacio acknowledged later aside,
as Orach gave his reasons. "I thank you in fact," he offered with no animosity.
The fleet had already its standing orders. There was nothing left but the tide
to rendezvous with the army on the sun after next, off the coast of Laconia.
Horacio had no need to lead a cleanup mission to stroke his pride.
For the first time in many years he was free, here off the shores of Ionia,
and bonds now loosened, his heart longed to follow Venus's cornucopia.

His quest beckoned.
With letters of marque in good standing,
he and Oruch shook hands, as comrades in that second.
"May Allah guide you," Oruch offered, notwithstanding
Horacio's pagan faith. "And you," he returned the goodwill,
as the Crescent Moon set off into a direction freestanding
from the struggle of imperial wars and will.
As the sun rode low, the crew buried Khan, casting his body to the sea,
giving him all the proper funeral rites, as due his stature as a pirate admiral.
Horacio, following his custom, placed two gold coins on Khan's eyes to appease
the boatman, while offering up his own prayers to Lord Neptune.
"Father of the seas, take this body into your keeping," he lifted his plea.
"Guide his soul fruitfully, for never was a seaman more worthy of your boon."
Then, while staring out into the graying night, "This ship has a new purpose."
Meanwhile, as they sailed, from behind the Rock, Mendez sang another tune,
for in a bitter mood did he board his vessel, seeking revenge with all his force.
"An eye for an eye," he cried, as Os Dentes Serpente set an intercept course.

BOOK X

FROM THE DEPTHS

As mighty Neptune slept
beneath those Ionian waves,
the body of Khan made its descent
from where the deck of the Crescent Moon gave
in honor and offering, to both the man and the god,
their rightful tributes. Wrapped in fine linens fit for the grave,
the weighted corpse sank deeper into the abyss. As a seedpod
it entered the coral domain of where untold creatures of the sea lurk.
There, in the deep blue sea, a rippling tremor through the currents plod
as Neptune stirred, and in so doing laid the groundwork
for a cascading chain of events.
For all of brother Pluto's plotting work,
he still could not control the oceans, and though Neptune sent,
along with the Olympian gods, into a hibernating slumber,
the Oceanides and other sea nymphs were still virulent
in an anarchistic sort of way, each following their natural tumbler,
they helped to maintain the fluid flow of order.

When Neptune, one who bound in a coma sleep,
shifted, it was no small thing, for only great motivation
from within could have the power to move the god of the deep.
More than an omen, a command, the water deities understood as instruction,
their lord's contentment with the corsair's offering, that they were held in favor.
The shockwave wove throughout the entire sea, as an enunciation
vibrating along the undercurrents, subliminally altering the behavior
of the water itself as it pulsated, liquidly encompassing the tidal rush,
and in its wake, as the warming against the cold, there rose a misty vapor
upon the surface of the sea, which enveloped the evening's hush.
Beneath the waves, in mystery's crevice, where all manner of beast thrive,
a commotion was stirring that'd make even the most hardened sailor blush,
for the daughters of the ocean Titans, three thousand sea nymphs, came alive,
causing the sea to toss and tumble, as would commence a symphonic overture.
Gentle the notes at first appear, only to build momentum to a thunderous drive,
as on the horizon a storm was brewing with a murky ashen feature,
a prelude to what was yet to come from this torrential tempest creature.

Aboard ship, the seas were rough
as they battened down the hatches,
to ready themselves for swollen humidity's gruff.
"Prepare to come about," Horacio catches
a glimpse of the storm ahead, making ready to steer around,
when pointing astern, Avranos in urgent tones matches
with a command of his own, the alarms he did sound.
"Captain, look out! We have company approaching!"
From the rear, through the haze, at the limit of vision's bound,
a squadron of war vessels was fast encroaching
upon the open space between their stern and the cannon's range,
creating a life threatening dilemma, with them the game for poaching.
At the head of a contingent of three, sat Mendez, still in a rage,
sailing at full speed, he gave chase to his prey.
Horacio, caught between certain death and otherworldly strange,
countermanded his order and on course he decided to stay.
"Douse the lamps," he called, as they turned toward the darkening grey.

Through his one good eye,
squinting to extend his single scope,
Mendez caught sight of the Crescent Moon as she fly
into the approaching storm, a move of desperate hope.
"Full ahead! Give me more speed," he vengefully growled,
setting his course to pursue, as deck hands tightened the ropes.
Into the choppy void of night four ships prowled
with winds gaining force by the hour, increasing in might,
tossed between jolting sea lashes, the seamen scowled,
for they knew they'd be lucky to survive the night.
Below the surface, the seahorses raced,
jettisoning their milky white manes to light
upon those cresting, crashing waves that laced
that slippery slopping, seascape scene.
A line perpendicular to the water's onslaught they traced,
as to not be capsized by the twenty foot surging sheens
that washed over the deck between gusting windy screams.

"Man the jib downhaul!"
Horacio called from the helm.
"Topmast staysail halliards! Clear away the downhaul!
HOIST AWAY! Clear away the halliards! HAUL DOWN!" echoed his realm,
as the Crescent Moon came head to the wind.
He readied to ride out the storm, lest they be overwhelmed.
As night blackened the sky, thundercloud covered and rimmed,
from behind those threatening puffs, half moon glowed a haunting silhouette.
Sparks of lightning flashed, unnaturally it grinned,

whence the skies opened, in a downpour they were beset.
"Beat to port!" Horacio commanded, cutting an angle between the waves,
advancing sideways, for the lights behind he also could not forget,
he placed lateral distance between his ship and the approaching naves.
Using the dark of night as their cover,
the storm would now aid them in avoiding sunken graves.
Horacio, with an eye on the enemy's guide lights, transfixed as a lover,
lowered the sea anchor, slowing their advance, they slid undercover.

Beneath the horizon,
underneath the line of water,
more was on the rise than man could siphon,
for within all that seismic activity it was only getting hotter.
In the realm of the deep, not only did the deities stir,
when Neptune sent his tremor racing through the mater,
but so too did the demons, whose wrath it would spur.
In the distance, at the heart of the storm,
at the very epicenter of their present troubles, a slur
was moving with malcontent, ready to transform
the tempest skies to a fiery red, with crimson and ash
and the water with blood deform.
Unbeknownst, onward they sailed, the waves they'd slash,
through beating currents and gale force winds raging,
towards their present fate, bodies to deck they'd lash,
lest they be swept into the sea and all of her racing.
For those unhappy seamen, they had only begun their ranging.

The night gripped them like a wet rag,
clinging to bodies that defied sleep.
"Find them!" Mendez scowled as they lag,
the surging sea having swallowed in her keep
the prey they seek. Likewise, his squadron was scattered,
thrust about by squalls and the darkening deep,
each was left to their own resources, formations now all tattered.
"Heave to!" Captain Cardenas called from his own command,
having been rocked by a steady gust, his ship battered.
"Curse this ill fated chase," under his breath he damned,
for having been selected as a second for this mission.
The third faring no better, listing away from the windward hand,
struggled to right herself against the weather's harsh conditions.
And so the darkest hours swirled and thrashed,
as the storm they rode deeper into only gained in ambition.
One after another the waves they crashed
and in the red of morning on and on they bashed.

"It's an ominous sign, captain,"
one Spaniard called of the horizon's scarlet light.
"Steady on, sailor," Cardenas cautioned his man.
Though of a like mind, it was his duty to hold tight,
as example for the crew to follow, even if that be to their deaths.
For the Crescent Moon, the nightly maneuvers had paid off right,
for in the early blush, with waves surging fast across ocean's breadth,
they found themselves to the stern of one Spanish vessel,
where the other two were anyone could guess.
Approximately a tenth of a nautical mile back from their trestle,
the Crescent Moon lined up, with cannons at the ready.
The Spanish man-of-war, already off balance, joined with the sea in wrestle,
did not even see the doom approaching until too late, were thrown in the eddy.
Two shots of cannon fodder sliced through the air,
with lurching ships on a plunging ride, still one shot held steady,
smashing into the Spaniard's port quarter, a flooding hole it'd tear,
On her beam ends, the Spaniards rolled and fell, no longer able to fare.

"Let's finish them!" Butrus cheered
from the prow, manning a cannon.
"Belay that!" clear of the wreck Horacio steered.
"They're no longer a threat to us. Leave it, anon."
In tempest tossed, it was enough to gain safe passage,
for tempting the devil with added delays would serve none.
Be it minutes or seconds, gaining time was their earned advantage.
"Hear that!" Mendez jumped towards the sound of resonance,
searching frantically for the origin, nearing a rage.
"Hoy! Ten o'clock!" the lookout yelled with excited diligence,
pointing to a spot about half a league away off the port side.
"I saw their mussel flash!" he added to the morning's dissonance.
"Got you now!" Mendez greedily adjusted course. "You've nowhere left to hide."
Tacking, Os Dentes Serpente would now begin the chase,
while at a distance, Cardenas and his crew following behind.
With thunderous conditions, it would be a slow moving race,
a zagging, choppy course now would have to trace.

Coming first upon the jetsam,
and rowboats full of men, to hostile waters sent
from the flailing, sinking ship of the caravan,
only added more delay to their impediment
and the distance the Spaniards needed to recover.
For two full days exhausted, drenched men, already spent,
stood before the mast, muscles aching, turned to rubber,
fighting to survive, they inched their way forward.
The storm, with no sign of abatement, did hover

and as they approached its swirling center chord,
round the Isle of Sicilia, the sailors could see its swollen eye,
with a spewing red-yellow glow, all lit up to a fiery fjord.
In the days of old, before the counting of time on high,
when the domain of heaven above was yet unsettled,
when titans walked the land and did battle with the sky,
there lived a great creature born of Gaia Earth's kettle,
the terrible, outrageous and lawless Typhon, a monstrous devil.

With double serpent tails for leggings,
and one hundred fire breathing snakes
slithering from his shoulders grew, this fearsome dragon of legends,
with the force of hurricanes on his breath, the sky he shakes
with mighty wings to challenge Jupiter for the crown of Olympus
and Earth to rule. All before him would he take, highest be the stakes.
Then, upon the precipice of doom, surrounded by a frightened chorus,
Jupiter, summoning all his power, smote his enemy with a thunderbolt,
casting him down with a deafening crash, Earth shaking beneath his corpus.
By the strength of arms, mountains they threw at each other in the assault,
until, finally defeated, Jupiter buried the bloodied Typhon
beneath the weight of Mt. Etna, his eternal prison vault.
It is from here, due to Neptune's jarring, that the monster began to swoon,
and by erupting fire from his mouth, the volcano came alive,
with molten ash and flaming lava flows into the sky were strewn.
It was from this beast that the massive storm was fed and able to thrive
and before his door now it was that the opposing ships did arrive.

The Crescent Moon, first on the path,
sailed cautiously past this fiery gloom,
as melting shards of fire stone shot past,
hissing fast, as they splashed into the watery tomb.
"There is much evil in this place," Suleiman warned,
feeling in his bones the presence of doom.
"Yes," Horacio concurred, "I sense it too," he turned
the rudder to avoid more flaming stones. "Keep a sharp eye out,
there's much danger that lurks here." The sky burned
before them. Closing behind, the Spaniards were also thereabout,
just out of firing range. They followed the Crescent Moon
into those burning seas, still raging with cresting clout,
wild waves continued to smash an undaunted tune,
tossing about the remaining vessels that had ventured so far
into the dragon's lair, tempting fate and sheer ruin.
"Now I have them!" Mendez sneered, ready to finally spar.
"Commence firing! Press them hard!" he cried, then, "Ahrrr!"

From his post at the helm,
Mendez sent to Cardenas an order
to sweep around, in an attempt to overwhelm,
and from the landward side attack their starboard quarter.
Fore-cannons erupted, echoing in the night,
as they began their maneuvers through that black water.
"In coming!" Avranos shouted out a warning at the sight
of the cannon's flare, as the shots fell far short of their target.
"Prepare to come about!" Horacio called, ready for the fight.
Just then, as the boom swung around, they were beset
by a crashing round that cut into their flank.
Cardenas, on his mark, approaching fast, was set
on finishing the present business, its end he would thank
on his return voyage. Lining up a second shot, his cannons slang
forth another iron volley to smash into the wooden bank
of the Crescent Moon, striking down in the shrapnel's bang
two sailors, along with Evhad, for them the death bell rang.

In that moment,
with reverberations all around,
the anger of mighty Typhon ferment,
from his lungs he expelled a hideous sound
and into the air cast a torrent of flaming lava
from Mt. Etna's swollen pit, shaking the ground
and the sea with it; all three ships tossed in the drama.
From beneath the island, where the monster lie pinned,
he released his dreadful serpents, their breath a molten saliva,
searching for victims above in the currents, they skimmed
the water's surface, one hundred anacondas on a tide of blood.
Unaware of the forthcoming danger, Cardenas grinned
with his focus on the forward fight, the battle lines being scud.
"Another round," he ordered, lest he lose the present advantage.
Igniting the fuses, the cannons flared, yet falling moistly dud,
attracting attention would be the last mistake he would manage,
as the snakes drawn by the fire, on them would commence to ravage.

They attacked silently,
without any advertisement,
up the ship's side they patiently
slithered. Breathlessly came the retirement,
as the serpents struck with flame and gnash,
strangling the bodies and burning the rest in corposant.
Now fed, and ship a ball of flames spewing ash,
Typhon and his deadly serpents began to relax.
"Blessed Lord almighty!" one of Mendez's crew let out a gasp.

“Must ‘av been struck by the mountain,” another did wax.
“Steer clear, we’ve no need for her to pull us under,”
Mendez gave his order as the shifting seas still be a tax
to their forward motion, while above them roared thunder.
From the Crescent Moon it was a different celebration,
seeing the enemy, with them in the sights, go asunder,
a cheer rose up from the deck, watching the sudden ignition.
For the moment, it was they who were saved from cremation.

Just as the words, “Thank Jove,” had entered his mind,
Horacio could see the fireball heading in their direction.
Fast upon the wheel he turned, to put their stern to the wind,
riding the storm waters, in hopes of deflection.
Mendez too saw the molten stone-shot blast out
from the mouth of the volcano as a hostile projection.
“Hard to port!” he shouted, also needing to come about.
Like a meteorite, or some angry fallen star,
the blazing rock crashed down between their two ships, in a rout,
sending a cascading tidal wave, wide as a hectare,
in all directions. It struck with a magnitude force,
sweeping the ships up like toys in a bazaar,
only to then cast them back down along the course.
They went tumbling, strewn across the sea,
pushed to the very brink of their recourse.
Holding on for dear life, the crews prayed for mercy,
as they went racing across the water like flying debris.

Waking to daylight,
bobbing to and fro on calm seas,
the crew of the Crescent Moon shook off the night,
bewildered at still being alive, at the heavens hearing their pleas.
They staggered to their feet, as a drunk would after the party.
“Praise be, we’re still alive!” Nebi on the moment did seize.
“Yes, but where are we?” his brother Isa asked, quick on the parry.
Trackless they were, with no reference, floating on open water.
“Oh my head,” Butrus moaned, awakening partly,
having been struck by the boom during the night’s slaughter.
According to the gauges, they’d been thrown in a southerly direction,
which might put them anywhere off the coast of North Africa,
crossing the same harrowing route as Aeneas’s earlier congregation.
“Come about north by northwest,” Horacio turned the wheel,
putting their ship on the most probable course correction.
“Bosun, get me a damage report on the double, we’ve got no time to steal.”
“Aye captain,” Suleiman replied, hot on his heel.

After burying at sea their dead,
and with repairs busily underway,
the crew enjoying the first restful moments tread
for days on end. With sun towards the west already halfway,
and the ship presently out of danger, it was time to take the tally.
By pirate standards, the captain is elected by popular say,
and Horacio must present himself before the galley.
"Assemble the men," he instructed Suleiman,
who brought the ship to order and crew to rally.
"Hear me now," Horacio called to each man,
"there's a decision we must make, here today.
Now, we all mourn the loss of our captain, Reis-el-Khan,
but this ship has a new destiny and it's you who must choose the way.
If there are any among you who question my judgment,
or right to this station, who would suggest another in my stay,
speak now, I urge you make your voices abundant.
If grounds be made, here and now, we will make the adjustment."

Over the crew spread a silent hush,
as one of thoughtful contemplation.
Who amongst them in arms would dare rush
against him? His sword by now was reputation.
Who amongst them would challenge him as a seaman of the line?
From one end of the ship to the other, he had earned each station.
Few others would any of the men trust on board more with their lives,
as proven by the recent hours, yet in the back there was a murmur.
"Yes, you, speak up," Horacio pointed towards the rear. "Let's hear your mind."
"Well," a gruffly bearded sailor cleared his throat, to the eye son of a Berber.
"There is the question of you being an infidel," a stir the words did instill.
"An unbeliever as captain is not a simple thing," he spoke with fervor.
"How do we know the direction of your will?"
"No, that's a fair question," Horacio waved down the clamor of voices.
"It's true, that we do not prey to the same deities. That I grant you, I will.
So let us speak of what I intend, for the support of your voices,
I'll tell you all you want to know, then you make your choices."

After some debate,
and filling in of the edges,
the crew leaned more to hesitate
hearing of otherworldly pledges,
yet in the tale he told, there within the Trojan's story,
an enticement too did unfold, between the doubt it wedges
that with the quest too did come the promise of eternal glory.
"Enough!" it was Suleiman who broke up the dispute.
"It too is the will of Allah the state of our present inventory.

The decision has already been written. Who here would dare to refute?"
"It was Khan's final command," Baloch seconded. "I heard him. I was there,"
swaying more than enough uncommitted to fulfill the suit.
The strongest and best on board joined, standing square
behind Horacio. "Troy and Thrace together again,"
Avranos stood by his shoulder, showing solidarity between the pair.
"As it should be," Horacio replied, completing the refrain,
with the mantle of command none but his to retain.

Into their future and destiny,
the crew of the Crescent Moon sailed,
while from the past, in the deep recesses of the sea,
at the edges of where the vibrating current trailed,
the leviathan, Oceanus, hearing the call,
moved the tides in a direction favorably scaled
to the undertaking Horacio no longer wished to forestall.
With the sun riding low, Suleiman relieved Horacio at the wheel.
"Mendez is still out there," he wasn't long to recall.
"Yes, and he hasn't heard the last of us, my friend. I feel,"
Horacio hastened to add, "our blades will cross once more,
before the end is upon us. On that day he shall taste my steel.
On that you have my word," knowing for both of them the point was sore.
In those final moments of daylight, an orange horizon presented its wonder,
as they continued on their northerly course towards what lie in store,
giving into those few peaceful minutes, where the mind is left to ponder,
until at last a voice rang out, "Land ho!" the lookout pointed yonder.

BOOK XI

THE GHOSTS OF MALTA

In that trailing dusk,
with the final specs of daylight
mingling with the sea air's musk,
a spot of land presented itself to light
upon the horizon. "I know that island,"
Suleiman spoke, catching sight
of the silhouetted strip of land.
"It's Malta, a Christian stronghold
and the limit of Aragon's reach, our best plan
would be to sail around past her dark folds."
"Agreed," Horacio confirmed his right hand's opinion.
"Keep her to our flank," he gave his orders, as the wind gust cold.
"Aye," Suleiman confirmed from behind the helm's bastion,
setting his course, with the dark of night slowly enveloping the waters.
From the ship's railing came a voice raised in a whispering fashion
that caught Horacio's ear, drawing him in close as would do squatters,
for Kasim was recalling to Isa and Nebi a tale he once heard of these quarters.

"That island is haunted, they say,"
he began, his voice raw with scruff gravity.
"Once, long ago, a great civilization inhabited this lay,
with tracts of land stretching all the way to the coast of Sicily.
Great mammoth beasts walked this land and man was much the pagan
as is our good captain here. They influenced the region substantially,
from Greece to Cairo, laying the seeds for those mighty clans.
Yet, they were also given over to debauchery and superstition,
with wild orgies and blood sacrifice, the natural order forsaken,
and so the one, true God angered at their deprivation
swelled the seas, wiping out much of their race,
swallowing all the land, 'cept for these here islands, a mere partition
that remains as a reminder of their former glory, to trace
back to today. It is said that those who died unrepentant in the great flood
still haunt these shoals and on certain nights their spirits can be seen to race
across the waters, whispering prophesies for the exchange of blood,
by which way they can return to their long lost kingdom, now covered in mud.

"If you believe such things,"
Kasim summed up the lore,
ending it with a hint of skeptic tinge.
Nebi sat rattled at his place on the floor,
"Unnatural, it is. Accursed waters."
"Nonsense," Isa scolded next to him, keeping score,
"It's merely a story to frighten ill-witted daughters,"
rousing a laugh from those in the congregation.
"Alright, back to stations," Horacio jovially broke up the cluster.
"Isa, Nebi, why don't you take first watch tonight. Keep us clear of apparitions."
"Aye, aye capt'n," the two paired in unison, returning to duty.
"Kasim, walk with me," Horacio guided him to a secluded direction.
"How'd you come by such a yarn?" he asked once alone, peeked with curiosity.
"Ah, yes," Kasim shook his head rapidly, with a searching look in his eye.
"My grandfather was a fisherman on these waters back in the last century
and told me the tale of how he had seen them with his own eye,
on a night very much like this, when the water reflected the sky.

"He'd shown me the scar
from where his hand had bled
and in his words, was shown afar
into his future, predicting, he said,
that one day I too would go to sea,
to never again return to my homestead."
Ominous he sounded. Horacio counted to three,
"Probably best not to be telling that to the crew,
no need to rile up their senses, you agree?"
"Yes," Kasim thought for a moment, "I see your point of view."
"Good," Horacio gave him a pat on the shoulder.
"Carry on then," he left Kasim there, walking alone out of view.
There, towards the bow, his thoughts began to smolder,
staring out into the starry sky, as a mirror off the water's surface.
He could feel a chill in his bones, with the night growing colder.
The ship crested through the rippling liquid sky, as if in chase
of stars and the memory of time. Towards Malta the runny lines did race.

"Bring us further in,"
in lowered tones he instructed Suleiman,
returning to the helm. With confound and chagrin,
Suleiman returned a "Sir?" in question of the revised plan.
"Just do it," Horacio replied. "Keep a steady eye."
"Aye," Suleiman adjusted course to bring them closer to the island,
still some distance away as the crow would fly,
while Horacio took leave of the deck for his cabin.
In those early hours of night all remained calm under the sky,

as Isa and Nebi stood lookout over a sea of rolling black satin.
"This island gives me the shivers," Nebi let out as the coastline inched closer.
"It's just nerves. There's no such thing as ghosts," Isa reminded him,
placing no stock in the tale of an old seafarer.
Faintly, a bell could be heard in the distance.
"What's that?" Nebi spun on his feet, hand on his holster.
"What indeed?" from behind them Horacio made his stance.
Finger to his ear, he motioned for them to listen to the instance.

Fading, the ringing echoed,
trailing off into the icy half-lit night.
A church bell, somewhere on yonder island bestowed
beyond the apex crest of mountain peaked height
over the bay, stretching out into infinity,
and to their ears the hour of midnight.
"Not ghosts," Horacio intoned with hushed sanguinity.
"Not ghosts at all my friends, but spirits, the first spirits."
Drawing the brothers in close to his vicinity,
Horacio imparted upon them a few new pivots.
"Years ago, when I had only just ascended to my prior post,
Captain Khan, shared with me some very similar minutes,
of a great deluge, that wiped out all of civilization, almost.
Every tradition has similar tales of a horrible flood and destruction,
so by way of consensus and multiple sources the story's origin does boast
some merit. However, Khan went much further in his induction,
to also mention the legend of this specter apparition.

"He said that before the great flood
our species was primitive, living in direct
harmony with nature, and from that bud
rose the birth of our curiosity and intellect,
asking ourselves the eternal question,
'Where did we come from?' We began to collect
more and more information
in the only language we understood at the time
that of Mother Earth and the universe since its formation,
that being mathematics, the oldest and truest of all clime
of reason, a common tongue that bound us together,
and allowed us beyond safe boundaries to climb,
for in our search for knowledge we unlocked the tether
that kept us with nature in balance and harmony.
Too smart were we by half and changed this world forever,
for in our very first attempt to unravel the mysteries
we exposed the deepest secrets of all the hidden majesty.

"Through mathematics,
more than ten thousand years ago,
we, our species, broke through the matrix
to calculate the movement and cycles, to and fro
of the seasons and stars, putting us even on par
with the gods, able to predict when they would come and go,
and through the precision of the computations went as far
as to prove their own existence... at that moment we became self-aware."
Horacio paused in his telling to let the brothers absorb the memoir.
"Then what happened?" Nebi pressed with an eager stare.
"Well, then the gods became angered, furious at the race of man
for their boldness, for crossing the divide beyond land and air,
of their search for the heavens, of some master plan,
that they opened up the skies and engorged the seas,
covering, drinking and drowning most all of the land
pushing all life towards extinction, a near certainty,
until, at the very brink, hearing love's plea, we were shown mercy.

"The skies cleared
and the rains abated,
yet into our core being our fate was seared
to that singular catastrophe, for now we were separated,
not simply in distances by vast seas from other tribes,
but from nature itself, having broken through knowledge that dated
back to the very counting of time. Once done it was impossible to unsubscribe,
so as a result, instead of being one eternal with the universe,
in direct communication with the greater powers, we sat beside.
As reward, or punishment, it's hard to know if it wasn't a curse,
that event bestowed upon us our immortal souls, as individuals
we stood disconnected, forever in search of return to the source, to reverse
the course, yet blinded we were by the deluge, a trauma residual
that our memories were collectively erased, obscuring the ancient ways.
The sole recollection for these tribes of man aboriginal,
aside from the horrors of the great flood itself, belays
a voice in the head, with a warning for the end of all days.

"'By fire and water
it would come, if we did not change our ways.'
Those were the very last words creation would utter,
before our souls were ripped from the womb, placed into these mortal stays.
It was in that moment of amnesic confusion that the gods came into being,
for how else could we explain this collective induction that still plays
to this day? Lost, afraid and wandering, the tribes of man fleeing
the recently unknown, went into the world as strangers.
Mute, we created new tongues and dialects and ways of seeing,

that differentiated ourselves from other nomadic rangers,
creating barriers between ourselves and the one I Am.
In place of a home, the earth became a lodge full of dangers.
We forgot how to trust and so we prayed an endless 'Amen,'
as a way of explanation for what we could no longer understand.
Thus rose, over the centuries, the image of god as man;
the duality of fate and freewill, ultimately placing responsibility in our hands.
This is the story Khan shared with me," he spoke as if under a trance.

"What of the ghosts?"
Nebi quickly asked to see the connection.
"The spirits," Isa corrected, having not lost
his eye for detail. "Yes, yes, the spirits," Nebi confirmed the correction.
"What about the spirits? How do they fit into all of this?"
"Well, that's why," Horacio jumped on the point of attention,
"I believe there's some veracity to this story of his,
for after that he then went on to tell me how he came by this knowledge.
Khan's older brother, Kemal, was the real pirate in the family, whereas
he'd been a sea merchant's apprentice. His path was to work a trader's sledge.
Then, one day, when Khan was no older than myself of that year,
Kemal was taken prisoner by the Christians and brought to dredge
upon a dungeon cell on this very island of Malta here.
Determined to free him, Khan outfitted a ship and a crew ready to fight,
making haste to this very place on what could only be a suicide venture.
Reaching the coast, having entered the prison vault under cover of night
and there, breaking the locks, finding Kemal, they made ready their flight.

"However, moments into their escape,
discovered, the alarm bells rang out.
Stumbling down the hillside, they fled chase.
Under fire, Kemal was struck in the side by a lance during the bout.
Having barely survived to the rowboat, Khan paddled back to the waiting ship;
his brother, bleeding his life into the waters, when they came about.
From underneath there appeared a swirling hue, and before he knew it,
they were surrounded on all sides by an otherworldly spread.
'Spirits,' he said. Out of nowhere appeared these spirits,
cascading along the shallow sea bed,
speaking in strange tongues to the ear,
racing across the water like incandescent blue lit threads.
Reaching up, they touched him, taking him by the hand and there
reading his soul, and his deepest longings, granted him sight,
a vision of the path he must follow to achieve his greatest desire.
Then as if in a dream, the haunted spirits vanished into the night.
Unconscious, Khan awoke, sprawled upon the deck of his ship now in flight.

"Kemal died that night,
and Khan, with a new found vengeance,
was born, vowing to make right
what had gone wrong as his earthly penance,
and thus began his war with Christendom,
for he blamed all of Christianity in the death sentence
of his brother. But, as his heart there hardened, so too in his ear did come
a final prophesy from the spirits, that the next time his ship would cross
this stretch of water, so too would he be dead." Hearts beat as a drum,
as Horacio recounted the tale. "And so here we are," he looked across
at the two brothers. "Now, I don't know if this story is true or not,
but not once in all my years did Khan sail by this way. For the heavens to toss
us here as the very first stop upon his passing gives need for thought,
for there must be some portent in the meaning."
"All that happens is by Allah's will," Isa inserted at that spot.
"So," Horacio queried, "everything happens for a reason, you are saying?"
"Well," Isa paused a moment, "yes, that would be one way of explaining."

"Good, so we're in agreement,"
Horacio then hastened to add.
"Sir?" Isa asked, foreseeing the commitment.
"If there's any chance," Horacio confided in his comrades,
"that this story has merit; if the spirits of the first peoples
of Earth inhabit these waters, imparting visions clad
in ancient knowledge of the universe and all its steeples,
with prophesies of the future that may help our current voyage,
then we are obliged to investigate for samples."
"What is it you're suggesting?" Nebi's curiosity took the stage.
"That we call these spirits here to us tonight and see for own eyes,
if the legend holds weight," Horacio sized up their courage.
"I need your assistance. Are you with me?" he asked. Ready were the "Ayes!"
from the brothers, overcoming doubt and fear with a sense of mission.
"What can we do?" Isa asked, ready to aide his captain in attaining his prize.
"Maintain a steady watch, ready at your stations."
Extracting a short knife, Horacio prepared his position.

With the heavens looking down,
Horacio gathered his thoughts and reasons,
staring out onto the rippling sea that cascaded off the bow.
A frosty air caressed his breath out of season,
as he spoke over waves to the powers therein.
"Hear me, brothers and sisters of old, light your beacons
once more. Share with me the wisdom you hold and wherein
the future be told. I pray you bless and guide this most noble quest
with your favor." Then lifting his free hand to the night sky, "Herein,

I offer tribute to your souls in the manner you would request."
Placing blade to flesh, he then sliced the palm of his hand.
Clenching, it dripped red into the sea, the legend to test.
A held breath and frozen silence met them where they stand,
unchanged the dark of night stood still before them all,
while under the darkened silhouette of Maltese land
the Crescent Moon made her path along her creviced wall,
a shadow it crept upon the sea beneath the stars and all.

"Ah! Just as I'd mentioned,"
Isa mounted the pregnant moment.
"A story is all it has ever been, though well fashioned,
a story all the same," feeling pragmatic pride in his comment.
Then, as he spoke those words he eyed his captain,
gaze bleeding into the horizon with a touch of disappointment.
"Perhaps," Horacio spoke, eye focused on a point in the distant span
of night. "Perhaps," he turned, lowering his hand when a shudder filled the air.
"Did you feel that?" Nebi spun to the side, like a capstan.
"I did indeed," Horacio gathered his bearings, trying to ascertain from where
came the movement. "That makes three of us," Isa confirmed his accord,
muscles tensing for action. Beneath the ship from somewhere
arose a vibration, subtle harmonics that didn't waver a chord.
It passed through the ship and up to the heavens, gone, silent as before.
"What was that?" Nebi asked, hand gripping tight to a cord.
"I'm not sure," Horacio took command. "Keep your eyes on the fore,
I'm going aft to check on the score."

Making his way to the stern,
Horacio bandaged his left hand with a strip of cloth.
There, as an echo, the vibration made a return,
like a slow pulse or faint beacon, it called out with sloth
ringing the ship to an alternate frequency.
From beneath, as a looming cloud of goth,
lights began to dance, weaving a tapestry
of colors; of sapphires, jades and lavenders,
with an endless stream, a swirling delicacy,
it hypnotized, lulling the senses as venders
would at a carnival, drawing in their game.
A whisper rose, indecipherable to by-standers,
barely discernible to Horacio, which pulled at him the same
ever closer to the ship's rail, he stood upon the edge.
Heart racing, it pounded in his chest refusing to tame
as he stared out in awe at the wonder there upon the ledge,
for surrounded was he, caught in the center of a kaleidoscopic wedge.

Above him, the skies borealis,
presented an opposite illusion of optics
as one would be led to believe, beholding the chalice,
that the sky could reflect the seas, yet seize it here, his eyes not playing tricks,
from heights to depths, in the iris of the eye, he stood there encapsulated
in living color, the universe itself coming into human focus.
"Marvelous," Horacio breathed in the majesty, insulated
from all other cares, at one he felt with the galaxy,
as it swirled around and through him. Senses stimulated
though unable to move, his muscles slowed to the Nth degree
lagging behind his impulses, as though on another dimensional plane,
he was there simply to bear witness as would gravity.
There, as the stillness churned, he could feel his energy wax and wane,
when there to him came a voice and a vision.
... No, it was a memory, a memory to him came.
Only, it was not one of his own, but some other's incision
into the filament of his brain, projecting the timeline's revision.

There was an explosion,
a great wash of light and matter,
that expelled into the countless directions,
from where all life, all everything, began... to scatter.
Yet so too was it forever connected, for it was all one,
a single verse dig it, that spread so fast for so long that a hatter
might say it wasn't moving at all, so immense was it beyond the reckon,
the omnipresent, everywhere undertaking, its scope lie outside of measure.
There, on a single point of light, in the middle of all this, all of a sudden,
out of the destruction, first by fire, a phoenix burst amidst the pressure
to birth life... and there, over the count of billions grew
a race, one that was so intrinsically in tune with nature
that it was able to comprehend everything and through
this connection built great wonders, shaping the earth
to its own command and thus rose a civilization who knew
the inner workings of the universe from their humble hearth
and in this way vast was its reach and worth.

Through the eyes of a child,
Horacio, in what seemed like hours,
yet only seconds in his counting passed, with senses riled,
was transported, not to a place, but to a time by such powers
that be, that before him he could see the image of a great city by the sea.
Emerging from around and below, whence his ship floated above the bowers,
stone temples and public squares, etched upon the landscape jubilee,
down the gentle slope of foothills, coming to rest at the edge of wave crest.
A festival was there ongoing, which slipped into salacious activity.

It was the end of an eon for the galaxy, when each star aligned with all the rest
a resetting of the clocks, so to speak, as the gravitational forces shifted
setting off a chain reaction that from their world would wrest
a new beginning. It was not so much a voice as a silence that was lifted,
stilling the air and all within, as the sudden quiet sent shockwaves of terror
through every heart. So used to tuning in, now disconnected, they drifted
apart. Helpless, frozen with confusion, that's when they felt the mighty tremor.
"Think you're gods?" rose the all-pervading voice. "Now you'll pay for the error."

The earth then split open,
slashing a great crevice across the land,
in from which rushed a dreadful wave upon them.
Through screams and pleas a great many fell with the strike of a hand,
though only a warning, "The next time by fire and water shall your end come!"
then nothing as the seas swallowed all but the highest peaks of land.
He was drowning, in a sudden covered by water, heart a pounding drum,
hands clasping at bubbles, surrounded, pressure from all sides, pulled under,
convulsing, he blacked out, being sucked through a funnel of rum-a-tum-tum
in his head, and opening his eyes, not dead, but presented from asunder
with another reality. There on a fast forward spiral, the blur came into focus,
with him standing on the precipice of a great stone cliff. Thunder
roared around him with blood-curdling cries and many a cuss
shaking the air. The rush of running filled his lungs
through fronds of thick foliage away from the ruckus,
where upon such path befell the sound of hissing and foreign tongues
there before an opening in the stone, a tunnel entrance, a warning flung.

"Beware, ye who enter,"
rose a whisper upon the air.
There, a foot upon the threshold's center
took a step whence danger reared its head to blare,
"The first across to perish fast, the second's fate to linger."
Not a moment was there to contemplate the notice given, for from there
he was transported, shot off from a rocket, through a twisting cavernous finger,
to plunge on towards a molten sea, spewing gas and fire.
Snapping to, he hovered surrounded by a thousand tunnels, each a trigger,
one he would have to choose, but which led not to a funeral pyre
remained uncertain, and then a calling familiar came from the rear,
he spun to see, yet was once again delivered from the mire
to light again upon his ship, the passing vision once clear,
now it vanished, transpired, and from his wounded hand an apparition,
releasing, did retire, descending back onto the waters, which did bare
its soul. And as it parted a final word in his ear came as instruction,
"Before crossing the final gate, seek your true father to amend the omission."

Waking, the sun began to break
upon the horizon. From his cabin,
Horacio emerged groggy, his head did shake,
rattled from the night's vision, a slow stabbing
worked its way through his whole body. "What'd you make of all that?"
Suleiman he asked, ending his shift at the helm, which to him,
"A quiet night. Nothing to report," left him befuddled where he sat.
"Really?" Horacio came back. "What of all those lights?"
"Sir?" it was Suleiman now confused. "It was as clear a passage as any that
have come before." For Isa and Nebi, they too had no memory of the night
other than all signals clear, a quandary of which he kept silent
for it appeared only he could recall the mysterious rites
that had happened. Then to his left hand his attention he bent,
for a sore reminder remained, yet with scar tissue already healed over,
something beyond explanation was at work in these waters which lent
its aide. With Malta at the stern, fading far away, a single word held over,
trailing into silence, soft in his ear did whisper, "Trust," as if spoken to a lover.

BOOK XII

THE UNDERWORLD

Meanwhile,
in the underworld,
Lord Pluto was living in style.
Never before had so much tribute been unfurled
before his feet. If maybe not on every lip,
he was never far from mind. As the world's populace curled
into religion, he became that much more important, the biting end of the whip
that set people into motion. From his domain, he controlled the strings,
pulling the world from left to right, according to whim, as he saw fit,
the lives of men on Earth his playthings.
From up above there was nothing, only silence,
leaving up to man's interpretation the meaning of things.
Fallible, they shaped theology to suit their own structures of violence,
leaving Pluto, by whisper or direct involvement, to mold the world to his image.
Reaping from their fields of battle the spoils of blood and rising pestilence,
his kingdom continued to expand to cover the earth in a sorrowful age,
one in where wars unending roiled with rage.

From his palace,
dark and magnificent,
overlooking the Elysian Fields of grace,
Pluto contemplated in a manner quite reticent.
"You've changed," Proserpine, his beloved wife, spoke in a soft voice.
"How so?" he turned from his tower pane, looking at her, feeling reminiscent,
her beauty unfading in all the long years, since that fateful choice
on the day he abducted her, stealing her away from the fields,
bringing her to the realm of the underworld, where by bargain did rejoice
at their union, having been struck by Cupid's arrow, even death might yield
to love. "You seem withdrawn, more somber than usual of late,"
she confided in him. "Your humor, grim as it may be, no longer do you wield."
"It's nothing, just a passing phase," he deflected, sensing the bait.
"I've got a lot on my mind," he passed it off to responsibilities.
"Are you sure there's nothing else?" she implied, but would not grate
on him by saying aloud what she thought, and all the possibilities,
that he might feel somehow remorse for all his morbid activities.

"No, I'm fine, my love,"
he kissed her paling cheek.
His duties as lord and ruler must come above
other considerations. Close is the counsel he must keep
and no point is there in worrying her with matters of business.
"I have a busy day ahead is all." It was the season of herding the meek
and there was still the new war to instigate, no end was there to the stress...
but he also loved his work, no one could outperform his covert ops.
Taking hold of his bident scepter and helmet of invisibility, by way he'd nest
amongst mortals and gods alike undetected, a mighty gift from the Cyclops
given during the Titan Wars it was, endowing the bearer with great powers
of deception, he bid his wife farewell, for much distance and many stops
were on his agenda of late, with as always too few hours.
His first stop was to check in with the war council.
Oh, the blood! He can't forget the blood. Mixing a bottle of fresh and sour,
he corked it on the way out. Departing from his queen's counsel,
four midnight black steeds delivered him, speeding from the castle.

Along he raced,
skirting the fields of Elysium,
passing groves of wildflowers laced
with sparkling gold, silver and platinum,
where those fortunate to be judged as worthy
would spend the rest of eternity free from toil and oblivion.
Contrary to spiritual speculation and the doctrine of religious theory,
no one has ever met the "one true God" either before or after parting from life.
Those hopes were all part of the elaborate illusion designed for the earthly.
The best any mortal could wish to attain is access to this realm free from strife,
far away from the absentee landlord living in the clouds of the mind.
Dust shifted from under horse hooves, as Pluto, king of the afterlife,
plodded down the course, plotting his next moves to bind
all of mankind to his appetites and unique worldly vision.
There, arriving at the crossroads, as knew he would find,
rested the road to Tartarus, the pathway to perdition,
where those less fortunate suffered an ever-lasting torment and derision.

Turning left,
he headed away, towards his kingdom's gate,
passing the throngs of newly dead mournfully bereft
in their misery and sorrow, already judged, they staggered to their fate.
With a crimson and black overcast, it was turning out to be a splendid day.
In the approaching distance the walls of his sovereignty loomed high and great,
as he made good time on his journey. Moaning cries from a disheveled fray,
offset the sound of whips and snarls and shouting commands with perfect
harmony, as a demonic rhapsody filling the air with a tortured musical play,

orchestrated his entrance with mighty flare. Halting before the office of prefect,
Pluto descended from his ebony chariot, greeted by his faithful dog, Cerberus.
Three heads bobbing with drool, snarling, the great beast flung his respect
upon his master. Pluto petted the monster and threw him a femur, thus
he went sprinting off to fight amongst himself for the bone.
In long black robes, Pluto tailored a macabre, most perilous
stature, with helmet and scepter. A sturdy ring of keys on hip shone,
dangling from his waist belt, the keys of his kingdom, for his hand alone.

Gruesome guards on either side
bowed their heads as Pluto marched past,
entering the halls of bureaucracy, all stonewall fortified.
There, in his expansive gothic office, overlooking the River Styx, he cast
his eye upon his current dilemma. From the fireplace roared a blaze,
as he stamped the bottle he carried down upon the table, saying at last,
“Drink up, my friend. It’s a special blend suited to your taste.”
In his plot against his brothers and the other gods above, Pluto
ran into one little snag that could not be avoided as he raze
the heavens. For in the greater vision, he knew, one other god must forego
his punishment, who would also grow stronger as a result of the coup d’état;
one who it would not take too much wooing to secure a pact to tow
the needed line… as long as he stay manageable, and for that, voila,
was a state of permanent drunkenness. For though aggressive, Mars he knew
was not a simple brute, given away to unwarranted destruction, from it far.
No, he required the proper stimulus, and like all the sharks in oceans grew,
he too had a similar affliction, for which his sword he drew.

The taste of blood,
even the scent of it, put him in a frenzy
and once riled, it poured forth to flood
all in its wake. This Pluto wished to unleash in plenty.
“Come on, we have work to do,” Pluto pressed the cup.
The God of War sat groggily, having not slept in over a century.
Bleary eyed, from his seat at the table, he pushed himself up
to an erect position. Taking hold of the goblet presented,
he wet his lips. With a sudden transformation, as if one corrupt,
Mars there changed complexion, and speaking in a voice fully scented
he said, “Oh, that’s good!” The first taste was always the best.
“There’s plenty more where that came from,” Pluto’s smile remained undented.
The pusher man, always draped as a friend, allowed his pigeon no rest.
“But I need you to do something for me first,” he baited the lore.
“Well, count me in,” Mars revived, felt the bluster growing in his chest.
“My sword hand itches and grows restless for battle’s allure.”
“Excellent,” Pluto led his nephew by the shoulder towards the door.

Exchanging his chariot,
they mounted together a midnight black carriage.
Pulled driverless by the same four raven sheen stallions, neighing nefarious,
hitched in pairs, their hooves scratched at the dirt, as if digging at carnage,
they prepared the start of the journey, while the two gods inside conspired.
“Tell me uncle,” Mars spoke with an arrogant air. “What’s the latest scourge
you’ve got brewing?” There sparkled a telling look in his eye, as one inspired.
As he drank, teasing his appetite, in some ways too did he become more sober,
his natural state of clarity being itself a bit off balance, with reason retired.
“Why do you hurt me so?” Pluto feigned injury to his honor.
“Everything I’ve done has been only to your advantage.”
“Oh how humble,” Mars laughed, but not long, just a brief tumbler.
“You know,” he picked his place up, seeing from his vantage
over Pluto’s right shoulder the Veil of Mourning as they passed,
with the River Styx behind cutting a snake, full of pain and disadvantage.
“I don’t entirely approve of your unilateral actions,” he said at last.
With hands in the air, Pluto asked, “Why must you always bring up the past?”

“What’s done is done,”
he shrugged off the complaint with his shoulders.
“We should be looking to the future, of all that can be won.”
Though both an eternity, Pluto plied his craft, as wisdom from the elders.
Without completely buying his line, Mars did not attempt to refute.
In the back of his mind he knew the matter wouldn’t stay buried in the embers,
yet his uncle was right on one point, he had substantially reaped the fruit.
He saw the benefits unfold for himself in the turning of a blind eye,
so why should he rise to protest a *fait accompli* and losing suit?
Yet, he wasn’t ignorant, the other eye he knew he would have to rely
on for keeping a watch over his own back. For the foreseeable future
however it would appear that his own usefulness none could deny.
And then again, he didn’t entirely disapprove of his uncle’s plotting humor
either. “Fine,” he blurted, faintly smug, turning his attention out the window.
The jagged grey of mountain crag grew large on the horizon like a tumor.
Galloping over a secret bridge, one of many hidden portals, known only to Pluto
and a select handful, they crossed Kokytos, the river of tears and sorrow.

From the heights
far off in the distance,
Mars, the war god, witnessed a frightening sight,
the red and amber glow of the Pyriphlegethon in her fiery, shriek-filled dance
towards Tartarus and the bowels of hell, to where none who venture return.
“So why all the suspense?” Mars turned back to Pluto with a glance.
“When are you going to let me in on the plan?” Pluto looked taciturn.
He would have to tell him eventually. “Alright,” he confided, leaning forward.
“I want you to go up and ally yourself with the Spaniards, upturn

the balance... not much, just enough to give them an edge." Mars looked bored.
"Is that all? Sounds like a waste of my talents? Why offer them your favor?"
"Ah!" Pluto chuckled. "Because unintended consequences lie in wait, stored
in their looming future. Not everything is as flat as it would seem. Savor
that we're on the brink of unleashing the genie from its bottle onto the masses,
and it will be by the driving ambition of these followers of the savior
that will expand the conquest beyond the confines of these present clashes
to another level, exponential, you and I, our powers will grow like the grasses."

If anything,
Pluto was a salesman.
He really knew how to push an idea, like shoveling manure with a sling.
Mars took another pull from the bottle. It was the bittersweet taste of the plan
that made him long for more. "Alright, I'll do it," Mars acquiesced.
"But I have a few conditions of my own that must be met," he lifted a hand.
"Of course," a crafty smile Pluto added, as the negotiator slid in to wrest
the terms of the agreement. Of all his functions as Lord of the Underworld,
cutting the deal gave him the greatest pleasure, it was for him the very best.
Regardless the details, he was the house and the house always won. In a world
where the game is escape, when there is no escape, even if he loses he wins.
Every now and then he lets a small fish off the hook, the illusion unfurled
that draws gamblers to his doorstep, yet there's no cheating at death's inn,
you can however always negotiate the language of the contract,
to add a personal touch and such when bartering future incursions.
For dealings with gods, the stakes were of course higher, yet he had a knack
of getting what he wanted, and Pluto did have a want that was a fact.

"Go on," he pressed Mars to begin.
"Well, the crux of the matter, dear uncle, is that I don't trust you."
"Good on you!" Pluto smiled at his nephew as he commended him.
"Nor should you, if we're talking as businessmen, it's understood to be true
that we'd each start off by looking out for our own personal interests.
Thus we deal with binding engagements that tie both me and you."
Pluto had a shrewd way with words which twisted the contexts.
Mars felt unsure of whether he should be flattered or angry.
These were the times when his caution prevailed, his patience to test.
"I need some assurances," he began, assessing by his uncle's ante
the strength of his hand to play. "Of course," Pluto remained nonchalant.
"What possible guarantee could I make to calm your anxiety?"
Mars thought hard on this question. What indeed could his uncle recant
to quell his concerns of betrayal? It'd have to be something he held most dear.
Then, leaning back, his eye rested upon the desired item of want,
knowing then in that moment that he'd accept no less than his chosen fare,
he grinned. "Your helmet," Mars then in the eye to his uncle did declare.

Pluto, sincerely taken aback,
coughing, stuttered and mumbled.
Confirming his ears, he uttered, "Come again, what's that?"
"You heard me right," Mars gloated, as if having caught a ball fumbled,
"I want your helmet. That is the price of my cooperation."
Wielding his helmet of invisibility, Mars would become the most unhumbled,
Pluto knew, truly an equal, able to avoid even death's own observation.
He didn't like it, a heavy price it was to pay, but pay it he would.
"Very well," Pluto declared, hand to it still clasped firm, "with two conditions."
"Speak," Mars smiled, having seen that he'd prevailed, now he could
be gracious in his victory. "What's the caveat you'd throw to me as a bone?"
Pluto admitted a pinch of pride in the manner with which his nephew stood,
they would do great and terrible things together, more than either on their own,
a natural symbiosis they maintained, yet, like the other he too did not trust
his nephew not to try to abuse his power, for advantage to hone,
and so, "First, you agree not to use this to hide from my person, this is a must,
and secondly, you will come and fight for me when I call, that is only just."

Mars considered the rub,
it was an annoyance, but no more than he'd already been willing to commit.
"Done!" he sealed the pact with his hand. "Welcome to the club,"
Pluto shook, handing over to his nephew the prized helmet.
Thus enabling thereafter, those of greed and blind ambition, the leverage
to manipulate the mighty forces of destruction for their personal benefit,
while war no longer was held constraint to defined lines of scrimmage,
but flowed freely, blurred between the boundaries of the acceptable,
invisibly it crossed from noble house into the arena of the savage,
attaining such magnificent heights, at a cost though most terrible.
"It will make a fine addition to my armor," Mars beamed at his trophy,
holding it out as if on display. "Indeed," Pluto remained affable
though already tinged with remorse for his loss. Of course this was not the only
way for Pluto to become invisible, death had many tricks, it was that he just
resented being even in a little way bested. The mountains grew smoky
in the distance, as their carriage approached the Gate of Dusk,
pulling to a halt before the sealed arch, embedded in a gapping crevice of rust.

There they descended
before those immeasurable doors,
impenetrable, yet so too easily they opened
from without, for naught in Hades, least of all this threshold forged of iron ores,
stood to bar one's entry, quite to the contrary, they presented a ready welcome.
Return though was entirely another matter, for once washed upon the shores
of Pluto's realm, only he might grant passage back to whence thou had come.
Fingering his ring of keys, he selected the proper one to fit this gate,
a thick skeleton, bony as a finger bent, which he slid into the lock's drum.

Twisting it, the metal wheels within they groaned, as the bolts began to grate.
On thick, heavy hinges the doors swung open, letting in a whiff of fresh air,
from the long spiraling tunnel that carved a rocky path to Earth's upper plate.
From here as many trails as could be imagined, one for every soul is there,
merged, leading to all the hidden crevices of Earth, yet to this point
they all returned. For Pluto though, a gateway it was to any destination where
he so desired. "So, where are we off to?" Mars attempted to pinpoint
his uncle's thoughts. "Different directions," Pluto twisted a shoulder joint.

There was a mission
that Pluto needed fulfilled
in order to succeed with his grander vision.
Having humbled the heavens, other beasts now must be quelled.
Thus his eye turned towards the seas, for him to truly be the omnipotent
he must gain control over this holdout bastion. Where oceans dwelled,
perhaps he would never be its master, however that would only prevent
him for so long. Pluto vowed to tame the seas for his bidding and for that Mars
would help lead the charge to victory. Depicting a look of one content,
he eyed the tidings of war. "Wreak havoc, my lad. with scourge and scars."
With a wave of his hand, Pluto opened the portal for his nephew's destination.
"To sea?" Mars asked, seeing his port of call a coastal stretch below the stars.
"Yes, prepare their navy. Build for them an armada," Pluto gave his instruction.
"Make them great in battle." "Fair enough," Mars thought his task not much,
a holiday in fact, he considered. "And for you?" he desired a greater induction.
"Oh, I have some things I must attend to," Pluto was vague as always in such.
As Mars departed, aside to himself he whispered, "Perhaps a woman's touch?"

BOOK XIII

A RETURN TO CARTHAGE

On Fortune's wings they flew,
over the open sea, with the wind at their stern
and spirits running high, the Crescent Moon and her crew
skirted the Christian sphere of influence. Setting a course north-western,
they trimmed sail to make the most of the prevailing air current.
"Steady on," Horacio felt the wind stream through his hair, as he turn
to look upon the horizon. If they kept their pace going at the present
rate they'd make the Tyrrhenian by nightfall, and hopefully pass undetected
up the Italian coastline. "Captain," Suleiman, on an aside, asked for a moment.
"Is it true, you search out the doorway to the afterworld? That selected
for a mission have you been, by the gods you worship, no less?"
There was a deeper question lingering unspoken, yet still detected
in the air. Horacio regarded his friend and first mate, sure of the duress
that must weigh with some of the crew on the course chosen for the ship.
"Got no choice but te trust thems guardin' yer back," Khan would often stress.
"En the end though they're all a bunch of cutthroats who'd throw yer te the fish,
so regardless the yarn ye care te weave, remember te press the point of profit."

"Yes,"
Horacio looked him in the eye.
In seven years of service pressed,
he had never felt more at home amongst family. With a sigh
he confessed, "All I can speak of for my life is of that which I've seen,
of that which I've done, everything else is speculation. This journey by
way of leagues and many miles has led me to where I am, somewhere between
where I was and where I must be and to that end I am drawn, not so simple,
nor as deep, as belief, for it goes far beyond that to something so clean
it could be described as fact." He put a hand to the sword sheathed as official,
"This sword is real. The things I've done with it are real, and when at night
I see those I've killed, at the point of this sword, I know too that this riddle
I'm chasing is real, for if not this sword wouldn't be here, and by that same bite
neither would I. The sword is real, and therefore too must be the quest."
Suleiman thought hard on the words he'd heard, for what he knew as right
was that he believed in people, in the consistencies of character to test
the qualities of the man, this for him is where the answers rest.

In these long years,
he watched Horacio grow,
working side by side as peers
and never once had cause been given to show
to question Horacio, in either his loyalty or judgment,
so standing by the decision he said, "Then to the very gates we go."
"Thank you, my friend," Horacio took his hand, sealing the corsair's sacrament.
Having pledged his word, now curiosity began, "So what's the plan?"
Suleiman asked of his captain. "The vision," Horacio shared his testament,
"showed me an isle of evergreen and copper, surrounded by a turquoise span.
Aethalia it's called, for the smoke filled plumes which rise from its surface.
The god Vulcan called this place home, where he'd forge many a great weapon,
from the ores and deposits he'd smelt in what ancients named Hades' Furnace.
It is known too by several other names, but this is the one the goddess gave,
and the one that shall be recorded, set down in my ledger, for if to glance
underneath to the root and its meaning, it may serve me well to save
and remember that Aethalia be both a beautiful and deadly enclave."

"I know this place,"
Suleiman then declared.
"It was good for raiding back in the days."
"Really?" Horacio could feel his pulse as it flared.
"How is it that Khan never ventured this way?" he asked.
"There've been too many warships present these last years to be dared,"
Suleiman clarified the situation. "Genoa, France and Spain have all cast
their nets, fighting to take this island as their own, to claim her rich deposits."
Considering this vital, new piece of information, Horacio then spoke at last,
"So then, you might know the best way for us to approach it?"
"Aye sir. I could draw you a map if you'd like?" Over the course of seven years,
Horacio had kept Venus's mission to himself, silent was he with the secret,
fearing none would believe, or worse would believe him to have loosened gears,
and pitch him over the side to save their hides as a simple precaution.
How different his destiny would unfold had he been sold on that day in Algiers,
instead of being held in the gods' good graces, to reverse his situation,
to find that after all that time, all along, sitting next to him was the solution.

"By Jove, yes!"
Hoarcio smiled to his second,
thanking the gods for it was he that they bless.
Over the ship's charts, Suleiman drew the line which he reckoned
would be their necessary course. "We continue northwest," he pointed a finger.
"Until we see the lights of Bizerte, avoiding where the shallows beckon,
we cut a course due north, putting us in the blind from where the sea's bigger,
between the Italian and Sardinian coastlines, to this point here."
Over a speck on the map he paused and for a moment began to linger.

"Mons Jovis," he said. "Avoiding enemy patrols, this is the first chance to seer
our position. This location is used as a watch post, so we'll need to slip past
at night. Then, if we go behind the penal colony, the Isle of Pianosa, here,
clear of the shipping lanes, we could make it all the way undetected at last
to the narrow waistline and darkened side of the island you seek."
As he listened, Horacio could already see the die of his fortune being cast.
"What do you mean by the darkened side?" Horacio urged Suleiman to speak.
"Oh, you haven't heard?" Suleiman spoke as if a secret he were about to leak.

"At the opposite end,"
Suleiman showed the location on the charts,
"great fires burn, lighting up the skies at night, to fend
off the approach of enemy vessels and thieving upstarts.
Long dead stories rumored that these flames framed the entrance to hell,
that this island of beauty also hid perilous dangers in many of its parts.
Though none can claim to have seen with their own eyes anything unnatural,
long has it been told that demons once roamed this point of land."
"And what do you believe?" Horacio tested his second for what he would tell.
"I believe," Suleiman, the pragmatic, looked up to his captain,
"that the French and Genoese have had difficulty gaining a foothold
in these waters and those furnaces help to ward off their prying the island
away from the Spaniards. Ground worth protecting is this stronghold,"
Suleiman hastened to add. "For a thousand years it has fed the Roman Empire
with iron ore for its armies. Great fortunes lie within her folds."
"So the crew would not raise objection," Horacio added to inquire,
"if in its finding a raiding party we would require?"

"On the contrary,"
Suleiman confirmed,
"that would boost morale quite definitely."
"Good, then make the necessary preparations," Horacio returned.
"Aye captain," Suleiman took his leave of the stateroom,
while Horacio stayed to contemplate what he'd just learned.
The legends spoke of the way he seek, while his vision foretold of a tomb,
that of Pluto's Shrine. On such path must be where the doorway lie,
and he one step closer to fulfilling his mission to the halls of doom.
Approaching Cape Bon, at the Gulf of Tunis, with the sun riding high
above their shoulders, an idea in Horacio's mind began to smolder.
Returning to the helm, overlooking the stretch of coastline, he let out a sigh.
To Suleiman he then turned, seeking advice from the seafaring elder.
"How long did you say the run would take from here to our destination?"
"At our current pace," Suleiman replied, eyeing the waves growing bolder,
"it should take us no more than a full day's duration.
Twenty-four hours, barring any unforeseen complication."

"Yes," Horacio agreed.
"That too was my calculation,"
confirming the opinion his second decreed.
"Bring us about port, ninety degrees," he made his notation.
"Aye sir," Suleiman turned the wheel to change their course,
as the Crescent Moon swung about, angling to enter the gulf in its rotation.
"What's in your head, captain?" his words pulling, as if by gravitational force.
"If we want our arrival to go unnoticed, under the cover of night,
then from our position here, we're at least twelve hours off course."
"Aye," Suleiman confirmed. "A delay would give us an advantage alright."
"And then there's something Khan had told me that stuck in my head,"
Horacio mentioned an addition to his reasoning that shed more light.
"An enemy with fangs should never be backed into a corner," he said.
"Whenever possible leave them an escape and take them on the run."
"Sir?" Suleiman questioned, uncertain as to where this all led.
"There are those on board who actively oppose what we've begun.
When we make port they'll jump ship. In the end, that'll be better for everyone."

Suleiman considered his captain's words,
and the wisdom that they held. "It is proper,"
he could find no fault in the decision. Onwards, towards
the coast they looked. In the distance, the last safe harbor
before their turn northward. Here they could also gain some needed repairs.
In their list of battles, having just recovered from the storming coffer
of Typhon's wrath, the Crescent Moon was sailing worse for wares.
Here, Carthage, behind her massive, impenetrably long walls,
maintained the largest, most important military harbor in regional affairs.
Like Algiers, the Maghreb of the Hafsid Dynasty, of which Carthage falls,
was independent in nature, torn between the world's great empires.
Having supported the Ottoman corsairs in the past, her majestic halls
open more in recent days to those of Venice and Aragon, as diplomacy requires.
The caliph, Uthman of Ifriqiya, having brought the Hafsid house
to the zenith of its rule, now looked to expand commerce beyond the fires
of war. Still, on eastern, Berber slopes, Carthage in tradition remained souce.
With letters of marque, Horacio and crew could rebuke any defiant rouse.

"Assemble the crew,"
Horacio gave his command.
"Aye, aye." Suleiman replied, a breath he drew.
"Listen up!" bringing to attention the corsair band,
he then stepped aside to give Horacio the floor.
"We're going to make port within the hour," the captain began,
a cheerful murmur lifted. "Before doing so, we need to take a full score
of the damages. Ali Abbas," he addressed the ship's carpenter,
"prepare the inventory and work crews. Those not assigned may go ashore,

but don't get too comfortable, we sail again on the night tide's harbinger.
That is all," he kept his message brief, passing on only the needed information.
In the foreground sat their last reprieve before being cast to Fate's arbiter,
it was a moment to reflect upon the road ahead and their final destination.
Horacio gazed upon the horizon, from where he stood at the starboard rail,
greeted by a welcoming coastline, a bountiful, serene temptation.
Trees of olive, fig and pomegranate, of almond, date and palm lined their trail.
Lush green gardens led to the mighty walls of Carthage, past which they sail.

All was tranquil
in that moment of sunlight.
Hovering there, the crew took in their fill.
Horacio remained pensive however looking upon the sight,
feeling the weight of destiny upon him, "Beautiful, is it not?"
Avranos stood by his side. "Indeed," Horacio agreed to be polite,
yet his tone betrayed an inner conflict. "Still, you seem distraught,"
continued the archer. "What troubles you?" he looked upon his captain.
"Nothing, my friend. It's just the waiting on the edge that's got me caught.
The uncertainty of what is still to come. You and I are men of action
and fare best when in motion. To be hovering here on the brink,
helpless but to count the moments, has my head spinning like a capstan."
Avranos nodded with understanding, "Yes, it's true, time is the greatest link
to all our frustrations. Either there's too much or too little of it to wield,
for what we need to do. Still, when the moment's upon us, we do not shrink
and that's what sets us apart. Far already you have taken us upon the field
and the path may yet be long, but trust that to the end your men will not yield.

"By your side we stand."
Horacio, well heartened by his friend's words,
let out a sigh to the wind, as their view of Carthage began to expand.
From the sea, the mighty walls were impressive, reaching towards
the heavens a full thirteen meters high, protecting the industrial center
in the north, which fed the once powerful city-state, from invading hoards.
Caressing the coastline, along the fortified isthmus, they angled to enter
the sole sea gate, a narrow neck opening which fed the mercantile harbor.
Here is where the landscape truly did open to an extraordinary tenor.
Overlooking the entire city, high up on the northern hill, akin to a huge arbor,
sat the columned citadel, the Byrsa, site of the Temple of Eshmun,
the healing god, at the top of a stairway of sixty steps. Here with fiery ardor
and fierce combat befell the destruction of the once great city to Roman
rage in 146 BC. Sloping down the hillside of the lesser Byrsa, towards the sea,
sat a temple of Tanit, the former city's queen goddess, now lying in ruin.
Beyond spread public squares, a religious area, markets, the council see,
towers, a theater, and four equally sized residential areas before the quay.

Most impressive though,
opening wide directly before the crew's eye,
was the military cothon. With an expansive radius, the fortifications did grow,
round and tiered as the coliseum of Rome, with walls standing doubly high,
it was a shipyard for vessels of war. Towards this harbor is where they sail,
passing straight by the slips for common merchant craft and thereby
announced themselves as a master among the weak and frail.
At the center of the military harbor sat a command post, like a large rotunda,
it stretched in staged layers upward, spiraling higher, as the point to a tail,
where lookouts surveyed the entire radius of Carthage from a circular veranda.
At either end of the harbor gates, with stone doors wide open, tall sentry towers
scrutinized the vessels making port, eyes now on the Crescent Moon's agenda.
She sail past, entering the fortified nest, heads held high, flaunting the powers
they earned as battle hardened warriors. Guided towards an open slip,
the crew made fast the docking lines securing her side to the anchorage bowers.
With letters in hand they announced themselves to the harbor master's grip,
who noted their arrival in the daily logs, as a matter of duty for stewardship.

Ali Abbas, making his inventory,
noted the needed supplies and presented his checklist
of timber, nails and canvass, as well as bandages within the category
of materials required. Suleiman added gunpowder and food stocks to the list,
assembling a party of hands to accompany him for making the procurements.
While the more hardened seamen for work crews Ali Abbas did enlist,
the fighting men, completing their duties, unneeded for further assignments
were granted leave to go ashore. Among these Isa and Nebi took advantage
of the opportunity, for with their eyes to take the famed city's measurements.
The long cobbled and dusty streets opened to them as they began to manage
their path away from the port. Up the slope, towards the Byrsa they'd roam
stopping occasionally at the random trading market, where goods would stage
from the Saharan caravans that journeyed from as far as their Egyptian home.
Examining fine linens, papyrus and ivory handled knives of Cairo design,
the brothers haggled with the merchants that crossed their trail, as they comb
the streets, in a mood for making deals. "You there," a gypsy girl did pine,
covered in veils a many hue, head to toe, apart from her eyes' piercing shine.

With a voice
both raspy and melodic,
she drew the brothers in closer by the spell of her vice.
"A mirror you present to all the world, yet beneath the outward optic
there is a chasm greater than the infinite sky which divides your true souls."
Startled, yet immobile, the brothers were captured by her enchanted rhapsodic.
Isa was the first to stutter, breaking the silence of their new found roles.
"Dear maiden," he began well natured, "as much as it grieves me to gainsay
the reputation of your profound intuition, my brother and I are matching scrolls,

with perhaps the sole exception…" with a hand raised she cut him off to say,
"That he's too trusting, whereas you trust too little," she stole his words
mid-sentence. *Yes,* Isa refused to admit. "It's quite evident my young stray.
That's the reason I called you to me," she pulled them with a glance forwards.
"I have something that each of you needs," peeking their curiosity.
"Is that so?" Nebi lifted an eyebrow as he took a step towards.
"Hold on," Isa, with a hand restraining his brother, tamed his velocity.
"What could you possibly have that we might need?" he tested her precocity.

"Something that might save your life,"
the gypsy smiled through her eyes in a knowing fashion.
Isa considered a moment, "Lead the way," his hand tested the hilt of his knife.
Stepping into the storefront shelter, the dim light casting a feature ashen,
they gathered around a small table. The room, a cacophony of trinket artifacts,
felt of a stew in the witch's caldron. In the corner, a grizzled ration
of a figure sat, black robed and lined face, eyes white and blinded by cataracts.
She moaned a mantra spell, indistinguishable in its purpose and vocabulary.
The brothers drew back out of reflex. "Fear not," the gypsy noted the impacts.
"Grandmother will not curse you. You are safe here as in any sanctuary."
Her voice, in soothing tones, causing them to once again settle.
"Show me your hands," she drew them, studying palms as if books in a library.
"Yes," she whispered intently, "there is much ahead to threaten your fettle.
Yet, I have something here that may offer you the needed protection."
"At what price?" Isa the more watchful, considered the amount of jingling metal.
"Perhaps," the gypsy glimpsed his eye, "it is the color of your hair's reflection,
or maybe the taste of the final breath on which your soul severs its connection?"

She spoke hauntingly, in a way that tempted,
seducing their interests, while remaining vague in her offer.
"For you though," she coaxed with a wily glance that intercepted,
"let us agree to, at a time most imperative, the equitable return of the favor?"
Nebi, already enticed, thought not once nor twice, enchanted, said, "Done."
"Um, ah," Isa looked with a sudden turn of his head towards his brother,
and as though if to rebuke, then shaking off the doubtful shudder, "Done,"
he exhaled, matching the other, with more than a little hesitation in his tone,
resigning himself to the deal struck. Pleased with the covenant newly spun,
the gypsy then lifted a hand from which hung two fraternal amulets of stone.
The first to Isa, she strung around his neck, was black as midnight's pitch,
"For the brother, who doubts his senses," she softly laid the chain of bone,
"take this ebony gem, whose core, a dragon's heart, fiery crimson stitch,
will glow red when danger rears its head." To Nebi, then she turned
with the other pendant in her hand. "And for you," said the gypsy witch,
"whose trusting nature hazard welcomes, a gift of lapis lazuli earned,
which with truth grows cold, but warm with answer false, the lie be burned."

The brothers two
regarded the gifts they had just been offered,
considering the enchantment accompanying each. Looking askew,
first at each other then towards the fortuneteller, feeling awkward,
fell for a moment speechless. Isa, being the first to break the silence,
ventured to ask, "How can we be sure..." "That what I have proffered
is true?" the girl completed the thought. "Well, yes?" Isa held his stance.
"Simply ask yourselves," her eyes grinned to Nebi, the stone around his neck
already growing an icy cold. "Aye, feel that," he began to shiver off balance.
Touching the amulet, Isa felt how it shifted from neutral to a bitter check.
"It's true," he confirmed, "the stone did change in temperature.
These are powerful gifts indeed." Isa gestured, within his eyes a grateful fleck,
seeing how these talisman could save their lives in a questionable venture.
"And in return?" Isa desiring with a sense of duty to balance the scale.
"Honor the bargain struck when called upon is the sole expenditure."
"You have our word," the brothers pledged. "In this we shall not fail."
Then suddenly, from the corner, the crumpled old lady with gruff voice did flail.

"Dido's curse is still upon you!" she crooned, and then, "Behind you!"
shaking their fortitude the sightless aged woman let out a croaking forewarning.
The brothers turned quickly to see through the doorway a member of their crew,
who passed unaware of their observation. "Go quickly, follow him," with burning
urgency, pointing a crooked finger long, the grandmother gave them instruction.
Sensing the honest urgency of the call, the brothers stepped to, conforming.
From behind the parted curtain, they peered their eyes with cautious intuition.
Taking up a trailing posture, they hastily left their newly found benefactor.
Not quite understanding the reasoning behind the current situation,
Isa and Nebi maintained a safe distance, recognizing the new actor
as being Jamel, the same bearded sailor who had questioned harshly
their captain. Whispering, "I've got a bad feeling about this character,"
Nebi confided. "That makes two of us," Isa agreed tersely.
Up the dusty hillside they climbed, without shadow under the afternoon sun,
the only cover to disguise their objective was to mingle smartly
with other passers-by. Behind a corner's edge, they watched as their prey spun
around to check his rear, before darting into a doorway, the game had begun.

"We should split up,"
Isa suggested. "You stay here and watch if anyone comes out,
I'm going to work my way around the other side to see close up."
"I don't know, what if it's a trap?" Nebi began to cast his doubt.
"That's why I have this," Isa placed a hand upon the ebony stone
hanging from his neck. "I'll know in advance if danger's about."
Not so reassured, Nebi agreed to the plan with a caveat of his own,
"Fine, but if you're not back in ten minutes, I'm coming after you,"
taking up his post, as Isa darted up an adjacent alley that split wishbone

around to the building's backside. Watching from the outside, Nebi drew
an impatient breath. His brother had only been away a few minutes,
yet he didn't like that he'd gone off alone. Too many variables and they too few.
All was quiet as he waited there, too quite by his estimates.
Then, from the same doorway a Spanish officer and two soldiers emerged.
Oh, this isn't good, Nebi told himself, his patience reaching its limits.
Then, a new idea, he grasped his amulet as thoughts on a question merged,
Is Isa in danger? he asked himself, to feel the tepid rock with icy cold it surged.

Hand on his dagger,
Nebi set off in the same direction
that his brother just a few moments earlier did swagger.
Halfway up the stretch, from a doorway in the building's hind section,
bursting through, fell Isa doubled over, rolling out onto the pavement.
To his feet he clamored. Nebi raced, as Isa opposite yelled a course correction.
"Run!" he bolted at speed Nebi's way, racing for any safe haven.
"What's happening?" Nebi tried to question his brother to no reply,
running side by side towards the harbor, Isa looking pale and craven.
They sped down the staircase, in situ, built into the slope of the hillside
to compensate for the natural grade of the landscape. Not being followed,
now at a safe distance, Nebi halted their progress for himself to decide
what exactly was going on. "Isa," taking his brother by the arm, a look hollowed
with fear and panic returned in the other's stare. "What happened in there?"
Panting, with only two words discernible between heaves his breath allowed,
"Danger" and "unnatural," Isa gasped, trying to pull in another lungful of air.
"They're coming for us. We must warn the others. There's no time to spare."

BOOK XIV

DIDO'S CURSE

Around his neck
the stone of red returned to black.
For the moment, it seemed that danger had been put in check.
Quickly the brothers, retracing their path to the harbor, made their way back
to their ship, the Crescent Moon, where the crew was busily making repairs.
"Captain," Isa for the pair spoke, "we must sail with all haste." Fearing attack,
they pulled Horacio aside, relaying the encounter that caused them such cares.
Telling the story about the gypsy girl and her gifts, they then recounted
the following of Jamel, and what then befell tracing him to secret lairs.
"Entering from the rear of the building, I observed them undetected,"
Isa began his report. "I saw that traitor talking low with three Spaniards,
one a ranking officer, the other two his adjutants," from what he counted.
"And so the Spanish know we're here?" Horacio considered those cards.
"That's unfortunate for sure, though I doubt they'd dare to make a strike
in such a fortified harbor?" "Nay sir, there's more," Isa's voice broke to shards.
"They seemed little interested until he mentioned your heritage, then like a pike
they became rigid with attention, taking a stance serious and businesslike.

"'A Trojan?'
asked their leader, a great significance he placed on those words.
'We must deal with this at once,' he told the others. And that's when it began."
Isa, unlike himself, visibly blanched and weakened, with wavering vocal chords.
A shudder passed through him as he tried to regain his composure.
"Isa, are you alright?" Horacio now equally concerned leaned forward.
"Yes sir," Isa righted himself. "It's just that's when it happened. What for sure
though I cannot say. Jamel demanded compensation, and overly it was given.
The officer nodded to his companions, who before my very eyes changed color.
They turned from flesh and blood to a ghostly grey, to something not living.
At that moment, the stone around my neck took on a glow of deep scarlet,
and Jamel, as if the life had been sucked right out of him, his soul driven,
turned white, aged in an instant and fell there dead, most unnaturally forfeit.
For my part, overcome and frozen with fear, I was unable to even twitch.
Had they noticed my presence I too would have been slain, an easy target.
Then, just before departing, I heard them confirm the words of the old witch.
'The queen shall have her revenge this night,' their leader did pitch."

"The queen?"
Horacio lifted an eyebrow, questioning the two.
"Dido," Nebi broke in. "That's what the old woman had said to intervene.
'Dido's curse is still upon you.' I swear those are the words that she blew."
"Yes," Isa confirmed his brother's ear. "I hadn't thought much of it at the time,
with everything happening so fast, but what Nebi speaks is true."
Horacio thought back upon the lore that foretold a warning to the Trojan line
of how broken by love and seared by fire, Dido ceaseless in her vengeance
declared a war everlasting between her race and that of Aeneas's vine.
"But Rome defeated Carthage long ago. None now remain to demand penance,"
Horacio spoke in sideward tones, reflecting for himself where lie the meaning.
"Still her spirit pervades these ruins, perhaps enough, with you, the essence
of her hatred, here within the fold of her walls, to raise an unwanted demon?"
Avranos spoke from the doorway, having overheard the conversation.
"If that's the case," Hoarcio looked up, making sense of the reason,
"it's possible we have unknowingly sailed into a trap." He felt growing vexation.
"Captain," Suleiman appeared, "we've got visitors approaching our location."

Horacio rose to his feet,
"Alert the crew to be on their guard, but do it quietly.
I don't want to see any scrambling, let's maintain a tempered beat.
Isa, Nebi, you're with me. Avranos, in the nest, keep your eye reliably."
"Aye captain," the group concurred falling out to take up their positions.
From a distance of fifty paces, a party, not Spanish, but of Berber notoriety,
evergreen robed and white turbaned, as befitting the Hafsid traditions,
marched in formation to their location. A single dignitary, with a guard
posted at each of the four corners, drew near. "Ahoy!" from their stations
called out the principal as they arrived to the edge of the gangplank, as a bard
would be put to theater. "Who is it that calls upon our vessel to pay homage?"
Horacio returned in a jovial manner, playing along, already wise to the charade.
"Greetings from His Excellency, Abu Umar Uthman ben Abul Hasan Muhammad,"
the courtier gave a full recital, as a means to either deceive or impress.
"It was brought to our attention that you're friend of the great Sultan Mehmed."
"Yes, it is true, we sail under his protection," Horacio made the point to stress
their credentials. "Very good. In that case, there is an offer I wish to address.

"Permission to come aboard?"
the visitor requested, as the norms of seamanship demanded.
"Granted," Horacio allowed. "Though you may leave your guards ashore,
you will have no need for them on this vessel," on his answer he expanded.
"That is much appreciated," the man, it was obvious a middling functionary,
there to deliver a message, stepped upon the brow, his men, as commanded,
stayed on the wharf below. Placing a foot upon deck, he stated the necessary,
"It's an honor dear captain to make your acquaintance. Any friend of the sultan
is a friend of Carthage," his smile too broad by half. Horacio returned the parry,

"The honor's all mine, but come, your visit today is by the caliph's compulsion.
Please tell me, what service may I render?" Horacio cut direct to the point.
"Ah," the dignitary gestured dramatically, as if notes he were consulting.
"To the contrary," he flourished, "it is His Excellency who wishes to appoint
a boon to cap your visit to this territory. This evening, up at the royal citadel,
you and your crew are all invited to dine as his special guests to anoint
and reconfirm the longstanding friendship between the great and noble
Ottoman Empire and that of the Hafsid Kingdom, prior to your farewell."

From several paces back,
Nebi, at his position on watch,
began to twitch uncomfortably, taken aback
by the sudden warming sensation, a burning notch
along his chest, emanating from the rock that hung there as a warning
that something was not at all correct. Horacio, not having to be told to dodge
was already formulating his rejoinder. "Well this is indeed a heart-warming
invitation. On behalf of not just myself and the crew, but of our benefactor,
the sultan, as well, we gratefully acknowledge such a generous rewarding.
It is therefore, as you can imagine, with great dismay to extenuating factors
that we must sadly decline the offer. As you see, we're undertaking with speed
needed repairs. Tasked are we to rejoin the fleet with haste, such is the fact, for
we must sail on the coming tide." The turnabout dismayed the courier indeed,
as a look of consternation crept upon his brow. "Oh, that is disappointing,"
he sighed with a heavy weight, "for I was told in no way to concede,
that for your presence we must insist." "Insist?" Horacio repeated the enjoining
phrase. With a nod, the dignitary confirmed that it was an order he was coining.

"Well, in that case,"
Horacio, maintaining his composure,
knowing full well that his acquiescence would be put in place
by force, if not freely volunteered, "it would of course be my pleasure,
with one small condition." "Name your desire," the caliph's emissary
spoke disarmingly, remaining gracious, at least outwardly in his posture.
"I'm sure you understand, as a man who serves a master, the burden we carry,
for if both we aim to please, then my ship must sail directly after the banquet.
So, if you agree, I along with my lieutenant will attend, while to the contrary
the crew continues their work onboard, ensuring that we remain on target?"
The royal ambassador stretched out a broad smile in compliance.
"That would be most agreeable dear captain. Please, prepare your junket.
My men and I will wait here as your official escort, for your convenience."
With the stage and rules of engagement now officially established,
Horacio excused himself to change into more appropriate vestments, whence
in his cabin his most trusted gathered, in turn their concerns they brandished
with declarations, their positions published.

"You cannot do this,"
Nebi, as habit led him, jumped in. "It's a trap."
"I concur," Suleiman with lowered tones agreed. "You'd be remiss
to follow this course. An ambush awaits," seconds and thirds his best did snap.
"Of course it is," Horacio held the same opinion as them all. "Yet, here's the rub.
That central command post controls the locks. If we run, those gates will slap
shut before we can even clear the exit, then we're just sitting ducks in a tub.
My guess is there's more eyes on us than we can count, we need a diversion."
"What do you have in mind?" Baloch, the Pashtun, inquired of the nub.
"To start," Horacio flashed a grin, "put on a clean tunic my dear Persian,
you're coming with me, as my second." Baloch bowed his head, in reverence
to the honor. Although it could verily spell his own death, he held no aversion
to performing the required duty, for it spoke highly of his esteemed excellence.
"Then, we'll give them exactly what they desire," referring to himself as bait.
"They want me, not the ship, As soon as we depart you'll have your chance.
Suleiman, I want you to maneuver the ship into open waters, do not hesitate.
Steer clear of the harbor, that's an order. Do not fail, in your hands is our fate."

"Aye sir," Suleiman bit his tongue,
in his heart uncomfortable with such an arrangement.
"Once past the gates, head north, with speed be sprung."
"Captain," Suleiman unable to contain himself with such estrangement.
"We shall not abandon you here." "Nay, you shall not," Horacio duly consoled.
"Around the bend, beyond the last tower, make your encampment.
Hold your position until the dark of night, at which point your path refold
taking up station at the promontory, just south of the harbor."
Then, turning to Avranos and the two brothers, "Hope you're feeling bold?"
"Aye," they all agreed. "Good, for now's the time to make ready your armor."
Departing their ship under escort, Horacio and Baloch were marched
ceremoniously away, with all the pomp of royalty on parade. Around, a clamor
of festive onlookers grew as they proceeded to climb the slope that arched
up towards the Byrsa peak which housed the citadel palace.
A strange sensation filled the air and sun-baked streets, all parched
in the late afternoon. "Do you get the feeling," Baloch noted the callous
cheers that rose, with an eerie dread, "that the entire city's been expecting us?"

"Yes, I get that too."
Horacio eyed with increased anxiety,
how the crowds with mounting fervor grew.
"It's as if they're possessed," he said with all sobriety.
"Something unnatural seems to be at work in these parts."
What at first appeared as joyful merriment now seemed tinged with hostility,
as the taunting of a bull being led to slaughter. "You think maybe the dark arts
have been employed to confuse their wits?" Baloch pondered the rising jeers
around them. "I'm not sure, but stay alert. Trouble's brewing in their hearts,

and that's a bad omen by any account." Horacio checked his own fears,
to maintain an outward appearance of calm, secure in the knowledge
that whatever was to come, this was only the first of several spheres
through which they would have to pass. Sensing the challenge,
he considered the path they would have to weave in order to survive.
"Wave to them," he turned to his second. "Wave?" as if to acknowledge,
Baloch raised the question. "Yes, we must belay their fears. If we strive
to show them friendship, a little longer it just might keep us alive."

"War is based upon deception."
This was one of the greatest lessons Khan had taught
to his young apprentice. Now, on the way to their reception,
Horacio would apply what he had learnt, so as not to be caught
in unnecessary crossfire. With broad smiles they greeted the crowd,
as would celebrities. "It's working," Baloch turned no longer fraught,
seeing that the disposition of the masses was evolving to be less proud.
Long forgotten memories of Rome flashed through Horacio's head,
"It's rule of the mob, turning on or for you in a heartbeat. They live unbowed
to any authority, except for the whims of their own emotions, so instead
of reason and intellect, you must appeal to their passion for vanity."
Indeed, the attitude had shifted, at least momentarily, in their favor ahead
of the pending trials, as they projected goodwill through their anxiety.
Applause rose as they completed the final steps towards the open gates
of the citadel fortress high upon the Byrsa hill. Feeling the swirl of true insanity
all around them, Horacio let out a sigh of relief, "At least these straits
were easily navigated. Now let's see what sway the ox has with the Fates."

Meanwhile,
in the harbor below,
the crew of the Crescent Moon was preparing for their own trial.
"Cast off those lines," Suleiman gave the deckhands an order to let go,
unhitching the ship from its moorings, as they slipped away from the dock.
"Hoist those sails." A squad of sweaty men pulled at ropes for canvass to grow
upon the foremast. Just as headway they began to make, there came to knock,
a moment too late, a full platoon of soldiers advancing upon their berthing.
Lined up, a hundred meters of water between their position and the gate's lock,
an alarm bell rang out from the central rotunda, a commotion unearthing.
"Look there!" Butrus called with urgency from his station at the fore.
Up high on both left and right towers the capstans spun, reversing
course the portal entrance to close the massive harbor doors and therefore
isolate those within from those without, to trap the Crescent Moon inside.
"Full speed! Pull those oars!" Suleiman shouted his commands as urgency bore
down upon them. In a battle to save their lives, the crew pushed back the tide,
bringing all their strength to bare, as against the odds they did collide.

“Row, you dogs!”
Suleiman berated the crew, pushing them faster,
as the walls inched closer together with the turning of the cogs.
The drumbeat pounded in their chests, hearing the voice of their master,
echoing with urgency, as the daylight narrowed before the ship’s bow.
“Ahhrr!” the crew strained with each successive pull at the oar, racing disaster
to the sound of the cracking whip, they lurched forward, as would a plough
cutting through the water. Without an inch to spare, they gasped and squeezed
through an opening no wider than their breadth. Scraping the portal’s brow,
their stern quarter shot forth as a cork from a well shaken bottle unsheathed.
Relief they exhaled, while from the tall towers, swords rattled and flailed
having lost their prey by mere centimeters. A hail of curses taunted and teased
from the battlements, as the Crescent Moon through the harbor exit scaled
their way out unto open sea, hearts still throbbing from exertion and labor.
Turning hard the rudder north, on the course Horacio had ordered, they sailed
out of range of the walled city towards the safety of a secluded shore’s favor.
“What now?” Kasim then asked. “We wait for dark,” Suleiman did not waver.

Up high, within the citadel,
the celebration was only just underway.
The banquet hall, decked in splendor, as before them wreaths of flowers fell,
delicacies lined the tables, with wine in every goblet, while musicians at play
filled the chamber with floating chords of symphonic harmony and grace.
“Does it feel to you a bit much?” Baloch shared a confidence Horacio’s way.
“Perhaps the final meal for a prized bull?” he returned with just a trace
of irony. “Yes, there does seem to be the lull of overcompensation
designed to woo us into a sense of false security. Something with this place
that I cannot put my finger on is deeply troubling. I’ve got a sensation
that somewhere apart from all these spectators we are being closely watched.”
Just then the trumpet sounded as His Excellency, the caliph, took his station.
“Greetings,” he bellowed, standing at the table’s head. Then, as he notched
his gaze upon his guests, “And to you, dear friends of Carthage and Tunisia,
I bid you a welcome return.” Horacio and Baloch bowing their heads, botched
their rejoinder in that moment, struck by hesitation due to a tense kinesthesia.
“Thank you and forgive me Your Highness, I seem to be struck by amnesia.”

Horacio challenged the ruler’s greeting,
“I do not recall having set foot before in this land.”
“Ah,” the caliph smiled, “but I do recall a moment, once fleeting.”
His eyes took on an eerie glow. “For if I am not mistaken, my young firebrand,
by the reports that reach my ears, Trojan blood runs in your veins?”
A thunderous silence descended on the great hall and in all directions fanned,
as the lights by some hidden force of their own accord dimmed, the only flames
in a halo ring, encircling our two beleaguered heroes. “Yes, that is true,”
Horacio, firm in his posture, confirmed the charges leveled upon their manes.

A sudden gasp struck the room, collectively a breath they drew.
"He admits it!" a voice among the shadows could be heard, as if in rapture.
"The prophesy is fulfilled!" from across the room another quaver flew.
"Ah yes, as has been foretold," Uthman applauded, standing tall in his stature.
"You have come back to us, to make amends and appease our beloved queen.
Behold, people of Carthage, the fugitive has returned to bond the fracture!
Our return to glory is now at hand!" A bellowing roar rose from sights unseen.
"They must be all under some evil spell," Baloch made of the unnatural scene.

"Or completely crazy,"
Horacio countered with an assessment of his own.
As if through a swelling fog, all around them began to turn hazy.
"I regret to say," Horacio took a cautious step backward, keeping an even tone.
"We're pressed for time and must depart from your kind hospitality forthwith."
"Oh, I think that is not possible," the caliph laughed from his banquet throne.
"I was afraid you were going to say that." Seeing they were facing the scythe,
Horacio and Baloch drew their swords, covering each other's back.
"I wish you no offense," Horacio attempted to offer a final olive withe,
"but we'll be leaving now." He readied his stance for the pending attack.
From Uthman's throat an ominous howl grew shaking the citadel's foundation,
mocking such a feeble attempt to deny their long awaited payback.
From the shadows two tall cloaked figures emerged, with menacing predation.
Beneath their hoods, faces hidden, only a smoky outline of dread presented
the hint of their features. "Take them!" Uthman commanded from his station.
Without an opposing arm in contest, encircled, our heroes became disoriented,
as the two looming figures from across the hall exuded a vibration tormented.

An overwhelming distress
filled the hearts of these bravest two,
as Hoarcio and Baloch, unable to control the excess
of fear building within themselves sheathed their swords and threw
their bodies upon the floor, writhing and contorted in vicious agony.
Easily they were lifted and carried by the nearest hands before they even knew
what had happened. Hands and feet tied, victims to some sorcerer's alchemy,
they were transported, held high above the heads of their captors.
A chorus followed, as they were carted from the hall to the outer balcony,
a massive terrace on top of the Byrsa heights, where many chapters
of Carthaginian history had already been written, beneath this very starlit choir
and the watchful eyes of the gods stretching eons back. Hungry as raptors
for their victims' blood, Horacio and Baloch were brought to the waiting pyre,
while temple priestesses gathered, chanting ancient hymns to their lost queen,
Dido, whose flesh burnt at this very spot, cursing Troy on that flaming fire.
Here, at the Tophet, the burning place, where the followers would convene,
making sacrifices to the Punic goddess Tanit, our heroes awoke to the scene.

"What the...? How did...?"
Horacio squirmed within his restraints,
as the daze from the seizure wore off. Attempting to rid
himself of the ropes that bound him to no avail, the constraints
held fast, as he was placed upon the sacrificial bier constructed of olive wood.
Turning his head, Baloch confided, "Captain, I'm not one for complaints,
but I must say I've got a bad feeling about this situation. Perhaps we should
rethink our strategy?" "Aye," Horacio chuckled, "I think you may have a point."
Just then the high priest rose to give the eulogy. Before the pyre he stood,
hands raised to the moon, eyes lifted, ready with prayers to anoint
the sacrifice. With a deep ethereal voice he performed the ritual invocation.
"O Tanit, mother of the waters, goddess of the moon, fertility and war, conjoint
to Mars, conveyor of bitter tears through flame and ash, hear this incantation.
We offer here the souls of the unrepentant, who have given great offense
to your most beloved. Take upon the winds the essence of this cremation,
and carry their spirits unto the inferno to appease Queen Dido, in recompense
for the injury, so to lift the curse and return Carthage to her rightful tense."

"Oh they're raving mad!"
Baloch could not contain himself amidst such foolishness.
"Loosen these bonds and I'll show you the meaning of offense, you cad,"
he struggled to no avail. Yet, Horacio, maintaining his calm effusiveness,
lifted his own righteous petition, seeing a flint of red through the corner
of his eye. "Mother Venus, just let his aim be true," he prayed, seeing luminous
the torch the high priest lifted, setting aglow the hollow features of the coroner.
"I now commit your flesh to flame," the priest bellowed, holding the fire aloft.
"Now!" Horacio yelled from the top of his lungs, as a swish grazed in due order
the air above them, planting an arrow's shaft into the priest, who dropped soft
to the ground before the alter. Amid the cries and clamor, losing not a beat,
Horacio, clutching Baloch's ropes, rolled to the side. Toppling from the loft,
they struck earth with a thump, one on top of the other, as Isa and Nebi
rushed to their sides, cutting free their ties, striking down the nearest guard.
Drawing swords, still surrounded, Horacio and Baloch took to their feet.
"Just in time," Horacio commended the pair, "though we'll be pressed hard
to make it out of here alive," he stood fast, having played his final card.

Striking with all the furies,
the four lashed out with great bravado,
taking the fight directly to the surrounding sentries,
who blocked their path. Battling blades raged to a heightened crescendo,
as the thicket around them only grew. From beyond a hush ensued.
Encircled, a voice above the din penetrated all within with a great vibrato.
"There's no escape. You've only delayed the inevitable," the ghostly knell cooed,
from where they could not tell. The air around them stilled, as from the rear
the two demonic shades reappeared, making clear their apparition, hued

in a charcoal glow that sapped all hope and drained all cheer.
"Not again," Horacio sounded his fret, unable to contend with the supernatural.
From his notch on the rooftop above, Avranos let a flying shard loose to tear
into the nearest of the two fiends. To no avail, the arrow's effect, merely lateral,
only succeeded in increasing the devil's wrath. Yanking the shaft
from his side, the beast with intent extended his reach in a direction unilateral
towards the archer's niche, and with an unworldly form of witchcraft
swept his hand, causing Avranos to slip and fall onto those below with a crash.

Wrestling through the crowd,
he was pushed into the center of the circle to join the rest of the crew.
A quiet determination, unexpected in such chaos, with a silence so loud
it swept over those assembled, while the five corsairs struggled through
a wave of despair that cursed their courage, feeling as though the very life
was being sucked out of them. "Ahhrr," Isa rolled in pain, as memories grew
of his first encounter. Nebi at his shoulder, held at length his fighting knife,
while with one hand supporting his brother. "We have to resist this evil,"
he said falling to a knee. Horacio and the rest prepared to meet the afterlife,
hope having been threshed from their souls, they felt a touch most lethal.
Just then, with life fading, as though falling through a star exploding,
a white light plumed mushroom, evaporating the night with radiant upheaval,
consuming all within the courtyard mall, and with that the spell eroding,
the general populace shook as from a dream now waking. All became undone.
A screaming disorder befell the crowd, with wide spread confusion corroding
their will. In every direction panic fled, two cloaked villains momentarily stun,
as the girl with hypnotic eyes took Horacio's hand, "Why are you waiting? Run!"

BOOK XV

CHAOS AND BALANCE

"Run!"
the gypsy's voice echoed in his head,
as Horacio, and the rest, thoroughly unstrung,
regained their senses. With the entire square in disarray, on foot they fled.
"This way," she guided their escape. The six scrambled across the square,
disappearing into the throng, towards the exits the rushing multitudes led,
pulling the escapees along in the current. Horns blowing in alarm did blare,
too late, as they exited the citadel walls making quick of pace their flight.
"What just happened there?" Horacio questioned on the run, as they tear
down the outlying slopes. "And who are you?" he wanted to know alright.
"This is the girl we told you about," Nebi offered up the solution.
"That's the second time she's helped us today," Isa said, shedding some light.
"Why though?" Horacio needed to know how came about this evolution.
"What's going on here? What were those creatures?"
"Those are fear and dread," she spoke of the two by attribution.
"By the names Timor and Formido they are known. Demonic spirits, curs
from the afterworld risen. Shape shifters who can take on many features.

"Yet, they are only a precursor
for a much greater evil is still to come. In the shadow,
lurking close by, hides their master, who will lead us to an unending war.
Only you can stop him," she dropped the words on Horacio like a heavy blow.
Startled by the account, Horacio took her arm, stopping all in their tracks.
"What do you mean only I can stop him?" he pressed her. "How do you know?"
"I have seen it?" she said twisting free. "There's no time." From their backs
soldiers were giving chase. They were still far from being out of danger.
"We must go, before it's too late," she urged them on, as thunder cracks.
"Through here, we must try for the side gate," she said, no stranger
to the half-lit back streets and hidden alleyways of Carthage.
Down a long and dusty cobbled passage, with footfall's clanger,
she steered them on safe paths across the city. "Here we use our advantage,
this gate is seldom used and lightly guarded. It's not far. Move quickly."
A hundred meters to the rear, a squad of twenty were on the charge,
closing in, not a moment could they delay. As promised, the side entry,
an arching double door, on either end had posted at each only one sentry.

Overwhelming,
they rushed the portal,
striking down the guards with no trouble. Compelling
the doors, unbarred they swung open. The road they hit full throttle.
With combatants still in chase, they needed to put some distance between
themselves and the city walls. Towards the waiting sea immortal,
running fast, past the open fields, they approached the nocturnal scene.
Facing the final obstacle, there a bone yard necropolis blocked their path.
"Right where we want them," a shadow in the background sighed as they glean
sight of their prey, standing before the *Tophet of Salammbô,* in whose wrath
they shall meet their doom. Here, as legend states, at the *Sanctuary of Tanit,*
rests the everlasting soul of the goddess Tanit herself and sacred soil hadst
best not be disturbed lest consequence befall. What better place to let
bleed a sacrifice befit a queen, than to lie it right there before her very feet?
"We must enter here to access the coast, but careful, this graveyard we beset
guards the city's southern most flank," she warned without dropping a beat.
"Spirits rest here that those in their right minds should hope to never meet."

Maintaining pace between the narrow
weaving space that separated ancient gravestones,
the crew dodged mounds of earth beneath the drifting moon shadow.
Pushing from the rear, just minutes behind, rose the aggravated tones
of the posse on their heels. Labyrinth, they twisted through the maze
of corridors and passageways that interlaced the footpaths of crossbones.
Here, at the center of the burial ground, through streaks of moonlight haze,
where crooked branches scrawled their way across the graveyard scene,
there came a stop before them, a darkened marble monument stays
their path. Laced with weeds and draping ivy, a placard could be seen.
Engraved, it read: *Quis Enim Illa Flet,* for she who weeps.
"We mustn't linger here," urgently, their guide pressed to reconvene.
Then, as a mist rolled in from all directions, "Wait," a hissing seeps
into the ear. "It's too late," she stops taking up a guarded position.
"What's happening?" Horacio, with sword in hand sweeps
around, instinctively taking stock of their condition.
"It's Tanit. She's coming," sounded the premonition.

With eyes at every angle,
the corsairs lined up drawing their weapons,
creating a forward edge in the shape of a triangle.
One way or another they would push through what beckons.
Out of the fog, murky figures covered in vapor slowly inched into view.
"Hold your positions!" Horacio urged patience for a few more seconds.
Emerging, out of the gloom, there wobbled, no taller than a foot or two,
the shades of children in the hundreds, spirits loosened from their coffins.
"Hold!" Horacio repeated his order, unready to commit hitherto

upon such heart-retching opponents. "What's this devilry that softens
our path?" he demanded of the gypsy. "These are her children," heavily
the girl responded. "They belong to Tanit. All the still-births and offerings
of Carthage. It is for they that she weeps." Around him, he felt the gravity.
"There's no way to fight such opponents." Horacio crooked his head to the side,
putting an eye behind, aware of the silence that lurked there menacingly.
Neither direction presented itself with favor, yet only ahead lie the tide.
"We must advance, there is no choice," Hoarcio let it ride.

"Stand aside. Let us pass,"
Horacio commanded, sheathing his sword.
"We shall not harm you, but you must make a path."
"Boldly spoken," Baloch followed suit, storing too his weapon in accord.
Before them, the statue of Tanit, molten, swayed between stone and flesh.
Over her shoulders, a large sea serpent slithered, looking out toward
their party. Eyes watching intensely, as the children continued to thresh.
Then, as if a breath had collapsed, she nodded her head in the affirmative.
Flicking its tongue, her snake at them hissed, "Granted be your wish."
"What was that?" Nebi shot with surprise, thinking his hearing selective,
yet sober, his stone cold held true in his hand. As though uncommitted,
before them the spirit saplings parted, swaying to either side as a collective,
forming a gauntlet passage down the center, obedience to her will submitted,
though not necessarily free-willingly. Hesitating, the gypsy surveyed the altar
then, gazed up at Horacio with new regard in her eye. "Our fate be acquitted.
Hurry, we must go." Feeling as if sailing through the Straits of Gibraltar,
the corsairs stepped to with caution, for no longer had they the room to falter.

Horacio in the lead,
with the gypsy flanking his side,
advanced, while of his surroundings taking heed.
The children, blue-hued, emaciated, extended and bent, swayed astride
as they pass. Deferent, they nodded their heads as Horacio went past,
the others however would have to suffer the taunting of jeers applied,
as from behind, the spirits quickly closed ranks, as a gate barring the path,
once again a barrier reef on which to stall. Slowly fading with the fog and fear,
they found themselves, on an open plain, overlooking a sea no longer overcast.
Pausing for breath and a quick debrief of battle, Horacio nearly lost a gear,
"What just happened? Tell us what you know!" he demanded of the gypsy.
Calming, through her veil, she looked at him, speaking soft and clear,
"You passed the first test. Venus will be pleased." Feeling slightly tipsy,
Horacio took a step backwards, and then regaining himself, "Say that again?"
"There's no time to explain," she resisted. "We must go quickly."
"Not until I get some answers," Horacio determined, took hold of the rein.
Very well, her eyes seemed to say, as she looked across at the Aegean.

"Tell him,"
a scratchy whisper touched the wind.
From out of the darkness, as the group spun to see, appeared the old grim.
"Tell him," the crooked old woman crooned." Horacio pointed now in the blind,
"Who's that? Some new witch?" reaching for his sword. "No, she's my sister,"
the girl softened even more. "Your sister?" Horacio looked with eyes pinned
to the extreme, from a ravishing beauty to this ogre creature draping sinister,
the two could not be more dissimilar. "How could this be? It's unbelievable."
"We are Isfet wa Ma'at," she gave as way of explaining herself and the spinster.
"She's always close by, somewhere in the shadows. We two are inseparable,"
Taken aback, Isa and Nebi trembled to recognize *the moaning of the Bedouin*,
as she was known. "Chaos and Balance," the two echoed in unison the parable.
"A dualistic power," Nebi committed. "A celestial paradox," Isa joined in,
"who rises to human form in times of great peril," each completed the other.
"If together harmony is maintained, yet apart there remains only bedlam,"
Isa completed the introduction to Egyptian tale. "Her nature is to bother,
stirring troublesome disorder, yet if on your side you'll never need another."

"So are you?"
Horacio asked the important question.
"Am I what?" she demanded, a defiant posture she drew.
The captain guarded her with more than a bit of curious introspection.
Finally, after a brief pause for reflection he rephrased, "Are you on my side?"
producing a glint of smile. *Perhaps,* spoke her eyes, daunting inspection.
Then, with a turn, almost dainty like, holding an air to the sky she replied,
"That's for you to decide?" leaving him bewildered in the afterthought.
"For now we have to make it to that boat," she took a commanding step astride,
aiming for the shoreline. "Oh, a shipload of trouble there you just bought,"
Baloch patted Horacio on the shoulder, as they began to move forward.
"Indeed," he let trail behind him. There at the beach, right on his spot,
waited Butrus captaining a dinghy, who seeing the approach waved toward
them. "Right on time," he jovially declared. "We've had one hell of a time."
"You don't say?" Horacio made light, happy just to see a friendly face seaward.
"Load up quick. We need to put some distance between us and this shoreline."
He guided the crew to make haste, pushing them double time.

As they cast off,
another situation there sat brewing.
To the return of a hand and dismissive scoff,
a question was laid at her feet, thereby ensuing,
"Why did you set them free?" a gravelly voice emerged from its tether.
Slowly, as cooling lava, Tanit oscillated fore and back, her words stewing,
until ready whence they came with a slither, "Because it is my pleasure."
"Is that what she said?" a rowdy voice nearly laughed, if not for the anger.
"Yes father," Formido nodded in answer, with his lord taking measure.

"She would," he pushed back. The embroidered chair he sat on, under
the pressure of shifting weight, slid an inch to the rear, scrapping floorboard.
"If I may," Timor entered. "Your consort is both a distraction and a danger."
"Yes. Yes," Mars slapped a palm down on his desk, striking an echoing chord.
"She pleases me," he declared. Standing, he gazed out night's open window,
framed by curtains of red velvet and tassels of gold, beyond to the distant fjord.
"Yet, there's something more behind this, I know. Never before has that widow
declined a gift. Prepare my warship. We're going to see what defies the billow."

Within the safety of his cabin,
with the Crescent Moon now well underway,
Horacio felt that the time had come to ask the question.
"So why are you here? Why help me?" he waited for what she had to convey.
"There's only one in Carthage who may bypass Tanit and avoid her wrath.
He who shares the bloodline of Aeneas, who over Dido still holds sway.
You truly are his rightful heir. As such, I'm charged to help you on the path."
Reconfirming much of what he already knew, Horacio required more from her.
"That still doesn't tell me why you're here? From whose hand are you cast?"
She smiled at that, through the veil that masked her beauty, to infer
her own pleasure at his direct manner. "I'm here because you're trouble,"
she divulged her natural attraction. "You disrupt the established order,"
she drew closer, "giving rise to a newborn balance emerging from the rubble.
Is it Chance, or Fate, or even Love that brings us together? I cannot tell,
but the winds brought you to my doorstep and now a single road is double."
"How do I know I can trust you?," inhaling her scent, the question did swell.
"You can't," she pressed coquettish. "I'll walk you to the very gates of hell."

For any other,
such a forewarning would be enough to scare the suitor away,
yet for Horacio it served more the opposite, drawing him in closer to her.
"Promise?" he whispered soft into her ear, in a gently ardent sort of way.
Eagerly pressing together, lips sealed the pact they made, kissing only *Yes*.
"They arrived not long before you did," later on deck her voice would betray,
telling the story of how they came, while under the gaze of moon's florescence.
"At dusk it was, when they appeared, by both sea and land they'd come.
From the west, out of dessert sand, with the sun at their backs, the essence
of two armored silhouettes grew. As the striking of bass on a heavy drum,
hope dissolved before them. These two, Timor and Formido, of which I spoke,
were they, who with shocking awe, terrified our nation overnight to become
pliant, with minds turning numb, finally overcome, they cast the final stroke.
Reviving ancient rituals, sacrifice was made with blood and ash, to release
Tanit from her grave. In the swooning debauchery that followed, there awoke
an indescribable evil. The next morning however, all again were at ease,
as though nothing had ever happened, all going about the day as they please."

Here, she shuddered.
Pausing a moment in the cold night air,
she drew in a breath and continuing the story she uttered,
"This is how, without even noticing, they were all caught in the snare,
slave to a power that none could see, but all could feel, enamored they became
to the very thought of war, possessing their hearts, their souls..." "Beware,
death rides a pale horse, and she's coming for us, I've seen it," a groaning came
from the dark folds interrupting. Horacio, startled, spun to find the elder sibling
among the crevices. "How long have you been there?" he asked of the dame.
"Forever," the spindly voice emerged from the shadows. Then, "Tell him,"
she flung a command to her other half. "Tell him what?" Horacio with curiosity
added, seeing the gypsy hesitate. "A new fleet they've started building,"
she let out with a heavy sigh. "Even now they ready to launch this atrocity,
to carry war to every corner of the map, unlike what has ever been seen."
Considering for a moment, Horacio shrugged off what luminosity
the information held. "So why should that concern me? War is routine.
It has always been and always will be. It's part of the never-ending machine."

"Why?"
the gypsy looked startled.
"Because you've caught its attention. That's why.
The pale horse is the command vessel for the entire flotilla, once rattled
she will chase her prey to oblivion," she let the words in his ear there linger.
"And how do you know this? What are you?" he seemed irked and embattled.
"Why are you alone immune to this power?" on the question he put his finger.
"For I can read more than tea leaves, my dear captain," she turned flirtatious.
"No spirit, I can assure, I'm flesh and blood as any, however with years of rigor,
as you well know, one can exceed the simply natural to become sagacious."
She paused, inching herself closer until they were merely a breath apart.
"Fear is simply a tool that can be overcome through action, by being vivacious.
I for one embrace the danger knowing it can do me no genuine harm. At heart
it is nothing more than an emotion wielded to control those who are weaker.
By confronting fear, you're able to see into the truth of all matters and start
to gain real courage, thereby freeing yourself in the process from the reaper...
mind you, not from death the inevitable, but of that which makes life meager."

Horacio listened,
feeling the weight of her words.
"And of this new danger you say that has risen,
you are sure it gives chase, eye intent, for battle it girds?"
"As sure as we stand here in this moment," Isfet looked him square in the eye.
Breathlessly, Horacio considered the warning. measuring his own next words.
"Very well." Turning, he broke off and stepped towards the helm to rectify
the situation. "Let's put some water between us and this devil plagued land.
Give me maximum speed, all that she's got," he relayed his orders, whereby

Suleiman set the crew to their labors, doubling the captain's command.
"Set them stuns'ls! Full speed! Trim the main sails!" the orders flew,
as all hands swiftly fell into motion. Well oiled for such an unruly band,
they got the ship moving at flank speed within a minute or two.
Still dark by the time they cleared the bay, they shot north off the coast
out onto open sea, a full hour passing before the first lights grew
off the horizon. A graying pink sunrise with clouds overhead was the host
to greet them on the new day, threatening rough waters ahead in riposte.

Scanning the lay,
their stern appeared clear, much to Horacio's relief.
"We should ease up, captain," Suleiman hastened to say.
"I don't like the look of that weather, it eyes us like a wandering thief."
"Agreed," Horacio concurred, confidence restored with the day. "Make it so."
As the crew began their task, the sorceress again joined his side to stir up grief.
"Blood will be spilt on this day. There's no avoiding the scarlet undertow,"
came the old woman's croon. "Bring it on," Horacio retorted with impatience.
"I prefer a straight fight to all of this witchcraft lurking in the shadow."
"Witchcraft?" she laughed with a biting scowl. "This is merely a pittance.
You have yet to see true witchcraft, my young man, but just you wait,
more is in store for you than you could ever imagine, have a little patience."
"Is she always this pleasant?" Horacio turned to ask the younger waif.
"Oh, Ma'at means well enough," Isfet defended her elder sister. "Her faction
is that of maintaining order and as such she tells what she sees most straight.
You would be wise to heed her counsel, for though blind, clear is her vision."
As if on cue, Avranos then sounded the alarm spotting a speck on the horizon.

"As you say,"
Horacio leaned in, recalling the earlier admission,
"I cannot trust you. So before we go any further, you must betray
the reason for why you are helping us. What is your true intension?"
Isfet, eyes piercing from beneath her veil, taking on an air most serious,
replied, "My dear captain, we are an evolving species with a new mission.
We've crossed the line between faith and knowledge. If you think it's curious
the expansion of all this violence, it's because war has taken control of science.
Since the apple we have learnt a great amount of information, yet notorious
is the fact that we have gained so little wisdom from it. It is our own defiance
of the truth which destroys us. We cannot go backwards, the box is now open.
Self-preservation dictates we take responsibility for what we know. An alliance
thus must be forged between those who have the ability, before all falls to ruin.
You can make the difference, but only if you bury forever the sword of war.
Search deep within your heart and you too will see the meaning of this omen."
Listening, Horacio considered her words, and finding no fault in the score,
gave his order, "Maintain your speed and bearing, we've a long day in store."

BOOK XVI

THE IDES OF WAR

As all the preceding fanned,
the Despot Thomas was making port in the famed Kingdom of Naples.
The city-state's defenses already in a clamor, as the regional barons panned
the succession of Ferdinand the First to the throne, and marched to topple
the monarch. Led by John of Anjou, who with the help of the Genoese,
landed troops in the south, capturing countryside towns that were staples
to the kingdom's riches, a definitive battle was brewing to crescendo for these
two competing forces. "Send an envoy," Thomas commanded as they docked.
"Announce our arrival, with letters of good conduct, signed by His Excellency
and Holiness, Pope Pius II," their mutual benefactor. Jolted, the ship rocked
into position, as lashings were made to the long wharf. "Si, at once, señor,"
the captain nodded, now in safe harbor. "Prepare an escort," he knocked
upon the floorboard with the toe of his boot. "Presently, I'll be going ashore.
When I do, you shall await further orders, I may still have need of your vessel.
Do nothing until you hear from me. Is that clear?" And the captain, "Si señor."
Though a rightful sovereign, Thomas knew that on Italian soil he was the vassal
and would do well to keep his options open, as the dust was yet to settle.

To balance in counter-point,
there was no such indecision with his valise,
who on such occasions of peril would make it a point
to adhere to one very simple code in order to avoid any malice,
such to that being, whenever there is doubt, keep the gold near.
"Leave one case behind," Thomas relayed before heading to the palace,
a fall back in the event all else failed. They stored a padded, locked box there,
beneath the head of the master's bed, hidden from chance and curiosity's due.
Departing with guarded escort, Thomas mounted a waiting carriage from where
he'd be transported the short distance to Castel Nuovo. A commanding view
of the harbor the castle held, with fortified column towers flanking the entrance
and every corner, as rooks would do, with notched caps for sentries to spy thru
and seek cover, presenting a mighty deterrent against which to make a stance.
Through two such columns the carriage now passed the fortified sentry gate,
where in future years Ferdinand would construct a triumphal arch to enhance
the stature and memory of the House of Aragon and that of Alfonso, his late
father, from whom he'd inherited the crown of Naples and a monarch's fate.

His Excellency,
the King of Naples and Jerusalem,
Ferdinand the First, at thirty-seven, was a young ruler established in recency,
outwardly in appearance to the naked eye a novice, yet there have been
few to mistake twice his ability, or for that the level of his ruthlessness.
For the moment, beneath the vaulted ceilings of the Baron's Hall, bedlam
was the course, as a group of regional rulers each competed to stress
their own particular grievances. "These so called modernization schemes
will bankrupt the provinces!" one frustrated regent turned to address
the monarch, backed by a mob of according voices. For his part in the scene,
Ferdinand sat pensively seething on his throne, as lesser men dared challenge
his right to rule over his own possessions. In the midst of such a ruckus sheen
did Thomas arrive to the palace and there presented, as he crossed the ledge,
entering the great meeting hall, he fell upon the King of Naples' gaze.
To his credit, Thomas himself holding no stake in the local claims and dredge,
found himself in the enviable position of being one of the few worthy of praise
in the monarch's eye, a neutral ally who posed no threat to his chaise.

"Thomas!"
Ferdinand bellowed, with a broad and uncharacteristic smile upon his face,
coming to his feet in a manner that for a king was quite unceremonious.
"You never come to visit anymore," genuinely pleased to see the trace
of someone his equal, who in this instance was also a person he could trust.
Regardless of circumstances, a fallen despot who maintained a similar taste
in world vision, was always a welcomed companion. Sharing too the thrust
of the church's might behind him, Thomas might also act as a worthy emissary
should need arise, as the relationship with Rome shifted on the prevailing dust,
with the whims of cardinals and their pontiff. For now, however cautionary
Ferdinand may be, he had a knack of spotting when Chance came knocking,
seeing in his new confidant a means to escape such bickering commentary.
"That's enough," Ferdinand brushed the feuding chieftains aside, blocking
their protests with a dismissive hand, his only gesture, turning his attention
to the guest. "It's so good to see you again. Come, walk with me." Cocking
his head, he led the Despot Thomas out and away from the present tension,
his guards sealing the doors behind them, as if a breath held in suspension.

"Wait for it,"
Ferdinand paused, holding the two there in silence.
Muffled, through the thick oak doors, came a sudden fit
and commotion, as the barons realized the cost of their defiance.
"Ah, I just love savoring those moments when an adversary discovers
that they've gone too far." Admittedly, there was not too much science
or thought behind such crude tactics, however when pulling back the covers
Ferdinand found that brute force was highly effective to get what he wanted.
He was a king both cunning and cruel, with a soft face suited more for lovers'

fare than the battlefield, who through scheming and strategy daunted
his rivals at every turn. "What will happen to them?" Thomas was curious,
as one professional would be to the other. "The dungeons to start," he flaunted.
"We'll see what information they have on these rebellions." He became furious
just thinking about it, a challenge to his throne. Though born out of wedlock,
his father, King Alfonso had taken steps to legitimize his son, the spurious,
leaving him the rightful heir to the title and crown. Yet now comes to knock
a pretender to his station, John, seed to that of the once deposed stock.

"Tell me though of your voyage?"
Ferdinand steered the conversation.
"What was seen by you and your entourage?"
He spoke of course of warring matters, Thomas knew, being called to station.
"Ah yes," the despot was eager to add to his approximate worth. "Surely though
you've heard about our little detour around the southern flank? The situation
is that we spotted no fewer than thirty loaded warships just south of Salerno."
"Thirty, you say?" Ferdinand listened with priestly attention as in confessional.
"Yes, from what we could make out at least that number strong, but know
we gave a wide berth on spotting their colors, deviating from the conventional
routes to make it safely to your port." The king considered these new details,
confirmed by prior reports, maintaining a manner both cold and professional.
"I see," he nodded thoughtfully. "Well, that's it then," reading the entrails,
a decision had been made. With determination in his gait, Ferdinand called
his guest to another, more private, chamber within the castle's inner rails.
Past a doubled sentry, they entered a room that was large and stone walled.
In the center, on a long and wide oak table, a tactical map lay sprawled.

Around the table,
his war council already stood gathered,
conferring on the best strategy to fight back the barons' rabble.
"Show me," Ferdinand waved his hand towards the map which lathered
their present concern. "Here," Thomas pointed to a stretch along the Amalfi
where, in the Gulf of Salerno, a position the ships of Anjou had captured.
"From a league away, we spotted their sails and turned to avoid calamity."
Reflecting on this new intelligence, Ferdinand counted a generous math,
"That puts around five thousand swords to our shore," measuring catastrophe.
In fact, at that moment John of Anjou was rallying troops on a northern path,
eye fixed on Nocera, from where would open to him the entire southern valley.
Studying the map, Ferdinand envisioned the best way to level his wrath.
"Launch the fleet here, in a picket formation," having studied Pompey,
he followed proven tactics. "Secure Capri and make her the pivot hinge,
extending patrols southwest for our ships to line up as far as Cagliari.
Give them no quarter in which to hide. Then sweep southeast to infringe
on all that lies before our ships. Run them to ground. Let their hulls singe."

There was something
truly remorseless about his manner.
While admiring the decisiveness, Thomas too heard the echo ring
of some unhealthy flaw, running like a vein through the king's character,
as though he actually enjoyed inflicting pain upon his enemies and opponents.
By no means without his own cruelties, for Thomas it was simply a matter
of business, while for Ferdinand it was where he lived among the elements.
"How soon can we have the army mustered?" he glanced towards his general.
"On your command, sire," ready was the reply, as hawks from the battlements.
"Make it so. We depart for Pompeii in three days. That should give us ample
time to prepare." Turning abruptly, he once again assumed the host's façade.
With a smile he addressed his counterpart, "It will be a magnificent funeral.
Come, my friend, we have more to discuss," he led them through an arcade
of stone passages, which cooled as they came closer to the surrounding moat.
"Remember this route," Ferdinand gave the royal tour, running roughshod
through passages known only by a select and trusted few. Stopping to gloat,
they came to rest upon one door, where Ferdinand, unable to resist thus quote:

"As they say,
'Keep your enemies near.'"
Unbolting the door, Ferdinand then offered, "You're not squeamish, I pray?"
Swinging open the portal, daylight flooded the gallery from around the sphere,
distorting shadow and perception with streaks of light, adding to the macabre.
"Welcome to my museum of mummies. Go on, you have nothing to fear."
Within a most ghastly sight, all dressed in costume lie the mummified cadavers
of slain and tortured enemies, embalmed and pickled with herbs, as a warning
to any who might come in later to oppose him. "I just love this one in lavender,"
Ferdinand reminisced. "It didn't suit him in life, but now, look at that coloring,
it's just perfect." He truly was demented, and made sure all knew the lengths
to which he would go to hold onto the reins of his power. Inwardly cowering,
Thomas felt the intended effect of the display Ferdinand kept in the depths
of Castel Nuovo. "Oh, but where are my manners, you must be famished?
Come, I'll show you to your quarters. Freshen up and regain your strengths,
then we shall take lunch in the garden." Ferdinand left him there banished
to his rooms, and turning once again spoke, before down the hall he vanished.

"*Benvenuto a mi casa.*"
Thomas watched as the red and white, candy striped robes departed,
tracing the corridor, until finally curving out of view. Heart racing, *Ya basta!*
he guarded his emotions, as royalty is wont to do when being outsmarted.
Within his towered suite, his servants in attendance, Thomas sat to gather
his thoughts, contemplating his next moves, being in waters now uncharted.
Signing a note, with signet ring sealed, he called upon one quick footed staffer.
"See this be delivered to the ship's captain at once. To him alone you hear me?"
With a stern eye Thomas held the servant's grasp. "Yes, my liege, to no other."

The courier hid the despot's envelope within the folds of his frock securely,
wishing that he'd not been chosen to accomplish this particular task.
"Wait," Thomas paused him mid-stride. "Take this, for tolls and duty,"
he pressed a small purse of pocket change, enough for his man to buy a flask.
"Oh thank you, my liege," the courier took the sac without having to think twice.
There are times to save and times to spend. This was the latter no need to ask.
When it came to personal safety, he knew better than to squabble over price.
For now there were appearances to maintain, to embrace the cold of ice.

"It's off season for pheasant,"
Ferdinand bemoaned the tale of his plate,
"Duck can substitute..." "... but it's not as pleasant,"
Thomas completed his thought. "Yes, that's right. Checkmate,"
the king heartedly agreed. "Which leaves us in our present circumstance,"
Ferdinand could change tempo without losing a beat. "I believe it to be fate
which has brought you to me, but I must know, are you a shield or a lance?"
"Beg pardon?" Thomas coughed buying time, uncertain. "Neither, I'd dare."
"Perhaps?" Ferdinand contemplated how to best gain advantage in this dance
of empire and conquest. "It's quite simple." He adjusted himself in the chair
to bring Thomas in close and intimate, and in a lowered voice revealed a secret.
"You have no choice. Come now, don't look so surprised, what I say is only fair.
Look at your situation. You're in desperate need of a benefactor, don't forget.
Between Naples and Rome there's nowhere left. Fortunately, you're in luck."
"How so?" Thomas repositioned, as he felt the growing pinch of regret.
"You still hold influence with the Holy See, and that's no simple deal struck.
As my proxy to the Vatican... well, let's say, you'll fare better than this duck."

The threat was implicit,
yet so too was the promise.
Ferdinand knew equally well how to reward those complicit,
as he did how to punish those who would dare against him rise.
"From what I understand, there are some lands, not so very far from here,
where the regional master has recently met with an untimely demise."
"Is that so?" Considering his options, Thomas felt there was more to hear,
perhaps his fortunes were turning? "Yes," Ferdinand sized up a morsel.
"And now I'm left to wonder who might be worthy to fill the vacancy there?"
"He would have to be trustworthy and capable," Thomas parried on the sell.
"Oh, much more than that," Ferdinand offered. setting the mark. "Loyal,"
he emphasized his most sought after trait. And Thomas, *What the hell?*
Why not? he thought to himself in earnest, it was all on par for being a royal.
As a ruler in exile, survival was based on striking alliances. What difference
was there really between this devil and the next to come? Having a claim to soil
was finally the only measure that truly mattered among the ranks of deference.
"So what are we talking about exactly?" he asked to know for reference.

"A mutual benefit,"
Ferdinand spoke to entice.
As the recognized Emperor of the East, Thomas had no obligation to submit
directly to another sovereign, his transit and safety would more than suffice.
Yet, in such a tumultuous world, the future could never be taken for certain.
Having the backing and favor of Naples could only go to help in practice,
so he listened, stroking his long red beard which split in a V from the chin.
"A pact between you and me... of friendship," Ferdinand placed on the table.
"For these recent troubles of yours in Morea," he drew back the curtain,
"both Genoa and Aragon came to your assistance. Yet, I see by the waybill
that you've arrived to this fair city in one of my vessels? If not, perhaps
this conversation would be taking place in French, eh? But no, we are able
to see that fate intervened. Your decision, the right one I might add, elapsed
when you boarded that ship and came to Naples. It was no chance or mistake.
So now it's merely confirming the choice you made a fortnight ago. Here, clasp
my hand and seal this bargain between rulers of men," being all that it'd take.
Not realizing it then, Ferdinand just saved his own life with that handshake.

Down at the port
it was an entirely different affair.
A bustle of activity was growing, as whispers report
of pending military actions. Boarding the caravel, Thomas's courier
anxiously tracked down the ship's captain, delivering the sealed note.
"My master says it's urgent," relayed the servant. Regarding the letter a snare,
the captain looked dubiously at it as he broke the wax to read what was wrote.
Consternation then crept upon his face, as he whispered to himself, "*Cabrón.*"
Knowing that there was little time before all ships of the line were set afloat
to war, in a gambit to secure the transport and preempt the military caldron,
Thomas sent orders to sail at once for the papal port of Fiumicino.
Uncertain of his host's intentions, Thomas would send his family on
ahead, while he secured a land route to meet them in Rome. Absent a veto,
the captain gave orders to hoist sail, as the crew un-tethered their mooring
from the dock. Making way, clearing the harbor and gulf, they wouldn't know
how close they'd just come to a southerly change of course and bearing,
as the navy was put on alert for maneuvers come first light the next morning.

The fleet of Aragon sailed,
as predestined by their king's orders,
forming a line of war vessels across the Tyrrhenian Sea, where they unveiled
their master's scheme, to cut off the shipping lanes with unnatural borders.
Here it was, on the open sea, as the lead ships carved a path southwest
that the lookouts spotted a lone craft advancing in their direction. Quarters
sounded, to prepare for their first encounter, the crew's metal they'd test.
As the distance narrowed, the lookout called again, "They're from Catalan!"
spotting the red and yellow stripped flag of their allies flying abreast.

"Hold to! At ease men," the officer of the deck gave the command.
"Signal them to lower their sails and present themselves for inspection."
Following protocol, no ship, friend or foe, was allowed to pass until they stand
the challenge. The signalman flagged along the message to no reception.
"Sir, they're not responding," caution rang in the sailor's voice.
"I see no activity at all," the lookout echoed concern with his own introspection.
"Stay alert, men," the commander remained solid as a vice.
"Prepare to come about," he ordered, locking in his choice.

The rogue ship continued on course,
with no movement onboard or in sight,
"Sir, I think she may be adrift?" They readied their force.
"Now, come about! Full rudder!" Spinning the wheel hard to the right,
the helmsman brought them about alongside the other vessel as she passed.
It was visible, now from close range, that the crew appeared to blight
upon the deck unconscious. "Prepare the hooks!" the commander pressed,
looking to board. "Steady on... Now! Loosen those grapples!" Then, "Well done,"
he called as the crew lashed their sides together, attention remaining steadfast.
Over the rails, the boarding party jumped to, finding the entire crew lying stun,
unconscious on deck, after having apparently survived some great battle.
Securing the ship, they tended next to reviving the sailors one by one,
looking to identify an officer capable of giving a report on the scuttle.
"Aye, that'd be me," a parched and cracking voice replied with dehydration.
"I'd speak to your captain," he looked up at his rescuers, as if they were cattle,
through his one good eye. Struggling to his feet, showing his frustration,
Captain Mendez, gathered his bearings, assessing the situation.

"That's an extraordinary tale,"
the commander of Aragon's fleet conferred upon his guest,
having heard the report of Morea and their subsequent trail.
"So after nearly being struck down by the volcano, from what you guess,
your ship and crew were overwhelmed and incapacitated, thrown to the wind?"
"Aye," Mendez concurred. "That sounds about right." With little left to wrest,
the officer in charge needed to make a decision. Already thick skinned
from years at sea, having heard yarns for a generation, the admiral knew life
was stranger than fiction, so absent any contradictory information pinned
to the file, he'd have to accept the report as noted. "You've escaped the knife,"
he began with his summary, "but I'm afraid not your duty." As an ally,
under the Catalonian flag, Mendez was obliged to assist in the strife
of the current military operations. "We'll have to commandeer your galley
and her crew for the duration of these maneuvers," he announced the verdict.
Considering his options, Mendez embraced the command, counting the tally.
"That suits me just fine," he concurred. "If I may just add to the edict,
that we ride point?" having skin still left in the conflict.

"Agreed"
the admiral granted his request.
It made no difference with him to let Mendez's ship be the first to bleed.
Heroes die young to win battles, while those like himself live long after the test.
Better too for him to lose the ship of another sovereign than of his own king.
Orders relayed, Mendez having been granted his commission, now all that rest
would be to get underway. Returning to vessel, Mendez let the ship's bell ring,
bringing the now revived crew to attention. "Listen up," he spoke to each sailor,
"You've proven yourselves well over the course of our trials. Each of you bring
honor to the crown. Now, we set out to complete what we've started. With valor
and courage you are charged to fulfill your duty. Every man to his station,
we have a victory to win!" His words, of course, were just game for the parlor,
with eye fixed tightly on one sole prey, revenge. Cutting loose from formation,
Os Dente Serpente, sailed into the lead, driving point for the fleet as a spade.
"Captain, what's in your head?" his first mate inquired from his bastion
at the helm. "This flotilla is a spear, by which nothing can get past once made.
Behind us lies only the shaft, yet in front... the enemy who'll taste our blade."

BOOK XVII

LUCK OF THE GODS

Through the rolling mist,
breaking a path over foam clad cresting waves they burst,
silently menacing, stalking the future, as the ever looming apocalypse,
came the towering forecastle and mighty pale arc of Hannibal's Thirst.
Sailing from Carthage upon the darkest hour, she longed for the taste of blood,
the scent of her prey guiding the helmsman's hand, as the heavens cursed.
At the prow stood her master, the God of War, who with a boot heeled thud
upon the deck, set his eye to the horizon. "That way," he inhaled deeply,
savoring the tang of haste and sweat that mixed with the flood
of sea salt on the air. "They're out there, just ahead of us, obliquely,
I can feel them." The helmsman adjusted course to come in line
with the direction Mars had set. When caught, the price would be steeply
paid, for once embarked upon, war could not so easily confine
itself, but instead would spread to every corner with carnage and destruction.
None were safe who crossed into this realm. "Bring me more wine!"
Mars called to his steward, his hunger swelling with a gnawing seduction,
as his sword hand itched to fulfill its own primary function.

"Ah, look at those streaks of scarlet,"
he eyed the first light of day as a good omen,
while pulling back a long swig from his goblet.
"Hunting season is upon us," he gave a broad smile. "Rouse the men.
Let them know there's knife work to be done today," he sent off his servant.
"That'll raise their spirits, eh?" he turned to his seconds, who shared an amen.
"It will indeed," Timor made his own declaration, equally fervent.
"All will tremor before us," Formido likewise echoed. "They shall perish,"
he spoke, as the three readied for battle, with eyes to the skyline, observant
to the direction in which fled their quarry. These were the moments to cherish,
with all the day's possibilities before them, contemplating their pending wrath.
"There! There she is!" Mars bellowed, pointing, standing tall and squarish,
as a speck several leagues away dented the horizon's lineal path.
"Prepare ye demons!" Formido hissed at the crew, eyes locked on their target,
as the finger puppets of the damned riled, anticipating the coming bloodbath.
"Shall we play with our food before we dine?" Mars, standing upon the parapet
considered the mouse, and in a feisty mood, he decided to affix his helmet.

"Where'd they go?"
Avranos called, suddenly perplex.
"They were there just a minute ago."
"Are you sure?" Horacio conferred with his lookout, seeing himself no specs
upon the seabed. "Yes sir. A ship was clearly there, gaining on our six,
then it just suddenly vanished." Horacio exhaled, each move more complex
than the one before, he would have to be twice as fast to avoid the tricks
being played. "Keep your eye sharp, let me know if you spot any changes."
Turning towards the helm, he conferred with his second, weighing the fix.
"Could be that we're the faster?" Suleiman confided. "Perhaps their range is
just beyond our vision?" "Maybe, but I wouldn't be too fast to lay a bet,"
Horacio considered. "Switch out half the oarsmen with fighters." Strange as
the order sounded to Suleiman's ears, Horacio made sense of his mindset.
"The lower decks have been sweating for hours, as our fighting men grow cold,
one end needs rest while the other warming. Let's ready all hands to be set
for when they're needed most. Make it so." "Aye," Suleiman did as he was told,
passing on the orders that got the crew moving within their stronghold.

Fresh, strong arms
added a notch to their vessel's speed,
coaxing a longer stride and more distance from the harms
that pursued. *Yet would it be enough?* the question lingered indeed
in Horacio's mind, as another ill fated omen on the air crooned.
"It will do you no good," with scratchy tones Ma'at in his ear did bleed.
"They are coming... and you sail towards the tip of their spear as a wound."
"What is it you say, old woman? Speak of what you see." Horacio spun.
"You are the antelope in the lion's den, being led. Soon you will be pruned
by what lies in wait." "What say you, there's another force ahead, that we run
into a trap?" "Such is true," Ma'at affirmed. Horacio unsure what to believe,
could not in his gut set aside the prophecy foretold to be done.
"What do you suggest?" he asked of what the old seer might hold up her sleeve.
"Time. It has always been your ally, therefore seek as much of it as you can."
Wise, he concurred with the suggestion. If an exit he could not retrieve,
perhaps he could postpone destiny long enough to turn the tide's plan?
"Come about five degrees northwest," he relayed his order to Suleiman.

"Aye captain.
Coming about, five degrees northwest," Suleiman adjusted course.
"You know, that will bring us within visual range of the island?"
Of Sardinia Suleiman spoke, and the lookouts that watched her bourse.
"Yes, it's a risk we have to take. Weave the thread to the very edge
of their view." "Aye captain, will do." It was a plan he could endorse.
As the hour grew old though, approaching Sardinia's southern ledge,
with the seas still a held breath of quiet, they would have to now commit
to having their port side compromised to a full stretch of land to hedge

them in on one side. It was a wager to which Horacio would have to submit,
if to stay true to the mission before him. "Helmsman, steady on. Take us in,"
he gave the command without hesitation, as the Crescent Moon softly lit
upon the far horizon. Then, at two bells, now completely hemmed in
the hunters to starboard did reveal themselves entering the race.
To the east, still leagues away, the outline of two warships, like a shark's fin,
pointed in their direction. "Full speed!" Horacio looked to the heavens for grace.
"To stations!" he called, as the oars strained to pull ahead of the chase.

"My lord,"
Formido approached the side of his father.
"The mortals are coming into range. Soon it will be time for the sword."
"Very good... Ah! So, Aragon has decided to join us after all. A little further
and we'd have had to take them ourselves," Mars eyed the geometry of vessels.
"Let's have some fun, shall we?" Mars, exuberantly drunk, decided rather
than to engage his men, to instead press the mortals into combat themselves,
equally enjoying to watch a fine spectacle. Still however, he could rejoice
in driving the opponents into each other's arms. "Prepare the shells,"
he spoke of cannonballs. Removing his magic helmet, with a bellowing voice,
he gave his command. "Let fly the fire! That should rile their bones."
Out of nowhere, at the Crescent Moon's stern, appeared an even deadlier choice,
in the form of a ghostly great white, with full blown sails and blustery tones.
Hannibal's Thirst emerging, announced itself with a roaring cannon's blare.
The fodder crashed seaward, without posing danger, yet produced the groans
Mars sought. "What was that?" crewmen turned in shock from the flare,
seeing the new threat that they'd have to bear.

"Steady on!"
Horacio in action, now a true soldier,
mustered the needed will of a leader to match his brawn.
"Keep your speed. We need to angle out those at our shoulder,
so not to get pinned in a corner," he pressed the oars. "Trim those sails!"
Suleiman then called out, to coax as much speed as they could bolster.
"What's this?" Mendez hissed, for his part in these tales,
looking through his good right eye, as Os Dentes Serpente eyed its prize,
with the Golden Harvest, a ship of the fleet, by her side. Along it's rails,
they prepared for a fight, loading the cannons, the battlements rise.
"She's mine!" Mendez cried. "To war!" he lifted his sword to the air,
to the cheer and scuffle of a battle toughened crew, holding a ready guise.
"Bring us closer!" Mars declared from his spectator's throne, enjoying his share
of the entertainment. "But hold back the cannons. There's no fun in killing
them right away." For him this was play. "As for you," he addressed the pair
of brotherly demons. "See what you can get up to," he ordered the willing,
as Timor and Formido both bowed, pleased with their billing.

A foul and evil wind then blew,
exuding from the deck of Hannibal's Thirst,
as Timor and Formido in celestial essence flew.
Vaporized, the spirits of fear and terror, at their worst,
took to the air and went forth screaming high pitched,
as a shudder running through the deep waters of Earth. Immersed,
the tremor struck hardest the crew of the Crescent Moon. Bewitched,
their fortitude slackened to despair, only her heroes still remained strong,
rallying to their captain. "It's upon us," Isa's stone to a blood red switched,
as the smell of fear floated across the deck, all sensing a change for the wrong.
"Hold tight as long as you can," Horacio fought back the dread, accustom
he was becoming to primal feelings. "It's all in the head," he sang like a song.
"Rally the crew. We mustn't let them outflank us due to this corruption."
Just then from the corner, the shadow of a woman began to chant,
"TERAKAJ SHAFAR TAKASKAJ JAKASHA," from an old Egyptian custom.
"What's she saying?" And Isfet, "It's an ancient spell of protection in cant.
It will strengthen the hearts of your crew, as long as she continues her rant."

"Carry on,"
Horacio gave his blessing.
"We can use as much help as can be won."
Saying these words, Horacio immediately saw the result of their pressing.
"We got 'em!" Avranos called out, noting the angle of the ships as definitive.
"There's no way they can cut us off at this distance," the case he was resting.
At the very least they'd not be boxed in, still they were far from a superlative.
Seeing this, Mars sat up. "How's this? Someone gives them assistance.
More speed!" he called, for the nature of this ship he was now most inquisitive.
For the ships of Aragon, they seethed falling behind, losing a sure chance
to end the battle quickly, now the pursuit could take all day, as the corsairs
made for open sea, successfully crossing the picket line in a defiant stance.
Shy of a "Horrah!" Avranos cut short the celebration from his crow lairs.
"Captain! Look there! Is that not the traitor's vessel?" he pointed to identify
Os Dentes Serpente as the enemy giving such chase, making rigid the hairs
of more than one crew member. Their captain's killer, their nemesis foe, to fie
on their back quarter, made all ponder this day as one on which worthy to die.

"To believe in something,"
Horacio pondered their current situation,
"even if it means sacrificing everything,
defines the character of man. Adjust our position,"
he gave the command. "We're coming about to attack."
A roar of accord rose in the air, as the fighting men took to station.
"Maybe your sister gave the men too much courage?" Suleiman began to tack,
bringing the ship about for battle. "Or maybe just enough," Isfet countered,
readying her own blades, a look of excitement in her eyes began to crack

from her veiled exterior. She too would join the warriors encountered,
to defend the Crescent Moon. "May Allah will my blade taste the traitor's flesh,"
Baloch, beside Horacio, gazed out yonder, across the sea's breech, downward,
searching for the unfinished enemy, whose insult still burnt his mind fresh.
"There will be a reckoning this day, my friend," Horacio sealed his pledge.
"Just keep your wits about you. Three against one hardly seems to mesh
with sound battle tactics. All we have to count on is surprise for an edge,
for here today shall fall hardest the hammer's sledge."

At that moment,
third from the stern,
Hannibal's Thirst again fell dormant,
vanishing a second time before their eyes, once more confusion to churn.
"Let's keep them guessing." Mars then grinned wide on the beat and added,
"Bring us in as close as you can," directing the helm, he desired to learn
more of this one, who acted so bold and fearless on confronting the dead.
"Look at how he turns to face the challenge. This one has guts!"
the war god nodded respect. The unexpected reversal maneuver led
to great chaos on those waters, as Mendez's force adjusted their struts,
trying to match the 180 degree turn. "Get us in front!" Mendez let out a scowl,
seeing the Golden Harvest now directly across their path. "Nuts!"
he shouted. "This one's ours!" Os Dentes Serpente pushed past her ally's prow,
their angles however distorted, as the range between the three vessels
narrowed. "Fire the fores!" Horacio commanded, making the cannons howl.
Two shots let out, striking their mark, leaving behind shards and tassels.
The first across the deck killing a sailor, the other smashing forecastles.

"Return fire!"
Mendez screamed.
Still unaligned however, his balls of steel struck only the mire
of a turbulent sea. As Aragon's ships turned, they were once again reamed
by another volley, this time taking out the helm of Os Dentes Serpente,
leaving a ship that had already been struggling coming completely unseamed.
It wasn't the crew or an unwillingness to battle, but a lack of epoxy,
which sealed the ship's doom. Too much damage, left only one chance
to still claim victory, as their bows were now in line. "Vamos, mi gente!"
Mendez rallied his men of the line. With grapples they readied to dance.
Cannon fire rang out once more from all sides, as three ships came to collide
with their destiny. Cunningly, Horacio angled the Crescent Moon to glance
the starboard side, putting Os Dente Serpente to center, while at the far side,
the Golden Harvest lie snookered, unable to directly join the engagement.
She would now have to make a wide radial turn against the tide,
before being able to enter the fight, evening the odds for the moment.
With a final rebuttal of cannon flare, all hands prepared their armament.

The two forces clashed,
as mortal enemies were want to do.
With venom and fury, swords they slashed,
cutting through the air, meeting the blades of those who drew
a hostile opponent. A clanging rattle enveloped every quarter of the scene,
as hero and common soldier fought alike to the death, with more than a few
on each side deserving of mention. Of our heroes, battling on the aquamarine,
the first on the line, as prow met stern, were the sailors and swordsmen.
This placed opposing captains at opposite ends. In the middle lie a screen
of sweat and gnash and bloodshed that they'd have to cross, for only then
would the business twixt them be settled. Kasim and Etci drew their blades,
scrapping with two sailors, when Mendez with his saber came upon them,
stabbing Kasim through the heart, fulfilling the prophesy of the shades.
Etci tried to jump to his aid, just to be beaten back with a long gash
across the bicep, saved only by an unsteady rock and the turbulent cascades
that rippled across the deck, as Hannibal's Thirst, invisible, set upon to lash
itself to Os Dentes Serpente's port quarter, jolting the ships with whiplash.

There, at the rear of battle,
Mars and his two filial accomplices
disembarked their vessel, moving silently towards the soundly brattle
of deadly combat to the fore. Here, advancing under his watchful auspices,
bedlam ensued. From the center, the fight raged the greatest along the rails.
Kismet, striking mighty blows with mace, fulfilled many of death's promises,
only to be felled himself when a lance ruptured his spleen, leaving trails
of blood on the scene. His would be a heavy loss for the Crescent Moon.
For their part in this contest, Isa and Nebi worked a pack below the mainsails.
Each covering the other's back, they would continue to outlive this afternoon.
At the opposite end, with a solid faction, the corsairs held the advantage.
Together, on one side Baloch and Butrus cleared a path most violently hewn,
while Horacio and Isfet made easy work of bloodshed at this early stage,
the namesake of Chaos being most in her element, bloomed a frenzied flower.
Suleiman, at the rear, guarded the helm and backs of the captain and sage,
with all going well, until the Golden Harvest finally decided to sour
their advance with an attack of their own, striking at the starboard bower.

Completing her maneuvers,
the Golden Harvest, with a full contingent
of reinforcements at their side now hovers.
With a second force to compete against, options became narrowly stringent.
Hoarcio would have to direct his effort towards stemming the starboard flow
of new soldiers, while at port the main battle fanned a crimson pungent.
He raged forth into the fray as the first line crossed the rail, entering the throe
of combat, striking the boarding party before they could gain a square foot.
Meanwhile, Mendez cut his way closer to the inevitable, forthcoming row,

set in his own determination. For the moment, neither side could put
a hand on victory, yet eventually one or the other would have to give.
Here it was that Mars, lucidly drunk at the height of his element, set afoot
to slaughter, emboldening the hearts of all comers who still wanted to live,
while terrorizing those of the weaker men, whose fate was just to die.
Through all this gore he watched and encouraged the combative,
marking out the principles, searching for where the captain lie,
until what he was looking for finally caught his eye.

Along the far side,
flanked by a moor and she-devil,
stood the master of this seafaring pride.
Fending off a wall of intruders almost by shear will,
they shored up the starboard, allowing their other heroes
more time. Of these, Baloch, on the forward lunge, came to revel,
face to face with Mendez. "Allah be praised," he raised, trading blows
with his mortal enemy. Slicing his thigh, Baloch was poised to claim victory,
when staying his hand, Mars, true to his word, un-evened the zeroes.
"This one's not yours," in the Pashtun's ear, he whispered maledictory,
casting Baloch aside with a reverberating thud, leaving him unconscious.
Staggering, Mendez limped forward, confused at his own luck in this story,
discovering then that he was merely being saved for something more nauseous.
Before him stood Horacio. Massing survivors from both sides encircled the two,
as the main event was about to take place, to settle on this day the promise
each gave for revenge, for blood and pride and glory. Giving honor its due
the two captains readied themselves for battle, each their swords they drew.

"You!"
Horacio's eyes lit with fire.
"Come and meet your doom!" Rushing with anger, Mendez flew
towards him, swinging high and wide with a blade that betrayed the liar.
Horacio, with a sweeping counter measure, disarmed Mendez below the elbow
and drove his sharpened point straight through the traitor's gut to finally retire
the killer of his captain and friend. A cheer rose up from stern to bow,
yet short lived was the celebration, as Fear took Suleiman, and Dread Isfet,
each by the throat they struck, immobilizing both with a single blow,
while Mars, now ready to reveal himself, removed and set aside his helmet.
With a mighty hand he took Horacio by the lapel and lifted him off his feet.
Just then a swoosh of air shimmered fast in his direction, as Avranos let
an arrow fly in defense of his captain. Without breaking stride, his fist beat
the dart, catching it by the shaft. Only then did Mars pivot his attention,
to cast the arrow back whence it came. Flinging it fast, as if on full retreat,
it impaled the archer to the top mast. "No!" Horacio added to the tension,
as Mars returned his gaze to the reason for this needed intervention.

“What makes you so special,
to warrant the protection of this witch?” Mars referenced his glance to Isfet.
“And for that matter the goddess, Tanit herself?” wanting to see the credential
of the one who caused him such trouble. “Why would you be made fit
for saving?” curiosity had gotten the better of him, pausing his natural instinct.
“Wait a minute, I know that sword! How did you get it?”
Mars spoke of the Sword of Troy that Horacio clutched tightly, his grip distinct
and strong. “It was given to me?” Horacio made curt his response.
“Is that so? Don’t toy with me,” Mars boiling, ready to make this mortal extinct,
would have the truth out of him, one way or another, when for the nonce
he was suddenly distracted, captured by the color of turquoise.
“Her eyes,” he said, heart suddenly softened, touched by the memory of once,
as Mars stared deeply into the sparkling pools of Horacio’s eyes.
Suddenly, without warning, Mars broke off, retreating so fast it was all a blur,
with Timor and Formido in tow, they returned with such utter surprise
that in their haste a fire erupted upon Os Dentes Serpente amidst the stir.
With that and the general confusion, no one knew exactly where they were.

Shook from shock,
Horacio made haste to gather his wits,
for now more than ever they were on the clock.
Raising his voice, he gave the order, “Cut loose the ships!”
While men under all colors rushed for the safe quarters of friendly craft,
the Crescent Moon made ready to get underway, chopping the strips
that moored their ships together, as Os Dente Serpent went up a flaming shaft.
“Fire all!” Horacio commanded taking the helm, adding a few nails to the coffin,
and a strafing gash to the Golden Harvest, making her little more than a raft.
“Ready, hard a starboard!” he shouted orders to a dazzled crew. With a spin
of the ship’s wheel to the right, he urged the Crescent Moon on in her flight,
wanting to put as much space between all these ships as possible to avert ruin.
Upon Hannibal’s Thirst, the crew of demons watched from afar the sight
of their quarry heading out for sea, as their master deliberated.
“Who is he, my lord?” Timor begged for insight.
“There is only one mortal, the God of War would not kill,” Isfet elaborated,
as she and Suleiman joined Horacio at the helm, in a mood most animated.

“My grandson,”
Mars exclaimed with a voice gone deadpan.
Taking a long swig from a bottle of fermented homespun,
he regained his equilibrium. “She never told me,” he spoke of Venus’s plan.
“The legitimate heir of Troy and Rome born from we, the gods of love and war.
Never before has such a mortal creature walked this Earth of man.”
Mars considered the implications and of everything that might hold in store,
when a question entered his thought process. “And what exactly is his role
in all of this?” he pondered, as Formido entered, taking the floor.

"Orders, my lord? They're getting away." "Well after them. Go on, let's roll!"
Then, after a pause, having searched thoroughly around, "Where's my helmet?"
"Oh, that isn't?" Isfet gasped, as Horacio stepped midship to take control
of the bounty that had fallen there, straight from the hand of a god. Isfet
recognized this immediately for what it was, "Pluto's helmet," she relayed,
noting the intricate artwork and markings. "You'd be wise beyond all merit,
to put that on," she spoke of great powers. As if before one's eyes betrayed,
Mars hollered out an indignant, "No!" as the Crescent Moon began to fade.

BOOK XVIII

ANCIENT HISTORY

Affixing Pluto's helmet,
Horacio felt a tingling sensation,
as if every fiber of his body were beset
by living energy. "Concealing you from observation,"
Isfet oriented him with the legendary powers of this fortunate gift,
"it will also envelop that which carries the wearer, making infiltration
a simple act. If dressed in this you stand close to any other, you may drift
a whisper in the ear, planting a subconscious suggestion in their head,
shaping ideas and opinions, manipulating foe and friend alike, to open a rift
or seal one, as you like." "So you are saying," Horacio followed the thread,
"that right now the entire ship is protected?" "Yes, we are all invisible,"
Isfet confirmed. "As long as the bearer is aboard ship, within this bulkhead,
none may detect our passing." "Jupiter be praised! How is this possible?"
Horacio asked rhetorically. "Nothing from on high," Isfet gave her surety,
telling of the Titan Wars. "This helmet was born of the darkest arts divisible.
During the war with the Titans, the Cyclopes gifted the brothers three mighty
tools. Jupiter was given thunder, Neptune his trident, and Pluto invisibility."

"There's more,"
the scratching voice of Ma'at pressed her sister.
"Tell them the entire story, of all that came before."
"Very well. In the beginning," Isfet began, words boiling like a blister,
"there was only Earth and Sky, beneath the shadow of the expanding Universe.
Together they birthed all form of creature imaginable, from glorious to sinister.
Yet the nature of Sky, the ruler of all the cosmos, by name of Caelus,
was jealous of sharing power. Growing fearsome of his offspring's strength,
Caelus locked the most powerful, the Hecatonchires and Cyclopes in Tartarus,
the deep abyss, a fiery dungeon prison of torment and suffering that at length
is an unspeakable torture chamber. Yet, Gaia, Mother Earth, sought reciprocity
for her imprisoned children. So recruiting her son, Saturn, who at tenth
and two was the youngest of all the early Titans, she unleashed his ferocity
with a well timed coup. With a great sickle Gaia had gifted, Saturn ambushed
his father, castrating him there in that moment, casting his loins to the sea,
from where sprung the goddess Venus. Finishing Caelus his blood rushed,
there taken by Gaia, from whom the Furies, Nymphs and Giants then gushed.

"Yet, just prior to that fatal blow,
Caelus made a prophecy that the same fate
would likewise befall Saturn when his children did grow,
who would rebel against his rule and, like himself, spate
their father. Taking up the throne, Saturn then secured his power
by re-imprisoning the Hecatonchires and Cyclopes behind Tartarus's gate.
Now, each of the gods and Titans possessed individual gifts to empower
their will. On slaying his father, Saturn was granted an attribute most unique,
which hadn't existed until the moment he threw Caelus from the tower,
being the power of Time. Until then all had existed infinitely in the mystique
of countlessness. Here though, in that act, Saturn set the clocks in motion.
Granted control over the flow of eons and seconds, turning time oblique,
he alone could step outside of its passing, to maneuver between the notion
displayed upon the dials, to even, if he pleased, make the moments freeze,
giving him a great advantage over any adversary. Yet as strong as this potion
of his was, even he could not change the past to recapture the lost breeze.
So the prophesy given, filling him with such fear, brought him to his knees.

"Having married Ops,
both his sister and the daughter of Caelus,
the Titan goddess of plenty, who looked over all earthly crops,
Saturn soon became a bountiful monarch, ruling over the glorious
Golden Age. However, eventually, when they decided to bear offspring,
Saturn was again overcome by the prediction of his poisoned genus,
and vowing not to share the fate of his father before him did spring
his solution. Upon their births, each child Saturn took and ate.
Five consecutively he swallowed whole to keep them from his ring.
In order the daughters, Vesta, Ceres and Juno went down his palate,
followed by the sons Pluto and Neptune, sharing the space in his gut.
Yet, as Saturn would soon discover, fear is often the driving cause of fate.
Ops, tricking Saturn, hid her youngest child, Jupiter, from view and put
in his place a rock dressed in swaddling clothes, wrapping it in a blanket,
which Saturn unsuspecting swallowed whole, believing his lineage now shut
within the lining of his stomach. Ops, now succeeding in her gambit,
whisked her son away, concealing him in a basket.

"To the island of Crete they flew.
Raised in secret by the tender goddess, Amalthea,
appearing at times in the form of a goat, Jupiter, the young god, grew.
There within a cave in Mount Aigaion, he was nurtured by cornucopia,
until reaching adulthood, when destiny returned him to his father's service,
masquerading as Saturn's cupbearer. Once established as a servant, myopia
of habit made him an undetectable threat. Then, securing a potion from Metis,
Jupiter served his father a mixture of mustard and wine which caused Saturn
to vomit his swallowed children. Having freed his siblings, adding to the circus,

Jupiter then let loose the prisoners of Tartarus, leading them all to churn
in rebellion against the Titans. A ten year war between them then ensued.
The Hecatonchires hurled stones as big as mountains, as the Cyclopes in turn
forged for Jupiter his bolts of lightning and thunder. For Neptune they imbued
all the powers of the sea into his trident, and for the eldest brother, Pluto,
they crafted perhaps the greatest gift of all, that of his helmet. For skewed
and erased from history was the elder's role in this unfolding epic canto,
where due to his invisible wit and cunning, Saturn turned a miming panto.

"As the war raged on
Saturn, in control of the power of Time,
was able to continually stay one move ahead of the usurping son.
With the mighty Atlas by his side, leading the Titan's defensive line,
they fought to a stalemate crescendo with the gods of the newer generation.
As always, from the beginning of time, power, the all consuming crime,
concedes nothing without a fight, and the Titans of old were no exception.
Until it came to Pluto, the eldest son, who conceived an entirely new stratagem.
Using his helmet of invisibility, he infiltrated Saturn's mind with misdirection,
making him by suggestion believe the future and past to be all one single item.
Saturn, then on skipping time, fell unconscious into a repeating feedback loop.
It was in this moment of vulnerability that Jupiter and his allies could hem
Saturn in, placing him into the Infinity Glass, a revolving prison coop,
which spun indefinitely the same one minute of time. Casting it forever
into the bowels of Tartarus, where it remains to this day, protected by a troop
of hundred-handed Hecatonchires, eternally guarding the entry gate's lever."
Isfet completed the telling, as Horacio contemplated his current endeavor.

"How do you know all this?"
Horacio questioned. These gypsy strangers remained a gnawing mystery.
Still unsure how far to believe her, "And what was that of being a witch?"
"Not a witch," Isfet glowed, her eyes magnetic, "but half nymph, half fury.
I was there, my sister too, born at that spontaneous moment of creation,
from Gaia's womb, when the blood of Caelus spilt, at hour zero of history.
We flourished in the Golden Age, growing strong with the passing damnation,
witnessing as gods and Titans battled for control of the heavens and Earth,
seeing, learning firsthand the plots and betrayals, the struggles for elevation
and sacred power. We learnt all their hidden secrets, and for what it's worth,
their weaknesses. What you see here, this flesh is merely an earthly vessel.
We come to you now from a time forgotten, to guide you through the dearth."
"But why help me?" Horacio remained suspicious, still with an internal wrestle.
"For only one reason," Isfet looked him sternly in the eye. "The goddess, Venus,
your patron and grandmother, is our blood sister, born from our father's tassel.
As her heir, a child of our lineage, we are bound by oath to protect her genus."
Horacio weighed these words, with the tales of Titanomachy and Genesis.

"So you are saying,"
Horacio confirmed his ear,
"that one of these monsters, a Hecatonchire, is staying
the path before the doors of Tartarus?" "No," Isfet drew near,
whispering, "Not one, but three, each with the strength of a hurricane."
"Into those winds of doom and danger, you hoist your sails to steer,"
Ma'at added to the storm that already swirled past Horacio's window pane.
"Then that be our course," Horacio stood fast by the commission bestowed,
the choice being made for him. "Clean up this deck," he called the crew to tame
the current situation. "Tend to the wounded and get all this trespass stowed.
I await damage reports from the officers. Where do we stand?"
Ali Abbas, with a bandaged, bleeding head himself, came forward and lowed
the woes of battle. "Eight dead, with twice that many wounded," he panned
his free hand towards the disheveled crew. "No telling yet how the lower decks
fared, but by the lean she's taken on some water." "Butrus, give him a hand,"
Horacio called on his strongest. "Get a team of able men on those buckets."
"Aye, captain," Butrus turned on the double to perform the required checks.

Baloch was just coming to,
hand cupping the back of his head.
pushing off of one knee, he took to his feet, staggering to
the right. "What hit me?" he said, and then suddenly realizing he was not dead,
"Did we win?" Then looking around, Horacio confirmed, noting the cost he said,
"Yes, yes we did. There lies the enemy slain," he pointed to the sprawling red
stain and carcass remains of Mendez despoiling the deck. "Many lives were laid
down today. Many friends were lost. Great is their honor, for they fell to avenge
our captain and friend, who may now rest knowing the debt in full is paid.
Nothing, can bring any of them back, but knowing that amends
have been made, we as men can move forward, for great too is our honor."
Horacio struck a sentimental note, knowing well how new losses can wrench
the soul. Yet, win the battle they did. As survivors of war's bloody horror,
they equally stood proud of this accomplishment, of simply being alive.
That was enough for the moment. As they made distance, out from the corner
was spotted the tail. The menacing white hull of Hannibal's Thirst on their five
renewed the crew's apprehension, as this new threat matched their stride.

"This is the direction,
they were last seen heading, my lord,"
Mars listened, as he scanned the watery section,
searching for a clue on the waves. "Due north," he stroked his sword.
"What's your game?" Mars asked the wind, casting rhetoric upon the air.
"Steady on, follow this course," Mars struck an uneasy chord.
"Keep all eyes peeled for any trace of their ship." Having slipped from his snare,
the God of War grew foul in temper, as he consulted his diagrams for any sign
of where the lost ship might be heading. Tables turned he was duly unaware

that his quarry sat directly before him, within his cannons range and line.
That however did not ease the crew of the Crescent Moon, who with trepidation
watched as Mars drew closer. "You're positive our location they cannot divine?"
Horacio pressed the sorceress nymph for an answer to his question.
"This ship and all aboard it are completely hidden," Isfet eased his fear.
Deciding to trust her, Horacio turned to his second, updating the situation.
"I want you to jettison the enemy's dead overboard, directly off our rear."
"Sir?" Suleiman raised a brow. "Set them a trail, off from which we'll steer."

The ploy was duly noted,
a ruse their hunters would likely not suspect.
Having dumped a string of bodies, leaving a fermented
path to follow, Horacio then called the helm to course correct.
"Turn northeast, forty-five degrees." "Aye captain, forty-five degrees northeast,"
the wheel spun the required torque. "Give an hour at this heading, then effect
a ninety degree correction northwest." "Aye captain," the helmsman repeats,
confirming that he heard the order. "Look there, my lord, in the water comes,"
one demon puppet pointed to the floating carcass debris, eager himself to feast.
Mars eyed the line they made, studying the trail of human breadcrumbs.
"Carry on," he pulled a swig adding to his swagger. "Maintain your bearing
and press the crew, we cannot be far behind. Soon they will succumb."
Mars then left the deck for his cabin, deep in thought, his inner voice swearing.
Where are you off to son? What is it that you seek? the internal monologue
kept the god in question. Then, with an eye upon his charts he was staring.
"What is it we have here?" he took another draft, to clear away the frog,
as the light began to show, breaking through the fog.

"What could you possibly want there?"
Mars, the warrior god, never one to believe in coincidence,
stared long at the emerald speck upon the map, recalling his long ago affair.
It began right there, on her pearl dropped island, beneath the starry silence
underneath her husband's very nose. Vulcan, the loveless, who left womb bare,
would not know that the heart of his bride be stolen, held in confidence
on the very night of their union. Under the light of this very moon, the pair
consummated their secret. This was where, in whose arms, he found peace.
Beyond the lines of war and battle, the love of Mars was Venus fair.
In addition to the brothers, Timor and Formido, each as if matching sleeves,
Venus bore to Mars a daughter, Concordia, the Goddess of Harmony,
who by inflaming love and taming rage, it could be said with ease
to be Mars's favorite. Aside from Venus, perhaps for she he'd stow his armory.
How long had it been since he last set eyes on his beloved child?
Mars thought back on her, on long ago, to what was now a fading memory,
to the early days of Rome, before imperial wars and turmoil riled
the world with conquests, to when Earth was still young and wild.

She was there at the founding,
at Juno's bitter, begrudging defeat,
when Aeneas, fresh from victory resounding,
laid down his sword for peace and, performing extraordinary feat,
planted the roots of Rome beneath his feet, flowering in all her greatness.
Though warring, Mars was not a jealous god, unlike others of the royal seed.
He had always many lovers, and knew full well that Venus too had countless
admirers, that she could never be his alone. This did not discourage Mars,
it was an arrangement that likewise suited him. So, seeing the rightness
of her mortal son's victory, his strength in battle and the courage of his arms,
it filled him too with a bit of pride. As a gift, Mars made to Venus a pledge,
to be the protector of her son's city. Filling his oath, descending from the stars,
Mars then fathered the earthly sons, Romulus and Remus, with the knowledge
that from them would be built the walls and foundations of the great city,
making immortal Rome, the fourth offspring from their loins. At the ledge,
hands gripping fast to wood railing, Mars stared out onto the mighty sea,
"Her eyes," he whispered, remembering their blue infinity.

BOOK XIX

VULCAN'S GATE

With Fortune's guiding hand,
having helped them narrowly escape ruin,
a duty was still required from the fleeing corsair band,
to honor their newly fallen lost in battle. Wrapped in cloth, each in turn
would be committed to the sea, a burial tribute befitting departed seamen.
The sun was setting a deep orange off their port angle, the moment to adjourn
the dead. "May you find peace, dear brothers," Horacio led the requiem,
as one after another were released to embark upon their final voyage.
For the last, Avranos, impaled through the chest with his own arrow, beaten
by a god no less, Horacio paused the bearers. With two coins for passage,
he placed them secure upon the bandaged eyes, "The others may not believe,
but for you my Thracian friend, I will see you again in Elysium." With leverage
the body slid into the sea, joining the rest as it sunk beneath the water's heave.
With a final salute, Horacio brought his attention back to matters pressing.
"Bosun, bring us about true north," he instructed the helm to weave
into position. "Aye sir, true north," Suleiman adjusted course, dressing
the wheel to bring them to a line that would keep the enemy guessing.

"Are you sure this is prudent?"
Suleiman questioned on an aside.
"It's the last place they'd expect to find us," Horacio would not repent
the decision made, as their ship maneuvered behind the hunter, to ride
her stern. "We're at a safe enough distance, and soon it will be night."
With dusk upon them, it wouldn't be long before a darkened sky would hide
all, with or without a helmet to disguise their true location. For now twilight
stretched a pale hue across the tired sky, longing to put the world to rest
in its everlasting cycle. Soon enough they would return to the fight,
for now the crew took respite in shifts, gathering strength for morning's quest.
At half an ancient league they followed, keeping a sharp eye for any sudden
change in heading or unexpected moves. "What does your heart suggest?"
Isfet stepped close to Horacio's ear, examining his look of sullen.
"Soon it will be the new moon," Horacio looked upon the waning crescent.
"I must be in place by then..." he trailed off. "To find the way that's hidden?"
Isfet completed his sentence. *Yes. It's true, you are far from innocent,*
Horacio thought to himself. "What do you know of the assent?"

"Only as much as you,"
Isfet had nothing new to reveal.
"That the way is dangerous and can be found by only a few..."
She stopped there in mid-thought, seeing how he turned the wheel,
eyebrows lifted, "So you intend to let one who already knows lead the way?
But how do you know he'll take you there?" his thoughts she'd like to steal.
"Because he's chasing me," frankly Horacio admitted, her curiosity to stay.
Meanwhile, further ahead, aboard the other vessel, with the die already cast,
Mars stopped looking in other directions, willed by his own questions to betray
safe passage, he set for them the path. "She calls to me," Mars said at last,
downing a bloodied bourbon, surrendering to the flow of his sons' questions.
"Besides, we lost the scent hours ago. All that still reeks is what's in the past,
behind us," Mars reset his priorities. "The only way forward is via her bastions,
to go where it all began. That's where I'll find my answers." "What about,"
the twins look first to each other before returning their gaze, as one mentions,
"the helmet?" "Well, obviously we have to get it back," Mars coughed, about
to spill his drink, on hearing the question which raised so much doubt.

"We'll set a trap,"
Mars waved a hand, dismissing.
"Let him come to us." Fingers, as if circling a fly, went snap.
Mars made a show of how little be needed to recover the item gone missing.
If Pluto found out though, he'd be furious. Shy of that it should not hinder
the overall plan. All that was proceeding better than expected, swishing
right along. Man hardly had need of his favors, more than enough tinder
was there already, just waiting to burn, that his absence would go unnoticed.
A few days off either way wouldn't change a thing, tomorrow the cinder
of war would still be waiting to cover the world with ash and woe. Well noticed
were the tribes of man, they had their options, but didn't listen. It was easy,
it was so easy just to take, to expand, by way of violence, like a psychosis
these mortals just fell into place. Eventually, they'd all kill themselves crazy,
himself as their catalyst, Earth as his playground. Man being ignorant
and deserving of their fate, Mars had no sympathy for the feuding, lazy,
careless mortals, who for sake of pride and earthly greed were indifferent
to common sense and morality. For him, immortal, twas just entertainment.

Still, it was true
that from time to time Mars would make an exception,
and momentarily get on the wagon, when one through merit drew
his attention and famed benevolence. Now was making for such a perception,
as Mars sat before his fireplace, staring into the roaring flicker of flame...
he considered this young... champion. If it were true, his initial conception,
then there was only one place where he'd find the answer for which he came,
within the Hall of Records. Through the night they sailed, the Crescent Moon
trailing. "They're steady on course," Suleiman reported. "Let's do the same,"

Horacio relieved him on watch, taking himself the final stretch to be in tune
come morning, now not far away. Somewhere before the darkest hour,
in the quiet dead, they approached an outlying island, floating like some rune
on the ocean. The silhouette of land jutted out its head, with a peak for tower
overlooking the sea. "That be Mons Jovis, with her giant oak trees that feed
the furnace fires of the old Roman port on the main island, supplying power
to the great smelting pots that have armed empires going back to seed."
Suleiman, unable to sleep, returned to speak of ancient Etruscan deed.

"Along the far side,
lies Pianosa, isle of the living dead,"
he pointed out the geography. "Once a pirate stronghold, now a sour tide,
the island, a prison in recent years it has become. Strong walls, Aragon spread
to fortify her banks. Unable to remove the corsair threat, the Spaniards boxed
them in, sending those captured to die in dungeon torture chambers instead.
If taken, that is where our last days will be spent." Suleiman waxed
the truth. Pointing to the route, "We need to sneak past, to make our landing."
"What of that other way?" Horacio asked, seeing how the ship ahead foxed
in the other direction. "Oh, we don't want to go that way." Understanding
where that way led, directly to a guarded port, Suleiman advised caution.
"The trail of blood," a whisper caught the air, expanding.
The pair spun to see Ma'at behind them, approaching as her fashion,
silently until wanting others to be aware. "What did you say?"
Horacio asked for repetition, remembering long ago instruction.
"It is known as the trail of blood," Ma'at retold, clear as day.
"From the port to the prison," Suleiman spoke of the way.

"That is by how this passage is known,"
he clarified the situation, giving context to the legend,
looking out onto the inky black. "Over time the stories have grown,
as I'm sure you can imagine, yet truer than any word spoken'd
be the fate of the prisoners here. We'd be prudent to sail the long and winding."
Wise Horacio knew his second spoke, yet in his head Venus's words beckoned,
Follow the trail of blood for safe landing
the omens are there to betray.
Her words more clear than ever, and binding
his decision, he left caution to the wind. "Belay,"
he instructed, turning towards Suleiman. "Trust me on this,"
he urged confidence. "Stay tight on her heels. Follow them in all the way."
Bearing to port, they entered the lane, hearts a balled up fist.
If not for the protection offered by the helmet, the night watch
would already be raising the alarm, yet thanks to this magic, a mist
disguised their silhouette, as they drifted past the sentry tower. A swatch
of sail ahead guiding the path, at last they approached the long sought notch.

With just a sliver of moonlight,
a blackened wall of high sea cliffs,
loomed over their starboard side, at a height
which eclipsed the sky. At this hour, the nooks and shifts
of beveled coastline portrayed simply a multiple variance of shadow,
which could only be fully appreciated in daylight, when the creviced rifts
of this hidden treasure were on display. As it was, they followed the flow
with quiet breath, turning to approach the northern side of the island,
where ships of commerce and war alike converged to the light of a distant glow.
“Now is the moment of greatest danger,” Iseft at Horacio’s side did stand,
passing a word, as they came within sight of the harbor. “The Iron Port,
it is called, but also known by another, more ancient name,” she lifted a hand.
“We’re approaching Vulcan’s Gate, my lord,” a demon lookout gave his report.
“Very good,” Mars caught sight of the growing light. “Bring us in to dock,”
he gave his order, as the helmsman maneuvered with the shifting wind’s retort.
Aethalia, Mars thought. *How long it’d been since last placing foot on this rock?*
With hand to wood, he thought of her again, giving the railing a knock.

Unlike mortals,
the gods were endowed
with a special capacity to cross, as if through portals,
from one realm of reality, within the ethereal plane to another, renowned
in the common tongue as multi-dimensionality. In short, this gift enabled
the gods to move between worlds, to see what had once been before, rewound,
to traverse beyond the sphere of man to lands all but forgotten and fabled,
while to mortal man much of what there’s to see is simply hidden and invisible.
Was to this interwoven crossroad Mars sailed, where the woes of man be tabled.
Were not for Pluto’s helmet, affixed to mortal head, it would be impossible
to continue the telling, for here the Cyclopes’ gift bespoke an unknown secret.
In addition to its cloaking powers, a doorway once opened made possible
for the bearer to trespass. Never before had man bore such an object,
and no godly possessor, having the natural ability, would even take notice,
so for eons this furtive endowment remained a mystery in such respect.
Only now, as Mars opened the gateway, to step across the precipice
did the universe reveal itself to Horacio as a flowering lotus.

Through the golden fire’s glow,
radiating a light of bronze and copper
in a reflective shimmer off of massive armored doors, moving slow,
Vulcan’s Gate opened the way into the harbor, as the ivory arc, known proper
as Hannibal’s Thirst, cleared passage to the Iron Port. Here was shone
Roman fortifications, overlooking a wide sweeping bay, guarded by copper,
as sentries patrolled points of entry. Along the far side, natural boundary hone
mountains high and deep with ore of bronze and iron, thick with forest mantle,
they were secure both in wealth and body from that direction, There, sewn

into niches, smelting pots the size of houses, glowed as lanterns on the mantel.
There, directly from the mines, would Vulcan with his hammer craft
all sorts of armaments, which flowed to the port as a line on an ant hill.
The rut-ta-tut-tun-tut-tun of bass drum echoed fore and aft,
as shimmering double doors, reflecting a bronze and golden hued light,
swung wide to greet the sky, on massive iron hinges born from mountain shaft.
Stitched into the metal work, an alloyed mural scene of gods engaged in fight,
as a volcano erupted its bounty in the background, radiant and bright.

Through Vulcan's Gate,
the wealth of the island flowed,
loaded upon the rows of merchant vessels that sat in wait
in the harbor. Mars, not always the most welcome guest who showed,
was nevertheless still the best customer. Where profits were to be made,
always was there a taker waiting in the wings, old grudges stowed.
Besides, Vulcan, God of Fire, with hot breath and his bludgeoning spade,
along with all the other gods of old, was at the moment, soundly fast asleep.
What was it...? Over a thousand years now...? Mars thought on the jade.
Has it really been that long? It seems just like yesterday, his mind took a leap
nostalgic, appreciating the past. They had a few good tussles, Mars chuckled,
as Hannibal's Thirst, in charcoal gray and scarlet, engraved on her ivory keep,
rolled past the common tradesmen still asleep at this hour. Cuckold...
Vulcan would be giving him no trouble this time around
and his servants, after so much time were more than capable to mold
any item... *except those required by a god, of course,* memory rebound.
"Damn it!" he knew he forgot something. *Well, perhaps another round?*

Meanwhile, on the Crescent Moon,
they trailed along unnoticed, riding behind in the wake,
with growing anxiety. "This is quite unusual," Suleiman led the tune.
"Even after all these years, I tell you, this port is not of the same make
as what was here before. There's something very different about this place.
Something I cannot put my finger on that haunts me." "It's not a mistake,"
Isfet concurred to ease the strain, seeing how minds began to race.
"What you're seeing is the Iron Port in her glory days, in the Golden Age
of the immortals." "How is this possible?" Horacio tried to keep pace
with the fury-nymph. "I cannot say," she admitted at this stage,
"but, I'd wager it's not by accident. Consider yourselves blessed,
rarely do mortals get to feast their eyes on the astral plane and engage
with other dimensions." Now the Crescent Moon would face the test,
crossing into the unknown, they'd have to rely on training and instinct.
"All hands stay alert, we're going in," Horacio kept the crew abreast
as they penetrated the barrier, entering a land thought long extinct,
there on the brink of uncharted waters, the future was theirs to be inked.

From the parapet,
the capital city of the Iron Port
swept upwards, to crescendo at the peak with coronet,
with a panoramic view, was the mountainous castle and fort.
Opposite their position, overlooking the harbor fjords,
built upon a sprawling green hilltop, was a Roman manor resort.
This was where Venus played in her day, upon the pleasure gourds
of pasture and bath, with moss lined trails to a turquoise sea.
Here, from her terrace, with an eye that looked out towards
her husband, to the rich mountains she offered as gift to keep him busy,
she could in confidence invite suitors for entertainment and play.
"There, let's make our way," Horacio guided the helmsman to their quay,
being a secluded cove at the far bend of the harbor, where said palace lay,
hidden by niche and arbor. "This should offer us some good cover,"
Horacio prepared the crew, "so once ashore, the ship we won't betray."
He couldn't have known then, there was no way for him to discover,
that he stumbled on the same cove Mars had used, when he was Venus's lover.

BOOK XX

AETHALIA

The sky broke red,
a maroon as ever there was,
each morning at the same hour tread,
with plum embossing underneath and silver bed, twas
an ominous way to start the day in paradise, as the first light reflecting
off of the precious metal deposits lining the eastern shores would cause
a spectrum of orange-red and burgundy to light upon the clouds, flecking
the sky with passionate color. Slowly the morning broke, across tranquil
sandy beaches, up rocky, eucalyptus slopes, with wild flowers specking
the rolling, rugged mountainsides to peak a thousand meters high, a triangle
to the heavens. Thus Aethalia woke. "Prepare the landing party," Horacio called
his best men forward. Baloch and Etci, stood, swords ready to wrangle,
as did the powerful Butrus and the twins, Isa and Nebi, likewise installed.
Equally too, Suleiman would not be divided, by his captain's side was he fixed.
At his shoulder, Isfet didn't need to remind him of her words, as he recalled,
"*...to the very gates of hell,*" promise made, the soundtrack of his mind remixed.
Pausing, Horacio took notice of this moment, gratefully transfixed.

"Ali Abbas,"
he called forward the ship's surgeon and carpenter.
"You're in command now, until our return." Then, looking across
to the men, Horacio took his hand as a friend, and focusing back to center,
"Keep your eyes sharp. Take good care of her and the crew," they shook.
"Aye captain, she's in good hands," Ali Abbas reassured, as he enter
the longboat, ready to row for the waiting beach. With a final look
backward, the party shoved off, Butrus pulling hard on the oar.
Crossing the cove, they came ankle deep in short order, a calm hidden nook
to greet them, as they hauled their boat the remaining few feet ashore.
Taking their first steps onto dry land, two things then happened.
First, Horacio from their vision disappeared, vacant his image bore.
"Captain?" his most sturdy looked around, bewildered and flattened.
"Relax," Isfet reassured the men. "Go on, take off the helmet."
Reappearing a moment later on the beach, before them stood their captain.
"This is astounding!" Horacio held the headdress, to the touch a metal velvet,
as his expression, along with the Crescent Moon before his eyes, there melted.

"What? Where'd she go?"
Horacio pointed to the empty waters that
just a moment earlier held their berth and home.
"They slipped back to the mortal dimension," Ma'at,
from out of nowhere, appeared aside the bushes.
"When you stepped upon land," Isfet as diplomat,
added for clarification, "the connecting energy that rushes
between the helmet and your ship was severed."
"So where is she now?" Horacio hotly blushes.
"Right where you left her," with a hand Isfet gestured,
suggesting he take a step back into the water,
where returning his helmet to cover his head, there stirred,
as he to his crew vanished, the Crescent Moon, in the very same quarter
as before, reappeared in front of him. "How can this be?" returning
to his natural guise, Horacio there on the beach asked of Isfet, Titan daughter.
"It's very simple," she held a moment with his eyes, turning,
as response to his question burning.

"There are four main elements,
common across all dimensions, those being fire, water, earth and air
that work as conduits throughout the astral plane. With specific resonance,
they effect each other and the gods' powers all differently. This is the where
and how your ship went astray, caught up in the workings of the mysteries.
There's no telling what we might find on the path ahead, so use that with care,"
she cautioned. On the stair, they wound up a garden slope through the trees.
Built with local granite and colored marble, the frescoed lane ascended,
past fields of olive up to the *Villa delle Grotte,* home to Venus's vestries
on the isle, a residential palace for entertaining, befitting a goddess descended
from Mt. Olympus. Vacant, this columned mansion built on expansive terraces,
with multiple wings and levels, a pleasure resort complete with scented
pools and fountains sculpted in her image, with many walkways and passages,
which led to a spa below, equipped with both calidarium and frigidarium.
The goddess of love spent many a summer's night here counting the traces
of stardust that trailed through the heavens, lounging in passion's delirium.
From here is where our party looked out upon the morning's blue aquarium.

"A good omen,"
Isfet signaled the group's attention,
"that your instincts led us to the goddess's home and
here, a safe haven from where to start this journey." Pausing in suspension,
Horacio took in the sight before him. "Perhaps, here we may find some clue?"
he considered, for their way forward was still towards a blind destination.
"Is there a map room or office on the grounds, a place where she drew
together her secrets?" "If anywhere," Isfet searched her memory,
"it would be in her private wing, here on the north side." Looking at the crew,

"Alright, spread out," Horacio instructed, keeping brief the summary.
"Search each floor, but be careful not to disturb anything. There's no pillaging
today," he made clear the order, keeping in check the natural pirate trajectory.
For Horacio, this location was sacred even though abandoned and aging.
Aside from the usual furnishings, a set of chairs, the odd divan,
there was not much to announce the once glorious and opulent staging,
all that had vanished with the scroll of time, lost to the marching span.
Not until reaching bedchamber, did the eye find its helmsman.

There,
in the privates of Venus chamber,
beholding a sunlit panoramic beyond compare,
stood a viewing table, sunken as though a miniature Roman theatre,
a model of the island, fashioned from stone and moss and clay,
in the center of what would be the stage, resting there in slumber.
"Is this what we're looking for?" Nebi called, first to spot the display.
"Well done. It just might be," Horacio eyed the newfound discovery.
With a hand upon the smooth, cold, hard surface, it began to give way
to a more intimate, tingling sensation, as if a living stone machinery.
"What a strange marble this is," Horacio reported what felt like a pulse.
"Because it's not marble, dear captain, but baetylus," identifying the refinery,
Isfet introduced the sacred stone precious to the gods. "Feel it convulse
beneath your touch, how it reacts. It does so for it is imbued with life,
directly from the ether." Horacio drew his hand away almost by impulse.
"Oh, don't worry, it's quiet safe. In fact, if you clear your mind of all the strife,
focusing on your question to the stone, it will sharpen the answer as a knife."

Horacio considered the advice
Isfet offered on the workings of ancient ways,
and trusting in her council, cleared his mind, to be concise
about what he was searching. As if almost a whisper, a memory plays
from long ago echoing in his head, *Pluto's Shrine is what you seek.*
The words fill him, focusing his meditation, on course he stays,
as the energy between man and object intertwine, and solid begins to leak,
becoming malleable, almost liquid, the model before him shifts and changes
until an inlet peninsular centered upon the stage, jagged and stony bleak,
west of their position, on the far coastal side of forestal mountain ranges.
"Enfola," Horacio whispered, seeing how the cordlike rock formation,
protruding to the sea, opened upward like a naval for heavenly exchanges.
"Here, this is our path," he informed the crew with a brief summation.
"Prepare to move out." Then, pausing he touched the stone again. In retort,
the baetylus shifted once more, giving answer to the captain's inner question.
Thoughtfully Horacio considered, looking hard at the divining stone's report
and then stepping back, went out onto the balcony to gaze upon the Iron Port.

Across the harbor,
in a line five kilometers away,
carving terraced up the hillside, as a branching arbor,
the stronghold city of the Iron Port grew. There, along the winding pathway,
up the rising granite staircase, within the city center, a god in red cape strode.
Determination filled his gait, as long in step he climbed the central stairway.
Coming to an assembly ground that overlooked the lower levels, he slowed,
facing the tall double oak doors belonging to the Hall of Records. Circular
and domed, the building imposed official as the bureaucratic abode,
charged with the duty of maintaining the ancient minutes, in particular
those of the gods and their doings. Here is where Mars would find the answer
to the question that was burning in his own mind, racing perpendicular.
With a shove from his mighty arms the doors swung open from the center
on thick iron hinges that trailed a long squeal in their rotation.
Footsteps echoing throughout the great hall, Mars, as master,
entered and proceeding, made his way to the proper station,
where the papers of love and war were kept in circulation.

Here it was that he found
the documents for which he was searching,
those that told of the final chapter of Aeneas, the renowned
and glorious father of Rome, as told by his daughter, Concordia. Reaching
for a lantern he sat himself amongst the papyrus scrolls and reams of paper,
which filled the ancient library. Opening the pages they began their preaching.
“Having defeating his enemy, slaying Turnus with a thrust from his rapier,
the final drop of blood required was spilt, and Aeneas, victorious, was grateful.
War had not been of his choosing, but forced upon him. Now that such caper
be done and behind him, he looked to put his sword away. Having seen his full
of bloodshed, he longed to trade his weapon in for a humble plowshare.”
Mars read on his daughter’s account of how she had watched the fateful
events unfold from the slopes of Mt. Olympus, and finding brother Aeneas fair,
planted fertile soil from her womb as a blessing into his marriage chamber,
where on taking Lavinia, daughter of King Latinius, Condordia would share
in the sowing moment to place her gifts to use in fanning the ember
of their passion. Sealing the union, they fell to slumber.

There,
as the lovers dreamt,
she whispered in his ear, as if a breath of air
had crossed his brow on a lazy summer’s day to supplement
perfection. “Know of peace now dear brother, your victory has been won.
No longer have you need for these,” she spoke of his warrior’s armament.
“In exchange for this,” she lifted his sword, “I have given you a son,
one who will rule after you are gone, leading the way for an empire
and a thousand years of balance. The prophesy fulfilled, now come

and witness your Trojan legacy, reborn from the ashes of funeral pyre
to merge the powers of love and war, yours shall find a place among the stars."
Then with a kiss upon his brow, the Goddess of Harmony did retire,
retreating with sword to the heavens. Concordia, child of Venus and Mars,
kept her secret, hidden within the eternal folds of wake and dream,
having made fertile her sibling seed, tipping the scales to parallel bars,
she entered the bloodline of Rome. "All that was told is not as it would seem,"
Mars closed the journal, now considering the flow of history's stream.

Could it be
that Concordia,
daughter and Goddess of Harmony,
had secretly, mothered and placed her diem
upon the sons of Rome? That she had stowed away
a Vulcan sword, made for the King of Troy? Mars pondered the idea.
No coincidence that the sword now be held by one who with her eyes betray.
One or the other alone by chance he could bypass, but not both there together.
There was more than random act before him, what role did she have to play?
For if Concordia truly be the missing sword's protector, then only through her
could this ship's captain come into possession of such a deadly prize.
Ergo, it stands to reason that through him he may also be able to get to her.
But then, where to find him? the question posed itself to rise.
For now, gifted from both sides of the aisle, the child held advantage.
Then to his feet Mars took, gazing out to where the seagull cries,
beyond the window's arched veneer, pointing his eye towards the old hermitage
across the bay, where he and Venus once consorted, now the center stage.

"To the villa,"
Mars declared in whisper,
remembering the very night they'd conceived of Concordia.
Mars and Venus each placing the best of themselves into her,
as a symbol of the depth of their affection, an exemplary match
for such polar opposites, neither being as much without the other,
they poured all their strengths and passions into the union, until by latch
they made fertile an immortal daughter, who stood equally worthy of both.
This goddess, Concordia, the bringer of balance, it is said, could snatch
victory from the jaws of defeat, simply with the wink of an eye, so wroth
the poet long ago. At war, she played by strategy, staying three moves ahead,
being able to win through position and diplomacy, cutting off the battle oath,
much to her father's chagrin. "If she's involved..." Mars shook his head
with dread. By casting herself as mother, equal to Rome as Romulus,
Concordia left herself a card to play. To the fate of those tired and huddled
masses, she'd be the deciding factor, as the mortal tribes reached peak nexus.
"There's no way she was acting alone," Mars felt the touch of Venus.

Ahead by half a day,
Horacio and crew mounted the pass.
From the villa there were dozens of trails that led away,
weaving along coastline and hillside, hidden in shade by a mass
of rough foliage, there were any number of means to effect an escape.
The goddess designed her forest particularly this way, in order to mask
her extra-marital adventures. Though a simple cuckold, similar to a large ape,
Vulcan was also a jealous brute of a husband and would not trust his wife
a fraction of the distance he could throw her, if he could ever get the shape
of his hands on her that is, which was so infrequent that for a mere trife
of her erotic charms, the God of Forges could be sent off delirious.
She liked to play with him this way, though she preferred more the wildlife,
than to endure his touch, and so made these branching pathways insidious
to anyone unfamiliar with their destination and twisting labyrinth scrawl.
Venus would giggle gingerly at the reports of how this drove Vulcan furious,
of how unable to locate his mistress, he would stomp and curse and scowl.
Oh, to be gifted the instrument made when back to his forge he did crawl.

Twas into these woods
that Horacio and his party did enter,
scaling their way out of sight, the blanket of foliage lifting their moods.
Their trail, alternating between rock and earth, carved a creviced denture
over hills, all part of a web-like network of passages crisscrossing the island.
At places it curved outward, glimpsing through the tree line on coastal water,
sparkling turquoise and sunlight; at other spots their road turned inland,
cutting back in on itself, until surrounded only by the quiet voice of forest.
“How can we be sure this is the right way?” Isa asked, wanting to understand
his captain’s confidence. “The stone tablet,” Horacio replied, “it pointed west
and showed to me the trailhead. Since then the path has stayed consistent.
I have no reason to doubt it.” “Of course, if you desire, there is another test?”
Isfet looked to the brother, Nebi, who bore the truth telling talisman. Content
to offer assistance, Nebi, clasping his necklaced rock to divine the temperature
variant, asked of it the question. Meanwhile, on the banks of coastal indent,
a landing party crew led by Mars was drawing towards the sandy aperture
of Venus’s private beach. Flanking sides, Timor and Formido ground denture.

“A traitor,”
Formido slithered,
speaking of his sister, while Timor,
brushing back his loin’s mane, heartedly concurred.
“I’ve never trusted her.” “Quiet, the two of you,” Mars chastised
the pair seeking to sow discord. Already aware of where the lines blurred,
he didn’t need to be reminded. Although the three were equally sized,
born from the exact same parentage, the twins, as vital elements of the father,
always felt his heart cared less for them than for Concordia, who they despised,

precisely because she held leverage over him, as a reminder of their mother.
They stepped ashore, determined to put an end to her relentless scheming.
"Let's go!" Mars barked abrupt, taking the lead, as the twins eyed each other.
Then, "My lord, a longboat!" a puppet-demon servant's voice teeming,
on seeing the beached craft among the brushes. A footed trail in the sand
led in their same direction, towards the villa, no longer farfetched dreaming.
"We found them," Formido declared, both brothers preparing to make a stand.
"Well done," Mars flanked over his shoulder. "Be ready on my command."

Entering the grounds,
Mars took in a healthy breath of air,
savoring the memory of flavor as he made the rounds,
knowing instinctively where to search for an answer from Venus fair.
Before the now twice visited bedchamber, Mars allowed himself a moment
to stand before her softly veiled mattress, a bed of clamshell and silk where
they would consummate their passions, hid far away from quotidian torment
of divinity. Laughing, remembering the past, "Did I ever tell you the time...?"
"Yes," the brothers trailed grim, remembering quiet clearly the testament
of how they came into being. Twas on this very sofa they committed the crime
of giving life to the pair of dark demons. It was not with intent, as was the union
between them which brought their sister to life, but of creating a being prime,
even greater, one to rival the almighty Jupiter, one who could be the fusion
of all the godly traits. Yet, as many a plan 'fore and hence, this one went astray.
Now the god Vulcan, we find it bears repeating to avoid any confusion,
was very jealous of his bride, and though not the brightest lamp out on display
he couldn't help but notice she'd given birth, yet they hadn't got past foreplay.

So at his forge,
he plied his retribution.
With ores from mountain mineshaft would he disgorge
to shape into an impenetrable net, for which he'd stake his reputation,
that not even a god could unwrap, and there about he set his trap,
placing the locks, so fine as to be unseen, on Venus's bedposts for repudiation.
And then, "Farewell, my love. I'm off to Lemnos," Vulcan playing the sap,
blew a kiss to his wifely maiden, making sure she watched his ship depart.
As it set sail upon the bay, Venus overjoyed at her deception let herself wrap
into Mars's arms, intertwined in the lover's embrace, and there, as they start
in play, fell upon her shell framed bed and caught up in the bronze webbing,
found themselves ensnared, unable to move beneath the weight of Vulcan's art.
"What devil of trick is this?" Mars scowled, from beneath the tangled bedding,
unable to move a limb. "Ha! Caught you!" on them Vulcan sprung
from behind the curtain. Boiling mad, "You and your faithless fibbing,"
he chastised Venus mercilessly. Filling her with fear and dread, he wrung
his hands, contemplating his next move at the top of a lung.

There it was
her egg was split,
forming twin demons, with fangs and claws,
in her abdomen, and though she'd love them, as was her writ,
they would always belong to the father. Vulcan, seeking compensation,
then called Jupiter and all the gods of Olympus to come down and visit,
to witness firsthand the betrayal. While laughing at the dispensation,
Apollo, Mercury and Neptune, enjoyed a bit of jest, "I wouldn't mind
to go second," Mercury joyfully teased, seeing the goddess's situation.
Jupiter, acknowledging Venus's infidelity and affectionate frailty, in kind
agrees to Vulcan's demand that his dowry be reinstated, thus Neptune pledged
support, as a second on Mars's behalf, if Vulcan would allow the net to unwind.
Freed, Venus fled out of embarrassment, while Mars, backed up and wedged
into a corner, made Vulcan a promise, "This is not the last you'll hear of this."
Storming out, Mars left the other gods to snicker, as to Thrace he hedged
his retreat. Hence, through not so much the blessings of marital bliss,
Timor and Formido auspiciously came to be. They sighed with a hiss.

Turning away
from conceptual thoughts,
Mars looked now upon the chamber, eyes coming finally
to rest upon that which had first brought him to these spots,
the Divining Stones of the gods. "Now we'll know the truth,"
Mars stepped across to the telling rocks to draw the lots,
and there unlock the riddle. From his place at the viewing booth,
he cleared his head to focus on the question, and when prepared
placed his hands upon the still ledge. Detecting as would a sleuth,
the energy within the baetylus took hold of the question he shared,
and for the God of War presented him with merely half the answer.
"Now, why would he be heading towards the caverns?" Mars stared
upon the hillsides halfway across the island. Shaking his head, he'd swear
that he was on to something, but exactly what he still couldn't place a finger.
The Divining Stones, as their nature, telling of where, but never the why, wear
only cold indifference. For the rest, Mars would have to catch this elusive figure,
now with a hefty head start. "Make haste!" he called. "We cannot linger."

BOOK XXI

GARGOYLE PASS

Venus
had many ways
of eluding her husband, thus
knowing how his sense of scent plays
heavily into her affairs, she employed nature's device
of spreading jasmine throughout her pleasure garden, which stays
her trail invisible to Vulcan's insidious sniffing, while she enjoyed her vice.
This here was the reason and cause of the delay, as the pair of grimly brothers
stood confused before the labyrinth of passageways. It would be rolling dice
to choose an entrance. "What's the hold up?" Mars upon them hovers.
"I can smell neither fear nor haste," Formido growls in frustration.
"We can't smell anything beyond these creeping weeds of mother's,"
Timor tried to clear his sinus of the fragrant shrub's menstruation,
to no avail. "Move aside," Mars brushed away the pair with his hand,
seeing that the circumstance would require his personal mediation.
Dropping to all fours, he closed his eyes and slowed his breath and
put his ear to the earth, allowing the way before him to expand.

"That way,"
Mars pointed to the right.
"I can feel the vibration of them running away.
Be quick, they've got a good head start to their flight."
His demon soldiers at double pace in earnest began the chase,
as their quarry entered upon the picture of an entirely different sight.
Coming to a break in the tree line, Horacio's crew looked upon the face
of the mountain. Bare and rocky, the pass curved up and around,
over nooks and crannies, following the seam of hill-scaped ranges that trace
the interior's breadth. With sun riding high on their backs, they wound
along the path, taking note of the strange formations that lined their trail.
"Look at this one," Butrus pointed to one stone growing out of the ground,
in the size and shape of a bear. "And this one," Nebi spoke, touching the tail
of a rock that looked like a giant footed serpent. "These are the Gargoyles
of Aethalia," Isfet took on the roll of narrator, as she began telling the tale
of how these creatures came to be. "Long ago, as today," the story she unfoils,
"Earth was unruly and full of danger, ripe were evil's spoils."

"But love
works in mysterious ways," Ma'at there interjected.
"Yes," her sister nodded in agreement. "Here it was that Venus from above
came to take her bath and in these very waters where Fate selected
that her necklace, made of seven of the finest pearls, would fall and scatter,
creating these seven isles. The most magnificent of course," she reflected,
"the centerpiece, becoming the Island of Venus, Aethalia, and for that matter,
as the plants and earth and rocks took shape, there were also many spirits
caught up within the transformation, and having been stirred into the batter
took form from the fertile soil of granite. Sitting here on the peaks as rivets,
they stand in guard against those who would bring harm to love."
"Ohhh... but that's not all," Ma'at with her bent back pivots.
"What is it?" Horacio pressed Isfet, who pausing was in need of a shove.
"Not all of the spirits," Isfet thought on the proper word to use, "are benevolent.
Several of the creatures are possessed with angry spirits not from above,
but by souls of trolls frozen in stone by the power of Venus, lying dormant
until such time as they can break free from their mineral interment."

"Press on, captain.
We should not linger,"
urged the voice of Suleiman,
uncomfortable with such strange terrain. Then, pointing a finger,
"We're being watched," Isa gasped on seeing what appeared a knight in armor,
mounted upon a steed. "See how that rider stalks our movement, with a stinger
held aloft." Isfet took half a step back. "No, that is not a man, but a Centaur.
Nonnus, is this one's name, one of Jupiter's creatures," carefully inspecting
the formation of rock, Isfet concluded. "You can tell by his horns this charmer,
easily mistaken as helmet. So this became his fate," she spoke aloud, reflecting
on his sudden appearance. "Well, that makes sense," she then surmised.
"It's well known that Jove lusted for the goddess Venus, and I'm suspecting
that Nonnus, born from Jupiter's spilt seed, was sent, becoming compromised
in the chase, and was hardened along with all the rest on the isle's formation.
Most worrisome is that dart he carries," Isfet was visibly surprised.
"Obviously a gift from his father, as a tool and means to outstation
the goddess and retrieve her for his own illicit elation."

Erect,
he stood before their party,
menacing, with his thunderbolt spear aimed direct
at their captain. "Let's move," Horacio motioned, "I care not to parry,"
uncomfortable with the frozen gesture. And then, as they continue along
the mountain, something changed in the stone idol that Isa carry,
turning to a crimson red. Behind their trail, a loosening of gravel song
crumbled in the ear. They swung around to see the monument had turned
and now, betraying an inner glow, the spear held high pointed long.

“Captain, look at how it follows your movement,” Butrus burned.
“It’s true, the statue does follow you,” Suleiman double downed,
stepping between him and the gargoyle. “He senses her,” Isfet churned.
“She lives in you, she does,” Ma’at’s trailing voice wound.
“Who?” Horacio shifted, taken off balance by the latest remarks.
“Venus, of course,” Isfet interjected. “Nonnus to her is still bound.”
“That doesn’t sound very good,” Nebi clenched tight to the barks
of knife handles. “It’s not,” Isfet concurred, as to the circling of sharks.

From within the spear,
the power of Jupiter intensified,
growing stronger, as a surging hum most clear,
gathering its energy. A tremble quaked, as crumbling rock fied
upon the mountain. “They’re coming alive,” Nebi sounded the alarm,
as around them all manner of stone creature with motions amplified
turned in their direction. “Move! Quickly!” Horacio, seeing the perilous harm
approach, commanded his crew to double their pace, lest they be squashed
in avalanche. Sprinting, the group fled the rumble that confused their calm,
as falling rock chased close behind them. Just then forward motion quashed,
as a bull made of granite came charging. “We’re trapped front and back,”
Etci drew his weapon, holding a guarded position, as gargoyles sloshed
towards them. “No, this is no place for blades,” Butrus pulled up the slack.
“Don’t you know that stones beat swords? You have to hit them with skin.”
And with that the strong man brushed the jouster aside, going on the attack.
Thrusting himself forward, Butrus rushed towards the mighty bull in tailspin,
his broad chest lifted high as though born of Herculean kin.

Slapping hard,
Butrus and the bull smashed together,
as two unstoppable objects collided in the forward.
Swept off his feet, striking the flat mantle of the bull’s forehead, in a lather,
Butrus stretched wide his powerful arms, and grabbing hold the giant horns,
he twisted, using momentum’s torque, to wrench the beast’s head, as a tether,
down towards the dust of Earth. “Hurry!” suppressing thrashing scorns,
Butrus called out. “I don’t know how long I can stave off this monster.”
The two wrestled in the dirt, as Horacio and crew scuttled past longhorns
and other roadway obstacles to regain an open path. As a boxer,
Butrus planted his fist down hard onto the creature’s temple.
Staggering, the bull shook, and in a daze rolling over in a sideways stir,
tumbled down the hillside. Throwing himself off with time barely ample,
Butrus scampered in the dirt and gravel to maintain his sure footing.
Brushing himself off, coughing, he lifted his fists to the air, as an example
to other daring opponents. “Yes!” he chuckled. “Well done!” the crew rooting,
they cheered him on for his gallant act of bull off putting.

But no delay
could they offer in celebration,
for from behind the gargoyles continued to advance to the crew's dismay.
"Press on! We have no time to waste," Horacio urged them from stagnation.
Ahead, perhaps five hundred meters, the path once again entered the tree line,
if only to make it that far they might be saved. Yet, to their frustration,
too fast the boulders came, closing the distance between the timberline
of safety and certain death. There emerged Nonnus, galloping in the lead,
stone hooves smacking rock and earth so hard that sparks did shine
in his passing. Lifting his spear on high, he aimed and threw to impede
their progress, casting a blast of thunder, which fell directly before them.
Halting fast, the party turned to face the oncoming stampede.
"Go captain. you and the rest make safe," Suleiman would not condemn
them all, but meant to defend the position to buy the others some time.
"Yes, you go," Butrus gave a second, lining up together the strongest men.
"No," Horacio wouldn't have it. "I commend your valorous chime,
but regardless the outcome we stand or fall together in this climb,"

There they stood,
defiant, with doom approaching.
Trailed by a cloud of dust and soot
in its wake, the gargoyles came encroaching
upon their position. "Steady," Horacio tensed for battle.
"Keep tight the ranks," he cautioned, knowing how easy the poaching
be for those who drifted away from the center mass. Nerves a rattle,
they prepared for the worst. Just then, at the edge of striking blows,
a she-wolf, twice the size in stone, drove between opposing forces a cattle
of fleshy baying mountain goats, tripping up in barricade the advancing throes.
Snarling with sharp teeth exposed, the she-wolf growled and threatened,
eyeing hard the Centaur, Nonnus, daring him with a nostril flaring nose,
the great monster held her ground. Seeing this the gargoyles hardened,
and Noonus, with riling agitation likewise he grew cold, turning rigid
once again he held his pose immobile. The sudden turnabout heartened
Horacio and crew, still they weren't into the woods yet, and before them fidget
a new possible danger. Holding their positions, the crew remained frigid.

Then,
just as unexpectedly,
the she-wolf turned her head again,
and regarding the entire crew collectedly,
found Horacio's eye. Softening, she eased her stance,
and as though in recognition of a mother to child, affectedly
purred a throaty thrum. Taking a careful forward prance,
the she-wolf moved in closer. "Easy, no sudden movements,"
Horacio cautioned, as he lifted a palm upward, slowly as in a trance,

showing the beast they meant no harm, and offering easing comments,
"It's alright, we won't hurt you," he gently lured the great creature.
"Sir?" Suleiman warningly whispered, wary of such amusements.
"No, it's OK," Isfet reassured, noting the steady black feature
to the rock Isa carry around his neck, signaling that all was clear.
Another step forward the great beast took sniffing out its treasure
and settling there before their captain drew near
placing her muzzle beside his ear.

Soft as feathered cement,
the fur ran a grainy fluid bristle beneath Horacio's hand
as he petted the monster. Into his hold her head she bent,
and then with a step backwards in regard, her snout she fanned,
pointing him towards the forest. "Captain?" Baloch questioned, urging.
"Yes, yes, we go," Horacio responded, the spell was broken, retreated the band.
Into the woods their path continued, as over his shoulder, attention diverging,
Horacio took a final glance at the she-wolf who presently guarded their back,
while around her a goat herd foraged and bayed, absent-mindedly converging.
Under cover, easing their pace, for the next few hours they continued on track,
marching attentively into the growing twilight, desiring to put as much space
as they could between themselves and the center of the recent attack.
It was just shy of midnight before they finally chose a resting place,
a nook in the trail that bent around a curve, exposing the shoreline.
"Tomorrow is the black moon," Horacio to Isfet the horizon did he trace,
pointing to the sliver of crescent above. "We must find Pluto's Shrine
by then." Having come so far, he now felt the pressing deadline.

"All that must happen will be,"
Isfet consoled the heaviness of his heart.
"Inshallah," Horacio repeated the refrain he oft heard at sea,
If God wills it, the meaning. For here, both is the end and the start,
the balance between chance and destiny, having the will to make it happen.
For a non-believer such as himself, following the call of a different mystic art,
Horacio understood the phrase with his own interpretation to pen,
being that the deities are there to guide, but you must have the will to act.
"The solution you seek," Isfet guided him to envision, "is to open
your inner eye. It has all been foreseen, in the dream of your mind into fact.
From everything that has already come, to the future path you will follow,
you have visualized these moments, which means there is a pact,
an understanding between your soul and the powers of the universe that allow
for the outcome you desire. By imagining, you bring your dreams into being."
Horacio contemplated her words, which fell not upon an ear hollow.
Already surviving thus far was proof that with belief and opportunity, seeing
victory was just a step in the natural progression of the spirit's own freeing.

"Yes, it is possible,"
Horacio with her agreed,
recalling the visions of the Cumaean Sibyl.
In his head, he saw an image of the path and deed
yet to come, and knew in his heart he was where he was needed. Patience
was now his best ally and friend. While he still drew breath, he'd never cede
in his quest, so always hope remained. In the same hour of this cadence,
as the crew settled in for a few moments of rest, back on the hillside,
where they had struggled to pass, Mars and his demons were pacing, hence...
"All over there's signs of disturbance," Timor glanced about from side to side.
"It's clear by this way they came," Formido for his part did mention.
Together they cleared the path, as the lesser henchmen in their wake did ride.
Striding down the center, with height and bulky force, came the ascension
of the God of War. He regarded the scene like a hunter, piecing together
the clues left behind. "Well, if it isn't Jupiter's tool?" caught was his attention
by Nonnus in passing. "You've seen better days," he jested to the ether,
when there he found his prize, guarding the passage to heather.

BOOK XXII

LILITH RISING

Meanwhile,
on an entirely different plane,
Pluto was busy plotting to beguile
yet another wayward soul into his misadventure. Here he came,
to the bowels of Babylon, standing before a dark castle overgrown with thorns.
Jackals scoured the haunches, while haunting at the edge of the dismal frame,
ostriches ducked and buried their heads in the sand. Howling wind scorns
the battlements, thick with thistles and briers. Satyrs can be heard whispering
to one another in the shadows, as wildcat beasts stalk the night. An owl adorns
the great mantle, quietly watching, guarding her eggs. With torches flickering
shadow and light off her unblinking eyes, she tucks into the secure obscurity
of her perching lair on high. Out of respect, the jackal started snickering.
Here it was that Pluto, the Lord of the Underworld, would set to test the purity
of faith, for here, in the dark and deserted recesses, is where he would find her.
Outcast and forgotten, temptress of the night, seductress of all impurity,
here was where Lilith, the first woman of Earth, did now reside. Too sure
a female for mortal men, she became a spirit of the night, a sultry whisper.

"What do you want?"
she brushed her head to the side,
staging the victim, using scoff as her taunt.
"It's been too long," Pluto appeasing took a forward stride.
"You can say that again," Lilith turned to face out the window,
as a grey fog rolled across the plain. "Come now, there's no need to hide
away like this in here," Pluto turned on his charm, eyes a wooing doe.
"You have always been like a daughter to me. There are always options
available for someone like yourself. I could be of help to you, you know."
"I don't need your kind of help," Lilith half spun to fling her opinions
over a shoulder blade, her raven black hair bounced a tangled mess.
"It doesn't have to be like this, we both want the same thing," Pluto cautions.
"And what's that?" Never one to mask emotions, her voice rang with distress.
Coming up close behind, as in the days of old, Pluto coiled an embrace
around her, and in her ear, with fork tongued eloquence, whispered, "Justice."
"Ha!" she scoffed. "For whom?" From his hold she began to unlace.
"This isn't my first rodeo with you," Lilith held her place.

"For us,"
Pluto wound back round her ear.
"For both of us. Come, there's much for us to discuss,"
he wouldn't take "No" for an answer, and with his arm let steer
her towards the terrace. "No one knows better than I how unfairly
you've been treated. I've never lied to you, there's never been a need, my dear,
you know as much. We've always seen eye to eye on such and are squarely
in agreement that you deserve your freedom. Why should you be punished,
ridiculed and scorned, traded away at auction for the price of a rib? So rarely
has Earth seen such high quality, to be cast aside and rudely banished,
simply because others don't have your courage to live? It's an outrage!"
the Lord of the Underworld declared. "So what would you suggest?" famished,
she stared back at him. "A second chance," Pluto tempted at this stage.
"How would you like to go back?" He plied his craft as only he could,
tempting Lilith with her hidden desire, to be reborn, released from her cage.
"In exchange for...?" she smiled knowingly, the contract understood,
as Pluto released a bellowing laugh, there, from where he stood.

"Oh, my child,
this here is a special contract,"
Pluto drew in close to her and smiled.
"You see, I believe in true equality and to be exact,
the gentler, wilder nature of the feminine, of which you represent...
being women, have for too long been given a subservient role in fact
and are in desperate need for... liberation. Now, if you would be so content
as to unleash your lust and fury, the likes of which hell hast never seen,
onto the realm of earthly man, I might be of such a mood of mind at present
to waive all remuneration. A truly free spirit," Pluto had Lilith caught between
caution and elation. Generous this was, maybe a little bit too generous.
A first, never had such an offer been made, it was unheard of, and unseen.
"No," Lilith looked sharp, taking Pluto aback. "You're a notorious
negotiator, my love and give nothing for free. Tell me where lies the hitch,
or it's no deal." Pluto grimaced at her spunk. Had he at all been curious
as to her ability to fulfill the mission, his doubts were now put to rest, to which
he decided to level with her as to the details of the switch.

"Yes!"
Pluto was elated.
"That's exactly what I want to stress...
self-determination. That's what the world of mortals sedated
has lost... its purpose. It needs to expand or it will die from stagnation.
Men have brought this world as far as they're going to take it. It is fated
that women will have to take the reins and you have that determination
to make it happen. You will inspire women to break the boundaries
established by men and propel the entire species to a higher vibration."

With sugar he wrapped the gift, presented as evolution. Still quandaries
remained for Lilith, as she thought on this proposed battle between the sexes.
"Free rein you say? And what do you get out of this?" inspecting the foundries,
she extracted Pluto's confession. "The fulfillment of a shared vision," he flexes
an eyebrow bent at her. "For this world to reach its highest potential.
Think of me as a benefactor, the first true... feminist, succumb to the reflexes
of nature itself. What I wish is to release Earth from being so deferential,
to give it a purpose, and with that freedom, to be something more substantial."

"You need my help,"
Lilith laughed, coming wise to his ploy.
"You have some illicit scheme growing like kelp
in your head, and you need me, don't you?" Pluto did enjoy
how her mind worked, she was a near equal in cunning he thought.
"Let's just say, there presents an opportunity for mutual advantage." Toy
as he may with the verbiage, Lilith saw the point, and neither sold nor bought,
she found that she had to agree, what Pluto offered was a deal far better
than her present circumstance, and already in his net, being caught,
it might be nice to get out and stretch her legs once again. Wetter,
her lips moistened at the idea of leading a cult. Finally, she turned
with a, "Done." Hands clasped, twinkle in the eye, a real go getter,
she was ready on the spot, having made the commitment, now she burned
to get started. "So, I assume you have a recommendation for where to begin?"
She shared a smile with her partner in crime. Alright, it's time she learned,
Pluto leaned in, "Well, now that you mention it..." he eyed his win,
while across his face there stretched a broad and telling grin.

"There's a child,"
Pluto began, "of the female sort,
which I think you'll find, though mild
in appearance, would make for an excellent cohort,
one who's in a position to gain great power, who could use... a mentor,
someone like yourself, who could help guide her ambition in the royal court,
to become the greatest mortal of influence, placing a woman at the center
of power on Earth." She liked the plan, it was simple and direct,
to take control from the very top. It was time for her to once again enter
the realm of man, only it wouldn't play out the same way it had in retrospect,
for this time around she would come to Earth unbound from the tether,
unconstrained from a master, it would be up to her to decide and select
the limits of her behavior, she'd release as a storm they'd have to weather.
"Tell me more," she pressed the dealer, wanting details on the plan.
"The grift, my dear, is called the long game, the cause and effect as to whether
such and such an outcome will manifest. Planting seeds across the span,
over time some take root and like weeds across a field they pan."

Then, with a finger raised,
"This particular lie took hold,"
Pluto almost snickering. "God be praised!
Religion! It was a hit, a huge success, a move strikingly bold.
Who knew? Who knew, these mortals would be so desperate to hear a story
that defined their own morality that they'd be willing to kill for it to be told?"
Pluto laughed outright. "The fools!" and catching his breath with an allegory,
"But what am I to do, the crop's sitting in the field, it's time for reaping?"
"And so I'm to play your reaper?" Lilith unsure if she liked the category.
"Oh, no my dear," Pluto quickly reassured, "Something quite more in keeping
with your truer nature. Think of yourself in the terms of... *a power broker*."
Oh, she liked the sound of that. It had a nice ring to it. Committed, leaping
forward on the idea, "So, tell me, this mark, who is she?" With a face for poker,
Pluto let out a sigh, regarding his new ally and friend in the business.
"An orphan of sorts," Pluto began. "Oh, they're the best to stoker,"
Lilith affirmed jumping in. "Indeed," Pluto agreed as one oft to witness.
"And this one deeply religious, who's in line to become a queen and empress."

"Oh my!
Sounds ripe for the taking."
Lilith toyed with the wherefores, the how and why,
extrapolating the motives and reasons that were baking
in Pluto's mind. "With the proper guide," he solemnly corrected.
"The western world is crumbling. Old alliances are steadily breaking.
The king, her half-brother in fact, is failing and already suspected
of gross incompetence, who simply bolsters himself with cheap rhetoric,
yet the finances don't lie, he will have a decade at most before being rejected,
and that's where Isabella will have the advantage. Although second by cleric
to the throne, behind her younger brother, I'm wagering she's got something
more to barter." "What's that?" Lilith was impatient. Brushing back a cowlick,
Pluto looked at her knowingly. "Oh... ha, yes," her laugh was a raunchy thing.
"Yes, my dear, her womanly ways. Already there is talk of a betrothal.
Princes and kings, from Portugal, Spain and Aragon, look to a wedding ring
and vows that will unite their forces, to bring the people wherewithal
together under a single crown and banner. This is what they wish to install."

"And you're going to help them?"
Lilith could not but ask the eternal question, "Why?"
She could of course see the allure of shaping the game, but then...
to what end? What did Pluto have to gain in helping man ally?
And under the hand of a woman no less? It was more than sport
that motivated this god of the dead, something which works to defy
her sense and reason... and still, the deal struck, she'd live in comfort,
so what did it matter the cause? Perhaps it would be nice for a woman
to lead a war for once? After all, who knows, maybe that's just the sort

of thing humans need? In any case, she'll have plenty of time to plan
out strategies later, right now she just wanted to stretch her wings.
"To Earth then," Lilith nodded. "Yes, I'll see you in Catalan,"
he watched as she opened herself to the night, and giving her his blessings,
Pluto slapped Lilith on the back. As sudden as a gasp and grasp for air,
he pitched her off into the inky black night, beyond her balcony railings,
into the enveloping mist below. Cast out of the underworld, Lilith spare
not a moment in rejoining her spirit to the realm which the mortals share.

Breathing, life
filled her lungs once more,
sweet as the dew of early morning, strife
forgotten in that second of oneness with the core,
and then as though floating, Lilith realized that she was free,
more than that and at the same time less, formless the shape she bore,
yet a living consciousness nonetheless, she shifted between solid body
and ethereal mass, connected at once to the overlapping intersections
of a multidimensional universe. Concentrate, she tried to focus directly
on a single form to take, overwhelmed by the infinite cross-sections
now at her disposal, a spirit, not holy... a not holy spirit, able to now inhabit
any form she so desired. "Oh, this is going to be fun!" Casting introspections
aside, Lilith swooned in all the possibilities, released from the mournful habit
of a dower and resigned existence, she could now aspire to a greater influence
over heaven and earth. How she itched to run through the fields like a rabbit,
given way to primordial instinct, yet for the moment she'd tame such effluence.
A bargain was struck, so now was the time for her to share her affluence.

Setting her sights
on the municipality of Arévalo,
and the impoverished agricultural sites
of Castilian rule, Lilith hovered like a ghostly halo
over a dull and barren castle. Here, in the confines, lurked
her first pupil, one of many to come, who would redefine the feminine credo.
Duende would she become, a heightened state of emotion, a spirit twerked
with mischief, consumed by passion, she would run the house.
Coming at night, and in the crevices of sleep filled moments, Lilith worked
her magic, whispering notions in secret, so quiet that even a mouse
would not notice her passing, and began to raise questions in the head,
of just what a woman's place was in this world, thus she made to rouse
a young girl's spirit with ambition to grow greater than a mere figurehead.
With clockwork set into motion, cogged wheels turning to the advancement
of time and the struggle for power to coalesce and coincide with a dread
hitherto undreamt of, the weaker sex would rise from defined placement
and reshape the world. And so Isabella, knelt to receive the sacrament.

Satisfied
with his handiwork,
Pluto, long in his stride,
pressed hands together and gave a knowing smirk.
"Now that's done," he congratulated himself on a job accomplished.
Making his way back through the stone corridors of timeless mason's work,
moist with night's sweating humidity, there was only one final thing he wished,
as he mounted his midnight black carriage. "Home," he called to the quartet
of horses, who neighed and scratched at the dirt, frightening an astonished
ostrich that ran in the opposite direction. Pluto, here at the rolling onset
of his ultimate victory, leaned back into the seating of plush velvet black.
"Nothing can stop me now," he waxed in confidence, considering if a tête-à-tête
was even necessary at this point. Mars, he knew, was more than capable to act
in matters of engagement. With this final piece in play, more was superfluous.
Perhaps, at last, he could take a day off, before launching the final attack?
Drifting in thought, Pluto, carried off, left the scene feeling magnanimous,
as hungry jackals lurking in the distance howled a cackling ominous.

BOOK XXIII

THE FINDING OF PLUTO'S SHRINE

Mars took a step forward,
"Ah, how I've missed you, my sweet Capitolina,"
he called the she-wolf creature by name. Coming toward
her with a free hand extended, he stepped into her arena.
With a look of recognition, the she-wolf bowed and nuzzled,
with a friendly growl, she welcomed her master, yielding to subpoena.
"I see you've been busy?" he looked around in a questioning manner, puzzled
by the surroundings. "What've you been up to?" Scratching the back of her ear,
Mars released the spell that bound her to stone, from which she bristled,
shaking a hairy black and brown mane of fur, and in tones only he could seer,
told the story of the visitors' crossing. "Is that so?" the God of War grooved,
listening to her lowered howling tones. "And you can lead me to them, I hear?"
to which the she-wolf nodded. "Oh, well done! I'll drink to that," Mars approved.
"Lead on!" he gave his children's nursing maid as much length as required,
trusting none more than this one faithful companion of old. It behooved
him to cut short the reunion, but matters pressing, to the trail they retired,
and in the dark of midnight forest, by scent and foot, the chase transpired.

Unaware
of the pursuit,
hot on their tail, Horacio and crew dare
to rest until daybreak, a red as ever to boot.
Yet, with grace's fortune, a night's crawl through the forest
is slow at best. At pace, they remained ahead a good three hours in their suit.
The crew, refreshed twice over, for having a few hours of rest,
stretched their legs on the inclining slope of an overgrown wilder trail
which wrapped along a tree line of eucalyptus, overlooking a crest
of cliff to eye-fall a watery shoreline a thousand meters below. Hail,
their souls gave praise for being witness to this brief moment of serenity.
Inhere lie the true magic of the island of Venus, for never would she fail
in the moment needed, to give cause for pause to admire her beauty.
Offerings equal in pleasure and danger; soft, seductive and vengeful
at once, as is the true nature of love's cradle, Aethalia, in all her vitality,
was the very embodiment of the goddess, Venus's idiom. Plentiful
in strength and frailty alike, yet everywhere it was beautiful.

Snaking,
the wooded trail U'ed,
turning back upon itself, forsaking
a direct line. slowing their pace, until becoming glued
once again they wandered the interior. "The path has not changed, yet,"
Baloch could not help but notice, "each step we take seems to be skewed?"
"As if we're being led in a circle." Etci felt as though swirled round a faucet.
"Well," Nebi chimed, plucking a wild berry, "at least she's bountiful."
"Yes," Isa pausingly agreed, then, "Captain..." he said, mouth an apricot wet,
the half eaten fruit in his hand, feeling himself uncertain as to how grateful
they should be at the moment, for his stone showed neither black nor red.
"I see it," Horacio called from the head of the line, as a mountain full
of vines intersected their path, cutting off forward progress, instead
it worked to funnel them down the slopes of a deep ravine and gorge.
"I don't like the looks of this," Suleiman said, sweat rolling off his head.
And Butrus, "Something feels funny," staggering, though as if on a forge,
when Ma'at trailed in, "Ah...! I see all have had a chance to gorge?"

"Oh, no!"
Isfet, lifted from a trance
of her own, having likewise been effected, did show
some understanding of their situation and current circumstance.
"Elderberries," she looked at her hand. "We have fallen victim to a spell,"
she cautioned the others, "one of powerful intoxication. There's a chance
that we've strayed past safe boundaries?" Her chaotic spirit she fought to quell,
as the elixir worked to rile up her own emotional state and equilibrium.
As a seductress, with countless charms, Venus found fragrance easy to propel,
as an aperitif in which to lure her prey and lovers. In her arboretum,
there grew many variety of flowering plant, each with special characteristics.
The wild chamomile she grew, for instance, the very same one in spectrum
of flower that lined their current path, widely known for its psycholinguistics,
for its drowsing, hallucinogenic effects, was one of Venus's favorite,
making suitors pliable to her whims and penchant for cunning linguistics.
The very smell of the flower, light and barely distinguishable, in its own right
could have a dozing effect, while sipping as tea, made one hers for the night.

And here,
they were surrounded by it.
Now to Isfet, the situation became clear.
The flower had lulled their senses, while on the fruit they bit,
drunken they'd become. To Horacio she looked, "We're in great danger.
Our senses, no longer can we trust." Swooning, she pointed out the culprit,
"Our very minds have become compromised on this tonic," she said. Stranger
things have come before to challenge, yet always their wits they could rely on
to see them through. Now they were on uncharted territory. A ranger

would be most welcome at that moment, as the trail presented gone
now leads them only in a downward spiral, straight into a dark abyss.
Summoning his focus, Horacio looked back to see the road they'd come on
was laced with pointed shoots and razor sharp thorns, making it remiss
for him to consider a backwards voyage. How oddly the path meant to lead
them in a singular direction, inhibiting their return. He could not dismiss
the warning signs all around him. But if fallen into a trap, which indeed
it would seem for certain, how could he be sure of his next move and deed?

"Nebi!"
he called at last,
bringing forth an impartial referee.
"Aye captain," the twin replied double fast.
"You can siphon false from fact, isn't that so?"
"From what this stone has shown so far, I'd trust it to be asked.
With cold is true, and lies grow hot, ask of it freely, what you'd like to know."
"So," Horacio began, "If I were to say, that the way back is closed?"
"You would be cold," Nebi replied, his hand feeling the frost of snow.
"OK..." Horacio took a moment. "And the way down's a trap?" he supposed
"Oh... yeah, that one's icy," Nebi confirmed what they already guessed as true.
Now his options were getting limited. Both forward and back posed
to them a danger. "Well, we can't go across this mess?" inadvertently he threw.
"Ah, captain... you're getting warmer." "Really?" looking at the tangle of vines,
weaving a sprawl as far as the eye could see. Hoarcio found no way through.
"No, that's not possible." Frustrated, Horacio examined the dangling spines.
The only worse way is up," he joked, to which Nebi abruptly whines.

"Ow!"
he jumped back,
releasing the stone. "Ow, ow ow,"
he kissed his palm, as a soothing shellac
to a burn. "I think you found it," Nebi declared.
Expressionlessly, the crew turned their gaze upon the upward track.
"Oh, you've got to be kiddin' me?" Butrus on the pending feat glared.
"You and me both," Horacio replied in agreement, taking stock of the climb.
Straight up into an equally dark mass as below, Horacio's eyes stared.
The vines, stretching at least a hundred meters, were some covered with slime,
some grown thick and hard as roots, petrified with ageless rigidity,
offered little flexibility for scaling hands. Short were they running on time,
as from below a growling sound, as though a slow stomach churning ditty,
could be heard to rise, with a ground shimmering tremor in its wake.
"What was that?" Baloch spun to take notice, as Etci lifted, "Allah have pity,"
as prayer. Horacio made his decision, "Nothing good from what I can make
of it. Come, let's move we've spent as much time here as we can take."

Further back,
by foot a good league,
Mars and his cohorts were catching up to the pack.
Following their scent, here they came upon the fateful intrigue
that turned Horacio's crew sideways. "Chamomile," Mars barked,
familiar was he with Venus's pharmacy and her use of herbs for fatigue.
"There, down that way goes their path," he studied how the garden pass arched
on a downward slope. "But they should have veered off to the side instead,"
he pointed to an offshoot, partially hidden by the trees. Trail unmarked,
perhaps purposely so, the turn was easily missed. "Surely they'll soon be dead,
following that flower?" Formido pressed the question, having guessed rightly
the reason behind the placement of such a fragrant lure and to where it led.
"The honey trap," Timor answered. "Once in, there's no escape. Good nightly."
The demons were in agreement that for all intents and purposes the chase
they were in was now over. All parties of interest would soon be packed tightly
in the grave. But not so fast, Capitolina, the she-wolf, began to sniff and pace.
Mars gently rubbed her snout, "A way through you say, back to the surface?"

Banding together,
the crew broke into pairs,
finding a partner to whom which to tether.
This time round Isa and Nebi would not be parted, theirs
a bond of brothers. Ma'at, Horacio placed with his strongest,
for Butrus would have to do the climbing for two. Taking cares,
he matched Isfet with Suleiman, his second, giving her the best
odds of success, leaving Baloch and Etci, his two finest swordsmen
tied in tandem. Great would be the loss if they died as one in this test.
Odd man out, Horacio would climb alone, covering the backs of his men.
Tugging on vines, as thick as a wrist and forearm, they each selected
the most sturdy they could find for weight bearing. Then, a haunting omen
befell their ears, as a gurgling sound rose from the darkened pit below, directed
like a belch, straight at them. "Hurry," Horacio urged. "We've no time to waste."
He got them all climbing, fearing their presence had not gone undetected.
Legs wrapped, as if round a cord, they used their arms to shimmy with haste,
pulling themselves upward. For their difficulties though, this was just a taste.

Looking upwards,
they could see the overgrowth
of forest, the crown of foliage that stretched up towards
the sky at the top of the tree line, the root of the draping vines' growth.
At the center, there was the clear blue firmament, as a circular perimeter,
where the top layer of the branches turned away from another. An oath
could be felt in the heart, for the effort required to move that hundred meter.
But that was just the shape of their course, a long and hyperbolic funnel,
there was still another obstacle to contend with, which worked to deter

their progress. The vines themselves, a symbiotic part of this living tunnel,
as pressure was exerted on them, would begin to secrete a sappy sort of gel,
which sweet like syrup, or that of honey, oozed to form a sticky runnel,
which clung to their bodies and clothing. "Oh, what's that smell?"
Butrus climbing steady in the lead, with Ma'at securely latched on behind,
was the first to notice the faint aroma. "It's something familiar, but I can't tell."
"It's that flower!" Baloch recognized it too. "Careful it doesn't trick your mind,"
Ma'at warned, scaling along, with surprisingly lithe agility for one nearly blind.

"This syrup,
it must be made of it,"
Isfet surmised, shaking her hand down and up,
as goo dripped off of her fingers, falling like a ball of spit
into the vacant below. Suddenly, as though tempting with candy a bear,
a vibrating roar then followed. Above, the tree tops, as if hands split,
now they came together, closing out the patch of sky that had hung there
like a carrot of hope. And so too pulling, the vines, no longer a wall,
but free hanging, also came to center, suspending our heroes in the air
directly above the nucleus of that dark and perilous, threatening fall.
"Hang tight!" Horacio attempted to rally, gripping fast the vine.
Just then, a tongue, long and froglike, protruded from the miring gall,
whetting itself on the drips and drops of honey, as a salivating wine.
It stretched ever higher, writhing it searched for a tasty morsel.
"Ah, ah... eh!" Isfet gasped as the monstrous tongue came to dine,
wrapping itself around her legs, now covered with the secreted gel,
which called the creature to feast, as if the ringing of a dinner bell.

"Ahhrrr!"
Isfet wretched while being pulled.
"I can't hold on much longer," Suleiman straining his arm,
clutched for dear life, wishing for him and his partner to not be culled.
Just then, as their luck appeared to be failing, with a flying holler came
Horacio, swinging across fast upon the vine, towards their position he bulled.
In moments of life and death Horacio never panicked, falling stony lame,
but rushed head long, not without thought, but for sure without over-thinking,
simply knowing by instinct and practice what was required to tame
the beast before him. With sword held high, he slashed at the serpentine thing
as he flew past. Turning back on pendulum, he prepared for another pass
at the monstrous tongue, for now he had gotten its attention. Tight to rigging,
Horacio swung the Sword of Troy striking hard the plant's fleshy sash.
Tasting the blade filled with such destiny, the honey trap creature
fell spellbound, recognizing immediately the sacred nature of the slash,
which could only come by way of the goddess Venus, its blessed creator.
Falling reflective, the giant plant then took on a more benevolent feature.

Retreating
its extended mandible,
the plant's posture relaxed, as though a memory fleeting,
and with branches pointed to the sky, becoming more expandable.
The vines, as though tackle fishing lines, recoiled to the high branches,
lifting the entire crew with them. The confusion of course was understandable,
as none but Horacio could fully appreciate the moment. To him, the chances
of his matron mother harming him were astronomical in his counting
that just as with the defending she-wolf, this moment only enhances
his profound belief that nature itself was working in his favor. Daunting
it may be, but in his heart Horacio knew this island could do him no wrong.
There, at the heights, exhausted from the effort, tree limbs mounting,
they found themselves climbing back onto safe land, at the end of a long,
bending plateau by the edge of a road. Regaining their strength on that cliff,
overlooking a deep forest, the crew would never have guessed that a throng
of hazards rested just below by looking. More so, on gazing at a passing whiff
of cloud and gentle horizon, they might venture the island a pleasure skiff.

Without notice,
Isfet turned in that moment,
giving Horacio a once in a lifetime kiss.
Heaving, with the taste of honey on lips ferment,
she parted, biting lower lip, restraining the rush of passion.
"That's for saving my life," she breathlessly savored the comment.
"Anytime," masking emotion, Horacio regarded her in a heart racing fashion.
Yet, a stolen moment was all they could afford, for now the quest beckoned.
"Enfola." Ma'at pointed a bony finger, as her voice trailed away to ration
upon the shore. Along the coastal stretch, there jutted, just around the second
bend, an unmistakable peninsula, surrounded by rocks covered with brine.
With a narrow connecting strip of land to a pyramid hillside, there reckoned
to be some portent to this place where in birth heaven, hell and earth did align.
The Navel of Earth stood there before their eyes, and within, a secret hidden,
a passage that'd lead Horacio to his long sought destiny. Directly in the line
of sight, the crew stood solemn, hearts racing staring at the sublime, ridden
with a sense of accomplishment for just making it this far beyond the bidden.

"Alright,"
Horacio stressed,
moving forward. "Let's keep it tight.
We still have a long ways to travel." Time pressed.
"I want to make the most of this light." And then, as they retook the path
a shudder stirred the air. A hand lifted, as a warning to be addressed.
"Something moves, the birds they are restless," Isfet noted a sense of wrath
in their cawing. And then, "Sir," I can hear movement approaching," Baloch,
confirmed from his station, with an ear to the ground, using vibration as math.

"Something, or someone, draws close," he rightly reckoned. By the clock
still out of striking range, Mars and his troops were closing the distance.
"The scent grows stronger. We're gaining on them," Timor urged on the flock
of demon soldiers in their pursuit, keeping a mournful pace and cadence,
with Capitolina leading the charge, they held the sense of gaining.
Formido, losing not a step to his brother added, "Leave nothing to chance
this time. What the pit hasn't swallowed, we'll finish with blood draining."
On they marched, on automatic, as soldiers given over to their training.

Mars though,
overseeing, was not yet committed
to giving the order for the letting of blood to flow.
He wasn't opposed, of course, but before a coffin be fitted
he'd like to see the measure of the man. Would it be as he held suspect?
Was he in fact chasing the son of Romulus and Concordia, one outfitted
in human form, born from the legacy of Aeneas? Oh, before all else, he'd inspect
the signs of lineage, to see for himself if the same blood ran in mortal veins
as did his own... then, then he'd know of which commands he'd select.
As the hour passed, their contingent came upon the disheveled remains
of where their quarry had come to ground, over the ledge of broken branches
and a mash of footprints. "Here," Mars surveyed the site for what it explains.
"They must have great strength and courage to crawl out of these haunches."
A touch of respect settled on his tone, as he looked over the edge into the pit.
Harmless enough, it looked from outside, but knowing better, one blanches
at the thought of being digested by this carnivorous flora, to finally submit
to being churned like butter, while roasting on a spit.

"Ah..."
the god reflected,
"but how else would one make ambrosia?"
The necessary evils, Mars considered, as he corrected
his footing away from the ledge. "Love giveth, and love taketh away,"
he sighed, knowing full well the sacrifices that daily plague those selected
to give their lives so that others may live. There is no other way,
the universe demands a rotation of the crop to preserve its own immortality.
To this, Mars considered himself on par with the farmer, ensuring they pay
the quota, he works the field sowing life into the earth, and with that stability,
keeping the balance in check, making way for life with an infinite future.
Tasting a drop of the honeyed ambrosia, "Ah, and here, the cure for mortality,"
he licked his finger, letting the sticky sweetness play on his tongue and lure
his senses into a state of powerful ecstasy. "The food of the gods, delicious."
Stepping back to expand his view, Mars took in the full scene, and then, sure
that he'd just stumbled on one of the answers that had plagued his conscious,
"I know where they're heading!" he gazed onto the horizon, feeling ferocious.

Twilight was fast approaching,
by the time Hoarcio and the others had scaled
their way across the island, for their feet to be encroaching
upon the length of land that jutted outward into the sea, railed
by winds and waves, a crashing sea salt spray, all too familiar,
lashing the shoreline. "There! I'm sure that's where we'll find our tale'd
object, on the far side of those rocks," so sure Hoaricio was to finding the lair.
Climbing upon rough boulders, hefty battlement blocks that prevented
a safe landing upon the seaward edge, they cut a trail full semi-circular
up and around the peninsula's tip, to where surging waves crashed and vented
into the air. Exhausted, driven by hope and faith, upon the final fading light,
they came to the seawall's outer edge. "Perhaps we've circumvented?"
Isa, pragmatic in his counsel, saw only cold, barren stone in his range of sight.
"No, it has to be here. This has to be the place," Horacio wouldn't be for naught
his entire lifetime's journey. "Look, it must be here," he searched into the night,
when around he turned and from behind he saw an obscure path, which shot
back to the mountain, and here, lying abandoned, the temple that they sought.

BOOK XXIV

OF THINGS IRON AND BRONZE

There,
in a decrepit state,
our crew stood to stare
at the columned and granite slate
temple of Pluto's Shrine, tucked into the desolation
of this lonely, far off corner, hidden from eyes both small and great,
lost from the memory of existence. Overgrown with weeds and isolation,
befitting the last spot one with life would care to visit, this place of worship
to the underworld, cold and barren, imbued the want for soul's salvation.
Perhaps as a sign, symbolic of his noble spirit, or maybe as a right sailing ship
would show alignment, Horacio took to a knee, placing it down at the altar,
giving the due, as would to Caesar, he lifted a silent prayer for safe stewardship
of the friends left behind and for safe passage on his journey, so as not to falter
on the path. A true distinction it showed in the character of the pagan way,
to ensure that prayer and homage be given... especially to the gods who'd alter
one's fortune over slight or whim. And so Horacio, to great Lord Pluto, did pray,
"If ever on this path we meet, all I ask, is for just a moment you look away."

Offerings made,
Horacio stood and reflected
upon the current situation. Covered in the shade
of night, the moon a blackened sphere as been predicted,
he cleared his mind to remember the words, of how and why
Venus had come to him so many years ago and there selected
him for these trials. There, again, her words returned with a gentle sigh:
"When in the darkest, moonless hour, look up from this hearth,
unto the vastness of the heavens in the sky,
and your path shall be unearthed."
There he stood, and heeding, turned his head to the heavens.
With the sky a pitch, inky dark, the stars above shone for all their worth,
tracing out the spiraling nature of the universe. And here, in the center havens,
where all light goes in, yet none returns, appeared a hole completely black,
hovering in the cosmos overhead. From heavy though it turned all sevens,
"Captain, do you see that?" Suleiman pointed to a light in the hilltop crag.
"Yes, yes I do," Horacio replied, seeing their party was now back on track.

Just a flicker,
now being noticed,
it shone bright all the quicker.
An orange-red glimmer, in the remotest
notch, at the highest peak, before them stood the path.
Windswept and narrow at best, an ancient, unused pass, gone unnoticed
for eons, led directly towards the heart of the prominence. As if from a bath,
steam rolled oddly off the stones the closer they approached the hillside,
creating a gentle mist, hanging as would a distant ring of Saturn that lath
the lower limits of the foothills, building up in the wee hours of night, to ride
out to sea, scarlet in the morning. Here is where the path between rock
and tree began to curve, spiraling a corkscrew around and up the side.
Though in the cold of night, the crew was sweating. "I don't mean to shock
anyone," Butrus made the observation, "but I think it's getting hotter?"
"It's not your imagination," Isfet answered. "It emanates from this hillock.
There must be a source underneath responsible for this temperate totter."
Though she stopped shy of airing all the whys swirling in the grey matter.

Soon enough,
they'd have all the answers sought,
as they made their way up the spiraling bluff,
into the blanketed peak of forest, which brought
them round the hill again. There at the top, with silence,
still and reaching, far above in the night sky, a streaking star was shot.
"Ah..." there came a collective reflection, yet broken quickly from the distance
they were, as from somewhere much closer a muffled thump began to whisper.
"What's that?" Nebi gave a jolting shudder, hearing first the unnatural science.
"Nothing lethal, I would hope," Isa counseled, his tenor only slightly chipper.
"No. I know that sound," Baloch was fast to recall, envisioning his homeland,
as the rhythm grew louder. "That's the blacksmith's hammer." By whiskers
they advanced, caution in every step, when bending round a point of land,
to the eye came a sputter, an inconsistent glow of light, as though the flame
of torch, coming from the dark of archway stones, intermittently fanned
with light. There, as a mine shaft, to a doorway in the mountain they came
and from what transpires after that, they'd never again be the same.

"This must be the way,"
Horacio stepped forward to challenge
the dark shadowed buttress that stood to stay
the courage of mortal men. Though outside established knowledge,
fear of the unknown, at this stage, was simply beyond his comprehension.
Keeping to the sides, the black of night helped to disguise their passage,
as they approached the mouth of this stone framed tunnel. With tension
they stepped across the threshold. "How easily they enter," barely discernible,
Ma'at's voice, under breath does linger in the head. "No such free pension

do I see for the journey back." She'd a way of saying what others were unable.
Once inside, the ringing thud of pounding metal only intensified,
a cacophonic soundtrack, with its own time and rhythm, forming a credible
drum, which kept everything in tune and moving, in a syncopated stride,
for the toiling labor of the busy working caste. For countless eons past,
the Coppersmiths of the mines, under Vulcan's watchful command, applied
their craft and famous skills to shape and form a bounty of prizes, cast
from the island's ores and mineral deposits, each more glorious than the last.

Endless
ran thick the veins
of iron and copper, to bless
both the gods and man, with the bounty of mountains
and all therein. Empires eternal have thrived and bled upon her treasures.
Diggers and craftsmen, the Coppersmiths lived at their stations, as trains
of carriages rolled constantly by, hauling off the completed wares. Measures
of iron and copper, nickel and zinc, tin and others too mouthful to mention,
sat in boxes nearby the boiling caldrons, where alchemists at their pleasure,
searched to unlock the mysteries of Earth. Bronze was the first great invention,
where they used a composite of copper and tin to fashion all manner of weapon,
and by doing so discovered the true secret of how to transform apprehension
into gold, ensuring in perpetuity the need for supply and demand. Deal done,
the ovens would remain lit a constant twenty-four hours for the rest of eternity.
Vulcan, of course, was the first to profit, forging the mighty mountain spun
objects that went out to the world, shaping the course of humanity
and the heavens evermore, stretching out into infinity.

Powerful
as he'd become,
with strength and wealth, full
of influence and bravado, Vulcan, in sum,
did not count on the cunning and craft of Lord Pluto.
Knowing the hot temper of this God of Fire and Forge, from
whom he'd have to constantly rely on for swords and other ammo,
who, stockpiling reserves, would always be in a position to rival,
it was simply the wisest course for Pluto to consolidate, rather than to go
always looking over his shoulder, awaiting the inevitable betrayal.
As sad as it was to lose such a good craftsman, it just made more sense,
from a business perspective, for his long term objective of a zero sum final,
to let poor Vulcan perish with all the rest, in the gods' sleep filled silence.
In his place, Pluto would raise a great factory, for the machine was the future.
Slowly at first the changes were implemented, through a restructuring lens,
presented as a change of management, maintaining the same basic structure,
only now with chains, nothing too heavy, made of copper, as an added feature.

Not slavery. Have pity
no, Pluto would not hear of that.
Instead it was called, *enhanced productivity.*
As with any advancement in technology driven by the plutocrat,
one must show the need, and in fact the benefit, of evolutionary servitude.
Sure, for a time, one would be fastened to a workstation, but only to combat
disobedience. After a short while, perhaps a few centuries of being imbued
directly to the mountain, the chains would become a partner symbiotic,
making them stronger, faster, more competent parts of the engine, accrued
with interest, as their copper shackles infuse directly into their very genetic
codes, altering their DNA structures, as modified organisms, the Coppersmiths,
an alloy of flesh and metal, became another piece of the equipment despotic.
With nerve and fiber a pure copper core, they were able to conduct the gifts
of lightning, transferring energy to and from any source. *Automation*
it was called. "A necessary evil... for the greater good..." the words of myths,
never more deceptively spoken by a politician, than when Pluto, in narration,
advocated for good and evil in terms of market based salvation.

Here,
the scene presented,
as Horacio and crew drew near.
Their entrance, a vent shaft dented
into the crest of hill peak. Once inside,
a short tunnel opened to a ledge. Cemented
stones, the size of a large head, walled as curbside,
waist high railing to prevent some unintentional disaster.
From the ledge, it cut a circular radius curve around the inside
of the pyramid's peak, overlooking a bismuth bronze and brass plaster
of light reflecting off every surface. Thick oak scaffolding framed the walls,
hollowed from inside, to creating a cone-like dome. A massive castor smelter
sat atop a fiery pit down below, rising up through the center to service the calls
of the Coppersmiths working busily at their stations. Spiraling up and around,
down the interior wood frames were rails for carts to go crossing past the stalls,
ascending and descending throughout the various tunnels of the underground
to where only they knew, making the circuit then back for another round.

Interwoven,
as would honeycomb
in the hive, and their would-be chosen
path, was a staircase that twisted round the inner dome
wedged between upper and lower sections of railway line rigging,
leading past, but out of sight of toiling Coppersmiths in their catacomb
workstations. "Come. This way," Horacio motioned, seeing the stair swinging
down, around to the left, keeping them in a constant rotation with the clock.
In a miracle of engineering, a second rail of carts, rolling in the opposing

direction, crisscross intersected the first. While one line brought to dock
raw materials for the hammer, in the other would the Coppersmiths deposit
their finished products, to be whisked away upon completion, keeping stock
flowing in counter rotations, looping up at the top, then back down to the pit.
The clatter of creaking wood and iron, to the kaleidoscopic rhythm of hammer
in counter point, created such a cacophony that they could run the gambit
and still pass by undetected. "Stay alert," Suleiman warned without stammer,
as their group on staircase tread carefully down into the glowing clamor.

Although,
once turning the first curve,
they had to leave behind the safety of their hollow
for a full frontal view across the factory cone, in a swerve
of panoramic, a dented golden-orange light pervading everywhere,
being draped in sullen tones, they held an obscure advantage that'd serve
their purpose. With aid of shadow, as mice they crept, Horacio there,
in the lead, setting the pace for his men, winding down the notched ratchet
of staircase. Had any of the Coppersmiths possessed a reason or care
to look up from their posts across the dome, it would have been a casket
for the intruders, who'd have been summarily executed as trespassing
thieves. Fortunate though, with mining carts flying as would a hatchet,
from above and below, with the closest Coppersmiths in range passing
completely out of view the nearer they drew, they continued on unnoticed.
A sweltering crawl, from top to bottom an hour full, with heat amassing
off the giant smelting pot in the center, as would a lava flow be focused
inside a volcano, the caldron stretched more than half the distance noted.

Extending from the pot,
as though sloping metal spines,
pointed at a downward angle, shot
off, one for every station, ran conduit lines
for molten metal, which flowed at the tug of a chain
into various weapon molds and mixing kettle confines,
where one might want to add some zinc, or tin, or if they so deign,
perhaps some cobalt, nickel or maybe even silver, depending on the need
of the project at hand. Descending the spiral of steps, a dizzying train,
eventually, with some pain, they finally came in sight of the bottom. Indeed,
it would not be long before reaching the final rung of steps. Here much caution
they would need to take, for several workers manned the stoves, to feed
the ovens with wood to fuel the fires, while others toiling in place at station
kept the mechanism in function. "There," Horacio whispered from the front,
scouting out their position. "I can see an opening," he spotted an option.
Bending at a curve around the central smelter, train rails wrapped a stunt,
as mining carts sped off into dark tunnels, as if on a treasure hunt.

“We’re almost clear,”
Nebi to Isa, hushed in lower tones,
feeling victorious, seeing they were so near
the exit, and so too might they have been, when, to the chill of bones,
a booming voice echoed, “Stop!” It was Mars standing high, at the pinnacle
from where they had just come, having followed their trail to these stones.
“You thought you could escape me?” his voice bellowed. As if rabbinical,
all action froze and sound fell to a pin drop. In unison, all heads snapped
to attention, Coppersmiths glaring up at the god, stunned, almost cynical,
yet alert and obedient. Just then, from underfoot, as gremlin booby trapped,
a creaking floorboard sang out, as Etci grimaced painfully, holding back
his breath. With a singular motion, all heads spun around and mapped
the crew’s location, every eye focused on them and their hidden cul-de-sac.
With a beat of suspension, all parties held the moment, as they calculate
the rush of new information. Then, in a flurry of “Let’s go!” and “Attack!”
competing orders rang out from the various quarters of late,
with the entire scene erupting, now to escalate.

Racing the last few steps,
the corsairs leapt onto a raised scaffold, hitting ground,
aiming, they ran full speed for the tunnels, burning quadriceps.
In their path however stood a group of bulky ashen workers bound
to intercept, blocking escape. Muscled bodies covered with soot and sweat,
all streaked in the red of copper, which defined their chiseled flesh. Round
these Coppersmiths turned to face them, with shovels and picks the threat.
From behind a swelling grew, as others released from their work stations
flocked into a bottleneck, attempting to converge upon them as a single net.
Swords drawn they had no choice, the fight was forward at the foundations.
Clashing metal, the forces collided. Engineering tools not a great challenge
against these pirate swords, however the skin of these hybrid creations
presented another type of danger. The flesh did not cut, but where orange
deflected, providing the Coppersmiths with a naturally protective armory.
Moreover through this alloyed integration, where ran the strips of metal flange,
through kinetic transference, they were able to funnel their built up energy,
releasing it as a static charge on contact with the enemy.

Swords sparked,
as they made first contact.
“Ahh!” Baloch jumped back, marked
by the voltage. “What kind of devil’s contract
created such a thing?” He was not alone in his shock.
All hands squared into a defensive posture, as blades retract,
guarding a pointed standoff. Over his shoulder, taking stock,
Horacio saw an entourage of these metal men moving to close fast.
“There’s no escape,” the creatures spoke with a collective voice to mock,

as if in some way they universally connected. From the front was cast
a testing launch, the Coppersmiths quick and strong moved to strike,
weaponless, took on swords barehanded. Flashes crackled to the last,
with every repelling trust met by a taxing rush of power spike
to make them tremble from within. Perhaps they'd have all fallen
then, due to shaking seizures, had not Horacio, using sword as pike,
jabbed his opponent through a soft quarter, who to knee dropped crestfallen,
prompting the other Coppersmiths to take a step back, all with a look of sullen.

"They have a weakness,"
Horacio held a fighting posture,
emboldened. "Stab at the fleshy opaqueness,
where metal joins to skin," he hoped they could prosper
from this show of strength. However, only a moment it would buy,
for the Coopersmiths didn't take kindly to one of theirs being sent to pasture.
"You will pay for that with your lives," they made an ominous sounding cry,
circling, as those with sword and mace and axe closed in from behind.
There, facing the end, approaching fast on the rail beneath, towards them fly
a mine trolley, three large carts, each loaded with armor, all combined
a fortune, on its parting journey. "Jump," Horacio made a split second call,
leaving the others befuddled. "We cannot defeat such a machine maligned.
We must jump we have no other choice." Seeing as the mine carts haul
down the track approaching fast, not a second they could afford to snooze.
"You heard the captain. Move!" Suleiman barked as only he could bawl.
Backed up to the edge of the platform, there was nothing else to choose,
so into the passing carts they dropped, with only their lives to lose.

Bruised,
though only in flesh,
they watched from below as their carts cruised
down the track, leaving their opponents flustered, fresh
with defeat, only able to watch as the intruders made their retreat
deeper into the mountain, to where her underground tunnels mesh
into a labyrinth of passageways, and any number of other ways to complete
their surrender to death. "Take that!" Butrus laughed in a taunting manner.
"Oh, my ass," Isa groaned, rubbing his backside, having landed his seat
upon the knob of a shield. "Hey, let me see that," Nebi pulled with enamor,
lifting the buckler from under his brother, "Oh, that's nice, you don't mind
if I claim that, do you?" Just then, slammed, penetrating the shield's armor,
the tip of a thrown lance stopped just short of his face. Looking at the find,
"It's all yours," Isa replied. "Ah, captain," Nebi turned his head with a stutter.
"I see it." Horacio called from his carriage. "We've got company behind!"
he warned the others of the coming assault, another they'd have to rebutter,
all while speeding down rails into the unknown, with hearts all aflutter.

Unable
to cross such a gap
by conventional means, Mars set his rabble
of demon soldiers into the mining carts to wrap
the entire course in minutes, and were already speeding
towards Horacio's position, when they'd jumped into a rolling trap
of their own. At high speed stakes soared, with each moment fleeting,
as any mistake could be the last. From behind, the first car of demons
gained, closing the distance between their two forces. Butrus, beading
with sweat, refusing to be out done by these other worldly seasons,
climbed to the rear, and taking hold of Nebi's shield, "Can I borrow
that for a sec?" "Be my guest," Nebi passed it, seeing Butrus had his reasons.
Ripping the lance from its facing, he handed it back to Nebi, "Here you go."
Then weighing the shield's balance, he squinted an eye aiming and flung
it long. Spinning like a dervish, it flew towards their enemy with great sorrow,
striking not their heads, but at the rails below, where their cart's wheels clung,
dislodging their trolley from the tracks, a shriek filled wail their last song sung.

"Bravo!"
Horacio cheered,
his man's heroic bravado,
seeing how the cart of demons reared,
flying off the tracks to crash unceremoniously
splaying blood and iron works, down the banks their ruins smeared.
The celebration however was only short lived as from behind feloniously
rushed two more cartloads in pursuit, among them the monstrous beings
that nearly did them in twice before. Leading the chase Mars ominously
rode in the front ready to pounce once within arm's reach. With fleeings
urgently needed and a route of escape, they sped into the cavernous reaches
of the underground. Then, rolling down the track with welcome greetings,
Horacio saw approaching a turnout with diverging sets of track. As screeches
loomed threateningly behind them, Horacio made a split decision. "Butrus,"
he called, relying on the one who saved them twice to again fill the breaches.
"We've got a junction coming up, do you think you can hit that lever for us
in passing?" Butrus gazed ahead to see the switch at the intersecting truss.

"Consider it done,"
Butrus responded turning to Nebi.
"Think I'm going to need that back," he spun,
reclaiming the spear. The demons were close as the swarming bee,
almost in striking distance, as their carts crossed the railway intersection.
Butrus, with Isa and Nebi in the back, was the last to approach the turn key,
and winding up his only chance, he held the long lance by the tail section,
readying his posture. Then, as they hit the juncture, with a loudly audible cry
of "Aargh!" Butrus swung for the fences, striking hard the switch in question,

changing the track's direction, breaking his spear in half. Letting out a sigh,
he fell back to sit, as he watched their opponents sail down the opposite track.
Furious with anger, Mars curved away, speeding the wrong way in goodbye,
he shouted after them, "This isn't over! I'll get you!" his voice faded back
into the expanse of the mine's labyrinth, as they rolled away out of view.
Leaning back, they breathed relief, finally coming to a pause from attack.
"Never in my life, would I imagine to witness such a mighty crew,"
Horacio commended his men, giving to each of them their due.

Opening wide,
the tunnel they traversed
now gave way to a massive cavernous divide
underneath the mountain. Walls of chiseled iron burst
into view, dominating the landscape. Granite archway pillars,
formed a bridge to transport them across a deep ravine, submerged
in total darkness. Here, a hollow cold presented itself as opposite mirrors
to the warmth of their latest adventure. Yet so too, aside from the sound
of a distant hammer, chipping away at raw metal, they were as caterpillars,
alone in their cocoon. Slowing by torchlight, they approached a staging ground,
and beyond that a pair of fortified iron doors stretching high to an archway
carved directly into thick, impenetrable walls of steal that stretched far round
the range of view. "Is this what we're looking for?" Suleiman eyed the doorway.
"I would think so," Horacio ventured to guess, as he and the rest reset,
climbing out of the carts to once again feel the surety of land and headway
in their effort. "Make ready, we must be close," Horacio prepared the onset,
as Ma'at, in her manner assured the crew, "Oh, you haven't seen anything yet."

BOOK XXV

TO THE GATES OF HELL

Before them stood
a pair of massive iron doors,
vaulted at the top like a pointed hood.
Reinforced with riveted sectionals and embossing scores
that portrayed two parallel stories. On the bottom rung
from left to right, stood an image of the mountain, and at the fores,
a group of working ores-men, while on the other panel, how it begun,
was a swirl on the inverse, as would a coiling serpent with many lands
and latitudes of being, from mild to menacing, those portrayed were flung
upon the landscape for the greater part in misery. Below the center stands
a darkened pit of ebony, while rivers snake an octopus carving out the scene.
"Erebos," Isfet's eyes grew wide. "This is a map of the underworld's badlands.
You'd be wise to make note of her markings. Here, above on the next screen,
is the great bearded Lord Pluto himself, eyes cold here as they are in the flesh.
You'd do well to avoid him. And there, next to this is the god Vulcan," a sheen
of psychotic, genius and rage held the beveled tones engraved in his thresh.
"This must be the intersection of where their two domains mesh."

Isfet took a step back
to examine the larger picture.
Above Vulcan, mounting the top track,
was embossed a mighty hammer, a symbolic tincture
of power and strength, while opposite, resting above Lord Pluto,
was an all-seeing eye, encased within a pyramid. They gazed upon the fixture
in wonder. Of the two, one door, Pluto's, was cracked open, and through it flow
a trailing wisp of air. "This is the path," Horacio took a confident step forward,
for having come so far there was only one direction left for him to go,
and so, setting the course, he lifted a torch and steadily moved onward.
Creaklessly, a well oiled hinge, one perhaps frequently called into service,
opened as Horacio put his hand upon the door's edge, pulling it outward.
"How odd?" Baloch noted of the quiet. "Not so," Isfet gave the others notice.
"Pluto likes to move around in silence." There, swinging wide the portal,
the crew showed amazement upon their faces, as from the deep crevice
there opened a mighty storeroom vault filled with treasures immortal,
a vast supply of tools and weapons, a wealth beyond a counting mortal.

"Eureka!"
Butrus exclaimed with laughter,
as he and the other pirates gazed upon the overflowing beaker.
"How much you think this is all worth?" Etci's eyes began to water
examining the riches. "More than you could earn in a hundred lifetimes,"
Suleiman sized up the take. "Pluto's treasure room," Ma'at crooned. "Hereafter,
you must answer for what you take," wising them to the penalty for crimes
against the master of the underworld. "Then Allah be praised we don't all follow
such deities," Etci scratched the scruff of his beard, as if these were the times
for pillage. "Hold up," Suleiman warned, keeping a leash on his fellow.
"No, it's alright," Horacio countermanded his second. "They've all earned
the right. Take only what you can usefully carry." He eyed how the hollow
was laden, overflowing with weapon and shield. "Is that wise?" Isfet turned
in whisper. "We're all in his bad graces as it is," Horacio gave comfort.
"Little difference will it make in the final judgment, while as will be learned
soon enough, a boost of moral it will present for such skilled men to comport
themselves and make use of these illustrious instruments of last resort."

None finer
for sure would their party
ever find on this or any other world, so for this minor
infraction, Horacio would look away as his men took a hearty
swig from the well, furnishing themselves with arms being fashioned
by Vulcan himself. Horacio looked on satisfied without partaking, already
happy with his sword of choice. That however didn't prevent the impassioned
others. Baloch for one found a companion for his curved Persian saber,
while Nebi found a replacement to his lost shield for his part of that rationed,
encrusted with a think bronze pyramid, reminding him of the famed labor
of his Egyptian home. For Isa, a set of brass knuckles and assorted throwing
knives, while Etci a new sword and dagger won. Butrus into his harbor
drew more the likes of mallet's allure, though unable to resist a pair of glowing
arm guards to accompany the blunt of his weapon. "What?" looking apologetic,
he addressed the others. "I scrape my elbows a lot." For his own showing,
Suleiman choose a notched battle axe, giving himself an optional esthetic
to counter his blade, able to wield both, being suitably athletic.

"Nothing for you sir?"
Suleiman asked, feeling the grip
of his new halberd. Like a cat, he thought he could feel it purr.
"I've got everything I need right here," Horacio made a sincere quip.
With pride he looked upon his men. "Almost," Isfet called his attention,
eyes beaming, as though having found the prize, her next word being, "Strip."
"Excuse me?" Horacio sounded pleasantly surprised. "As you gave mention,
you're already in so deep, you've got nothing left to lose. If you want to succeed,
you might as well wear the very best armor." Before them, held in suspension,

fitted upon a headless manikin, as though the hide of some saffron steed,
rested the breast plate and armor of Apollo. Light as skin, yet solid in fitting,
it allowed him flexible range of movement, without the bulkiness to impede.
"It's incomprehensible to me how this treasure could just be here sitting,"
Isfet acknowledged her own dilemma. "Though, if Pluto has somehow captured
this off the body of Apollo, the sun god, and stored it here, then it's befitting
to say that at some point you'll need it." Adjusting the straps, body sculptured
within the vest, Horacio could not help but feel enraptured.

"There's an energy
about this suit," muscles he flexed,
feeling a noticeable enhancement of power, in synergy
he was with this new battle garment. "How can this be?" he sounded perplexed.
"It is Apollo's after all," Isfet clarified the situation. "These fibers can harness
the power of the sun, absorbing the strength of both light and heat, annexed
back upon the wearer, sustaining one during extended periods of harshness,
hunger and drought, all to which you hasten to enter. No harm by fire
may be done to you, as long as you wear this armor, wherein the farness
of your journey passes you beyond such assured sunder, you may retire
safely into the flame." All this came quite suddenly to Horacio, and surely
he was only starting to realize the true depth of his endeavor, into what a mire
that they'd walked. Then it was that a wisp of air graced his cheek. Securely
in thought, his decision was made, when a moment after he noticed a shadow
creeping up a crevice, a hint of light behind. He saw what must be done, purely
for the sake of his mission. Around the corner, there crept up from the hollow,
a rigid staircase of limestone. From the scent, Horacio knew where it'd plateau.

"Suleiman,"
Horacio turned to his second.
"Aye sir," ready he was to reconvene with the plan.
Unready though was he for the next orders that beckoned.
"I want you to lead the men back out to safety. Follow that staircase
back up to land, carry what treasures you can to the ship. It's reckoned
that you've all earned your pay." "Nay, we won't abandon you to this place,"
Suleiman was this once ready to disobey. "The path clearly leads down
this other way." "For me it does," Horacio reassured, "but not in your case,
you must now lead the men. You're their new captain." Others gathered round,
as Horacio gave his final orders. "There's no way to complete this mission,
unless I go alone, from here I enter a domain where none wish to be found
and only I may pass unnoticed. Your stories will go on, just not in this edition."
"Just are the words he say," Ma'at trailed in the otherwise lingering silence.
"Captain?" Nebi questioned first, along with the domino of others in expression.
"No, this is right," Baloch, with greater foresight, concurred with the sentence
presented by Horacio. "From here, only he may pass through the entrance."

The crew collected cargo
and made their final farewells,
as together Suleiman and Horacio
shared their last words. "Avoid the swells
and aim for clear horizons," Horacio blessed the voyage.
"And you as well," Suleiman clasped Horacio's hand and in the eye he tells,
"I'll see you on the other side, my brother. May Allah guide your passage
and see to your safe return. It has been an honor sailing with you." "Likewise,
my friend, the honor has been mine. With you in charge the ship will manage
more than well. The crew is lucky to have you to lead them." Eyeing lengthwise
his path deeper underground, Horacio steadied his torch. "Let's move out!"
Suleiman hastened the men not to dally, much there was still to revise
before reaching safe quarter back aboard ship. Clearing away any doubt,
Isfet afforded Horacio a moment, as he faced the stony creviced deep.
A kiss they shared in private, then peeling back with a glancing scout,
to ensure they were alone, Isfet whispered a thought for him to keep,
"Remember to think of me, before you take the leap."

Such is the nature
of Chaos, she will always add confusion
the moment you think you're safe, yet, conversely may too nurture,
when your last hope has been forsaken, a paradox she is in conclusion.
"To the gates of hell?" Horacio recalled her promise from, what was it...
just days ago. And there, such is the nature of time, an invented illusion,
or a constantly fluidly forever, both always and never now. The eternal culprit,
enabling change to thrive. Together they can do both great and terrible things.
For now they say goodbye. "It's there, just in front of you," Isfet had to admit
she'd taken him as far as she could go. Her presence within the lower rings
was famous and would only draw attention. "But before you go, take this,"
she handed him a leather sachet. "What's this?" Horacio tugged the strings.
"Chamomile and elderberries. I saved some from the trap. While in the abyss
they may serve to help you. One being quite sublet, brings on a powerful sleep,
while the other, with a fruity taste, a state of incapacitating drunkenness.
Use them wisely," she pressed them to his hand. There, at the edge of the deep,
they parted, having to go, the seed being sown, now was the time to reap.

"Hurry up,
you two!" Suleiman barked
as Isa and Nebi sought to turn up
matching goblets. At the back they marked
the rear of the line, the last to mount the staircase.
"Oh, look at that, I think those are rubies," Isa remarked
on the stones encrusting his cup. Then, "I know just the place
for these," Nebi was downright cheerful, when Isfet rejoined the group.
"Well?" Suleiman asked as she drew near. "He's gone," she turned to trace

her eyes back the way they'd come, as a soft breath of air made to loop
gently past them. "The first one in to perish fast, the second's fate to linger,"
Ma'at swooned. "What was that?" Suleiman paused, halting the troop.
"A message on the air." she said. "I merely interpret, as would a singer."
"The captain!" Isa, thinking on Horacio, saw upon him his stone glow red
and without further notice turned and ran back towards the springer
stones below. "Isa wait!" Nebi called to no use behind his brother, and instead
of waiting himself took chase. "Damn it!" Suleiman cursed the disorderly bed.

"The rest of you,
continue on. We'll meet you at the top."
Suleiman commanded the others, as he then flew
back down the staircase. For Horacio's part he came to stop
just shy of an open portal, a door sized hole in a rock before him stood.
"*Many are the paths that lead beyond Hades' gate,*" he remembered the hilltop
prophesy of his youth. "*Yet only one, winding and narrow,*" he understood,
"*through which you may find the prize you seek, destined by Fate.*"
Here, before him, lie his doorway, a secret and ancient pass that could
be the answer to all his questions. And as he was about to step, "Captain wait!"
Isa rushed in to save him. However gallant, it was a bitter fruitless call,
for by the time the others had arrived to help it was already too late.
Stepping in front of Horacio, Isa unintentionally fell through the portal,
and setting off a trap left by Pluto, to ensure that all who passed were dead,
ran headlong into a row of jutting spikes the rose up to greet his fall.
"No!" Nebi screamed from the rear, witnessing the dread,
of his brother receiving a pike directly to his head.

Sorrowful
was the current scene.
The unnecessary loss of life. Once so full,
now just a moment later, was gone, vanished between
the pages. Nebi, beside himself distraught, fell upon his brother's remains,
sobbing. Horacio held him, his own heart felt broken, inward was his scream,
looking upon the fallen brother. No poignant soliloquy or meaningful refrains
to mark the scrolls of history; no last heart-wrenching words to melt
some future reader, just death, the silent unflinching, inflexible pains
of death to lull their senses with that vacant nothing that's left to belt
one sober with the cold reality of their own powerlessness in such plights.
Passing the brother to Suleiman, Horacio pried loose the punctured pelt,
that served as Isa's remains. "Make sure he receives the proper burial rites,"
the worst and most dreaded final command given by any seafaring captain.
"Aye sir," Suleiman sullen, helped Nebi to his feet and covering wounded bites,
lifts Isa's body, while together he and Nebi carry away the fallen wrapped in
his own blood. For Horacio, the taste of it grew bitter the more often it ran.

He tired of death,
already aged for his years,
the wanton, unending carnage bequeath
for war and glory, casting up the best to the point of spears,
for what? To fill the grave with those who all died before their time?
Yes, he tired of all this death, and now from recent vantage point it appears
he will be having more of it than for what he ever bargained. Readying to climb
the next level, he took and exhaled a breath, clearing his mind for the moment
of what would stay with him to his final days. With steps careful and sublime,
Horacio approached once more the doorway, adjusting to head his helmet,
invisible, he crossed over to the other side. Meanwhile, the raiding party
had reached the upper stone, and sliding back a slab tombstone bestowment
found themselves exiting though Pluto's very shrine. Taking in a lungful hearty,
Butrus roared with delight on reaching fresh air. "Look it's almost sunrise,"
he admired the eastern view, as others mounted the landing, standing smartly
counting plunder, when a sorrowful bellow took them by surprise.
"Behold, the morning sky is red, and another sailor dies."

BOOK XXVI

ENTERING EREBOS

On a different track,
the war god Mars and his company
careened lower into the mine shaft, down a crack
in the iron ore and granite foundations to accompany
the Coppersmith miners, busy with hammer and chisel in hand.
Scaffolding straddled a gorge-like mining cave, wide as a valley, abundantly
supporting the rail lines that circled and dipped throughout the expand.
"Finally we come to it," Mars scowled in a foul mood, for the opportunity lost.
Now they'd have to make up time and distance, for which they hadn't planned.
Spanning the cavern, their carts slowed of their own accord, as they crossed
a lengthy bridge to the other side. "End of the road," Mars spat from his berth.
"The Triple Walls of Bronze," Timor spoke with reverence, as embossed
before their eyes was the barrier separating the underworld from Earth.
"Impenetrable," Formido's voice trembled with its own sense of dread.
Mars shook his head, "Well, not really," holding information of worth.
"Formidable as they may be, these walls were not designed as a bulkhead
against entry. Come," he motioned forward. "The trail's only cold, not dead."

Gently on,
morning came,
across the Gate of Dawn
as Horacio stepped not into some monstrous frame
but onto a sprawling field of wildflowers that covered the hillside
looking out over Elysium, the blessed pastures of grace, whose fame
was only spoken of in story, but now before his eyes, just on the other side
of a calm and placid river. *This can't be right,* he thought to himself,
imagining that he would be surrounded by the dead in mourning tide,
and all sorts of gruesome demons. Instead he found misery put on the shelf
for some other season, while here fluttered butterflies within his field of vision.
It must be some trick, Horacio reconsidered all of what he knew, and the gulf
of all what was still unknown, and felt that it might be the wisest decision
not to remove his helmet. Down a hillock, a wooden footbridge arched
over the stream unto Elysium proper, the only crossing this side of the incision,
for few were the roads that led to this place free from the oblivion that marked
all other quarters of the underworld. Here was where the fortunate marched.

It was in this moment
that Horacio saw the hidden splendor
folded within that final human sacrament
of passing into the afterlife. Not all was as dour
as had been portrayed by mystic priests and ancient texts.
It's as large as the imagination, he heard it once said in an hour
of contemplation. *You put yourself where you need to be,* he seemed perplexed
with lost memories, thinking on the situation. *If there's only one path to reach
the needed location, then this was where I was meant to be to find the context
to this journey.* He reminded himself to stay alert for what this place may teach.
Not familiar with where he tread, this being one of Pluto's secret and private
passages, he couldn't truly know how vital this advice was, for here he breach
the inner sanctum, the Groves of Proserpine. Here, an always perfect climate,
an eternal springtime morning, with a gentle breeze and chirping sound,
fragrant amongst the olives. Here it was that the mysteries decided by Fate
wanted for him to have knowledge. For here, within a gazebo, sitting around
a tea cozy table and flowering gardenias, it was Proserpine herself he found.

Through a wood of aspen
and poplar, both white and black,
a second lady came to join her. Clasping
each other warmly, they sat together with the back
turned towards springing white roses over their shoulders
that were sacred to both death and the goddess. Nearing the garden shack,
Horacio crept within distance to hear. "Inside him something smolders,
I can feel it in my bones," Proserpine shared a secret in confidence.
"Are you sure, my sister?" it was Libera who asked, who to the elders
was her sibling alter likeness, the goddess of freedom and providence.
Proserpine sighed, "Ever since the pilgrim came to replace the poet,
something has changed inside him, something deep with consequence."
"Are you sure?" Libera took her hand. "Might it not be some female opponent?"
Proserpine withdrew considering the suggestion. "No, he knows better,"
she waved off the idea. "He knows I'd crush her to mint. No, this is more stoic,
some deeper transformation of his character that he's hiding from me." A fetter
she felt trapped to this place and looked to her trusted abettor.

"If you truly want to know,"
Libera gathered closer to her sister.
"There's only one place from which the answers flow."
"Yes," Proserpine already knew where to hear the whisper.
"Mnemosyne, within the Waters of Memory," she named the price.
"But to drink from those waters is to offer an equal part of your soul to blister."
"Only for a moment though," Libera was reassuring. "The effects of the sacrifice
are not permanent... but necessary, and only last the length of the vision."
Yes, Proserpine knew that truth was spoken, and solid was the advice,

yet still she lingered, the taste of fire was her weakness. To aid the decision,
Libera offered her sister another enticement. "What if I told you a secret?"
she tossed a mischievous look across the table towards the Elysian
banks of the Mnemosyne. "If you mix wine in with the water you seeketh,
the pain it inflicts is deadened." "Are you sure?" Proserpine looked hopeful.
Gently laughing, Libera teased, "Who would know better than me the sequent?"
"True enough you speak," Proserpine shared in the chuckle, feeling more joyful.
"It really is the only way to discover the truth. You've been more than helpful."

One step closer,
Horacio thought having eavesdropped
on the conversation. If looking for an answer
to his final destination then it would do him well if he too stopped
for a drink of water and slake his thirst for knowledge. Across the grove,
where the grass meets water, beneath the weeping willow trees, topped
by a shimmering glimmer, Horacio found himself before a great trove
of water, forming as a pool and outer boundary of the protected lands.
Beyond these banks, sat Lemnos and the Palace of Hades, past the mangrove
borders that formed an impassable barrier. Yet from here, where he stands,
it was not even possible to see the other side. Beneath the shade of willows,
to himself in seclusion, having no other container, he took into hands
Pluto's helmet, removing it from his head, and then dipped it in the shallows,
to retrieve a portion of this magic water. Following the goddess's instruction,
having no other viable substitution, from within his leather satchel he chose
a number of elderberries. *Just enough,* he counted to cause intoxication,
yet not too much to produce any cognitive obstruction.

Less is more,
he measured knowing the strength
of this vine, and pressing it into the water, to himself he swore
an oath in tribute and then, raising the cup, "Now show me at length
the plan, that of Pluto's secret, and of whom is this pilgrim they speak?"
Wetting his lips, Horacio drank heftily of the potion, leaving not even a tenth.
Collapsing, Horacio's head spun, overwhelmed by a lightning streak
of color and sound, every piece of information coming in was twisting vibrant,
an overload of the senses, as he tried to balance himself for what he seek,
thankful for mixing the chaser. As one he felt, both wise and ignorant,
knowing already what he was there to see, yet with a total lapse of memory,
opening his eyes, for the first time being reminded that neither important
nor insignificant was he. And there before him on the same trajectory
appeared a grey cloaked figure. It would be remiss, if we did not say,
exactly what this represented, for what hurt the gods most in summary
was to remember. Eternity was always in a constant state of dismay,
ever changing, yet in Hades, it was much more than just shades of gray.

Here,
as too was once Olympus,
from the point subjective all there
is was always a constant, the omnibus
never changed. Perspective was only ever counted
by wins and losses. So, if you live long enough, as does an immortal oculus,
having eventually come to see everything you might have cared about mounted
to the no more, remembering, as with Queen Proserpine, only presented pain.
Therefore, her reluctance. Yet Horacio, having through fortune surmounted, did
drink from Pluto's own helmet, thusly the waters showed to him a refrain
not of his own making, but that mixed with the thoughts and actions of the god
Pluto and his reclusive past. It is for this that now we catch a glimpse of plain
speaking from the mind of the most cunning craftsman that ever plod
through the universe. However, only a glimpse would he be allowed
to touch, a clue to lead him further, as great distance was he yet to trod
before reaching his prize, the journey had only begun for the avowed
servant and heir of Venus. A whisper in his ear then grew loud.

"The spirit you seek,
awaits you at Saturn's Cave,"
a disembodied voice into his ear did speak.
"The pilgrim," a hoarse toned Horacio tried to brave
a word, yet through these waters it was only the Muse
who had the power to lead the conversation. Though he crave
to move on his own, Horacio was only the passenger, unable to choose
the direction by which this dream unfurled. "Time and distance
have no power in this domain of death," the voice continued to infuse
instruction. "Forget all that you have learnt, none of that has importance.
See only what now is." Struggling to cope with all the horror, to face
all the suffering along the spiraling road, something more than circumstance,
a deeper plot uncovered, within the voice that spoke, led Horacio to trace
a memory of what lie before the is. There Horacio was certain that the voice
was none other than Pluto's, he was sure no one else could hold that place.
He was only being shown a fraction, what was put into head by choice,
yet there was another truth that Pluto was likewise trying to devoice.

"I understand,"
he gasped, coming back to life
within the land of the dead, and
opening his eyes, clasping hard his knife,
spun around in a state of confused bewilderment,
heart pounding inside his chest, surrounded by the afterlife,
and fortunately yet undiscovered, he thought hard upon his commitment.
Meanwhile, on another plane of existence, Mars had found his entrance.
A deep crack penetrated the Triple Walls of Bronze at an angle cross bent,

that of a sharp razor blade, which allowed only a single file in one chance
direction, that to the domain of death. "Let's go," Mars led the demonic faction,
without even stopping for breath, only one thing on his mind being vengeance.
"Only one direction the tunnels lead and I mean to discover the attraction
these earthlings have for visiting Hades and an early grave." The brothers,
Timor and Formido, heartedly agreed. "With such a blatant infraction,"
the former was quick to point out, "there's only one sentence that covers
the crime." Knowingly, nods and murmurs rose from the others.

"Silence,"
Mars was in no mood
for his sons' boastful compliance.
For him there was a singular crime that brood
in need of response, that of having been twice bested.
There shan't be a third, he marched on defiant. Swelling was a private feud,
one of ego and reputation. In each of the three walls, the crack crested
in perpendicular directions, further preventing a backward retreat.
By design all may enter, but return was a separate issue to be tested
and rested solely on the whim and pleasure of Pluto. To attempt a feat
in contradiction would simply be a fruitless endeavor and only serve
to increase one's torment to the exponential. Here, penetrating the pleat
in the final wall of the three, the party of Mars, with a gruesome verve
stepped onto a rocky, barren land with an ashen orange sky berating
overhead. Thunderclouds lingered on the horizon in the direction they curve.
Gazing out onto the landscape, Mars took his bearings, contemplating
the quickest path to take. Each option more than the last frustrating.

"That way,"
Mars finally decided,
pointing towards the dark mountains that stay
their path. *"Domos Hadou,"* in sullen tones, Formido provided
a name for the coming obstacle, being a range of treacherous cliffs
that led into the Dominion of Hades. Here it was the land collided
in an upward slant, crawling with vampire demons, whose gifts
of releasing bloodshed on wayward spirits was renowned throughout
the underworld as legendary. Pity on he, who from destined punishment shifts
his path to cross such ruinous terrain, for without so much as a doubt
would wind up shredded limb from limb by these hideous creatures.
"Onward," Mars commanded, unafraid of these crag hidden lout,
who being no match for such a mighty god and the war faring features
of his followers, would for their own sakes remain watchfully hidden
among the rocks. Off somewhere in the distance rose the cries of screechers,
howling on the wind, as their entourage crossed the passage forbidden
to all but those most courageous, who dare step upon the mounds of midden.

Standing upon the pinnacle,
overlooking the vast valley that stretched below,
with his twin sons, both looking at their best cynical,
and the she-wolf, Capitolina, by his side, Mars's eyes took on a glow
of determination. Beyond the barren foothills, bled the Orchards of Hades,
a wasted land of suffering, and further on to the destination they must go.
"What is it, my lord?" Timor asked, seeing how the blush of certainty fades
from his father's complexion. "Nothing," Mars shrugged off the question.
"All is as it must be." Desiring other options, he pondered the countless shades
on the horizon, many of whom he'd dealt with intimately in his profession.
No choice however presented itself in his deliberations, he must go headlong
into this confrontation. Yet, it gave him no pleasure to continue the procession,
merely showing himself was to admit defeat. More still, what if he were wrong?
No, there was no other path to take. God or not, it was now a matter of duty
for him to complete the mission he was on. Regardless of how far or long,
he must see through to the end what was started. "Come now, my beauty,"
he petted Capitolina. "To the palace," he led, followed by his trusted deputy.

BOOK XXVII

THE PILGRIM'S CONFESSION

Reinvigorated,
Horacio continued on his path,
with a soft moss underfoot that consecrated
each step taken in these blessed fields to bath
both foot and soul with velvet contentment. Shades
of the past, souls of the fortunate, free from the wrath
of the damned, busied themselves with leisure, as serenades
danced in the ear. For his part, Horacio made to go unnoticed
by wearing the cloak of his helmet, yet if eyes not playing charades,
he could not help but be tempted, for here by a glade in the remotest
part of the island, he came upon a soldier wearing Trojan armor.
By Jove, it was indeed ancestor Aeneas, and with him, he noticed
his own father, Anchises. If anyone Horacio could dare to trust to harbor
safe his secret within the underworld it would be this soul, who at one time
stood in his very shoes. Removing his helmet, Horacio approached with ardor
the father and son. "Lo, what's this?" the elder, Anchises began to chime.
"Who approaches, dressed as some god in his prime?"

"It's true,"
Aeneas seconded his father.
"This is no spirit," this much he knew.
"Who are you? What business do you further,
here in the underworld?" Overwhelmed with admiration,
Horacio knelt before the pair, and on his lips did gather,
"That for the service and duty of Troy," his citation.
"Oh really?" Aeneas and father seemed taken by surprise,
unaware of any such mission. "Please stand and make your declaration,"
Aeneas urged their visitor to join them as a friend, able already to surmise
that they held a common lineage. "Tell us, how may we be of assistance?"
Then, before Horacio could go any further, something caught the spirit's eyes.
"Wait, I know that sword!" Aeneas blurted out having seen at a close distance
the blade that once was his own. "But I gave that to..." he broke off suddenly
in mid-sentence. "Her eyes," Aeneas for a moment was shaken from his stance.
"It's you," nodding with a flash of recognition, Aeneas understood abundantly
the situation and with a warm smile welcomed Horacio to their company.

Having conferred
and receiving the blessings
of his ancestors, Horacio was referred
to Jupiter's Road, the pass that ran the full leggings
of the Elysian isle. "Follow that way to find Saturn's Cave,
though I don't know if he'll be there. Remember, his guessings
did our line no favors when he drew his breath, and now in the grave
it's said that he's full of regret, spending his time in contemplation."
Aeneas told of what was known of the pilgrim, and proud of how brave
and strong his seed had grown, he offered Horacio a final salutation.
"Take care my son, and keep your wits about you, the deeper you climb
the more treacherous becomes the slope." Though having some consternation,
with the most difficult tasks yet to be undertaken, and no sure paradigm
towards victory, the honor given to the House of Troy was still unmistaken.
One day, maybe soon, Horacio too would join the halls of his ancestral line,
to have songs about him written. Until then though no delay could be taken,
so giving his last farewell to kin, Horacio let the dust from his feet be shaken.

The road
was long, yet gentle,
as Horacio continued in the mode
of pedestrian on his journey. Seemingly continental,
the expanse of distance was greater than he'd imagined
it would be, yet from outward observation only incremental
in the passing of time. How strange it appeared to be fashioned
that the clock synchronized itself to his feet, remaining mostly constant,
in comparison to the world from which he'd come. As it so oddly happened,
the sun, and yes, although entering from underground, he became conscient
that the sun did shine on Hades, for not truly under-earth but on a realm
independent rested this berth of the dead, accessed through an infinite convent
of portals, and in it the sun moved so slowly that eternity could be held to helm
over the course of one single day. Stranger things would come to pass before
his time came due, so on he pressed, feeling blessed, only slightly to the whelm,
for coming into view, he could see the point of a tall tower in the fore.
Cautiously, he approached, unsure of what there lie in store.

Through a clearing,
Horacio saw what looked
like an enormous sundial, veering
towards the sky. At the far end a crooked
gnomon, a fashioned triangular blade, formed the structure,
which cast back down the shadow. Horacio stopped and overlooked
the scene. If his measurements were accurate then only a fracture
of time had passed, at best he figured it could only be ten in the morning,
yet it felt like he'd marched for days. *Amazing,* he thought on the sculpture

before him, and then at the base, which grew from the ground, forming
directly out of a natural mound, he saw a lone figure sitting in the grey frock
of a monk. *That must be him, the shade I seek,* Horacio felt hope soaring.
Approaching from behind, Horacio looked upon the still figure. Taking stock
he decided it was safe to proceed, and removing his helmet there addressed
the spirit. "Are you the one they call, 'The Pilgrim'?" From his sitting rock,
"Some have called me that," the spirit responded to the inquest,
solemnly without so much as a twitch more to be expressed.

"Then you are the guide I seek,"
Horacio took a step closer trying to examine
this spirit's hidden features. "Please, I ask you speak.
Reveal yourself to me." Slowly, as if some aging brahman,
the shade pulled back the hood that disguised his appearance.
"Wait, I know you!" Horacio with surprise felt grow within him
great excitement, having recognized the hard lined profile's emergence
from such a meager and lonely cloth. "Could it be the master Alighieri?"
"Call me Dante," urging the familiar, spoke the pilgrim born of Florence.
"But if I am not mistaken, we have never met before this allegory?"
"Yes, it's true," Horacio had to admit. "In person, we have never met,
but I've heard tell of your work. You're the one the scholars call a visionary.
Once when I was a child, I'd even seen your portrait. The product of your sweat
will live beyond you." "Ah, and so we have it," the spirit of Dante seemed
less than joyous in hearing news of the earthly success of his triplet.
"What troubles you signore? Your work is very well esteemed."
"Ah yes," Dante returned. "But not all is as I had dreamed."

"In that we have agreement,"
Horacio concurred with the lettered elder.
"Yet, whatever truly is? Do we not all make appeasement
with the gifts we have at hand? What counts is that you strove bolder
than any of the rest. Your contemporaries of the past have all but faded,
though your name lives on." To that he received only the shrug of shoulder.
"True perhaps, still damage I have done and for that I now am graded."
Dante spoke of regret and punishment as being the only reward
for his service. "How can that be?" confused Horacio traded.
"Did you not also in life, as sources claim, travel to cross the fjord
that separates earthly existence from the world of the hereafter?
Is it not true that you have an intricate knowledge stored
of these spiritual domains? Please tell me of the matter."
"Yes, what you say is accurate," nodding, Dante could not disagree.
"Yet, so too, is the account incomplete, for much that was sought after
was hidden from me. The vision given deliberately altered, and I, the enrollee,
a dupe, for a more sinister motive, told the lie, propelling a fictionalized story."

Dante sat reflective,
pondering the injury done.
"Do you know how truly selective
the sights to me were shone? Not one
single counterargument was to me given
than what was wanted to be told. Now begun,
the invention will take root and the world will be driven
away from the path of light." It was for this his soul did suffer.
For all his righteous intentions, Dante felt there was no way to be forgiven.
"Tell me, what exactly have you done to make the journey that much tougher?"
Horacio tried to understand what filled this spirit with such a deep despair.
"I gave to man an image," Dante looked up. "A picture drawn from sulfur
that will ignite the world in rally behind a false theology. Now, beyond repair,
this devil, Pluto, who fed to me the lies, will use this comedy for his own ends."
"Pluto, you say?" Horacio was sure this spirit had information beyond compare,
which could aid him in his purpose. "Yes," Dante replied. "It's he who sends
the dream to me, for which I now must make amends."

"If it's redemption
you seek," Horacio had a thought,
"perhaps by helping me find direction
on my quest, you too will be improving your lot?"
Dante was intrigued, "Speak clearly. To what am I agreeing?"
"I need a guide and all signs have led me to you, right here to this spot.
You know the labyrinth of the underworld better than any other being?"
"Better than most I would say. Moreover, I have access and safe passage
to, though not all, most of the foul quarters, it's my penance to be seeing,
if you understand, but most of the time I choose to be here amongst the sage."
"Choose to be here?" Horacio couldn't help but notice the phrase, it spoke
to him strangely of something beyond the grasp of his present knowledge.
"Are not all souls sent to their fate?" "Ha, ha," Dante laughed at the joke.
"No, no, there's much left to learn about the ways after death to tell.
The truth is we all pick our own destinations. If I may invoke
one such recent memory, that from my very first visit to hell,
it should sound for you most clearly, like the ringing of a bell.

"As with so many
writers who by muse present,
the beginning of their story
is quiet often very pleasant
and had the poet any sense
he'd cut the tale short in that moment,
saving us the need to go any further since
whatever follows will undoubtedly be worse
than from the point he began. In short, silence

is often the best and wisest way to break the curse.
And so too I am guilty. For when I put my quill to parchment,
to tell of what I'd seen, the very first of those with me to converse
were the souls of them who had reached such great achievement
in their own lifetimes, those who had inspired me the most from youth,
who for no fault other than being born prior to the baptismal sacrament
were denied their access to heaven. Yet, I must tell you, as a fellow sleuth,
it's only for the company you keep that makes paradise or hell in truth.

"So I choose
to stay with the rabble
of heroes and scholars, whose
lives were the most remarkable.
Yet, like all souls, I too carry the burden
of my earthly failings, of being incapable
of reaching my goal before the final curtain.
No matter how acclaimed may become my name,
I cannot completely rest until I know for certain
that my testament be true and untarnished. The same
is for all who strive to a higher purpose, so in penance
I am constantly revising, unable to put to bed my shame
of missing all the facts and therefore this is my sentence."
"To write and converse with all the great persons and minds of late?"
Horacio was not sure if that he considered punishment, but in substance
he understood the angst felt by the poet, being left to contemplate
the incompleteness of his life's great endeavor, his eternal fate.

"Tell me,"
Dante eyed his visitor,
cautious in believing what he see.
"What is the purpose of your quest, insofar
as to your motivation? What has brought you here?"
Horacio spoke with only one answer for the inquisitor,
"Love," he said in truth. "That is the rudder by which I steer."
Thoughtfully, Dante considered the message. "That's the only good reason
to do anything at all. I once too was on my journey and too as clear
as you, was riled into service by love. If not for the slight and treason
done onto me, by the Lord of the Underworld, my suit would have prevailed,
but there, having believed I found her, it was not until the very season
of my own departure that to me the illusion was finally revealed.
All the details were correct, but the devil arranged them for his own purpose,
using pieces of truth to tell an elaborate lie. It was the larger picture that failed,
painting a binary canvass of good and bad, so that from which after rose
one god and one evil, when in fact they are all one, thorns of the same rose.

"Ah, but love,"
Dante paused for breath,
"if ever there were a god above
it is for love the only reason. It seems that not even death
can defeat love and so yes, I'll be bound to make another journey."
"You do me great honor, signore," Horacio gladly welcomed him. As neareth
he could figure the best navigator of the underworld, short of the turnkey,
Pluto himself. "I am vowed to find and release Saturn from his prison vault.
Hoping that led to the cavern of his own namesake, that the tourney
would be close at hand?" "Oh, far from it," Dante would prove his salt.
"Though at one time, it's said that he inhabited this land, once residing
within this very same clock tower, long ago, I am told, he came under assault
and was driven far from here, placed into a hellish pit of his own presiding,
far away from any other soul. Though I am not allowed to visit this barbarous
haven, I know of the way and can bring you a great distance, providing..."
Dante paused so his warning might sound, "you understand how treacherous
is this undertaking? The path you request leads straight down to Tartarus."

Horacio thought hard
on the words that Dante gave.
He wouldn't sound so foolish as to play the card
of fearless. To be afraid is natural, but the only way to save
oneself is by overcoming that fear and rising to the challenge.
"Thank you. Your concern is duly noted. Eventually all paths lead to the grave,"
Horacio concluded. "It's what you do with the time held in the balance
that defines the value of one's life. Sometimes safe is not the way to play it."
"Well put," Dante approved of his gallantry, however, "just keep safe knowledge
of the horrors that you witness. If caught, that will be the minimum payment."
Horacio understood the meaning and risk he bore, yet would not turn away.
"Lead on," he was determined. "We shall take each obstacle, my dear poet,
as they present themselves. And where I must I'll hide myself in a way
most undetectable, for as once you did I too come by sanction
of writ, by the deities' instruction. If I were to now delay
my duty, a far greater damage would be made in comparison,
whereby even the darkest fate received wouldn't merit compassion."

"I shan't try
to dissuade you any further."
Dante saw how ardently Horacio ply
for a higher purpose, and would not bother
attempting to pull him in another direction.
His heart was pure. For this and no reason other
both the poet and the pilgrim applauded in reflection.
"The way is long, so prepared yourself," Dante adjusted his cloak
and taking hold his walking staff, cast aside any lingering objection.

"From here on out only danger and pitfalls shall we find," he spoke
in reassurance. "And of that, the greatest of them all you'll shortly see.
For if you wish to enter the place which is forbidden to all other folk
except the Lord of the Underworld himself, then you must obtain the key."
"The key?" Horacio turned to question. "Yes," Dante with a knowing look gave.
"Which Pluto keeps upon his person at all times, of this I can guarantee."
Hard news was this, for Pluto he wished most to avoid on this side of the grave,
yet such was his fate. "So be it," Horacio sighed, as they entered Saturn's Cave.

BOOK XXVIII

INTERSECTING ROADS

Through the Gate of Shades,
Pluto's horse driven carriage raced the night,
passing the throngs of newly dead ferried by blades
of curses and torment. From here is where the plight
of the ignorant masses flowed, funneled by way of this port
to their final judgment. Trampling past ranks of the departed that light
upon the banks of Acheron, the River of Woe, where huddled and contort
spirits file disheveled in their sorrow towards the boatman, Pluto approached
the dock, his steeds neighing at the rolling mist that accompanied their escort,
Charon, and his ferry across Avernus, the Lake of the Dead. Here reproached
were those waiting their turn, for the master of this realm took precedent
over the damned. "Welcome back," Charon in gruff tones encroached
his boat upon the landing. "It has been some time since your last descent,"
infrequent were the visits. "Yes, I had business in the Judeo-Christian orbit
and this was the nearest portal. Secure my stallions and equipment
for the passage home, I care not to dawdle." Obediently, Charon took the bit
and bridle, sheltering the team safely aboard his river barge for transit.

Ruffled
and flowing
his cowl shuffled
in the foul wind blowing
off the Acheron with a howl of misery
riding the wanton air. Ready with staff lowering
into the murky depths, Charon pushed off his floating livery.
His rugged, unkempt features and scraggly full length of beard
cast a haggard pall to offset his funeral pyre eyes with grim mystery,
as he guides the ship over thick grey waters. "What have you heard
during my absence?" Pluto kept tabs over his underworld domain
by means of eyes and ears lurking in every quarter. Volunteered,
Charon gave his answer. "Not heard, but seen. An electric stain,
lightning has struck far across the plane." "Lightning you say?"
Pluto, raised an eyebrow, knowing the meaning behind the refrain.
For when lightning strikes in Hades, a living soul has found a way
to cross beyond the astral plane, to bypass the normal gateway.

"Yes,
several times,"
Charon did confess.
Although these same crimes
the boatman had committed on multiple occasion,
having ferried souls of the living across the maritimes
of the River Styx, and of this he still kept secret, his oration
was not hindered by allegiance to conceal the actions of others.
If anything it emboldened him even greater, for to the orchestration
of death he was an equal partner, profiting handsomely beyond the coffers
of the grave. Any side business, was his business alone, and he liked to keep it
that way. Rightly, he was the gatekeeper for a reason. Those making offers,
he might entertain, if it suited his pleasure, yet none had the right to reap it
for themselves. So without hesitation he reported the lightning that he'd seen.
For him to do anything else would simply be a break from proper etiquette.
"We'll have to look into that," Pluto acknowledged through the misty sheen,
as somewhere in the distance a ghoul began to scream.

"What was that?"
Horacio asked, hearing
a wailing sound, like of a cat.
"Oh," Dante spoke of the jeering,
"those are the cries from the Waters of Oblivion,
where memories die before reincarnation. A necessary shearing
in order to forget." The sound had grown louder since crossing the meridian
separating Elysium from the Land of Dreams, *Demos Oneirio*, it was known.
Through Saturn's Cave they had followed a hidden pass, dark as obsidian,
to emerge in this terrible place. Now, down a slope to their right, it was shown,
a dark lake of forgetfulness, where the River Lethe pooled together to the size
of a lake, into which a great many souls were being driven and thrown,
their memories there stripped away. "Are you saying we once again rise,
like the Jesus of Christian faith?" "Oh, no," Dante beat back the confusion.
"Not some old wizard's trick, invented on parchment for a cleric's prize.
Rebirth is only one of the many possible outcomes, not some elaborate illusion.
Think of it like this if you want to understand the solution."

Then turning,
Dante caught Horacio's eye.
"For every living soul, there's a yearning
to find peace. The pathways to attain this are as numerously high
as are there are in the number of spirits. That would be the equivalent
to a sum total greater than all of the stars in the evening sky,
across the entire universe, stretching back to the very first instilment
of life, a number so large that it lies beyond mortal comprehension.
And each of these souls, to find their peace, to bask in the light benevolent,

must release the weight they carry. For some that is through ascension
back to life, to pay for the karma of their sins by taking rebirth in the skin
of those they have harmed in a previous existence, like a circle in suspension,
where perhaps the master becomes a servant, where life itself becomes akin
to punishment. There are some spirits who spend eternity in this manner,
spinning through the revolving door of life. Others might wind up destine
to be pinned to one of the pleasures of this domain, and in all candor
it's each one who decides their own fate in the matter."

Continuing on,
with the sky a graying overcast,
they skirted past the vast pool that spawn
rebirth to a new existence. "Careful not to cast
yourself too near the water, lest you wind up forgetting
who you are." Dante turned him round the course until at last
they came to a bleak and dreary forest. Horacio almost regretting
the path they were on asked his guide, "What is this hideous place?"
"Ah, this is what they call the Woodland of Lament and Sorrow." Setting
the record straight Dante added, "*Taxus baccata.* Where souls go to face
the loss of hope for a brighter tomorrow. Sprung as yew trees rooted
to a poisonous seed, they pay for lethargy in life by being forced to retrace,
their past, seeing all that could have been, had they not remained muted
with inaction. Each time the wind blows it whips up a new memory,
as their leaves and branches are stirred into motion. Painfully persecuted,
these spirit filled trees howl long their pitiful serenade of misery,
locked in the constraints of an immobile penitentiary."

"How horrible!"
Horacio's heart was overcome.
"Oh, there are things here much more terrible,"
Dante reassured him. "Hold your pity for what is yet to come."
"Oh! Look how they torment us!" a wailing yawl cursed the wind
from hidden sources, as they trod the wooded path. "The scum!"
another cry screeched through the air. "Damn you for moving about unpinned.
Showing off so! We have done nothing to you. Why do you torture us like this?"
"Hush you!" Dante snapped to the yew. "Save your curses for the woodwind.
You have put yourselves where you want to be. None other than you is
responsible for your predicament." Dante then turned to Horacio, "Disregard
these creatures. It's their self-punishment to blame others for what they miss."
"Yes, I'm sure you're right, dear spirit." Horacio replied. "Yet it's still quiet hard
to dismiss their suffering." "Well," Dante nodded, "that only goes to show
the depth of your character. I shan't fault you for that. Just keep your guard,
for the deeper we go, the more others will try to draw you in. Although
your heart is pure, I cannot say the same for those we'll meet below."

Wisdom,
Horacio understood
the instruction to be and welcome.
If to fail now by some grift, how much regret would
he carry with him planted, himself as some bitter tree in this forest,
forever to lament his lack of fortitude and courage, as the rest of the wood
before him. Yes, he would guard his steps, as the upcoming tests
were sure to be more perilous. "Thank you for your counsel,"
he acknowledged Dante's good judgment. "Come, we should not rest
long here," Dante pressed them on. "Before us lies another obstacle."
Here they came to a fog covered marshland with many trails twisting
throughout. "The Dream Brood," Dante warned. "We must cross this circle
to arrive at the bridge that leads us further down. Here there be existing
tribes of scavenger children, born from the likes of some foul witch's brew,
all wayward and unruly, they are spirits dreaming in nightmares persisting,
even with open eyes." Then he advised, "Draw your sword before we continue.
That will keep them at a distance, as we work our way through."

Doing as instructed,
Horacio drew his blade,
as the scrape of metal conducted
upon the scabbard, a shivering bayed,
cast a warning across the marshland fog.
"Do not be drawn off the main path through this everglade,"
Dante gripped tight his staff. "Else you will be trapped within the bog,
never to find your way out again." Somewhere through the vapor and mist,
just out of view, a scuttle of whispers was calling, along with the croak of frog.
In spell making tongues, voices streamed out to greet them with a hiss,
"If foky kek jins bute, ma sal at lende;
for sore mush jins chomany, that tute kek jins."
The trailing voice, like some raspy disembodied duende,
called to them. "Careful," Dante saw how the words made them yearn
to follow. "It's a summoning spell." "What are they saying?" And Dante,
"'Whatever ignorance men may show, from none disdainful turn;
for every one doth something know, which you have yet to learn.'

"It's an old gypsy trick,"
Dante spoke of his rough translation.
"They call to you, using what they know will stick,
an unquenchable thirst for knowledge. They offer temptation
to draw you in with the promise of teaching you something
you don't already know. But then, once lost in their lair of frustration,
after stripping you bare of all that you're worth, you'll find the one thing
that you weren't already familiar with in terms of insight and experience
is the taste of your own mortality, which to you they'll willingly bring."

"You say they mean to kill me?" Horaicio now alert, holding a solid defense,
thanks to Dante's proclamation. "Yes, that's the lesson they would share.
Have no fear. As long as you stay on the path they can only menace
with words." They continued on under the watchful stare
of wayward shades in the shadows, occasionally receiving a taunt,
yet nothing more than what they were able to bare, as their share
of the toll for the passage. Exiting this troublesome marsh of want
their path then led them out to cross the first truly dangerous haunt.

There,
as they approached a clearing,
Horacio and Dante stopped where
they could yet go unnoticed, fearing
what waited for them just beyond the curve.
"Hear me," Dante in low tones spoke solemn, steering
the conversation to the next important task. "Preserve
one thought, no matter what happens you must remain hidden.
This bridge we come to is guarded by frightful demons who serve
that devil Pluto. If they discover you, there'll be no safe quarter given,
all eyes in hell would be turned to you." "Understood. I'll keep safe
within my helmet. But what of you?" Horacio, showing concern, didn't
want any harm coming to Dante either. "No. do not worry for my sake, strafe
won't fall upon me here. They know I'm free to wander at my own discretion.
Though they'll scowl about and curse and spit, foam their mouths will lathe,
they'll still let me pass unscathed." "Very well," nothing was left to question.
Horacio affixed his helmet and disappeared, as Dante led the procession.

On top
of a wide stone bridge,
sweaty from steaming slop,
a squadron of red winged demons cringe
with spear and pitchfork under the glow of torch light.
"Ahhh! Get your head back under or I'll stab and singe
you again." A pair of these foul creatures laughed at the plight
of passers-by beneath the waters, while a third toyed in the corner.
"Halt!" a forth one snarled a command, seeing the pilgrim come into sight,
heading in their direction. "Malebranche," Dante whispered, eyeing the scorner.
"Stand aside you devils!" Dante scoffed belligerent, without slowing his pace.
"Oy! Who dares give commands other than me at this station?" No sooner,
did the demon scowl before all were posing for a fight. Evil Bush Face,
Malofaciebus, the hell-walker's name, for the thousand pricks of blight
that spotted his head and leathery appearance. Scaly lizard skin in place
of flesh covered this demon's body, making his touch as cold as night.
"Out of my way!" Dante stayed undaunted. "Oh, darkness flee the light!"

“Ay, I know this sod,”
cried one devil in the back.
It was Scarmiglione. “Still worshipping the ‘one, true God’?”
he laughed, as the other demons snickered, drool sliding off the black
of their tongues. “And under His protection,” Dante held fast. “Move aside,
or you will suffer for your defiance.” Malofaciebus, looked over the jack.
“What do you know of this?” he conferred with the others on the side.
“Aye,” Scarmiglione grudgingly confessed, “he does move with permission.
But what of it? Come on, let me eat him, just a little taste of his hide.”
“No, no,” Malofaciebus pushed away the petition. “So I can pay for the nutrition
of your belly? I don’t think so. Get back in line.” The other two demons flapped
their wings and scowled, for now they wouldn’t get to ply their perdition.
With pitchfork in hand, the taller of the two howled and slapped
a shade whose head popped above the water, gashing its face to the ear.
“Take that,” the foul monster broke wind, as his partner callously clapped.
“Enough,” Malofaciebus, called the miscreant devils around him to rear,
and with a flourishing bow and a gaff, “You may pass without any fear.”

Feigning reverence,
on one knee, the four ghoulish fiends
lowered their horn-pointed heads, as if in deference,
though presenting only half as sober by generous means,
they mocked their piety with taunting chortles and laughs.
“All praise, most noble one,” the Fork-Tongued Pig, Furcapolinga, leans
in scoffing as Dante mounts the stone bridge, readying his staff’s
end to reproach the demon. “You’d do well to give Him praise,
if you knew what was good for you,” Dante returns and chaffs
the demon, who scuttles an inch backwards, to then again raise,
“Oh! Have pity on us, Lord, we are but ignorants.” The pig then burped,
lifting a chuckle from the others, from which another weighs
in with, “Amen,” to a general clamor of agreement. “Enough!” slurped
Malofaciebus. “Pass already.” Waving Dante through, he tired of the game.
Behind his back a whisper, “But doesn’t he know the King has been usurped?”
“Shhh!” the porky demon poked his partner, sniggering in quiet all the same.
“What he don’t know is...” he broke off to go torture one of the floating lame.

With the bridge
now a shrinking background,
and with it the demons too a smidge,
with a hand on his shoulder, Horacio wound
a whisper in the ear that only his partner could hear.
“What was that all about?” The known was on shaky ground.
And Dante, glancing around to ensure that no one else was near,
“The illusion that must be maintained. As long as they believe
that I believe, the devils are forced to submit. They think it’s my cross to bear.

Have no fear in the face of danger. If a hundred and forty years to grieve
in the underworld has taught me anything, it's to have a thick skin."
Horacio enjoyed his first light moment since entering this cleave
of land. "You're full of fine tricks, signore." Smiling, he lost all of his chagrin.
Yet now, with great peril they came to enter the Inferno proper, *Domos Hadou*,
the Dominion of Hades, a wretched wasteland, both hostile and barren.
Here, their path skirted treacherous slopes along a jagged skew,
forming a ridge that stretched out as far as the eye could view.

Down the rocky foothills,
opening to a sprawling vast canyon,
Mars and his henchmen tramped past landfills
of rotting flesh, circled by scavengers and other carrion
creatures of the sky. "Come, it's not much further,"
Mars stamped, leading the others, his voice a bellowing clarion
that demanded obedience. His mood as foul as the vulture
that pecked at the scraps of carnage off on the desolate range.
His eye was fixed on his destination, betraying the look of murder.
"Just across the orchards," he said, marching towards the fields of strange.
Here, on the outskirts, pools of tar boiled in pockets that spotted the dusty soil.
In them sat stewing the polluters, fossil barons and their minions. In exchange
of water, the midget demons who tended these caldrons, funneled crude oil
down their throats. "Drink up," they sneer. "This is all that you desired in life,
so now you get it back in plenty. There's no water here to buy... eh, don't recoil,
or for dinner you'll get gold." A hollow moan rolled in waves, as the air rife
with carbon chocked out their pleas, while hot pokers added to their strive.

Entering the orchard,
little need was there for the twins,
as fear and terror, a stinking dread, swung hard
against the wind. From the limbs and branches, hanging for their sins,
dangled slave masters and oligarchs, traders of both flesh and labor,
the exploiters of others. By the neck they stretched long, until their skins
were as thin as parchments. From below, with torches devils would savor
the scorching of toes and feet to keep the swingers always in motion.
"No rest until we get every drop out of you," one red devil pointed a saber,
while the spirits of the fallen were being squeezed of their last ration
of blood, the rent to be paid to the tree for the noose of their lodgings.
From left to right this fetid fruit orchard stretched out like an ocean
to either side. Here was harvested the trees' scarlet orb droppings
that hatched into tiny cursing demon sprites. In passing, Capitolina growled,
at these mischievous fiends, who on seeing her jumped and went dodging
behind a line of trees, "Ehhhr!" they spat, taunting and teasing, then howled.
Before long, Mars and his party, came to the egress of these woods befouled.

There,
coming into view,
the Palace of Hades laid bare.
Distant no longer, the welcome was well overdue.
Having been ferried across the Acheron, Pluto retook his carriage,
whereby a hidden bridge, he traversed the Stygian Marsh, and coming through
the Asphodel Fields, passed the shades of the indifferent dead, who forage
peacefully, neither blessed nor damned, but somewhere of balance amidst
the storm. Having skirted the interior range, and coming around the final ridge,
Pluto sighed his first moment of comfort since having departed the abyss.
"Home at last," he felt relief as his team of stallions crossed the palace gate.
Yet that moment was destined to only be fleeting, as the coming of an eclipse,
for upon his doorstep, hell was breaking loose. Cerberus growling, in a spate,
was squaring off with the she-wolf Capitolina, each testing the other's resolve.
"What's this?" Pluto quelled the situation, ordering calm before it was too late.
"Forgive the clamor, my lord," the demon in charge groveled to himself absolve.
"Mars has just arrived." "Oh great," Pluto exhaled. "Another problem to solve."

BOOK XXIX

WITHIN THE PALACE OF HADES

Across the great plains
of suffering, where trapped were the wretched
hoards of interest merchants tormented by thirsty pains
after death, did Horacio and Dante pass. The view stretched
out beyond the horizon into an infinite haze of dust that swirled
around in great clouds, choking the throats of those who in life wrenched
away the world's resources for themselves alone. Chained by foot, they curled
against the biting dust that pecked at their faces. "This is where the bankers
and speculators are kept," Dante gave the tour. "The impoverishment unfurled
by their actions, the stripping of the essentials of life, has led them like cankers
to these fields. Here they are always cold and hungry, denied a place to sleep
and just when they think they'll get a moment of rest, along comes the rankers
of blue demons with sticks, to jab them in the side." "Look at this heap!"
balked one of the keepers, ready to throw a kick. "Where'd you find cardboard?
You think you're allowed such luxury?" the demon spat, snarling with teeth.
"Pay it no mind," Dante assured his companion. "It's the final reward
for their earthly investments." "And just," Horacio struck a chord.

Past these fields,
there came into view,
as if a tall mountain that yields
bone, a great ivory palace. Closer to this they drew,
merging with a road, wide and well travelled, that led to the halls
of Hades' justice. Here a ridged bureaucracy ruled, as if by some voodoo
to bewilder and confuse, an endless spiraling frustration of regulations befalls
the shades and souls awaiting their final judgment. It was on this road
that they began to cross the souls of those newly judged amidst their calls
for mercy. Yet none would be had for those being led to their new abode
amongst greyer pastures. Occasionally, a snarl would be cast Dante's way,
though none would care to bother, he wasn't of their concern as he strode
past, his companion hidden with sword beside him. It wasn't until they
approached the citadel's battlements that there arose any challenge
at all. Here, as Dante walked the cobblestone, haunted with cries to the flay
of whips and their cleaving, merely a few lengths away, a demon with talons
stopped him to say, "What are you doing here?" with a look most savage.

"Out of my way!"
Dante, showing more courage
than might be expected, hastened to say.
"I'm here on the Lord's work. Making revisions, you savage."
"Alright," the demon grumbled. "No need to get feisty, I was only checking."
"Well, maybe I'll check you with a blow from my staff?" Dante added damage
to his tone. "Never mind him," a second demon chided the first, deflecting
by tapping a finger to his head. "Oh, ha-ha, yeah," the first one backed away
and started to laugh. "One of those. Yeah, you may pass," without inspecting
him further. "If ever you want to join a buccaneer crew, all ya gotta do is say,"
Horacio whispered to Dante encouragement once they were in the clear.
"It's just a matter of being the first dog to bite." In reflection, Dante
probably would have chosen his words more carefully, for just as they veer
past the fiery moat, glowing with lava and brimstone, through the crested
palace gates, they see Pluto's carriage idle, with stallions neighing, and here,
on one side of the courtyard lounged the she-wolf, while on the other nested
Cerberus. Between the two was the gauntlet that would have to be bested.

Even though being invisible,
for Horacio, the entrance to the palace
was terrifying. If it had been permissible
he'd have avoided this obstacle altogether. Alas,
this was the course he'd have to follow. "Wait a minute, I know that hound,"
he gave fair warning. "If she catches my scent, I fear we'll both face malice."
"Alright," Dante thought, looking over the scene. "In that case we stay bound,
as close we can to the other side. Still, that three headed monster is as equally
dangerous, if not more so. Keep close to that file of dead," advice being sound,
as even in death the shades had a vile stench about them, like a potpourri
of putrescence that lingered. So treading carefully, keeping an even pace,
they crept past the sleeping beasts, and up the short stairs which naturally
led towards the pillar framed and marbled columned entrance. A place
of opulence and terror, this seat of underworld power, which carved upwards,
chiseled like some glorious cathedral of the night, was Pluto's palace.
As a mighty fjord, it stood there overwhelming the receding withering yards
of pain below, cast in a molten glow from the moat, reflecting vermilion shards.

"Hall of Records,"
Dante looked up at the gruff
character that stood before the entry, towards
the inner chambers. Giving him the once over enough,
the demon on duty by the door returned a gnarling, "Thirteenth floor."
Here they entered the heart of the Hades' bureaucracy, being the stuff
of which nightmares are made. Each and every single shade that comes before
the Court of Hades, must submit to presenting their case before the judge.
For this, they must make the Herculean journey to pass through the door

of their own lives, making account for all of their actions. So the spirits drudge
up the thirteen flights, there being no such thing as an elevator, to commence
the process of laying bare the soul. Here, in the Hall of Records, from a smudge
to a headline, it's all there to witness, objectively as an impartial observance,
laid bare. From there the guilt or innocence is a relative formality,
what is of interest though, what can vary wildly, is the penance,
for there are two types of punishment a spirit can receive in their finality,
those that are voluntary and those of mandatory legality.

That is why
the judges exist,
to ensure that by and by
no soul may escape justice,
to protect against the chance that some clever
shade might come by and be truly remorseless,
one who, regardless of right or wrong, would endeavor
to evade their destine fate, as would a narcissist simply not care,
sending himself to Elysium without a second thought. And so there is the lever,
the impartial, brutally fatal judges, Minos, Rhadamanthys, Aeacus, who stare
into your very soul, and at the root, know the truth of your core existence,
so that with surety, and the underlying principles of uncertainty, whether fair
or not, we each wind up where we need to be. So here, as the poet's remittance,
Horacio and Dante climbed the final steps leading to the thirteenth floor.
Nearly out of breath, both man and spirit, gave new meaning to persistence.
"This is as far as I'm able to travel in the palace," Dante pointed to the door.
"Beyond here, lies Pluto's private wing. I cannot be seen down that corridor."

"Fair enough,"
Horacio concurred with his guide.
"Will you be alright here?" not knowing how long or rough
might be his absence. "Oh don't you worry about me. I have no need to hide,"
Dante reassured him, "I brought a notebook with me to make some revisions.
I'll stay here assuming my disguise, while you make busy on the inside."
It was a good plan, and all they had to go with. "Beyond those partitions,
you must find a key in the shape of an hourglass. That's what opens the portal
you're searching for," Dante described the skeleton. "By all the prophet visions,
there's only one place he keeps it. Upon his person." Horacio felt mortal
as never before. "Well," Horacio considered the options, "if you see me back
here any time soon, don't worry, it's just my ghost checking in post-mortal.
Otherwise, I'll contact to you upon my return." Then, going on the attack,
Horacio left Dante making his way down the corridor into the private wing
of the palace, where Pluto kept his offices. Down this lonely marbled track,
set apart from the throngs of groaning spirits and other beastly offspring,
Horacio could hear approaching a voice being raised. "And another thing..."

It was Mars,
staking out his position.
“Ever since you closed Olympus from the stars,
I haven’t been able to just descend upon the opposition.
Now I have to chase them down. Sure I could cut them off,
if I knew where you kept all your secret doorways, magician,
but I don’t. Besides the whole point of being able to descend,” he began to scoff,
“is to have a place to descend from. To be able to step back and take a look
at the bigger picture... to evaluate the situation and see the tradeoff,
which you have prevented me from doing.” Now he was beginning to cook.
“All just temporary inconveniences,” Pluto poured a cup of Mars’s favorite wine.
“You’ve been saying that for a thousand years,” crossing the room like a rook,
Mars came up close to his uncle. “It’s time to pay that check,” being his line.
“Here,” Pluto, passing the goblet to Mars, took a few steps to give distance.
Turning, as though matter-of-factly, “You do make a valid point, that’s fine.
Come, let’s talk in the map room.” He guided Mars, as if rewarding insistence,
to an adjacent gallery, where a large tactical map gave them visual assistance.

“Look here,”
Pluto with the wave of a hand
gave a demonstration, a vision to share
with his partner of necessity. “Let me expand,”
Pluto made a gesture towards the table laden with diagrams,
images of new peoples and lands, territories far reaching and grand.
“Here will be founded the greatest empire yet to come. From fields of lambs
there’ll flourish a nation of lions that you’ll lead into the most glorious battles
ever seen. For not just the sake of brute force, my lad,” by inches and grams,
Pluto applied his craft, soothing just enough ego to balance between rattles
for destiny and fame. “Together, you and I will united the entire planet
under a single banner and through the subsequent power struggles,
our strength will grow to a magnitude hitherto unimaginable, truly titanic.”
“Then what?” Mars, with the taste for blood, took a sip from his chalice.
“Then,” Pluto looked out, across his majestic columned balcony to the magnet
that pulled at his thoughts, “the stars. To the ever expanding cosmos borealis.
From here we’re bound by no limits, the entire universe shall be our palace.”

Quietly,
Horacio infiltrated
their meeting, silently
listening in, as the gods debated
the conquest and, as a direct consequence,
lordship over all things both living and dead. Fascinated
by the sheer audacity of the plan, of how one could even commence
contemplating such a vast, far reaching endeavor, to be such a terribly large
being that one could hold the entire universe in the palm of their hand, whence

Death, the God of the Underworld, Pluto, was set on launching his barge
to verily become such an omnipotent creature, with Mars, the powers of war,
his strong arm and second. Surely, Horacio could not just simply charge
into battle and fight these gods alone, but there must be something more
that he could do about it, to prevent such an inglorious finishing line.
Then he thought, *Perhaps that's precisely my mission?* Scanning the score,
he looked for where the opportunity presented, and as if touched by the divine,
an idea came to mind, spotting Mars's full beaker of wine.

Reaching within
the pocket of his satchel,
Horacio withdrew from the sheepskin
the remainder of the elderberries gifted, and being not bashful
squeezed them into Mars's cup. "Quite impressive," Mars applauded
the plan, wetting his lips once again. "Yes," Pluto concurred. "So I grapple
with why, when we have so much important work already plotted,
that you'd go off and chase after some trifling mortal in the first place?"
Already feeling a bit intoxicated, Mars spoke most freely and lauded
Pluto with information that more sober lips might have kept safe as an ace.
"I think we're related." Horacio froze cold hearing the words, however Pluto
was warming with interest. "Is that so?" he turned and began to retrace
his path back into the interior chamber. "Well, I suppose congratulations go
to the father? One of your mortal spawn I'm assuming?" "Grandson in fact,"
Mars looked up from his goblet. "Concordia's child, I'm thinking." To know
that was something Pluto was very grateful for, something he'd keep to retract
at a most needed moment. But more was still to know before he would act.

"Tell me,"
he said, preparing
for a longer discussion, steeping a tea.
"What makes you so certain?" Pluto asked, glaring
across the distance that separated them. And Mars, already slightly
slurring, replied, "He has her eyes." Listening in disbelieve, with more daring
yet to be demanded, Horacio composed himself, the information to rightly
be processed later, still having a job to do. There, spotting his chance,
he crumpled some chamomile in with the other steaming herbs, so lightly
as not to be heard, and stepped out of the line of their banter. As circumstance
would have it, the knowledge was of both use and concern. "How interesting,"
Pluto spoke of the tell, as he gathered his cup, and sipping resumed his stance.
From opposite chairs the two gods sat facing each other, "Go on, I'm listening,"
Pluto continued. The last thing he'd want is for Harmony to mess with his plan,
yet it was still highly inconclusive. On his hip, his key ring jingled, the sting
was yet to come, as he settled in comfortable, questioning Mars. "Can
you tell me why this offspring is worth the bother? He is after all just a man?"

Dizzily,
Mars made to answer,
and leaning in quite busily,
"He found Aethalia," he managed to swear.
"Really?" Pluto yawned. "And the passage though the mines?"
"That's where I lost him," Mars's head slapped the table like a flamenco dancer.
"What's wrong with you?" Pluto, feeling weary himself succumbs and reclines,
finally nodding off in no time. With one god slobbering and the other asleep,
this was the moment he'd been awaiting. As a spider dropping from the vines,
Horacio approached most cautiously in silence. There, by Pluto's side he creep,
and seeing the ring of keys, spotted one very different. *This must be it.* Sure
he was of the find. With teeth in the shape of an hourglass, only one did leap
to the eye. Working the latch that secured the ring, with intention to procure
needed item, Horacio froze as Pluto shifted in his slumber, his pounding heart
enough to set off the alarm bells. Yet through such terror he would endure
and unhooking the key, Horacio stepped back slowly as he made to depart,
and stashing it upon his person, he retraced his footsteps back to the start.

Meanwhile,
at the Hall of Records
Dante was keeping track of the lines of dead that file
past his refrain. It was truly a cog-like mechanism, with each of the wards
of the court having to take precise measurements, right down to the nanobyte,
of their souls, weighing to which side of the scale they fell, striking chords
of fret through many a shade, as the agony of waiting was only a slight
better than, in quite a few cases, of knowing one's fate, a punishment
in its own right, for those who were only human. To his left and his right,
the sounds of calculator and abacus tapped out their reports to supplement
the wrenching footsteps of the mechanism that turned the soul robotic.
An essential part of the workings of hell, Dante noted down as a comment
in his ledger, *is that it's fundamentally a zero-sum game. Individuals sporadic,
move up and down, but the masses don't matter. All important is the machine,
keeping the whole thing moving. The masses are just food and the product, sic.*
So it is written, he scrawled in his notebook, in detail describing the scene.
There, Dante, the scribe of the afterlife, had his eye on the screen.

Behind it all,
stared a holographic eye,
emanating off some distant back wall,
observing everything, as an ever present spy
and overlord, silently watching, here, in the brain of the beast,
in the prism where all knowledge was stored and collected, rested the why.
It is not for one's sins we're all examined, Dante's words rose as would yeast
upon the paper, *but for a matter much more dark and sinister. Information birth
the key to this infernal Hades' power. Only by knowing all from the deceased,*

all of their weaknesses, may Pluto maintain absolute control over the hearth of damnation, he closed his journal. *Fortunate are the living they have no such ability to consolidate so much information, or it would likewise be a hell on Earth,* he thought to himself in reflection, as from out of nowhere he felt a touch.
"Time to go," Horacio whispered in his ear with a sense of hurried urgency.
"Right," Dante shook. "Didn't see you coming," he gathered himself in a rush and made for the exit. "Thirteen flights down, I hope it's not an emergency?"
Dante noted on an aside. "Me too, but let's not wait for an insurgency."

Horacio pushed them on.
And Dante, "But also not too quick.
Nothing stands out more than someone
making a break for the door. You've got to be slick
about it." Horacio could not argue with the reasoning,
they had to be patient taking the stairs at the same click
as all the rest of the spirits, Horacio's heart internally secreting
to burst from his chest, biting his lip at the thought that at any moment
an alarm could sound, and they within the palace trapped. Yet the seasoning
was still in his favor, as they finally arrived, without so much as a comment
from any of the demons guarding the passages, back at the ground floor.
Here time moved, not that it even existed in the underworld, but, like cement,
at this moment it moved incrementally as they made for the archway door.
Exiting the palace, the same demon as the one before, grunted to acknowledge
Dante's leaving, but made no move to stop him. And then, taking once more
to the stairs that fed out to the courtyard, forgetting the scent of his mileage,
Horacio passed the she-wolf, who still drowsy sniffed the air with knowledge.

"Tell me you got it?"
Dante asked as they cleared the palace,
now heading south, down a slope that dotted
away from their present dangers and into an atlas
of even greater misfortune than any would care to witness.
"Right here," Horacio patted the fold of his tunic, where out of malice
he kept safe his prize. "Yet, that is not all there is to this business,"
he recalled the revelations of his true lineage, as recounted by Mars.
"Stranger things have been known to happen," Dante spoke as an eyewitness,
weighing what the omens foretell. "If I read the meaning of these aligning stars,
if it is true what you say, that Pluto has taken an interest in you, then sooner,
more likely than later, he will find you and when he does it will be no farce,
he will lay all his power to bear upon you." Not wishing to be the crooner
of ill fortune, Dante thought on a solution. "There may be a light in the dark,"
he spoke with a modicum hope, remembering a legend older than lunar.
"We must get to the River Styx. It's your only chance, and that being stark."
As Dante spoke those words, in the distance behind them, a dog began to bark.

BOOK XXX

CROSSING THE RIVER STYX

From high up in the palace,
the sounds of barking below could be heard
echoing upward. Mars, stirring with aching head, was feeling callous
and staggered to the terrace to see what was the matter. "Quiet!" was the word
he mustered, seeing Capitolina acting flustered. "And you two," he scolded
Timor and Formido, who were busying themselves, frightening the cursed herd.
"Make yourselves useful and stop torturing the already damned." Arms folded
akimbo, he turned back away from the balcony's view to then again stumble
inside. "Oh my head," he muttered, having spent the last while molded
to a table and chair, now he was worse for wear. At the same time a rumble
was brewing, as Pluto likewise awoke from his slumber. "What happened?"
he wondered aloud, not feeling quite himself after such an unexpected tumble
with sleep. Groggily, he sat up. "Looks like you tied one on too," Mars penned
from behind, reentering the map room. "Indeed," Pluto regained his composure,
trying to make sense of the scene, when suddenly his own mood blackened.
Sniffing, the memory of fragrance came to him, a scent of familiar exposure
that he just couldn't place. "Chamomile," he finally recalled, now being sure.

"Bad blood,"
Mars then said, looking to his goblet.
"What was that?" Pluto asked, already hearing the thud.
"Bad blood," he repeated. "Look, it's coagulated, almost like chocolate,"
showing the dregs of his cup. Eyes narrowing, Pluto sniffed and stood all tense.
"That's not blood, you idiot! It's elderberries!" he spoke of the droplet.
"Elderberries?" Mars took a double take, trying to make sense,
while Pluto quickly added up the figures, rushing to his pot, counting herb.
"Son of a..." he muttered and spat. Pivoting, having dropped all pretense,
death turned to war, as Pluto asked, "This offspring you say you couldn't curb,
was last seen on Aethalia?" "Ah yes," Mars coughed. "Why do you ask?"
Pluto, stepped closer, very close, eyeing Mars up and down, cursing a verb
in his head he asked, "Where is my helmet?" And Mars, trying to mask
the obvious, said, "Oh yes, about that." Pausing, thinking how best to break
the news, Mars considered his words. "It's not something that should tax
you," he went for nonchalant, "but I seem to have misplaced it in the wake
of all these events." "Misplaced?" Pluto exhaled to release the fumes he make.

“Of all the irresponsible...”
Pluto stepped back, lest all he’d been building be for naught.
“It’s not lost exactly, that is I know where it is,” Mars spoke as if not impossible
the retrieval. “Or rather, who has it,” his story began to unravel on the spot.
“How is this even possible?” Then, Pluto again on second thought, “Never mind,
I don’t want to know. What I do want is for this bastard to be caught,
so I can question him myself.” Then, looking at Mars sternly, “We must find
him forthwith and you’d better pray that he didn’t get the ambrosia.”
“I’m on it,” Mars didn’t need to be told twice, already his feet inclined
towards the door, desiring to leave well enough alone. And then for nostalgia
instead he leapt off the terrace. Ah, he loved descending, it’s something
the gods did best, so much better than taking the stairs. “Aethalia,”
he might have known, Pluto paced back and forth in his quarters, wondering
what Love had to do with it? That was the question circling round his head,
“What did he truly know about Venus?” Could she be somehow posturing?
Anything Concordia’s involved in, she’s only doing in her mother’s stead.
But why would she be sending a mortal to the land of the dead?

Even for Pluto,
this was confounding.
“Women should never be underestimated,” didn’t he know?
This for him was common knowledge, something he often found astounding,
but now, tables turned, there was a riddle to decipher. “Information.
I need more information. Why risk coming all the way here?” Rounding
a turn, he thought on the sound as the keys on his belt jangled. “Damnation!”
he swore. Below, Mars had already departed, having picked up a scent
of his own. “Well done,” he petted the she-wolf, as she led the congregation
south into the badlands. “I’ll have to deal with this myself,” Pluto bent,
turned away from the balcony’s ledge, reaching for his bident scepter,
and called for his battle chariot, for speed there now needs to be spent
in order to cut off the challenge to his rule above and below, this specter
of hope must be crushed. On he rushed, mounting his chariot, down
the road four horses raced bound for the deep of Tartarus. The collector
of the dead had one more soul to reap. Well ahead of the crackdown,
yet not far enough by half, Horacio and Dante came to the ghost town.

Here,
in the Asphodel Fields,
where shades of the indifferent appear
to wander aimlessly through a darkness that never yields,
lost amidst the illusion, the pair came to be. “Few demons ever cross
through here,” Dante gave reason for their course. “In here what wields
power is the mind. Nothing you see is real. These spirits are all at a loss.
All would be needed is to open one’s eyes to be granted passage to Elysium,
yet trapped are they in their own thoughts of despair, that out they toss

any idea of happiness." "Much as it be in life," Horacio noted the delirium
brought on by floating too long on trackless seas. "If only one might choose
a direction?" "So be it," Dante agreed, seeing the spirits as fish in an aquarium,
swimming in circles forgetting each moment what was the last, to use
what time they had with useless meandering, a fate as sad as many a story
that have come before. "There's no purpose in trying to light a fuse
here, none would even take notice," Dante pressed. "Yet even such purgatory
might offer us some assistance to our own quest migratory."

"How so?"
Horacio's interest was piqued.
"That wolf that bayed on our departure," Dante let Horacio know
the source of his apprehension. "Undoubtedly, there'll be others tweaked
by our doings and the trail will lead them straight to these very meadows,"
he spoke of a *fait accompli.* "And this is where they'll stay." Streaked
across the vast horizon were the countless hordes of lost shadows
and Dante planned to make use of them. "Remove your shirt,"
he instructed. "Excuse me?" Horacio added, considering his clothes.
"For bait," Dante clarified. "Cut it into strips, so your scent we can divert
into multiple directions." "Right!" Horacio understood the tactician,
slicing his chemise to ribbons. Then with so many bands of cloth for skirt,
the pair fastened the musky smelling strips of fabric as an addition
to many a spirits' wears, while they muddled by in their endless streams
of sloth. "Well done," Dante watched, as each shade trailed on to perdition
tailored to distract the hounds. "Now, my friend," he continued, "it seems
that we have a mission to complete." Bound were they for the extremes.

Through the valley,
they turned, cutting east,
in effect setting a course squarely
perpendicular to their current line of sight, creased
directly towards their objective, the River Styx, and beyond
down the fiery Pyriphlegethon to Tartarus, occupied by Hades' fiercest beasts.
A plum and violet twilight greeted them, as a storm being spawned,
when they reached the descending slope that looked out over the river's murk.
"Hurry, we need to get there before the boatman's return," seeing how dawned
the night, Dante was want to make speed. Sensing something more at work,
Horacio beckoned, "Tell me signore, since we left the palace, you appear
most troubled. Is it the risk ahead that weighs on you?" Dante, not with irk,
but with urgence, waved Horacio on. "Come, I'll tell you as we go," he steer
them down the slope. "It's not fear of what's ahead, but of that we left behind
that drives me so," Dante had to acknowledge. "Not for myself, to be clear,
but for you." Touched, Horacio felt the need to respond in kind.
"That is greatly appreciated, and for your safety I'm of similar mind."

"No, you misunderstand,"
Dante corrected the record.
"If what you say about your heritage will stand,
that you are born from the line of an immortal chord,
then you are in terrible danger." Just then, from somewhere across the plain
came to their ears the lingering howl of a wolf, the momentary calm scored
by fright, as the chase commenced in earnest. Back still a ways, Mars strain
to find the path. "My lord," reported Timor, "the ground is a mash with prints."
"And Capitolina remains undecided," Formido likewise added to their pain.
It was true the she-wolf was flummoxed, with each direction leaving hints,
she could not say for sure where her suckling lay, causing her to howl
in her longing. "Leave it," Mars chided the noise. "Give me silence," he glints.
There, as they do, Timor, the fear, and Formido, the dread, scowl
forth leaving nothing but the stillness of terror in their wake.
"Where would I go?" Mars thought in quiet to distill the answer. "Yowl!"
in the eye of the storm, he found his solution and the road he needed to take.
"We travel east." he finally commanded, beneath them the ground to shake.

"They mean to kill you,"
Dante was most clear on the topic.
"As a man, you're no match for the gods. Yet there are a few,
and the signs say you're one, who from a certain optic
may still lay waste to their plans, who may right a wrong,
might even change a perspective, to redefine the objective, sic.
So it is written," Dante say. "Even though mortal, a soul that is strong,
has the power to change the world, and with it the destiny of the stars,
thereby living on." Horacio drew inspiration from such a noble song,
"You seem to speak of honor and not a fate most terrible and sparse."
"True there's that too, but greater still the responsibility then becomes
to balance the scales just right. You're the unknown, there are no bars,
you are what they fear, the unknown possibility that drums and drums
in their ears, of just what would happen if all those lost souls in the fields
suddenly at once all opened their eyes and demanded their own Elysium.
What do you think would happen if that power Pluto no longer wields?
That's why my friend," Dante paused, "your destiny lies on these battlefields."

"It sounds as if you speak from experience?"
Horacio hasten to ask, recognizing the courage and knowledge
his companion had shown this entire way. "Yes, it is true, in a sense,"
Dante admitted, "I am, as you've guessed, a free spirit. One of a college
of sorts, of those few who instead of fearing the strength of power,
have learnt to conduct it, like water, taking the shape of whichever wedge
that presents itself, letting it flow while directing the current. However,
every one of us is different in their own way, as you and I are each unique.
Though I have access and am free from harassment, as if hell's own wallflower,

there's little I can do but scribble and observe, that is the weave that I pique.
You however... ah well, you truly frighten these gods and their ruling elite.
That's why we have to get you to these waters before a certain clique
catches up with you. Right now, you're still vulnerable, just meat.
If caught in the interval, dead. But in a skin mortal, descendent
of the gods no less, there is a way by ancient ritual that can defeat
even death, and though not immortal, would make you transcendent
to that of an invincible, unconquerable ascendant."

"Come again?"
a startled Horacio checked
his hearing. "What's this that you've lain
before me?" "Yes, the word I speak is correct,"
Dante reassured. "By ancient scrolls it is told,
the secret of River Styx, that any mortal subject
to these waters, shall inherit these power foretold,
of invulnerability in combat. It is therefore with haste
we must make for this place on the coast before the cold
hand of death befalls you." Now too did Horacio have the taste
for speed, redoubled his motivation. If maybe not to best, but to at least
hold his own against these powerful gods, perhaps it wouldn't be such a waste
to partake in this Stygian baptism? And here, within distance their eyes feast
already on the waters, where Horacio must face an unusual challenge.
For here on the banks, safely wrapped in armor that could fend off any beast,
blanketed with the gift of invisibility, enabling him with extraordinary carriage,
he must now strip down bare, discarding it all, vulnerability the rite of passage.

"Hurry now,"
Dante urged, "the mist grows
on the far off bank. Soon it will plow
our way carrying the boatman and his crows,
delivering the dead to these banks. The hour is late."
Horacio exhaled, holding the moment, to savor the final flows
of this stage of his life. No matter what happens in the course of his fate,
he'd never be able to go back to this instant standing on the brink
of such a life changing choice. And done in his mind, he did not hesitate.
What had life been, if not to lead him here from whence he wouldn't shrink?
First his vest, then his boots and legging and breastplate. His sword,
in scabbard, he laid carefully down, and all the rest until the final link,
the helmet concealing his presence. "Now I feel truly naked," he gave his word,
laying it on top of his clothing. "Quick now, complete the ritual plunge,"
Dante urged, on the lookout for any rogue demons. Horacio, in accord
dove into the waters of Styx, and as through the liquid his body lunge,
his muscled soaked up its power, as though like a sponge.

Just as Thetis,
was there to hold her son,
Achilles, when submerged into quietus
Hades and River Styx, he the heir of Myrmidon,
so too had come Concordia, to be there with Horacio
in his own transformative moment. There, as about he spun
in those waters, she appeared to him as a vision whispering in stereo.
"Here, as you are blessed with the strength of these waters, dear child,
do not forget the pledges made in order to attain such power. The ratio
of your worth, is the measure of your word. Stay true, no matter how wild,
and the gods will be there to protect you." Then, trailing off hauntingly, "Soon,"
was her final word. Concordia swept off with the current, as Horacio styled
his hand, reaching out for her, when there by the wrist he was taken as boon,
pulled out of the water. "Thought you were going to drown, you were in there
so long." Dante helped him back to solid footing. On the air there rose a croon.
"Those are the crows that fore-call the boatman. Quickly, on with your wear."
Now, fog arriving and two again one, Horacio slipped Dante coin for the fare.

Docking,
streams of the dead
and damned came flocking
to the shores. New sheep to be led
to Asphodel and the slow march of oblivion.
"Look at how these wrathful and sullen tread
along the muddy riverbank, gnawing an angry idiom,"
Dante revisited a sight he'd sooner forget. "Come, we descend,"
he spoke, seeing that the last had disembarked having crossed the Stygian.
"It's time to meet your brother." "My what?" Horacio whispered from his end.
"Well, half in any case, another father's son." Such introduction would suffice
for the moment, if passage they were to barter. "Say Phlegyas, let me bend
your ear a moment," Dante called to the boatman. "What would be the price
for transit?" "Ha," Phlegyas horned and bearded turned, eyes to estimate
the petitioner. "You know souls may not go back across. This is not the device."
"Ah, but I only wish to go further on," Dante pressed, "to the lower climate."
"Didn't you see enough your last time through?" Phlegyas held the stalemate.

"Ah, what difference
does that make to you?"
Dante shot back in his defense.
"I'm here to make revisions. Besides, as your due,
I can offer you silver." He showed the glimmer of coin.
"Where'd you get that?" Phlegyas shot, as Dante drew
back from his clutch. "None of your business, but allow me to join
and it's yours." "Er... very well," the boatman grunted and let out a mutter,
claiming his prize, he let his passenger enter. Casting off, he set to rejoin

the water's current. "To Tartarus and the lower realm," he then did utter.
"The consequences are all your own." Phlegyas clad in flowing robes that clung
as the wind gusted and blew, stood at the bow using his long oar as a rudder,
pushing past the bobbing clumps of shade that fought each other for a lung
of air, before being pushed back under. "Too bad they're not still mortal,"
Phlegyas did jest, "else wise, they'd all be invincible, and we'd be flung
in the water to join them." Dante looked up, "Indeed," he spoke with a chortle.
"That would be something to see, this far beyond the portal."

"Ah, but shades
don't have that advantage,"
Phlegyas, thought on his time in Hades.
"Had I such opportunity in life, much I'd manage
quite different," he spat bitter, rubbing the sore of his wound.
"Where Apollo shot you?" Dante inquired. "Yes, the disadvantage
of being born only mortal. The gods can strike at whim. But no longer bound
am I to stone, that in itself a blessing. I much prefer my present employment,
ferrying souls by the pull of my oar, work that is both honest and sound."
Deep into the marsh they wove, with cries and moans for their enjoyment,
as the souls of those forever tormented, drowning in debt, unable ever to pay
the boatman treaded and sank in turn. Above, looking over this entertainment,
Mars and his company came to the ledge, a little too late their arrival this day.
Unable to intervene, they watched as Phlegyas ferried a lone hooded figure
across the Styx. "Should we give chase, my lord?" Timor asked if he may,
but Mars had other intentions. "No. From here we cannot lay a finger.
We must cut him off at the pass to Tartarus. Come, there's no time to linger."

BOOK XXXI

BY FIRE AND GNASH

The first test
of his heightened ability
would come much sooner than he'd have guessed.
For as they curved the Stygian, there grew a volatility
to the waves, just past where the white rock of Leucas connects
the marshes to the river of flame, the Pyriphlegethon, and all of her hostility,
as she flows towards the bowels of hell. The water around them, in context,
was bubbling, as from underneath the heat began to rise, when by surprise,
Phlegyas declares, "The still living had better show himself to me, or the next
thing that will happen is I'll deliver the both of you to Pluto myself." With sighs
of, "What do you mean?" Dante deflects, yet to no avail, the jig was up.
"You think I don't know the weight of my own boat?" he scowls and cries
visibly vexed. "Look how it drags in the current. There's living mass in my cup.
Show yourself now, or you'll only wish to be sent to Tartarus." Discovered,
Horacio had no choice but to remove his helmet, yet this was only the windup.
Once becoming visible to the naked eye, there was a moment that hovered,
as momentarily stun, Phlegyas ducked and covered.

"Lord Apollo!"
the boatman groveled.
Seeing the breastplate's glow
upon Horacio's torso, Phlegyas swallowed
the thought that it was the sun god himself,
returned from the missing, having him followed
beyond the grave, to put more punishment on his shelf.
"Forgive me, I did not know it was you," his lesson well learnt
within the walls of Tartarus, to honor and respect the gods in self.
"Oh no, you've got it all wrong," Horacio adjusted the current.
"I'm not Apollo, and I wish you no ill will..." was about as much
as he had managed to say, for Phlegyas, smoldering with eyebrows bent,
realizing the err of his ways, and being equally embarrassed and such,
yawped with fury, and from a lowered stance lunged out full throttle.
It was more the suddenness of the attack than the boatman's touch
that threw Horacio off balance. Yet unharmed, it was Phlegyas failing to dawdle
who jammed his shoulder and dazed, he fell, pitched overboard like a bottle.

Throwing out curses,
with his one good arm he paddled
to a nearby jutting rock, where verses
left Phlegyas nursing his wounded pride. Embattled,
Horacio took hold of the single oar, righting the boat which threshed
to every bump in the water. Safe onboard, the new crew now settled.
Before them, pinkish orange waters to a flickering red they stretched
down a twisting slope that burned a molten river. Screams of phosphorous
would haunt Horacio to his dying day, hearing the tormented as they meshed
with the lava. Ahead, rose into view, the foundry cliffs, a cascading chorus
of fire-falls, that plunged ever deeper into Tartarus, to the most lowest rings.
"By Jove," Horacio was crestfallen seeing such despair being solely prosperous.
"What have we gotten into?" the true danger of his mission now strings
perilously in sight. "This is the path," Dante assures him. "It's not a pretty one.
There," he pointed. "Guide the boat to dock. This is as far as she brings
us, from here we must manage by foot." Steering by oar, completing the run,
Horacio brought them to port, tied to the wharf, helmet on, ready, they begun.

A sweaty, stone cliff
greeted them, as they disembarked.
Over the edge, there fell the fiery pit. To sift
through such a sight would require a ledger earmarked
for its own. The glowing demon sprites and jagged toothed monsters
slithered, like a snake pit over one another in some living Botticelli, embarked
upon a furious mission. Gnawing on the closest catch, in the pit there stirs
a host of evil spirits, clawing from their terraces, all with malicious intent.
As even the bravest may show doubt, Horacio too felt the biting spurs
of fear cut into him, looking out in that moment. "What horror," he bent
a whisper, if for no one other than himself. "Come," Dante urged.
"The way is steep and fraught with danger. No time can be spent
resting in deliberation." "Yes, you're right. Lead on," Horacio purged
any lingering thoughts, except that to see through to the end his mission.
With sweat greasing the brow from the rising temperatures that surged
the closer they'd get to the core, they proceed along the downward incision,
as steam glowed, rising as a magenta smoke out from the furnace's emission.

"How long
will it take to complete
this path?" Horacio eyed the throng
below. "Oh, time is all relative here," Dante beat
back the notion to laugh. "Years can pass by in an instant,
while seconds a lifetime and more. The question you should instead repeat
is, 'What is it I must still endure, to achieve the dream I seek?' Constant
is this struggle, that's sure, and it will continue long after we're both just dry
dust upon the wind. What matters more is whether or not you're persistent

in using well the time given, for one way or another the end will come, if by
the design you imagine, or by another yet to be seen, the finish line is there
before you. All that's left to be known is whether you can cross it, or nigh?"
Dante in answering one question raised so many more. Yet, to be fair,
it was exactly what Horacio needed to hear. Time is not so subjective,
he understood this to be true. A straight line may not always be where
the quickest path lie, and so too with time, being lineal in the perspective
may not always lead one to their desired objective.

Refocused,
on the path ahead,
in short order they came to a sprawl of locusts.
"Then from the smoke came locusts," Dante quoted from his head.
"They were given power like the power of scorpions of the earth... Amen."
He spoke of Revelations, words once prophesized, here a plague upon the dead.
"They were allowed to torment them for five months, but not to kill them,
and their torment was like the torment of a scorpion when it stings someone.
And in those days people will seek death and will not find it," to sharpen
the point he said. "They will long to die, but death will flee from them." Spun
from tale, here the story true, as glowing demon sprites tormented those spirits
fallen by the wayside, before their very eyes. "What's this?" a buzz begun
amidst the demonic clatter. "Fresh meat, I see. Sharpen the stingers and spits."
"Not so fast," Dante called to rebuke. "You shall have no fun today, you fiends.
Pass I will without delay. I'm not the menu, but here to report on you culprits."
Known Dante was in these parts, and bitterly despised was he for past deeds,
telling of their secrets, still he was protected, for that they stuck to the weeds.

This was the time
when Horacio needed to remain
especially silent, tiptoeing as a mime
along this funnel of despair. Not for his own mane,
but for the sake of his companion, for he knew that the only restraint
keeping the sprites and larger demons at bay, was the fear of becoming a stain
in his ledger. Astonished, Horacio saw the power of this ink to make faint
more adversaries than ever his sword could manage to quell. Still, the warning
rang in his head. If suspected for a moment that he varied off script, the paint
on his portrait might just dry a darker shade of red come the new morning.
So with a hand close to his knife, Horacio advanced along these foul quarters,
following the lead of his guide. Onward, there was a new found spawning
of dread, as there opened before them the steaming and sweltry hot mortars
of the City of Dis. Encircled by glowing red brick, as though settling magma,
the fortifications presented themselves an unwelcoming front, with supporters,
a vicious flock, mounting the ramparts, swearing their rhetoric and dogma,
casting their curses and stones upon those below, entering this gated stigma.

Before the walls,
amidst rows of empty coffins,
awaiting which spirit what befalls
the torment of a sunken grave for their sins,
Dante motioned Horacio close and in lowered tones did mention,
"This here is a place of great illusion, do not trust all of what spins
before your eyes within this dark city of the lower realms. Many a notion
was shown once to me inside these walls, and by far not all of it honest."
"How so?" Horacio asked for more, but amid a more pressing tension,
his answer would have to wait. "Anon," Dante lifted his hand lest
they be overheard. "We approach the gate, guarded by Furies most vile.
Stay alert, they will stop us if they can." Just then appeared their latest test,
three winged Valkyrie-like demons, female creatures with snakes that rile
in place of hair and a bitter scowl that passed for face, with wrinkled brow,
holding brass spear and pitchfork. Here they watched, spitting a spiteful guile,
as spirits destined to the pit of hell marched past in an unevenly staggered row.
Ducking, they cowered their heads from many a real and feigned blow.

"Well, look who it is?"
the first to see Dante scowled.
It was Magaera, upon the battlements of Dis,
who called out the traveler. "Returning once again to be fouled
I see, no longer wearing life. What do you want here, so far below your station?"
rose her challenge. "Aye," Tisiphone, punisher of murder, in second howled,
beating her wings in a threatening manner. "And without your Dalmatian,
so far from home." "Perhaps, we should pinch him, to make sure he's really
dead this time?" Allecto sneered, stepping forward with angry vexation,
pointing her sharpened tip his way. Not to be outdone by these three shrilly
vipers, Dante had prepared for this moment, knowing that soon enough
would it come. "Try it," he scoffed, lowering his hood. "I move about freely,
and if you think not, I'll call once more on my protector's grace, to snuff
you three out again, just as had been done before." With bold words Dante
took another step forward, causing the furious Erinyes to doubt. "It's a bluff!
Go on, stick him!" Magaera called from up on top of the tower. "Avanti!"
Hearing the urging, Allecto, with venomous intent, lifted her pike andante.

"Yes!"
Tisiphone encouraged.
"Show this pilgrim not to mess
where he doesn't belong." Steaming, enraged,
Magaera taunted, "Do it! Do it!" as Allecto snarling,
with bloodshot eyes, showed her fangs. There, as she leaned back estranged,
like a cat ready to pounce, when a thunder clap in the midst of this quarreling
there boomed a disembodied voice. "Enough! Clear the way!" came the sound.
Terrified and shaking, the three Furies fell about themselves, gnarling

and gnashing their teeth. "Eek!" Magaera toppled from her tower, round
and over herself she spun, before stretching out her wings to fly right.
"I thought you said that God was dead?" she flapped to avoid the ground.
"He is, or at least that's what Dis had said," Allecto looked a frightful sight,
unsure of what to do, she scrambled backward, looking angry and confused.
"This is all your fault," Tisiphone, cursed her sister for starting the fight.
Then to Dante, "We'll get you!" She backed away into the night, diffused
amid the darkness, as did her other sisters, their egos being bruised.

Through the gates,
Dante passed without even looking back.
His outward calm did nothing for how his heart now palpates.
Had he turned in that moment from his narrow strait, he fear there be attack,
for his eyes surely betrayed what raced through him, that of his own disbelief
in his good fortune. "What, you thought I was going to let anything so black
befall you?" Horacio whispered, hand upon Dante's shoulder. From grief
there turned a renewed feeling of strength. "I never doubted for a second,"
Dante grinned, a shade happier for not getting skewered. From this relief
though, in a place like hell, it can only again turn sour. There beckoned
another sight, one he'd seen before, but not in the proper lighting.
"Look here," Dante made an annotation. "See how once there reckoned
heretics in this soil, now the vale lifted from my eyes, as if struck by lightning,"
he was more excited now than Horacio had yet to see him. "The scoundrels
that had once inhabited this place are gone. In their place a frightening
assortment of clergy and king, Constantine himself caught in these tendrils."
Dante looked upon these purveyors of religion, as if they were entrails.

"These are the ones,
to solidify their own wealth and glory,
sacrificed the safety and lives of millions,
who told once and again the original lie, the story,
just to radicalize the masses, to stir up hate and derision,
so that man and brother would turn on another, when the only allegory
that makes any difference in the end, is who profited from the collusion
of infusing religion and war into the government to begin with?"
Dante looked to where he thought Horacio's eye to be to avoid any confusion,
"This whole thing ends and begins where it's always been, with the myth
of religion. Jesus, Jehobah, Mohammad, Allah, even the Buddha are all correct
in that they speak of love and of unity amongst all people. Yet the scythe,
Pluto, Dis, Beelzebub, or the Devil, whichever incantation you choose to select,
are merely the reflections of what these sultans and kings, popes and rulers,
all these titans of war and commerce represent. Yet, you never suspect
you're being duped, too busy hating someone you never met. These pushers
and sellers of religion have their own special place carved out in their futures.

“These are the true heretics,”
Dante said in conclusion. “Using ‘God’ to turn belief
into the excuse for hatred and wars, when the true objective only ever is
for their own earthly gains, taking what others have, as would do a thief.
By murder and intimidation do they rise to power and so too shall they fall.”
Dante kicked at the embers that smoldered around one fiery tomb of grief.
“Whose tomb is that?” Horacio had to ask seeing the flaming spikes that wall
the unrestful place. “Oh, that’s for the next to come. There’s never a shortage
of tyrants posing as salvation.” “Excuse me, signore,” Horacio couldn’t forestall
the question any longer. “Your current positions seem to refute the reportage
of faith for which you’re widely known. Help me understand this discrepancy?”
“Oh, that’s easy,” Dante smiled, moving on, he shared a piece of knowledge.
“Things look a lot different when you’re dead,” he said with full transparency.
“The living don’t always see the whole picture, time is too short and subjective,
but when you’ve been dead as long as I have, well, there’s much less obscurity.
Just because you’ve died doesn’t mean you lose your ability to be reflective,
in many ways it’s merely an opportunity to enhance one’s perspective.”

“So, it’s true, what the Fury said?”
Horacio hurried beside Dante, down the smoldering path.
“What?” Dante paused. “When she said that God is dead?”
“Yes, precisely?” Horacio was most curious. “Barring any holy wrath,”
Dante checked over his shoulder. “It’s hard to say if one ever existed at all.”
“But...” taken aback, Horacio stalled in his motion, as Dante let out a laugh.
“Oh, you misunderstand me again. It must seem as a break with protocol
to speak in such a manner. For if there is no God, what kind of paradox
would we be in? But worry not my friend, the universe is big enough to crawl
with as many gods as you desire... and even none at all. It’s a Pandora’s Box,
full of possibilities to choose from, and this, oh this just scratches the surface.”
“How do you know all this to be true?” Horacio stepped around cinder blocks.
“Ah, that’s easy,” Dante lifted a finger. “Because I follow the Muse to trace
back history. I simply report what I see and hear. Come, we’re not at leisure
to debate,” Dante led. “The road’s still long.” Meanwhile, in a darker place,
flickering moist and cavernous, Pluto whispered rhapsodic, “Come my treasure,
I have a job for you.” Slithering, Medusa appeared, “It would be my pleasure.”

BOOK XXXII

MEDUSA

Storming the gates,
Mars drew fast upon Dis,
to catch sight of what the Fates
had decided. There, in a clamor, the Furies
were most excited, backing with claws and fangs exposed,
as would a pack of rats trapped in a corner. Magaera scurries
to the rear, pushing Allecto forward. "What happened here?" Mars posed
before them a bristled stature, in no humor for kowtowing excuses.
"It was God. He's risen again," Magaera bawled from the rear, she supposed.
"Or one of His angles at least," Tisiphone by her sister's side accuses.
"What nonsense is this?" Mars scowls at them all, ready to unleash
his anger. "It's true," Allecto backed the story. "We all heard the abuses,
clear as you and I right here." "Heard?" the god was not amused. "Sheesh!"
he held up his hand to silence the background chatter. "What do you mean,
'heard'?" he looked hard on the Fury Allecto. "What I said," from her leash
she hissed in answer. "There was no body, just this booming voice unseen,
commanding us to clear the path for the poet Florentine."

"Poet,
you say?"
Mars didn't know what to make of it.
"Who is this poet you mention? Come now I don't have all day!"
"The one that's known as Dante," Tisiphone shared the information.
"He scorned us once and we were just having a little fun to make him pay,"
Magaera filled in the blank. "That's when we heard the angel's incantation,"
Allecto confirmed what her sisters had said. "So, that's who's helping
him," Mars spoke to himself, connecting the dots. "That was no incarnation,
you fools. You've been had," he boiled. "Which way did they go?" Yelping,
the three Furies pointed down the spiraling road. "Now get back to your posts,"
he waved a dismissive hand, having his fill of the three. "No more whelping."
With that he left the Furies to secure the portal of Dis, where the ghosts
of those damned still wandered around unchecked. Allowing for the delay,
ground they were gaining, and so Mars continued to press, as he roasts
with anxiety over making the catch. For too long his quarry has gotten away,
and now in the Underworld he's outlived, and only just begun, his stay.

In other sectors,
Pluto was securing his trap,
a sort of negotiation of the vectors
for which the pending confrontation will wrap.
"What I need from you my dear," Pluto began the exchange,
"is a bit more than what we are usually accustomed to. This mousetrap
calls for something a little more potent than your typical poison, in the range
of epidemic." Sputtering torchlight casting shadow and glow, the only source
of illumination within the cave, shed an ominous shade, meant to estrange
those falling prey to this lair. "What did you have in mind?" Medusa of course
was game for whatever mayhem would allow her to torture and maim
her victims. "Something that might earn you your beauty again, if you endorse
my bargain." A stir rumbled from within the niche she was hiding, a frame
just outside of view. "Tell me what it is you desire?" came her raspy accord.
The torches around crackled, as even the fire brought to attention its flame,
hearing the details of the agreement. "Very well," Medusa sighed heavy toward
what was being required. "Don't fail me, and you shall receive your reward."

With a glow in his eye,
Pluto began the incantation,
calling forth spirits of the dark and the deep, he ply
the mystic powers, with a trance in his voice and humming vibration,
he summoned forth the transformation. With a reverberating thump and flash
the deed was done, as a wave of energy rolled through all of damnation,
and Pluto threw up a cheer. "Oh, that'll do nicely," he curled his moustache.
Meanwhile, Horacio and Dante were plotting their path through the lower ring.
"There are three challenges coming that you must face before your clash
here is done. The first is to face Medusa, by eluding her deadly sting.
For only through the labyrinth of her cave, can you arrive at the second
obstacle, that of the wall of fire, an impenetrable barrier of living
flame which no one, mortal or shade, may pass." There, Dante reckoned,
the journey would come to an end. "Even if somehow you manage to defeat
the first beast, there's no way for either of us to cross that Armageddon.
Then," Dante laid out the final impediment, "if by some true miracle you beat
these first two impossible tests, you'd still end up mincemeat.

"Before the doors,
guarding the entrance to Saturn's Tomb,
are three monstrous giants, older than the dinosaurs,
the fifty-headed, hundred-handed Hecatoncheires, who loom
over the passage, ready to pounce. Not with an army could they be trodden."
"That doesn't sound very promising," Horacio had to admit of the doom
foretold. "Well, I never swore to victory," Dante spoke of the pending burden.
"Only that I'd show you the way." "True enough," Horacio agreed,
"and for that you have my gratitude. Do not to worry, I'm not downtrodden.

We will take each battle as they come. That's the only way to succeed.
Each step will lead to the next opportunity," with that they were in harmony.
On they pressed, for close at hand was the first of these three dangers decreed.
"Just on the other side of this hillock lies the entrance to the cave, if memory
has not failed me," Dante then gave the caveat. "Now we just have to elude
the Minotaur, for he is a foul and angry creature who would in summary
put an end to both of us in a heartbeat. Like the Furies, this crude
and bullish beast holds no love for me," he spoke with certitude.

"Then we find a way around,"
Horacio was determined, now more than ever,
knowing how close he was to his goal. Then, out of sight, a sound
of horrendous freight came rolling over their position as never
had he heard before. "Quick, we must take cover behind those rocks,"
Dante urged imperative. "It's a stampede that threatens our endeavor."
From the opposite side of the knoll, there came a rush most unorthodox,
as a multitude of shades fled, running with speed in their direction.
The rush was led by none other than the Minotaur himself, as if a pox
drove them from the field. "Save yourselves," a shade with ghostlike complexion
ran past, as the Minotaur taking cover, very much out of character,
spotted Dante to say, "Welcome back. You've picked a fine day for inspection.
Go on, I'm feeling generous today. You may pass," as chased by some predator,
a flood of souls ran by, going the opposite way. "What's the cause of the fright?"
Dante had to ask the bull, who was preparing to charge away. The Minotaur
looked up at him, "An evil so rank and deadly that none are able to fight.
It's Medusa. She has taken the form of a basilisk. Your only salvation is flight."

Sharing the information,
the Minotaur then scratched at the ground,
and scared went running away. From their hidden station,
behind a fortification of rocks atop the ridge, the alarm did Dante sound.
"Oh, there's no hope here. As much as I sympathize with your quest,
there's simply no way to surpass such a monster, nor can we go around.
That cave is the only entrance. If a basilisk guards it, then at the very best
you can ask for a quick and easy death." "No, there must be a way," Horacio
wouldn't quit now having come so far. "Tell me of this creature unblessed?
What are its strengths and weaknesses?" Dante shook his head in woe.
"The basilisk," he said, "is a horrific menace. A part dragon, part serpent
and part cockerel. But that's not even the worst. This most terrible foe
has five ways to kill you, without even spreading its wings. Repent
now, before you go any further. Confronting this beast is suicide.
If you manage to avoid its gaze, which is certain death, your life will be spent
on its noxious fiery breath, or on venom so toxic it can kill at a meter outside,
if you can get that close, of course touching it is death. My advice is hide."

Just then,
came a shrilling hiss,
half-bird, half-snake. The sound meant to madden
all in its wake. "EEH-YA!" Dante shrieked, covering his
ears, beginning to shake. Somehow, it didn't affect Horacio the same,
perhaps he thought due to his helmet, which covered his ears from this
torment. Already he had found a chink in the armor. The sound began to tame
as Dante slowly recovered. "Oh, yes, I forgot to mention the lovely singing voice,
which can paralyze and, if near enough, kill. Luckily, to here it'd only maim."
Dante shook off the ringing sensation in his ears, with nothing to rejoice.
"I do not doubt your courage," he said, "but I think we've reached an impasse.
There's just no way to proceed beyond this ledge, I see no viable choice.
To advance is to die." Horacio took to heart the words. If the dead fear to pass,
what chance does a mortal in Hades have? But then in his head another bell
rang, a voice long ago from the past. "No, I have come too far, alas.
There is no turning back." A spirit in his chest began to swell.
"I thank you signore, for bringing me this far through hell."

Removing his helmet,
Horacio knelt next to his companion.
"It has truly been an honor, I'll never forget,"
he took Dante's hand, there behind the stone walled expansion.
"And I," Dante held him there a moment longer. "Thank you for the opportunity
to correct my own ledger. Long have I waited to put to rest this canon.
Now perhaps, I too may be at peace." Then as Horacio turned to face impunity,
"Wait," Dante stopped him once more. "You wouldn't happen to have a mirror?"
"No, why do you ask?" Horacio looked back. "Oh, for that's the one immunity
the basilisk doesn't have. It will die upon seeing its own reflection. Yet before
you get excited, there are none below, for shades cannot use them. With grief,
the condition is no better." "Actually," in the place of the previous horror,
Horacio began to show a glimmer of understanding, "that's helpful relief."
Replacing his helmet he again vanished, before mounting the hillock's peak.
Over the edge he crawled, making note of the terrible scene in brief.
As forewarned, in front of the entrance to the cave he seek,
there rested a hideous, monstrous freak.

Medusa,
transformed into a basilisk
by the hand of the underworld producer,
was even more terrible than anything he risk
before. Standing tall, at six or seven meters high,
this evil creature with a snake's tail and talon picks
for feet, had a feathered body, hard as scales. Able to fly
with dragon's wings, it could spit fire from the sky. Atop this creature
sat the Gorgon's head, pregnant with squirming vipers that hiss and cry

on their own behalf. About the gigantic fiend was not a single kind feature
that Horacio could place. The only advantage that Horacio presently held
was of being unseen, yet it still might not be enough to best such a reaper.
Again she let out a terrible shriek, by which even the trees may be felled,
yet Horacio stood fast, the helmet did truly protect him from the noise
the basilisk made. Approaching, he maintained a distance, as he smelled
the sulfur of dragon's breath scorching a wide perimeter. The fire destroys
every last blade of grass in its path, while Horacio quietly maintains his poise.

Testing,
he picks up a loose rock
and flings it to behind where the beast was resting.
Violently, the basilisk, Medusa, swung around surprised at the knock
and taking to air, floated ten feet above, spewing fire upon the granite mount
which bore the cave's doorway. *I have to lure it away,* Horacio took stock
of the situation. *Only then will I be able to enter.* Making his next move count,
Horacio took hold of a second rock and flung it to the side. Hearing the clank
of falling debris clatter, Medusa turned once more with fire taking into account
that an intruder was somewhere around. Twisting its stare, the viper was rank
with venom. Triangulating, Medusa clucked, racing on foot to Horacio's general
direction. And there, recalling the once upon instructions by which he'd bank
his entire life, the prophesy of Cumaean Sibyl came rushing, as either funeral
or salvation, *When others prepare to die,* she'd said, *stand your ground and look
the Gorgon in the eye.* In a move tantamount to suicide, following the ethereal
command, Horacio stood fast and removing his helmet, with a fist he shook,
"Come and get me!" catching the stare of the creature's eye being all it took.

Keeling over,
Medusa, gorgon and basilisk,
fell dead on the spot, where there sprung a leaf of clover.
As if his heart had dropped right out of his chest, Horacio overcoming risk
of such great proportion could make no sense of the gambit that had left
him standing and such a lethal opponent dead on the ground. Yet, by a whisk
of more than good fortune, he knew the gods played some role in this theft
of victory from death's hand, for his survival defied even his own logic.
Giving wide berth for the still warm carcass, Horacio cut a generous cleft
around, cautious not to be avenged by some lingering venom still toxic
to all life. And thus he approached the opening to the gorgon's cave,
stepping carefully lest he set off some trap designed for a most tragic
ending in this gothic, unholy place. Entering, the stone walls gave
off a glistening, as if sweating with the orange reflection of torchlight.
With helmet still in hand, even his breath was visible, as though the grave
was watching him, he drew his sword at last, to give himself a fright,
when turning towards a niche, a swarm of bats swept in from the night.

"Aargh!"
Horacio swinging, was caught off guard
by these flying rodents, as they flutter about in a bog,
before trailing off down a tunnel passage. Catching his breath it was hard
to know in which direction he was going in, for now he was spun around,
with several possible channels open before him. "This way," a whispering shard
off a torch lit alley trailed. Horacio moved forward, holding his ground,
though remaining a skeptic that this be the way to go. Still the lowering slope
made this as likely the path as any. To a rotunda this came, massively round
with a hundred portals, all feeding into and off of this one point to telescope
into just as many directions and only one of which for him to choose.
"Something too is familiar about this place." At least that would give him hope.
He was sure he'd been here. The same molten pit in the center with hues
of fiery yellows and reds came back to him, as if from a long forgotten dream,
where he knew the ending, but it was just out of reach. Searching for clues,
he spun around the center, each door resembling the next. Ready to scream
he froze, hearing her voice again, "Behind you." Nothing was as it did seem.

BOOK XXXIII

BAPTIZED IN FLAME

The secret to harmony
was to be able to see the perspective
through another's eyes, to be a mirror in fact, an irony
that was not lost upon the gods, whose vision, often selective,
rarely extended beyond their own walls and desires. How refreshing
it was therefore, when Venus and Mars added Concordia as an elective
to the pantheon of the gods, for she alone had the ability inside her threshing,
to unite the others around a common cause. A being truly in balance between
the power of love and the force of war, Concordia, neither timid nor thrashing,
was not afraid to fight in combat, yet too held in her the empathy to glean
the wisdom of the olive branch. It was said to look into her eyes was to find
peace, for in her stare, her eyes became the true reflection there to be seen
of the other's soul. Translucently variable, her gaze was the mirror to blind
her opponent. In the mortal realm, what would causally be attributed to luck,
for the gods was a vital tool to be wielded, for to ally with her was to bind
oneself to victory. Yet, for over a thousand years she'd been missing, struck
from all memory of existence. Now her eyes returned, and they were stuck.

Before him
was a vast pool of fire.
All around in every direction swim
an ocean of doors and not one to which he could safely retire.
"Behind you," the voice had called, but all Horacio could see in that direction
was the lava pit below. His heart raced, trying to make sense of this mire,
when through the fire he saw a strange and darkened collection,
an image of a fortified archway with massive black doors blocking the entry
to some unknown place. The walls all obsidian soaked up the reflection
of fire bubbling off the moat. Before the gates the shadow of what he didn't see,
lurking somewhere in the niches just out of view, there waited an omnibus
of pain for him, of that he knew. Just as quickly the vision gone, in a frenzy
the fire flicked its flame, as again the voice came whispering softly sonorous.
"Trust," it said. There and then Horacio understood the meaning to the riddle.
His path lie through the flame, a leap of faith if ever there was one so ominous,
for if mistaken, even the slightest bit, his remains would be charred and brittle.
With a heavy breath, he climbed the ledge, tense was the sound of the fiddle.

Holding, he exhaled,
gathering some appropriate thought,
and ready, he made to place his helmet on when there wailed,
“Not so fast!” It was Mars who appeared from behind, having finally caught
his allusive opponent. “We have a few things to discuss first,” he grinned
as his demons covered the various directions. “It seems someone has taught
you well, maybe too well for your own benefit.” Absent a drink, he was ginned
up and ready. “Do you know who I am, boy?” Mars paced with swagger.
“Well, I believe we have had the pleasure,” Horacio stepping, twinned
the god’s movement, carefully guarding his flank against a dagger.
“Good, then you should know better than to trifle with the gods,” the volcano
began to warm. “Only when I’m not in their service,” Horacio topped the agger
wall, maintaining the high ground position. “Ah!” Mars was pleased to know.
“So you serve the gods, you say?” “Such is true,” Horacio would not refute
the fact. “Well, you can start then,” Mars looked at him sternly, “by letting go
of that helmet.” Horacio with visible consternations saw the coming dispute.
“Yeah, I don’t think that’s possible at the moment,” he held tight to the loot.

From either side,
the cowled figures of Timor and Formido
stepped forward, advancing in an attempt to deride
his resolve, yet evolved from their earlier encounter, Horacio
was no longer affected by fear and showed the least amount of dread
for his situation. “I won’t ask a second time,” Mars, ready to slay the doe,
showed his impatience. “If you want it,” Horacio drew his sword and instead
of bucking, rebuked the god, “you’ll have to come and get it.” Laughing roundly,
Mars unsheathed his own metal, “I thought you’d never ask.” he said,
mounting the wall with a lunge. Swords clashing they squared off soundly,
rattling steal with flashing sparks, they fought on the very edge of the fiery pit.
“You know you cannot win,” Mars parried, swiping high a wide boundary,
barely missing his head. Not knowing his own skill, Horacio made a pivot,
leaning away at the last second, he spun, blade up to block, and landed
an elbow to the jaw, stunning Mars, and himself, for a second that split,
as they righted themselves. “And apparently, neither can I lose,” he handed
Mars the response of a pirate, for which he’d have to be reprimanded.

“Don’t get too cocky, kid,”
Mars spat, tasting the nudge to his jaw.
“You don’t want to get on my bad side,” he was being candid.
Up to this moment he was just having fun, testing the chutzpah
of this mortal who’d dare challenge the gods to battle, to be worthy
of his lineage. Yes, Mars did like his spunk, it would be a shame to saw
him in half. But so too would he not accept insolence from a mere earthly
man, so with his sword he lashed again, as they clang from the left to the right.
“Unnatural it is,” Mars, failing to strike a blow, was at the end of his mercy.

"You've bathed in the River Styx," he could tell by the strength of his fight.
Invulnerable this mortal had become. "Yes, that's right," Horacio admitted
what the god seemed to already know. "Instead of fighting all night,
might I suggest a draw?" "Hardly," Mars scoffed. "Though it would be permitted
to talk." He saved face enough, confronted by the choice of a long and fruitless
scuffle, one where neither could win, so for the moment, being acquitted
from battle, Mars settled for discourse in place of his normally blunt hubris.
"As you like," Horacio agreed, to do otherwise would be pointless.

A step they each took to back away,
giving each other the space to safely retire.
"Why don't you begin?" Horacio offered the right of way.
"Well, I see you've some skill," Mars looked at him, coldly with fire,
"with that sword. Pray tell, where did you get it?" Horacio considered
the question. "It was passed on to me as my birthright," not being a liar,
he reveled as little as possible. "I know that sword," Mars offered.
"As you should," the Trojan replied. "I have no quarrel with you... yet,"
the god kept score. "But you're out of your depths here," delivered
was the truth. "In fact, the only reason your life hasn't already been forfeit..."
Horacio there interjected, "Is because we're related?" "Oh, you are a cheeky
bugger, aren't you? Now, where did you hear that?" Mars began to regret
the parley, when "Oh," he remembered. "You'll have to pay for that," meekly
Mars brushed off the hangover, and "Yes," he admitted, "There's that.
Still it doesn't absolve you from your trespass. Now," with a heavy tone, bleakly
he lays down the ultimatum. With an arm extended, "Hand over the hat,"
he says, "and I might just forgive you this spat.

"Defy me now,
and not even Apollo's armor
will save you from my retribution," Mars did vow.
Sheathing his sword, Horacio thought on the offer with ardor,
holding the helmet out with both hands. There he remembered her
and his pledge. Knowing in his heart there could be no other safe harbor,
he did the impossible thing. "There's another reason why I'm still alive to spur
on, when rightly I should be dead," he corrected the God of War's account.
"Oh really, and why is that?" Mars played along, hand awaiting the transfer.
"Because without this helmet, you can't pass the wall of fire." On the count
of one, Horacio placed the helmet back on his head and dropped into the pit.
Above him a reverberating "No!" could be heard trailing down from the mount
that looked over the fire. Disappearing through the flaming wall, Horacio quit
the cavern, leaving Mars fuming. "Damn it, I was that close," he stomped irate.
"Not a word," he turned, forewarning the brothers, feeling the miles and grit,
as the two looked upon one another. Having failed in their mandate,
now only one option remained, to leave the outcome to fate.

Hellfire
is a curious thing.
This Horacio was soon to discover, as he retire
his body to the blaze. Yes, it consumes with a scorching sting,
yet more than that, it thinks. Micro-organisms within the flame,
alive and sentient, flow together between gas and liquid to bring
about a form of life known as the Archaea, which thrives on the very same
hydrogen and sulfur that feeds the fire. At extreme temperatures and pressure,
these creatures bind together, reassembling at will. Without a nucleus to tame
and determine their shape, they freely transform into a countless mixture
of possibilities. Instead of words, they communication with a sort of telepathic
feeling, transmitting information by touch, commonly in the measure
of human understanding known as a burn. A more accurate graphic
however would be that of a melding of the minds, for once in contact
with another object, just as does water, the Archaea, on pilot automatic,
take on the inverse of that form, which is why they were currently stacked
together as the hollowed mirror of Horacio, with a look of shock on impact.

As a comet,
shooting through a sky,
wet in a red and orange sunset,
Horacio dove through fire on the fly.
Now, unconsumed, his mind began to make reason,
for to suddenly realize that he wasn't dead, and with his own eye
to see the eternal flame, swimming all around him, brilliant as the sun,
he gave thanks and praise to Apollo, for it was his armor that vouchsafed
the promise. Moreover, all about him it began to glow a brilliant white beacon,
harmonizing to the flow of energy and heat that, from the Archaea, strafed
his body, all to no avail. And right too was Horacio in his calculated guess
that the helmet he wore was the key to this doorway. For just as they'd tasted
Aethalia's shore by way of its connection to the elements, so too the headdress
would open a connection directly to the hellfire. Without this, the thought
he'd need would most likely escape him, and with that his means of success.
For the more he moved forward, the less distance he got, slowing to naught,
and without this helmet to pick the lock, forever in a fiery grave he'd be caught.

With it,
he could think
as the fire thought, to wit,
with the Archaea he held a mental link.
The more still he was, the calmer they became,
and likewise the more agitated he was, the tighter the chink
in the armor. If he pushed at them, to him they would do the same.
Somehow, it was still he though who directed the traffic. He that had the power
to control its flow, yet he still needed to learn how to steer through the flame.

That's when the epiphany came. Closing his eyes, he pictured the dower
black doors that bore his third challenge, and pulling at the blazing swell,
he made himself as small as he could, and with that he fell like a shower.
The fire having matched his motif, dissipating before his path, it quell
to a flickering flame, a mere candle in the night. Into the black abyss
Horacio fell far, as if seemingly forever, until he could not even tell
if at all he were moving, or in fact when and how he came to stop on this
cold, hard slab of pitch black granite, here in the bowels and pit of Dis.

And so the key
for this fortunate mortal,
for unlocked was a another mystery,
that of the element of air. For this invisible portal
connecting all in the material, air played a vital role
in the secret mystic arts. What other element could throttle
sound so effectively, to allow the helmet's barer to simply stroll
though the most dangerous lairs unheard? Oh no, air was a willing accomplice
and wouldn't let harm come to the one who wore this divine means of control.
To that, a pocket of air, insulating his fall, left him lying there conscious,
yet unaware of ever making such a soft landing. Opening his eyes, a sheen
of amber from somewhere below lit upwards to show a deep canyon precipice
straddled by a narrow sliver of stone that bridged the long divide between
here and there. No sign was there of any other creature blocking his route,
and that's what worried him. "What's wrong?" Timor was the first one seen
to break the silence. Turning his head, Mars grimaced a troubled pout.
"That mortal," he said, "was only half right in that which he spout."

An immortal
he knew, despite the assertion,
could still pass through this portal
of fire, even without Pluto's helmet. Certain
was this, however, unlike the clean passage Horacio enjoyed,
without the helmet, he'd have to swim the distance with great exertion,
something quite frankly, if possible he would have preferred to avoid.
Now he was eyeing fire. "Fine," he muttered, popping the top of his flask.
"I'll do it myself." He took a full swig and then regarding the blazing void,
saluted his men. "See you all in hell," he turned to complete the needed task
and checking himself once over, dove head long into the fire. "Make way!"
he commanded the flame, as he passed out of sight. Now in his own mask
of fire, Mars would have to face the long slog through. *Oh, he's going to pay!*
was a repeated refrain in his head, as he wove through what was like burning
spider webs, slowing every advance that he made, with a scorching overlay.
Even though a god and immortal healed instantly, the sensation of churning
pain left an impression none would forget, and a favor he'd soon be returning.

Meanwhile,
Horacio with little time to spare,
advanced through the dark, towards the stony defile
outlined by a molten underflow. Across the expanse were a pair
of arching black doors, set into the same frame he had seen through the flames
before, yet now in front of his eyes. He could not help the feeling as he stare
across that ravine, that even though well hidden through the divine claims
of his helmet, that still he was being watched. Everywhere there were shadows,
and in every shadow eyes. They couldn't see him, but for him twas sames,
the monsters foretold by his companion, perhaps lurking right under his nose,
were alas for now undetectable, and that weighed on Horacio, for wherever
they were, he knew they were watching. Sword hand to the fold of his clothes,
he checked that the key he had pilfered was still there, and as he hover
in pause reassuring himself that maybe he'd got lucky, there on the brink
he took a few cautious steps forward. On the bridge, closer he felt than ever
to his goal, when out of shadows came a baritone. "Oh, what's that stink?"
the voice called out, as simultaneously three hundred eyes did blink.

BOOK XXXIV

THE HUNDRED-HANDED-ONES

The Hecatoncheires,
Briareus, the strong, Kottos, the punch
and Gyges, the curved, were three anarchistic curs,
as ever there were. If any three could make up a bunch,
it would be them, for there was a reason why a gathering of baboons
was called a congress. The only thing they could seem to agree on was lunch.
Then again, with fifty heads each, and just as many hands per side as spoons,
they were lucky to share only one stomach a piece, or nothing would ever
get done. As it was, when one started, the entire buck and a half croons,
and then it's a jumbling mess. "Bacon," cried one fiftieth of the clever
one, Gyges. "Sure does," an equal proportion of Briareus conquered.
"Smells like fried up pig." "Oh, what I wouldn't give," spoke a head in fervor
on the shoulders of Kottos, "for some nice juicy ribs. All we ever get cornered
is bats." "And them's just blind chickens," his neighbor nooded, taking a whiff.
"Yup, like singed little pig hairs. That's what I smells." And it just went forward
from there, each in his turn postulating on the menu. From the side of the cliff
a rumble of movement came in waves, as the Hecatoncheires all began to sniff.

Through all of this,
Horacio remained frozen,
unsure of what would be called for and what be remiss.
Amongst the many black niches, heads popped out by the dozen,
searching for the source of dinner. From above, like a spider clung
one, a hundred hands clutching to stone. Freshly woken from dozing,
Gyges this one, stretched his eyes and a score of limbs, taking in a lung
full of air, half of him yawned, while the rest surveyed the cavern.
This was his preferred station, from a bird's eye view above, where he flung
down on intruders unexpected. Most cunning of the three, he chose to govern
from a distance to see the whole picture, though he was not the leader.
That duty fell to Briareus, who being the strongest of the three in the tavern,
decided that was how it should be. He sat beside the door, planted as cedar,
figuring that just his presence there would be enough of a barrier to prevent
anyone from passing. So still had he become that his own presence was neither
felt nor seen, he'd simply blended into the scenery. In the unlikely event
however, that anyone made it that far, he'd be there to ensure they repent.

Kottos,
in the middle of the three,
was always on his fingers and toes.
Neither as bright as Gyges, nor as strong as Briareus, he
however was probably the most dangerous. Being unpredictable,
he crawled like a crab, from crag to crag, being both arrogant and brawny
he liked to pounce and fight. For the sake of argument, he'd ridicule and label,
antagonizing victim and ally the same, until turmoil finally ensued.
"Hey," one of his heads then said. "You know what smells as unforgettable
as a pig?" "What?" a few heads down, curious as to the riddle, screwed
his gaze over to one fiftieth. "Humans!" the head laughed to a chorus.
"Oh, that's a good one. They really do," Gyges chuckled, as twenty eyes skewed.
"Now that would be a treat," Briareus joined in. "You know, it's curious..."
Slowly, they were starting to reach consensus to the origin of the smell.
Gyges shifted, as a sideways moving caterpillar, sniffing at the odorous
air around Horacio's position. As anarchists, they did not agree very well,
yet, for the stomachs, there was always solidarity around the dinner bell.

This was when
Horacio had to make his move.
With two of these centimanes closing in,
his only option was to make for the mouth of the stove.
Taking advantage, his only one, that there linger some confusion
over his presence, that they were only being led by the nose, it might prove
useful to dissipate the scent, and the only direction he had any allusion
of heading in was forward. Therefore on he went, there was no other choice
to make. Kottos, the first to arrive, climbing up the cliff's rocky protrusion,
clung to the side of the bridge. "Something was here," a dozen gave voice
to the discovery. Shimmying the rounded cavern roof, Gyges followed the trail
of scent as it rises. "This way. Down the bridge," he urged Kottos on twice.
"Hey! Save some for me!" Briareus picked up a village sized stone as he wail.
"Maybe a nice hindquarter?" "I don't see anything," Kottos challenged
his brother. "Are you sure we've got something?" unable to find head or tail.
"When have these noses ever been wrong?" the plurality of Gyges managed.
"Yes, you have a point," the deferring side of Kottos acknowledged.

"But where is the swine?"
Briareus hurled his boulder over the cliff,
it making a magma splash, burping up lava bits as brine.
Horacio saw no end to this, the net it still drew tighter, when as if
by chance came the needed distraction to buy him an extra moment.
"But it's true!" one of Kottos's heads had gotten into some kind of tiff
with a faction of Gyges. "You're always sticking your noses in. Never content
to give a guy any peace. Sniffing this, smelling that. Easy for you, I'm stuck
in the middle next to these guys. I don't smell a damn thing unless I'm bent

face down into it." "Yeah, well how much flesh have you found for us?" struck
back Gyges's far left head, encouraged by a neighbor. "Don't pay him no mind,
at least you don't have to sleep next to him." "Just you wait a minute, buck.
What do you mean by that?" Kottos's middleman, his teeth began to grind.
"You snore," Gyges's flank declared. "Oh, I do not! That's a lie," the head
didn't know which way to turn. "Oh, yes you do," Gyges then refined
his rebuttal. "All night long. You keep the whole cave awake," he said.
Then a caucus laughing, "He snores so loud he could wake the dead."

"Oooo,"
Briareus moaned.
"That's a good one. So,
what's up with the pig?" his stomach groaned.
"No, I think you're right," spoke up Gyges's top head.
"See, I don't snore," interjecting, Kottos's antagonist honed
in on the chance. "That it smelt like human," Gyges completed his thread.
"Ah, see what I told you," Kottos's better half said. Now totally confused,
Briareus grumbled, "So which is it?" To which, one of Kottos's own said,
"Oh yeah, he snores." "Huh?" went Briareus, when Gyges infused,
"Human!" Like a series of light bulbs, some dim, some more bright,
that suddenly all lit, these titan killers no longer seemed so bemused,
as ready for combat instead. "Where, where?" Kottos itching for a fight
echoed, "Lemme at him!" Gyges, following the rocky ceiling's curve,
let his nose lead the way. "Somewhere on the bridge, just out of sight.
Keep going, the scent's getting stronger." Briareus to his rock pile, "What nerve
some human's got. Come on, lead him to me. Dinner will be ready to serve."

Briareus taunted
with a dozen rocks on the right
and just as many left, he stood ready and flaunted
his strength. "Nothing gets by me," he showed off his might,
while walking directly past Horacio, he stood guard at the mouth of the bridge.
Then, just as both Kottos and Gyges drew near, that's when they saw the light.
With a flash and a crash came the yawp. "Son of a ..." Mars had a burning itch,
as he fell through the wall of fire, the portal to this domain. Unlike Horacio,
his entrance was not so quiet, turning a hundred and fifty heads to the ridge
at the far end of the cave where he dropped in. The sudden change of scenario,
turned everything around. Gyges and Kottos, flipping, went scurrying back
in the opposite direction, leaving Briareus alone to man the gateway's patio.
Sulking, he watched as they raced across the cave to claim the meaty snack.
Letting a few stones drop in disappointment, he said to himself in all sincerity,
"You know they're not going to leave us any?" Giving him the needed whack,
his stomach cried foul. "Wait," he trailed after the others calling for austerity.
"Save some for me!" he jogged down the bridge with caterpillar dexterity.

Mars was neither
in the mood nor prepared
for what was to come next from the ether.
For now the Hecatoncheires, primed and ready, glared
down onto his position. As was their fashion, they simply attacked first,
any questions they may have could always be left to the wishbone. So stared
at with hundreds of eyes, in a frenzy, none would even blink at such an outburst
twice, and so they unleashed their fury. Hurling stones, scores at a time
they buried Mars beneath a mountain of boulders, doing their worst,
envisioning a flattened man pancake, being that squished flat as a dime
was the best way to stretch them out, with so many mouths to feed.
So, it came as a bit of a surprise, when rumbling, the stones played ragtime
down the slope, as they descended in avalanche before a bursting stampede
befell. Like all the gods, strength was not his weakness, and Mars now furious,
ready himself for a fight, whether or not he could have just done the deed
of announcing himself and clearing up this misunderstanding, was injurious
in that moment and would settle it the old fashion way, for anyone curious.

The gods, although
technically unable to fly,
were very good at jumping, and could plough
a great distance when the moment came nigh.
This is how Mars, standing atop of the rock heap,
came to be airborne. Leaping, he threw himself into the sky.
With sword drawn, he laid into Kottos. Slicing, he made a sweep
of the air, before striking a stone wielding hand. "Ow! The thing bit me!"
Kottos snapped surprised, winding up a score of fists, with which to reap
his retaliation. He swung, missing, as Mars used his shoulders like a tree
for climbing, landing a punch that sent ten skulls smacking into just as many
jaws, necks stretching accordion. "Argh!" came the mouths of bit lips three,
screaming, as a backhand caught Mars coming around, as good as any
that have come before, smacking him back, tumbling towards the rafter.
There, Gyges was waiting to have a crack of his own, with plenty
of hands free for the tearing. Not to be underestimated, Mars a crafter
of battlefield tactics, saw the rush coming and the opportunity he was after.

Though
having a hundred hands each, and in wrestle
greatly outmatched, there was a weakness that Mars did know,
that they still only had two knees. Being top heavy, in a tussle
the Hecatoncheires could be knocked off balance. Now, upside downed
wasn't really one of Mars's favorite positions to fight in. Yet, as he nestle
there, bouncing off the cavern's ceiling, knowing he was eventually bound
to give way to gravity's pull, he didn't have many options available.
Then came the rocks and with it his battle plan. From the ground,

Kottos was throwing boulders thirty feet wide, big enough for Mars to be able
to get a running start, and on the move it was merely a matter of keeping
his pace. Sheathing his sword, he picked up a few stones, himself capable
of launching a pitching offensive, and seeing Gyges hanging there creeping,
aimed his throws for the gripping hands that clung to the top of the cavern,
weakening his position. As they drew closer, Mars shot himself, sweeping
forward, sword extended, like an arrow from the bow, how the tide can turn.
Seeing the dart, Gyges, startled, pulled back, trying to dodge the concern.

Taking a leg,
Mars struck with the force of a cannonball,
as Gyges, losing his balance, toppled like a loose peg
from its socket. Grabbing Gyges by the ankle as he fall,
the two tumbled together in a downward somersault.
Heading straight for Kottos, Gyges curled up into a ball
and struck the other square in the chest. Crashing to a halt,
all three lie scattered on the ground, dazed from the shock of impact,
before the foot of the bridge, as Briareus arrived, ready to join the assault.
As all this transpired, Horacio made use of the distraction, to enact
a bit of subterfuge of his own. Mounting the doorstep, he felt into the folds
of his clothes and retracted the long protected key. Metal teeth an exact
match to the hourglass, and her infinite flow of sand. There he holds
for a moment, his heart racing fast, with no time left to think,
he slips the key into the lock, careful to not make a scratch. Rolled,
the key turns, as his fist works the latch. Slowly, there on the brink
the door glides open, just enough for him to make an inward slink.

"And just what do you think
you're doing here?" Briareus questioned Mars, recognizing the god
as neither man nor pig. A single head turned backwards, hearing the clink.
"Chasing an intruder. Now lay off!" he pushed back against the squad
of hands that restrained him. "Only one who's been through here is you,"
Briareus grumbled, loosening his grip. "Yeah, that's right," Kottos lifted a rod,
"You're the only trespasser who's come by this way," a punched head blew
in retort. "Oh, that's gonna leave a scar," his neighbor regarded the black eye,
on the whole ready to finish the fight. "Ah guys," stacking the cue,
one of Briareus's heads tried to interject, being cut off by more outcry,
"And we're not even allowed to eat you." Gyges, recovering slowly
from his lumps, limped over to sniff Mars, for his own reasons why.
"Who did you say you were after?" he asked in tones that were wholly
menacing. "A human," Mars spat back, his own voice sour and gruff.
"Ah ha!" Briareus for the most part seeming pleased with himself, solely
on the knowledge that what they'd smelt wasn't a pig being enough.
"Guys!" the lone head on the side then began to huff.

"What?"
all eyes were focused
on him, with a single arm jut
out pointing, as a magician hocus-pocused,
and said, "Is that door supposed to be open?"
From across the stone bridge, eyes like a swarm of locusts
fell upon the open door that should have been securely locked, when
with a clank it then did again close. "AHHH!" was the look of shock
and surprise that swept across every face. None the least frozen
was Mars, with his swelled up anger, as he was the first off the block,
bounding to cross the gulf that divided each side, with a "Damn!" and a curse
on his lip. Close on his heal was Briareus, each racing toward a dock
that was shut. "How do you open this?" he slammed his fist terse
to the metal that absorbed the blow without the slightest tremor or dent.
"You don't," Briareus grunted. "Not without the key," being his final verse.
Taking up his post again, alongside the rock pile he normally frequent,
leaving Mars standing there before the door fuming hell bent.

BOOK XXXV

INSIDE THE CLOCKWORK OF TIME

Horacio entered
the dark prison vault.
Off in the distance there centered
a warm glow, of brass and gold and cobalt,
which penetrated the shadows in streaks of refraction.
A mechanical hum, of rotating drums accompanied a default
of clicks and clacks that pinged in a steady rhythmic contraction,
Here, in the heart of the machine that regulated the flow of eternity
and the passage of countless eons, is where he'd find his prize. The extraction
of which was still though in doubt, for the course was anything but a certainty.
Spinning cogs and rotating gears made of it a circular journey across.
From the center, as if the movement of planets, seemingly still with serenity
underfoot, the further outward one reached, greater the curving arch did toss,
with speed that defied all reason. Measured in time, what for one was a second,
for the second, in that same instant would be a lifetime of years to cross
to reach the destination. Horacio at the very edge and starting point reckoned
that there must be some way to traverse this obstacle that beckoned.

To look upon such a highway
of revolving cogs and blades, if he wasn't sliced
in half by one, he'd be crushed by the notches of the other, either way
an untimely end for one who has travelled so far. Calming his mind he spliced
a memory, a warning, something his guide Dante had said. *"This here is a place
of great illusion, do not trust all of what spins before your eyes..."* He priced
the words with value, for what was time but not the great illusion, to trace
to infinity a singular moment, which may or may not have even existed
at all? Perhaps, this was all just an intricate illusion designed to replace
what was real? Yet to know and believe are distinctly different, insisted
his mind. The eyes can be betrayed, for what they see they will believe.
What if they're only shown a fraction of the evidence? Twisted
would become their view, and with it reality. No, he must weave
another path through, one that was in harmony, ruled by the mind.
So, calming himself, he let himself breath, slowing his lungs to heave
in a controlled rhythm, and as foretold in the prophesies of mankind
he focused on the light, and now could see he who was once blind.

All that was known,
of matter and space, energy,
and the soul, was only shown
through a narrowly filtered elegy,
a snapshot and solely a sliver of time
that defined the possible as a singular effigy.
When in reality, the totality of everything there is to climb
far exceeds the imagination. Here, Horacio began to tap into some of that.
As he focused his breathing, concentrating thought upon his objective prime,
opening his mind, in tune with the shifts and harmony of his current habitat,
where time was fluid and could fold in upon itself to be multi-dimensional,
replacing the lineal concurrently. Horacio stilled himself there to combat
the urge of rushing in, for this puzzle required patience. Sensational,
there was a feel to time, a pulse that it generated, that Horacio was beginning
to touch. It sped to slow to pause to speed up to slow down again. Rotational,
it fed back on itself in a motion perpetual, and in this was the underpinning
of how the entire pendulum of time kept spinning.

What this meant in the practical
was that by feeling the rhythm of the machine,
Horacio could match its motion, so that in a position tactical
it was as if nothing was moving at all and Horacio in a manner unforeseen
simply crossed the distance in the breath between beats, along the spine
of a cog, which brought him directly to center, where shimmered to be seen,
an hourglass of sparkling crystal, held aloft as if by intervention of some divine
power to defy gravity itself, or perhaps this was its center? For this Horacio
knew was the object of his search for all these long years. This one shrine
being none other than the Infinity Glass and in it, within the sand that flow,
Saturn, the God of Time and father to all the gods immortal, imprisoned
an eternity ago, now the only hope for restoring the true balance and ratio
between the powers that be, to free not just the gods as envisioned,
but release Love itself, to bring Venus and the power of love back to humanity.
Needed was this now more than ever and Horacio, as commissioned
would bring love back from oblivion. Though some might call it insanity,
he drew his sword and readied to strike the glass containing infinity.

Just then, he remembered his pledge
to the Cumaean Sibyl, and her ghostly plea
to finally be put to rest and there at the very edge
of fulfilling his quest, he would not forsake the esprit,
who had shown him his first steps, now that he stands at the last.
Helmetless, sword in hand, facing the crystal glass, his word a guarantee,
Horacio addressed the prisoner. "O Lord Saturn, god over future and past,
I've come to release you from your tomb of glass, and though I ask nothing
for myself, I do request you grant the same freedom to the Sibyl, who cast

me on the fruitful road, that has led me here today." The stirring sand blushing
in the glass added a hue of mauve, and creating a vibration against the crystal,
sounded in words Horacio could hear. "I have seen this future ever rushing
to the now, since my first immortal breath, seeing you before me so wishful,
and I will grant it for my release, but before I do you must know that the act
requires an exchange that only you can give. An equal amount of bristle
and tears in number of years must be your burden to prophet, to retract
the spell placed upon the Sibyl. That will be your pact."

Flushed,
the impact of those words
gave Horacio a reason to pause. Rushed
could not be such a decision. In that breath played countless chords
of indecision, but one thought rose above the rest, that if it were all an illusion,
that time itself did not exist in any form outside the imagination, then forwards
or back would simply be relative and all that really mattered in conclusion
was the character and strength of one's word. So, yes Horacio stepped
forward, albeit with some initial hesitation, and for that only clearer his vision
to do what he knew was right. So in his heart and on his breath, word kept
he said, "Agreed." And there, drawing back his sword, ready to strike,
he was frozen to the sound of applause, as a single pair of hands clapped,
filling the void like thunder. "Oh, well done," Pluto always did like
good entertainment. Revealing himself from the dark creviced shadows,
Pluto marched forward, pronounced was the clang of his boot, as the pike
in his hand, his bident scepter, hummed with a vibration full of sorrows.
"I especially liked the part about sacrifice," his smile straight from the gallows.

"Now, if I'm not mistaken,"
Pluto took his time to examine the catch.
"You're the thief who broke into my sanctum, and has taken
what isn't rightfully his? So, I think that before I dispatch
you to the carnival of pleasures that I have in store just waiting
for you, I'll take back what you stole." Waving a hand as though to snatch,
the helmet voluntarily detached from Horacio's grasp, and went skating
through the air to Pluto's possession. "What, did you think I didn't have power
greater than this? That I am not the master over my own realm?" Berating
Horacio, he gave a scoff. "Oh, but you will come to learn." With a sour
look upon his face, he aimed his scepter towards the door, which did open
as if by will. "Come, join us," he invited Mars to enter. "Many an hour
you've spent on the hunt, my friend. It's only right that you're here when
it comes time for the kill." Mars strode into that dungeon clockwork,
an equal shade of doom as Pluto. After being singed and beaten
he had his mind set on retribution for all of the pain and irk
this mortal had caused him, along with all the extra work.

"Not so arrogant now?"
Mars showed his anger, sword hand clenched
as he approached threatening. "Tell me," an eyebrow
bent. "Why did you come here? Who sent you? Was it her?" he drenched
Horacio with questions. For his part, Horacio, held in suspension,
struggled to move, so tightly was he seized by Pluto's grip. Benched
to inaction, the most he could muster, a single word from his detention,
that being, "Love." "What is it you say?" Pluto turned to him suspicious,
"Come let me hear it again," he pressed. Horacio visibly stressed under tension
spoke, "For love. Venus sent me." "No. That cannot be. It must be fictitious,"
Pluto showed visible pain, his own dread coming to pass. "She died long ago,
with all of the rest." Mars too was shaken on hearing the auspicious
account from his lips. Horacio laughing there sincerely with words apropos
said, "You can't kill love. Didn't you know that? Love is a power eternal."
Pluto's eyes narrowed as he considered the rebuke and even though
he couldn't deny the truth of it, to be reminded of it, and by some vernal
man, was not the kind of ridicule he'd likely suffer, not in his domain infernal.

"Perhaps,"
Pluto was done playing this game.
"But I can still kill you," in return he snaps,
plunging the bident spikes of his scepter through his human frame.
"No!" Mars shouts. "I wasn't done questioning him," likewise unsure
he was if he'd wanted to take it that far. A huge annoyance, all the same,
Horacio still sprung from his loin. Now too late, Pluto with a free hand, secure
in his thinking, took him by the vest. "Oh, did you think that the River Styx
would protect you from me? No mortal is invulnerable from death," a grin pure
satanic washed over his face, seeing life in Horacio begin to fade, to intermix
with death. "Yes," he said, "you and I will become good friends with much time
to contemplate your punishment." Then, as an afterthought added to the mix,
he turned his head towards Mars, and in a heavy voice suited to the crime
Pluto said, "Oh look you're right, he does have her eyes." Removing his scepter
he stepped aside content with his work, as Horacio slumped over as a mime
to his knees. Rushing in, Mars grabbed Horacio by the lapel, to be the receptor
of his final words, shaking for the answer, one who'd share the fate of Hector.

"Where is she?"
Mars rattled Horacio roughly.
"Where's my daughter?" his angry plea,
as he shook Horacio's dying body toughly.
Concordia remained a mystery for all anyone knew.
With the fall of Rome, so too did fall Harmony. As the world collapsed, gruffly
descending into chaos, taking the heavens with it, and a singular deity in view,
the mysteries of heaven and earth began to unravel. The future looked bleak
for the gods of old well before Constantine made his decree, or Pluto his coup.

Concordia was simply the first of the gods to disappear. Like a flashing streak
that raced across a starlit sky, first she was there and then she was gone.
By the time Pluto had come to ascend no one even noticed that her physique
was missing from the pantheon of Mt. Olympus. With the last breath drawn
Mars would have his answer from the only one who could possibly know.
Horacio, feeling his end, saw that in the final equation he was a simple pawn
to the clockwork of time and now his time had come. There, in his dying throe,
Horacio looked up at Mars with eyes aglow.

"Right behind you,"
a familiar voice crooned,
as both Mars and Pluto, like corkscrew,
spun around in their places, leaving Horacio marooned
and alone. "What better way to find you then by loaning away my eyes?"
It was Ma'at, who by surprise, in her fashion, from the shadows was pruned.
"I saw what you were up to," she addressed Pluto, revealing her disguise.
"So I went to the one place I knew you wouldn't search, back to the pharaohs
of the past, to the sands of Egypt and the desert, awaiting the time to arise.
Pluto and Mars looked aghast, especially Pluto whose own eyes, like arrows,
were pointing her way. "My dear, you have no business here," Pluto deflected
in his usual manner. "On the contrary, it's you who's forgotten the marrows
and reasons for existence. The ends never justify the means," she corrected,
standing her ground. "The business you engage in is very much mine."
"But what of your former radiance?" Mars paternally inflected,
seeing that her power, more dour of late, frail, didn't truly shine.
Weak, he thought. For all her time away in exile, she must be in decline.

"All in due course,"
she lifted a hand, as if to expunge
any thought that she might not be a force
with which they'd have to reckon. Like a sponge,
she fed off opposing energy as if it were life giving water,
calming the seas before a storm could rise with waves at her to lunge.
"In order to survive the contradictions of the desert, with all the slaughter
of the ancient and mystic ways, falling to decay at the feet of a new religion,
of a single theological existence, I found it necessary to squatter
into this form before you." What she didn't say was that in the region
of Cairo, where the goddess finally settled, as the power of Rome diminished,
and she, like this land, went forgotten, as slowly over time the legion,
as with everything else was enveloped into the sand and finished,
Concordia saw the opportunity to start again, under the guise of multiple
personalities, and thereby twinning herself as sister, there flourished
the spirit of Isfet wa Ma'at, Chaos and Balance, the rightly incorruptible
pairing of Venus and Mars, who together were virtually indestructible.

Where one was
the other was never far away.
Of those present, this was a fact that only Horacio had cause
for knowing. And as he thought on this, remembering Isfet, the way
she had kissed him, now as he was hunched over the edge of his final crossing,
the leap from life to death, he knew that this was where he was meant to stay
in that final thought with her, there, in that moment forever. As if embossing
the impossible, thinking about her gave him added strength, for a memory,
a taste came back to him, as the air lifted his lungs. As if the frosting
to a delicate cake, her lips and his exchanged the sweetest alimentary
embrace. Though the idea itself gave him strength, he felt a return of vigor,
life no longer racing out of him. He couldn't say why, but he knew this energy
renewing his power had to do with that kiss. Distracted, turned by the figure
of Ma'at, both Pluto and Mars had their backs to him, blinded by supernova.
As though Isfet were there lifting him to his feet, Horacio strong now with rigor,
his wounds healed, as by some power divine, lifted his sword for the coda.
Seeing a speck in the corner of his eye, Mars thought of the word, "Ambrosia."

Few things
were as sacred to the gods
as ambrosia. For on the wings
of doves came this nourishment to Olympus. At odds
with death, it was the very source of their famed immortality.
For any mortal to taste of this divine consumption, the sustenance lauds
them with long life, yet if given to by a god or goddess, more than longevity
it bestows, as with Hercules, a place in the pantheon of the immortals.
Here as Isfet, an equal part of Concordia, the Goddess of Harmony,
had ambrosia on her lips and on that kiss transferred to Horacio the laurels
reserved for the gods, and in so doing opened for him the door to the stars.
When Pluto stuck him with his scepter, it merely put to sleep the mortal's
shell and awoke the birth of a god. This, as mentioned, was seen by Mars,
the glint of a sword lifted was enough to forewarn one who was a soldier,
but then again, Mars didn't necessarily agree with Pluto either. Wars
would always be there, if he had anything to say about it. For the beholder,
it was a win either way, so in that fateful moment, he let turn a shoulder.

There,
as Horacio rose,
with his blade lifted in the air,
ready to strike the Infinity Glass and finally close
his quest to free the gods, Ma'at there called on Pluto's attention.
"Now, is the time, and the time is now, to wake from this repose,
so yes, I will show myself. Look into my eyes." Watching in suspension,
Ma'at all wrinkled and bent straightened her bones, as youth returned,
she retook her goddess body. Eyes no longer cloudy blind, absent of retention,

now they sparkled as mirrors shine, reflecting back the soul they burned,
mesmerizing their gaze held as did Narcissus's pools of sparkling water.
There, in her eyes, Pluto saw too his fate, what was needed to be learned.
For too late in reflection, he saw the swing from he who survived manslaughter.
And just as the word "No!" would rise in Pluto, like some barbaric battle cry,
Horacio, son and Rome and Troy, with the help of Venus and her daughter,
holding tight the Sword of Troy, the legacy of his forefathers, gave reason why
to believe in Destiny, the Fates and Love, as shattering glass began fly.

BOOK XXXVI

TO INFINITY AND BEYOND

As the Infinity Glass,
prison of Saturn, Father of Time,
shattered and sprayed a trespass
of fragments, releasing an expanding chime
of sands, sparkling effervescent, from their confinement,
like an explosion, the power of creation spilled forth prime
upon the under-haven. Pluto and Mars, and all under consignment,
were frozen to an immovable pause in time, as the universe realigned,
rebooting such things as Wisdom, Compassion and Love. With refinement,
each god to their core element restored, evolved to a higher purpose of mind,
as elemental beings throughout the cosmos, there to influence and guide.
Yes too, Jupiter would get his revenge, and more on that is yet to unwind,
for now, let's turn to Saturn though, for in his story there's much to confide.
Most of all, Lord Saturn bared a grudge upon all of his children, in particular
the three, who placed him into his cell. Now released, he would preside
over their punishment, which justly he felt it should be both orbicular
and long, a revolving cycle, as to match his own torment perpendicular.

Holding them all the same,
each deity guilty in their own degree,
for how could any of them avoid the blame
of working in their own self interest? So came the decree,
"Jupiter, Neptune and Pluto, the three of you have done me wrong.
As punishment and for my entertainment, you will be subject to an eternity
of combat against one another, confined to the boundaries of Earth. For as long
as it takes for one of you to vanquish the others you shall fight. And to ensure
you're constantly at each other's throats Mars to you will be chained along
as overseer to keep you in constant turmoil. Be warned, for anyone to endure
all the way to victory and domination over the others will come at the cost
of losing everything you hold dear and with this knowledge firmly secure
you will still be cursed continually on to battle and just when all is lost,
the pawns will rise against you. That is the moment you'll come to realize
the single truth that today is beyond your comprehension, as you're tossed
to your prison, that your own destinies are tied to the fate of this prize
over which you fight and all its inhabitants. Its failure will be your demise."

Then to Horacio he turned,
"For a man you have shown extraordinary courage,
and though your reward may not be as you had planned, you've earned
your place among the stars alongside the gods who inhabit and flourish
the space from which time began. Yet, before you can rise to take your seat,
Horacio, Keeper and Scribe of Time, there's a pledge that has come of age
which now must as fulfilled. An era of man in human years to complete,
to witness and transcribe. As the Sibyl did, the prophet's eye shall illuminate
your mind with visions of what is yet to come, for better or worse, replete
will be the knowledge and for you to decide what information to disseminate,
what to acknowledge and what to hold back, a responsibility most heavy
the burden you'll have to bear. Yet, unlike the Sibyl, left to disintegrate,
you, a new immortal, will live on into the expansion, remaining steady
to witness the passage of time." Then, as the sands continued to swirl,
each grain as if a star and in the space between stardust, sweet and heady
glittered, encompassing everything with Horacio sucked up into the whirl
of cosmic power all around, as mysteries eternal before him began to unfurl.

As if floating,
amidst the stars,
careening through bloating
galaxies, spinning around supernova fires
and through black holes in the celestial firmament
above, then plunged out the other side, the enormity of memoirs
packed into each breath that streaked past in this astral testament
was truly too overwhelming to put into words. To concentrate and focus,
Horacio had to summon great energy from within, and still no permanent
image came to rest inside his head, so much was there, so much onus,
for him in that spin of time to digest that he had to just let the ocean
wash over and through, dragging him away with the current of the opus.
It was in that flow, which he saw how time was merely a construct of notion,
the result of cause, the past, and effect, the future, and the choice right now,
the only present in which to decide on the multiple possibilities set into motion.
Here, he opened his mind's eye and looked out from a perspective of wow,
stepped back far enough to see how all the pieces played together somehow.

Then,
with Horacio standing still,
watching irrespective of as to when,
time simply skipped past him, folding at will
from season to season, as fluttering picture frames,
while he gave witness to the changes in probable downhill
outcomes with each passing rotation around the sun. Flames
in his heart did burn with passion, seeing consequences with credibility
for seeds that had already been sown. For although this Pluto of many names

stood there in defeat, the sequence of events started was still an inevitability.
His master plan now so obviously on display, which would eventually fail
due to Horacio's own intervention, yet as a rolling ship has a forward sensibility
and is not easily stopped once set in motion, so too does speed the pale
course of history past his visual vortex. Seeing the flowering poison seed
of religion that Pluto had planted over fifteen centuries past, now a tale
most firmly believed, it'd take too long now to reverse the course he'd
started, before the entire world to his treachery would cede.

Worse too
was revealed his secret,
of a sacred land where grew
pyramids the likes of those in Egypt,
except these were surrounded by a sea of trees, a forest
where a people, unknown to Mediterranean civilization, kept
a spiritual connection, unsevered from the energy of the universe. Here rest
the one chance to foil the plots of darkness for good, yet he was now merely
a witness. Time forwards and the flag of the cross has crossed the great test
of the mighty Atlantic, under Spanish authority wielding steel with clearly
one purpose, to conquer and enslave for profit. Great fleets more powerful
than he'd ever before seen, ships that dwarf his galleass, and would barely
a moment pass before the entire of Europe had her eyes on the bountiful
west. Millions would be conquered and subjugated, enslaved in a flash,
as invading hordes, drooled to the promises of riches and gold in a wonderful
infinite land where one could just take what they wanted and such mash
as it would take to fill every last vessel with scoundrels to burn and slash.

"Boom!"
battles and bloodshed
more death than ever could be counted zoom
before his eyes as each consecutive battle, worse than the one before, led
to the next, and the next and years by the dozens passed in exactly the same
manner, as soldiers and colonists followed one another, an expansion that fed
constantly upon the fears and prejudices of the masses, who for some claim
of the church would massacre native peoples at a time by the thousands,
with a hunger for conquest that unquenchable never had enough to tame
the need for more. Wars unimaginable swelled and swept over the lands,
as rulers from all of Earth's kingdoms fought to compete for the spoils,
while the poor continued to bleed. This was Pluto's vision, one that expands
to an endless flow of carnage, his own coffers filled, brimming with royals
and peasants alike, for completing his quota they were all equal in the end.
With unstoppable expansion and a seemingly endless supply of earthly toils,
great cities and capitals Horacio could see emerge as an obvious trend,
until to the very last corner the ruling classes' reach would extend.

It was this insatiable greed,
this expanding quest for power,
like some parasitical corrupted need
that infested the hearts of man so dower,
as some residual after effect left over and contracted
from Pluto, who having such a head start in that early hour
that he'd infected all who'd come in contact, and now protracted
over centuries, with ever greater populations to control, the inevitable
outcome was that it would grow so big, that eventually impacted
would be the survival of all life on Earth. Images flashed of improbable
weapons of savagery, as both Jupiter and Neptune fought to compete
growing in intensity their own counter abilities, in order to fight multiple
wars at a time. Jupiter, controlling the heights from his mountain seat,
through his influence, the very secrets of air itself would be unleashed,
gifting the art of science to mankind, great machines of flying to drumbeat
even grander acts of carnage, dropping death from the skies that besieged
the guilty and innocent alike as the reasons for war would never go impeached.

So terrible
and great became
the powers of man that possible
it was to compare their wield with that of these same
gods, for how could such capacity for destruction be attributed
to anything other than that of some super natural being? Then came
the explosion, the very first in a chain that crossed the line undisputed
between crazy and sane. A cloud of fire rose from the earth, as if a mountain
of flame, destroying entire cities in its wake. The death toll widely distributed
to the ranks of impoverished civilians, turned to fodder and ash, to sustain
the luxury and excess of a few. The sight shook Horacio to the very core,
for though a great warrior himself, this child of love could not refrain
from feeling the pangs of heartbreak and sorrow, as he witness all in store
for the future of man. Yet more there was to come before the reversal,
for the roots Pluto had planted ran deep. If fated was a never ending war,
then with it came a degradation of life so complete that on a scale universal
the planet itself would weep to make all that came before merely a rehearsal.

Plumes of smoke
would rise like veins from the earth,
as the very air they breathe turns a toxic cloud to choke
and poison all life on the planet. Water running black the girth
of the globe, would bubble and ignite into fire, as fish would be consumed
by waste products, disappeared from the once mighty, thought limitless hearth
of the oceans, and so proving the fact that knowledge cannot be assumed
as an equal to wisdom. Yet too late would come such obvious revelations,
for ignorant the line of man would become, blinded by faith presumed.

Thinking themselves a master race, walking about with warped imaginations
that somehow they were the image of God, it is they who would soon discover
that actions have consequences, that the blooming flower of Gaia's gestations
would come from the seeds which were sown. And so, his eyes to cover
Horacio wished, for in having such knowledge, a blessing be also a curse.
In all of this, there was no happy ending, for how can one ever recover
from watching what they love the most burn, and to that much worse
for there are no winners on a dead planet. The situation he had to reverse.

Along the entire timeline,
moving forward from the moment of now,
where as bad as it might appear in the instant from his place on the vine,
perspective was an important ally, for seeing the larger scale and how
all the pieces fit in, the world of the moment, though a wild, unruly
and dangerous place, was at its peak and would only diminish somehow,
to be less than what is was right now, that this was the greatest truly
the world would ever get, for clean was the air, the water and land,
safe was the food and drink, free was a man in spirit, and surly
if he had an enemy he knew him on sight, and for why to make a stand.
The only true sin arrived with religion, to justify the damage done by rulers
and kings, to sever the connection between nature and man, to demand
of him unspeakable things, all in the name of the one worshipped. Intruders
into the spirit were these cults of religion, changing the natural order of things.
The only chance he saw the future had was to start a few of his own rumors,
to tell the real story from the point where history springs,
and for that he'd need help to pull a few strings.

And this is where
the story begins, the moment
the warrior puts down his sword to dare
change course by picking up the pen. Spent
Horacio was, having seen such an overwhelming vision,
but so too did the knowledge reinvigorate him, for now bent
was this newly ordained spirit to use his gift in order to field a commission
of his own, and so to the ether he went. The crew, led now by Suleiman,
having ascended through the doorway of Pluto's Shrine, faced the decision
of having to bury Isa, their fallen comrade in arms. Leaving their kinsman
facing the sea, under a burial mound, where Nebi wept the loss of his twin,
crestfallen he spoke a few words in private. "I'll see you again, you can plan
on it," he spoke over his brother's grave. "When you see the sunrise akin
to as it is now, look to the sea and you will find me. Never far away
will I be, brother, for always our ships will sail a parallel course." When
he was finished, the crew, mustered and ready, under the light of a new day,
no longer hunted, stepped lighter returning upon that rocky pathway.

Aethalia,
the flower that she was, bloomed
for them as if Venus herself had smiled down upon the crew via
fragrant bird song, easing their return along the winding trail resumed.
Crossing the island, through a break in the foliage, they spotted
their landing craft, beached right where they had left it. Consumed
with relief, it was only then, with sand under their feet that dotted
the shore, that anyone noticed that Isfet wa Ma'at had gone. Yet,
Suleiman, following instruction, knew it was in the design. Plotted
was the one way journey from which not everyone would return. Set
was their course, the true test of which would now come. Entering the sea,
as foretold, the barrier between planes of existence crossed, they were beset
by a most welcome sight, the reappearance of the Crescent Moon. Glee
they felt, boarding their vessel, ready to set sail. Looking upon the horizon,
Baloch then asked, "Which way, Captain?" and Suleiman, who gifted by Nebi,
wearing the brother's amulet around his neck, began in his head to siphon
instructions that in the voice of Horacio said, "West, to the land of the Mayan."